MISTER BOGGIE

DEAN PATRICK

2026, TWB Press
https://www.twbpress.com

Mister Boogie

Edited by Terry Wright

Cover Art by Markee Books www.markeebooks.com

ISBN: 978-1-967888-22-1

Dedicated to:

Chris Kennedy

Dave Foley

Joshua Nielsen

Susan Nielsen

My publisher, Terry Wright and TWB Press

And my beloved wife always, Lisa Montoya

Contents

Introduction and Acknowledgements

I wrote this novel for every one of us who has ever been bullied, and for those of us who have carried the consequences of that bullying far beyond childhood. Bullying comes in many forms. It's not always loud or physical. It's not always the bigger, meaner kid who takes your lunch money, slams you into the wall, and then walks away laughing with his or her comrades. Sometimes it's much more subtle in workplaces, family gatherings, friendships, marriages. Wrapped in authority that allows certain people to harm others without ever being questioned. This novel is a story about when the pendulum swings in the other direction.

I was bullied when I was younger, and like many people, I learned early how power can move unchecked through a room. The person who changed my childhood was my mother, Susan Nielsen; she noticed and saw that bullying was taking place. She went into action and put me in martial arts classes. It was a decision that made all the difference. Martial arts taught me courage before it taught strength. It taught awareness and an understanding that violence is not always chaos, but choice. Over the years, I have had the privilege of training with some of the finest martial artists in Houston and in Ogden.

Specifically, I want to thank first, Chris Kennedy, who is the inspiration for Rex Brody. The idea for this novel came when I watched him one day grappling with many of Foley's MMA best amateur fighters. One after the other, almost effortlessly he displayed absolute domination and skill in jujitsu. Outside the ring, Chris is one of the most gentle and loving souls I have ever met, and it has been an honor knowing him. I walked away that day and wondered what could happen if such a fighter had gone through childhood trauma, like me, and decided to go in a much different direction...

Over the past 10 years, I have also had the privilege of training with Dave Foley of Foley's MMA. Dave is the inspiration for another character in my books, Burke Macey, and it is through his training me in boxing and jujitsu that I have been able to overcome so many demons, not only from my childhood, but also the bully that is addiction, which my route in life had taken.

My brother, Joshua Nielsen, is the inspiration for Marion Paul, the fearless cop in my previous novels (also here in his rookie year) who faces the evils of the Terra Drake underworld, and never, not once, backs away from the horrors he faces. Josh has been the constant fact-checker for every police scene I have explored in every story I've written. He has been with me on this journey every step of the way.

Most importantly for this novel, as well as every effort up to this point, nothing I have written, nothing I have had published, nothing that I have ever expressed at public speaking events, on podcasts, or during interviews, nothing would have been possible without my wife, Lisa Montoya. She is my constant companion and the pure voice of love and encouragement who has believed in me since the moment I met her.

Over the course of my writing career with TWB Press, I must give thanks to Terry Wright who decided, with my first novel, to give me a chance to be a published author and a voice in horror. Over the years, he has become a true friend and mentor.

Mister Boogie comes from a place of understanding.

Rex Brody is not a hero, but he is not a simple villain either. He is an anti-hero of sorts, forged by neglect, humiliation, and sanctioned cruelty, shaped by discipline rather than impulse. He is what happens when survival becomes methodical, when pain is not erased but refined. This is a story about consequences, but it is also about redemption, though not the kind that arrives cleanly or without cost.

This novel exists within the Terra Drake universe, a prequel to "The Lady Mephistopheles" and it stands wholly on its own. You do not need to have read the other books to understand this story, though those who have read them may recognize their shadows moving at the edges of *Mister Boogie.* This book is a study of how far a person can turn. Far enough to where monsters are reality.

I'm not interested in comforting explanations of evil. I'm interested in its origins, in how it organizes itself, and in how easily it is ignored until it becomes impossible to deny. Monsters are not born in a vacuum. They are assembled slowly, often with the cooperation or indifference of the world around them.

If you are looking for easy answers, *Mister Boogie* doesn't have them. But if you have ever wondered how far someone might go once they stop believing that anyone is coming to save them, then you already understand why this story needed to be written.

Read carefully.

Enjoy, my fine readers.

1: HUMBLE BEGINNINGS

In one of its smallest and cruelest corners of a typical social services office in Houston, an event took place, heated as a matchbook strike seen across the universe from a world that no longer cared for outcome.

But this outcome would be far different.

In the social services conference room sat Rex Brody with his dad, Sam Brody, his dad's skank girlfriend, Kathy, his Grandpa Charles and Grandma Mary (both their spouses, Lena and Mitch), his aunt Anna Stannis, and his uncle Ty. Young Rex sat and listened to what was being said about his immediate future. Not only his own, but sister, Emma's, and his brother's, Don. Rex knew nothing to say when the case workers asked him what he liked about his dad's house and how things were going, and if he wanted to live with his dad, or if there was someplace better to go.

What Rex knew for certain was that a level of hate that he couldn't understand was brewing inside and causing his mind and body to react to things that he also couldn't understand. It was 1983; Rex was 9 years old. Don was 12, Emma 13. In the background outside the conference room's cheap pale walls, KC and the Sunshine Band's "I'm Your Boogie Man" could be heard playing on a staticky radio like some sick echo of what was actually taking place inside the conference room where, he knew, his dad was going to give up on his children's lives.

"It's okay, Rex, just tell everyone what you think. What is it about your dad that you like most, and what do you like most about living with him?" The caseworker, Rachel, had just turned 21. Rex thought she looked closer to his sister's age. Even though Emma was 13, she had developed as a woman far too quickly. Don sat next to Rex, hunched forward, his fingers intertwined, looking like he wanted to disappear into the cracked vinyl chair beneath him. He never did like speaking, especially to strangers, and he hated confrontation.

Rachel was new, with an optimism that wasn't yet rusting over by the heartbreak of her job. Her boss, Cynthia, was also in the room: a composed 26-year-old with sharp eyes and a shaper pen with a clipboard of paper ready for notes.

Rex didn't answer right away. Instead, he turned to look at Emma. She had long brown hair and eyes too large for her small face; she looked a lot like her grandma. Emma wore baggy clothes to conceal her woman's body, always conscious how people looked at her. How men looked at her. She barely spoke, and when she did, her voice was soft, as though she were afraid the world would scream at her if she spoke too loudly. Rex had taken on the role of protector.

Don certainly couldn't do it, though at 12, he barely understood what that meant. He believed he could protect Emma, regardless of his age. And if he ever couldn't, he believed that the day would come when he would make everyone pay for everything. Whatever was going to take place in the pitiful and empty space of the conference room, Rex knew a day would come when nothing could stop him from protecting her. Don, too. Just not that day.

Emma shrugged in response to the same questions, her shoulders rising and falling in resignation. That gesture—the helplessness of it—felt like a crack splitting through Rex's chest. It was a silent pain that he couldn't ignore.

Rachel smiled nervously and folded her hands over the stack of papers in front of her. She believed in second and third and fourth chances, never wanting to see families torn apart. She was still naive enough to believe she could patch broken families with soft words and careful questions. "It's important that you're honest, Rex. We want to make sure you, Don, and Emma are somewhere you feel safe; that is the purpose here today, to find someplace that's good for you."

Rex's grandparents chimed in with encouragements that everything would be okay, so did his Uncle Ty. His Aunt Anna's words were pure ambivalence, each of her words landing perfect strikes of doubt and beratement; she wanted her brother, Sam, to feel he was the worst piece of shit a man could be, certainly the worst father a father could be: a man who failed at every level to provide for her niece and nephews.

Rex hated her for talking about his dad that way. He made a commitment that day to find a way to tell her exactly how he had felt, to make her feel what he felt. That one day he would even show her how he felt in a way she would never forget.

As for safe: The word landed in his mind like a stone carelessly tossed into deep water. He and his siblings knew their dad's house wasn't safe. It was suffocating. But not for the reasons everyone in the conference room tried to pin on him. Sam Brody wasn't an addict or a raging drunk or a bully or physically violent. Sam had no heart for such behavior. He wasn't cruel in the way most people expected. No, his dad's failures were quieter, insidious in their ordinariness.

Sam Brody was sick, though no one had the language for it back then. Mental illness wasn't something anyone understood or talked about, especially in their Lake City neighborhood where dogmatic Christian beliefs were constantly stated as the cure-all. If divorce was imminent, go to church. If drugs were an issue, go to church. If your home was filled with violence and mayhem, the church would repair it all. If someone's wife was raped or someone's home burglarized, it was the church where all would be made as right as rain.

Rex knew Sam wasn't a monster; he was a man who

had slipped into his own mind where he couldn't escape. Emma knew it, too. And Don, despite his quiet demeanor, understood better than anyone. He took on more responsibility than he ever should have had to, trying to fill in the gaps where Sam failed. He was the one to scrounge for food, keep Emma from crying at night, calm Rex's outbursts when the hunger and frustration boiled over.

Sam couldn't hold down a job, not because he was lazy, but because the weight of the world crushed him in ways no one could see. At times he'd try. He'd show up with big plans and ideas, but within weeks, something inside him unraveled. He spent days locked in his ruined thoughts, staring blankly at the walls, lost in a fog that no amount of love or pleading could penetrate.

When things fell completely apart, when he lost another job, when the bills kept piling into heaps that were scattered all over the portable folding plastic table with dented legs set on filthy linoleum floors, he was the prime coward in the fight for his children. He retreated into the comfort of skanky Kathy, who Sam had quickly glommed onto just a few weeks after the children's mother, Teresa, had killed herself by swallowing several bottles of pain pills to forever cease such pain.

Kathy laughed too loudly and filled the silence of their hoarder's home with cheap television and loud music. She was Sam's escape from the crushing responsibility of raising three children that he knew nothing of how to care for and didn't want to care for because his drug-addict wife left him alone by taking the easy way out.

The house itself told the story of neglect. The floors were caked with grime, the faint, sour scent of ancient spills clung to the air. Dishes were piled in the sink and on the counters, coated with the remains of long-forgotten meals, and the fridge hummed emptily; most of the time its only contents a half-carton of spoiled milk and an expired ketchup bottle. There was no food in the pantry, just empty cereal boxes and cans that had rusted at the edges. Trash bags that should have been taken out weeks ago sat piled in the corner, their contents threatening to burst out. Flies buzzed lazily in the heat, claiming the space as their own, or lay dead, gathered in groups in the corners of window shelves in the cold months.

Rex knew his dad loved his kids in his own way, but it was far from enough. It was never enough. Rex wasn't old enough to understand the complexity of his dad's illness, but he felt the absence. He felt it in every missed dinner, every forced smile, and every long silence that hung between them.

Sam Brody wanted to be anywhere but inside the conference room with the case workers and immediate family who appeared ready to breathe down his neck every mistake and bad choice he'd made since his own birth, furthering the suffocation that squeezed away all last hairs of dignity. The weight of parenthood was simply too much for Sam, and the crowd of family gathered around him felt more like pillars of stone leaning in where there was no light.

The caseworkers waited patiently for Rex's answer, paying no real attention to what the other family members said, their pens poised over their papers like starved crows. He clenched his small fists beneath the table, wishing he could tear the whole world apart for making him choose. His heart pounded in his chest like a large jumping bean, and the venom of his frustration boiled over. But he kept his composure.

"It's fine." His voice barely more than a whisper sounded more like a hiss. "I like living with my dad."

He felt Emma and Don's eyes on him, wide and searching, but he couldn't look at them. He knew what Emma wanted him to say—that she wanted to be brave enough for all of them. But bravery was a luxury they couldn't afford. Plus, it would take too much time and effort. Don Stared straight ahead, stone faced. More than his own sister's eyes, Rex felt his aunt Anna's eyes even heavier.

Though it was Rex's Grandma Mary who made the initial call to social services one night deep into the holiday season, it was his Aunt Anna who started this whole chain of events where she called night after night, wailing about how horrible her brother was, how awful were the kids' living conditions. On and on she went for several months in her self-righteous façade, only trying to mask her own miserable failure she had been to her own daughter. Every time Rex heard his aunt speak, it blistered his very spirit. He knew he would have to take care of her one day. Protect the world from her.

Anna Stannis also hated everyone and everything due to her own circumstances of endless broken relationships that she bounced around constantly in shameful promiscuity. Anna blamed her entire life's failings on her mother and father divorcing when she was a blooming teenager, doing her best to cause as much damage as possible to everything she touched in her life: from married men to her daughter to her mother to hopeless boyfriends she'd string along for months. Anna Stannis was the epitome of reckless narcissistic sabotage.

Rex hated her. That was a piece of the hate that was brewing inside him that he could understand at a young age. A piece of the hate he would one day handle.

It wasn't just her words; it was how she said them. The know-it-all tone, the self-righteous curl of her lips. Aunt Anna didn't just want her brother to feel like a failure. She wanted everyone in that room to watch him collapse under the weight of it. She reveled in it, drinking in her brother's humiliation like it was her goddamn right, but he was still Rex's goddamn father, regardless of how he felt about him.

Rex clenched his fists under the table, nails pressing into his palms so hard he thought they might break the skin. He imagined grabbing one of the pens off the table and jamming it into her thigh, not to kill her, just to hear her scream, to watch her eyes peel back in fear, the same fear she probably thought she could only inspire in others. He then imagined he had a large knife. A hunting knife and what it could do to the sorry bitch.

A small, sick thrill ran through him at the thought. It wasn't normal, but nothing about this was normal. Nothing about him was normal and he knew it since his first memory.

Anna caught his stare and smirked again. A knowing, smug little twitch of a smirk. Like she knew she had already won. Like she knew that whatever was happening in this room was already set in stone like a new commandment he remembered being created when his dad had him and his siblings watch that movie with Charlton Heston on Easter Sunday.

Rex ground his teeth, his jaw so tight he thought it would crack. One day, he wouldn't just hate her. One day, he would show her what hate could really do to her.

But for now, he was just another powerless child being shuffled through a broken system, surrounded by vultures picking apart his life before his eyes.

It would change one day, he knew this. Felt it searing through his veins. One day, no one would ever speak to him like that again.

Rachel's smile softened, but something flickered behind her eyes with an understanding she wasn't supposed to show. She nodded and scribbled something in her notes. "Okay, Rex. Thank you."

The rest of the meeting dissolved into background noise. *Custody* and *visitation* floated meaninglessly in the over-air-conditioned air. His dad sat slouched in his chair, staring at the wall behind the caseworkers, Kathy snapping her gum as if she was bored to tears.

The others in the meeting, especially his Uncle Ty, who Rex had just gotten to know as he showed instant concern when Grandma Mary had to call social services several weeks ago because things were simply unraveling to a dangerous level, never came to his dad's rescue. Rex loved his grandma and knew she was trying to protect him and his siblings. Still, no one offered any solace to his dad as Sam Brody just shrunk more under the weight of shame...and anger.

When it all ended, they stepped out into the searing Texas sun. The heat pressed down on them like a slug of iron. Sam lit a cigarette as soon as they reached his truck, exhaling a cloud of smoke that lingered in the thick air, looking almost as haggard as Sam himself.

"You did good in there, buddy." Sam ruffled Rex's hair with a hand that smelled of nicotine and sweat. "Real good."

Rex didn't respond. He climbed into the cab with Emma and Don and stared out the window as the world passed by in a blur of rusted storefronts and cracked sidewalks. The radio crackled with static before cutting on with more KC like a cruel, cosmic joke.

Their house felt like a tomb. Sam tossed his keys on the counter and sank into the couch, manically flipping through channels until the noise drowned out the silence. Kathy followed suit, propping her feet on the coffee table like the pig she was as the TV blared.

Rex led Don and Emma to their room they all shared at the back of the house, where the humid air was stifling. Paint on the walls was cracked and curling, the lone window overlooking a yard where an old swing set sagged like broken bones and frayed nerve endings.

In the room was a double-bed mattress that sat on a block of cheap foam. Emma sat cross-legged on the bed, her hands twisting in her lap. "Why didn't you tell them?" Her voice trembled.

Don sat on his hands and said nothing.

Rex sat beside Emma and stared at the floor. All three siblings sitting together for the last time. "Because they'd split us up."

Emma nodded, but tears welled in her eyes. She trusted him, but the weight of that trust felt suffocating.

That night, after the house fell into its usual quiet, Rex lay awake in the dark. He listened to Emma's soft, steady breathing and stared at the ceiling, tracing the jagged cracks like a map leading to nowhere. Don was in a deep enough sleep that a small snore escaped from his nose every third breath or so.

The walls closed in. The weight of the air pressed against his chest, making it harder to breathe. He turned onto his side. His fingers curled into a fist against the filthy mattress. The sheets smelled like old sweat and cigarette smoke. Everything in this house was rotting: the floors, the walls, the people inside it.

Rex ground his teeth until he felt them start to give. He hated this house, hated everything about it, the stained walls, the pissed-on ragged carpet, the holes in the ceiling, the rampant stench no fragrance could mask. He thought about his dad sitting in the other room, useless, leaching onto the television, drowning himself in the noise like it could erase the world's decision that his kids weren't worth the fight. The way he slouched, the way he avoided eye contact. Pathetic and worthless, just as his bitch aunt made him feel.

Rex's stomach was a set of knots pulled so tight he wanted to vomit but didn't know how. He wanted to hate him but couldn't. Not fully. Hate required something more than disappointment; it required energy, and his dad wasn't worth the effort.

So back to Anna. The bitch. The "C" word his dad had called her many times. Aunt Anna was a different animal altogether.

He closed his eyes, and there she was, standing in that shitty conference room, yakking like a wind-up doll, putting on her little show. It wasn't enough that their family was being torn apart like stuffed puppets with loose strings, she needed the whole goddamn world to know that she was the one holding the knife. Look at me and all I've done to save these children from such a monster.

His nails dug into his palm as he wished he could rip that smirk off her face like a fresh strip of duct tape off a piece of rotted tile. He imagined it. He imagined much worse, like what it would look like if someone took a hot poker and drove it down her throat, searing the top layer off her lips, torching her esophagus. The thought made his heart slow, the anger inside him settling into something cold, something steady. Something...comfortable.

One day, she wouldn't be able to smirk at him. She wouldn't be able to smirk at anyone. She would be the one sitting frozen in fear and panic. Terrified of him. A lot of people would feel the same way.

His breathing evened out, but the heat in his chest resisted. It felt like something was waking up inside him, stretching, hungry, curious. He didn't know what it was yet, not fully, but knew it had been there for a long time.

He glanced at Emma's sleeping form. She was curled into herself, small, fragile. She shouldn't be that way. She shouldn't have to be afraid of the world; the world should be afraid of her.

He looked over at Don, peaceful in his sleep, unaware of how much weaker they were going to be tomorrow. How much worse things could get.

Rex wasn't like Don. He wasn't going to let himself be pushed around, dragged from place to place like some stray dog.

The world wasn't going to decide his fate. He would, only some different version of him.

His gaze went back to the ceiling, followed the jagged cracks again, this time seeing something different. It was no longer a map leading to nowhere, it was one leading to war.

The day would come when he'd be strong enough to make everyone pay.

Hate simmered beneath his skin like settled acid blots. More hate fumed at his dad for being too weak to hold on. Hate for the caseworkers and their practiced sympathy. Hate for the whole gangrenous world for pretending things could ever change.

Suddenly, the quiet cauldrons inside his thinking zapped cool by the sound of knocking: loud, urgent, extreme. Rex sat up, his heart thudding in his chest. In the front room, his dad groaned as the knocking grew louder. The door opened, and unfamiliar voices filled the house.

"Mister Brody, we have a state-issued protective order for removal." The voice was calm but firm.

Rex heard his dad mumble obnoxious and empty threats as heavy footsteps moved through the house. Moments later, the doorway filled with the figures of two officers and a caseworker holding a clipboard. Rex couldn't remember if it was Rachel, but it looked like her.

"Rex, Emma, Don. It's time to go."

Emma's breath caught; a small whimper escaped her lips. Rex stood slowly, fists clenched at his sides. Don stood motionless, tears forming in sky blue eyes.

"Let's make this easy, okay?" The caseworker's expression was soft but resolute and forced.

Rex said nothing. He stood in the middle of Don and Emma and held their hands, squeezing them tight as they were led out of the house. The night air carried the same endless, thick scent of heavy asphalt and heat. The flashing red and blue lights painted the world in chaotic colors and shadows dancing around manically from the flashes.

As they were guided into the waiting cruiser, Rex's gaze drifted back to the house, his dad still standing in the doorway, blank-eyed and stupid. Useless as well as unusable. Something inside Rex broke completely, and in its place, a monster slipped, wide awake.

Rex Brody's survival was built on hate.

***

His path was never linear. It was a relentless fight

against the constraints of ordinary life, a series of restless leaps across continents and into combat, all in search of mastery and meaning. But the roots of that journey began long before he boarded a plane to Cambodia or stepped into a cage fight. It began in that bleak social services room in 1983 where he sat helpless as his world was systematically dismantled piece by piece.

The police car that fetched his siblings and him away from their dad's house might as well have been a hearse. Every mile felt like another bit drilling away any innocence he had left. Emma cried softly the entire drive. Don was paralyzed in fear. Rex stayed silent but with a focus that knew would one day become unmatched. He kept his eyes locked on the passing streets of Lake City, memorizing every detail as though he were mapping his hatred for later use. It wasn't just his dad who had failed him, it was the whole goddamn world. When such abandonment took place, there were two choices Rex faced: break, or break out.

The foster homes that followed in the 80s were prisons of their own. Every house had its own brand of hell, every adult another rusted link in a rotted chain. Rex never feared the adults; it was the silence that did it, as his mind would drift back to that final day in his dad's house, to the emptiness of the fridge, the broken promises, the smell of cigarette smoke clinging to his skin. The demon inside him—whoever it was—whispered: *They will always betray you. The only way to survive is by force.*

The day they were separated was the day something inside him extinguished forever. Probably his soul. The police had come in the night like executioners and pulled them from their father's rotting house, but that had been nothing compared to the hollow-faced caseworker who split them up like cattle at an auction. Rex still thought it was Rachel but couldn't be certain of it. No matter, it would be Rachel, too, like the rest of them, who would also pay.

Emma was the first to go. The foster mother was older,

soft-spoken, with a false warmth that Rex knew was snake's breath. She touched Emma's shoulder as if she was a stray cat she wasn't sure about. Rex wanted to slowly slit her throat.

"Say your goodbyes," the caseworker told them, as if their sister was being erased from their lives right in front of them.

Emma's lip trembled, but she gave every effort to remain dignified. Rex could see in her eyes that her soul was stripped bare. She hugged Don first, whispering something; he didn't answer. She turned to Rex in a whisper. "I'll see you soon." It was a lie, but she needed to say it. She also knew Rex needed to hear it.

She was then led out the door like she'd been nothing more than a sleepover friend. Rex never knew what happened to her, not that day nor the years that passed by, but his commitment to find her was as real as his inner demon. They would both find her.

Rex and Don were driven to another house, one with crumbled paint and sheetrock and a porch that sagged with secrets. The couple who took them in didn't speak much beyond instructions: where to sleep, where not to go, how not to be a burden, to stay out of everyone's way. There was already another foster boy there, a lanky 15-year-old with eyes like charcoal and cheeks covered in angry zits, called Herman. He watched Rex and Don with the kind of detached amusement of someone who had already learned that any hope had died long ago with the secrets hidden under the rotting porch.

The first night, he lay awake in the top bunk in a room that smelled of cat piss and Listerine. Don below him, trapped in perpetual shock. There were strange clicking sounds in the walls, like cockroaches planning an all-nighter. Rex tried to listen to Don's breathing.

The door creaked open.

Herman's shadow moved in the doorway. He didn't say

anything, just stood there. Watching, one of his hands rubbing his cheeks too harshly.

Rex felt his muscles coil, but Don was already shifting in the bunk below. His brother sat up, staring the older boy down. Neither spoke. The air was syrupy and sick. Ugly.

Finally, the shadow in the doorway smirked. "See you around." After what seemed an eternity Herman slinked back into the dark hallway.

Neither brother slept that night.

So, it went month after endless month. Sometimes Herman would come in and just sit on the floor in the dark, watching Rex and Don. Sometimes he'd pull out his dick and play around with it, then tuck it back, giggling in a way that made Rex want to vomit. On and on until one night when it happened, Rex hopped off the top bunk and screamed as loud as his young throat could manage. Herman went bleach white and panicked to shut him up, but Rex grabbed him by his balls, squeezed them with all his strength until Herman couldn't breathe or move, and whispered into Herman's greasy ear that he would murder him in his sleep if he ever bothered his brother and him again.

Herman never did.

***

The second foster home was worse. The first house had at least been quiet. If the rules were followed. The second one was a circus of screaming children, slamming doors, and a foster father, Jimbo Torrington, whose patience was measured in beer cans. Rex had bruises on his ribs within a week. Don got it worse.

Worse than that, there was the school bully, Dale Barker, they had to deal with. Day in day out, night in night out, Rex and Don's life seemed impossible to ever break the torment. Until one particular day during summer break while still in Foster Fuck Home Number Two.

It was the day Don's bike had been destroyed by Dale Barker and his thugs. He had felt powerless, as terrified as his brother, which was never the case. Unable to act. But then, as he and Don and their friend, Greg Lubbock (who also stood in shock fear) trudged home in silence, something changed.

While walking home in defeat they came upon a woman lying out in the sun in her backyard, just beyond the bayou that separated the neighborhoods. The yards in that area had no fencing, leaving her fully visible to anyone passing by. She was wearing a black string bikini, her body stretched out on a towel like something sculpted from stone.

She motioned for Rex to come closer. He looked back at Don, who still had the ghost of humiliation on his face, and then at Greg Lubbock, their odd neighbor who had watched it all happen. Greg, who was easily as big and strong as the bully Dale but did nothing as all cowards do. Rex's hate for Dale had turned south toward Greg in those moments of being broken and exposed, but now he faced something he knew was far different than the school bully or the school coward.

Rex hesitated to approach her at first. He'd never seen a full-grown woman lying nearly naked ,but with a confidence that scared him in a way he never knew possible. He stepped forward. When he was close enough, he saw her eyes beneath dark sunglasses: striking, violet, with a strange wire-thin glow that lassoed around the frightful color, impossibly vibrant.

"Would you like me to slit that boy's throat open with my straight razor?" Her voice was low and deliberate, sending a long cold wire down his back. "The one I use to shave my legs so close? If you say the word, I will get up right now, go to his house, and slit him from ear to ear."

The long cold wire turned to ice. He wanted to say something, anything, but words failed him.

The woman tilted her head, her impossible body

propped up on her elbows. "Do you think I am joking?" Though she whispered, it was a voice that Rex believed he would hear over the sound of a car wreck or even a locomotive racing through the night.

He slowly shuffled backward to Don and Greg, shaking his head. "I don't think that's needed."

She smirked, then her lips curled downward. "That's a shame."

Rex kept creeping backward, one careful step at a time, his eyes fixed on the woman and everything about her. He finally turned from her and walked back to Don and Greg, never looking back.

"Holy shit, Rex, who is that?" Don's voice trembled.

"Yeah...I mean, whoa. I've never seen her before. She's like Playboy in real life." Greg's leering comment was nothing more than to get back in Rex's grace, but Rex had none of it.

"She's more fucking scary than Dale Barker, and now you want to play it cool? Really?"

Greg lowered his head and stared at the ground as they all three walked away from the woman as Lake City's summer heat paled in comparison.

"Come on, Rex, he was just tryin' to—"

"Don't give him any pass, Donny. Doesn't matter anyway. Forget about Dale. Forget about what happened." Rex stopped, put his hands on his hips and looked back at the woman. They were far enough away to where she looked like a bikini-clad toy Barbie Doll. He could tell she was looking straight up into the sun.

"Did you notice anything about her, Donny? I mean... Did you feel anything that was...I don't know...bad? And I don't want to hear any of your bullshit, Greg. I'm not talking about your porn shit."

Greg kept his head down, but his eyes moved up toward Rex and Don. "I wasn't gonna say anything."

Rex looked at his brother, searching his eyes.

"Yeah. Yeah. I don't know what it was, but I know what you're saying. I think we should just get as far away from her as we can. Now."

Rex nodded in agreement and led the three of them farther down the bayou toward home.

He wondered if he would ever see the woman again, but at that moment, he knew he would spend his life searching for that same power, that same unwavering fearlessness she displayed. He was committed to finding it any way possible regardless of any consequence.

A few days later, Don finally lost it; finally snapped after a particularly bad night where the foster father had thrown him against the wall. He fought back. He wasn't a fighter like Rex, but rage made up for skill. He managed one solid punch when Jimbo was staggering before the man put him down hard, cracking his head against the floor.

The next morning, Don was gone.

The caseworker—this time he knew it was Rachel—gave Rex the same dead-eyed false sympathy she had given Emma. "Your brother is being placed elsewhere." She said it as though discussing a piece of broken furniture that needed taking out on Tuesday Trash Day.

Rex didn't cry nor argue. He just sat in silence as the last tether to his family was ripped away.

Everything inside him continued the same twisting, like a set of large steel-tipped hooks that were attached to his guts, the twisting giving way to tearing.

What kept Rex from completely losing his mind was the image of the strange woman that hot summer day after Dale Barker's rampage.

***

When Rex hit high school, he had been through four foster homes, three group homes, and more nights alone than he could count. He didn't make friends. He didn't trust a soul, nor did he believe he had a soul. He fought often. Not because he lost control, but because control was all he had left. That, plus he was naturally gifted in self-defense. Naturally strong and fabulously athletic.

As his years aged, such skills began to make violence feel as natural as his ability to inflict it.

One late afternoon, in the middle of his junior year, a group of seniors cornered him in the locker room after gym class. Three of them. Big, cocky super Jocks. The kind of guys who thought the world owed them every goddamn silver coin placed in the silver spoon.

"Word is, you're a tough guy," one said and sneered. "Think you're some badass, bitch?"

Rex didn't answer. He watched them, calculating. Watching their throats, their knees, their elbows, their temples, lower back areas; every vulnerable spot.

The first punch came fast. Rex slipped it, letting the kid's momentum carry him forward. A quick strike to the sternum collapsed him like a sad sack, gasping for his next breath. The second one swung wild, like almost everyone did who had no training or any concept of how to fight. Rex stepped inside, grabbed his arm, and twisted until his shoulder dislocated, probably worse.

The third one hesitated. That was a mistake.

Rex's elbow connected with his jaw before he could react. The kid crumpled, unconscious before he hit the tile.

When it was over—all of it happening within a few seconds, tops—Rex stood over their groaning bodies, heart steady, breath even.

He smiled and crouched down low to the one jaw-dropped. "Come at me again. Please. I will fucking come after everything you have ever loved."

That was the first day he realized the world was filled with weak people, and that he was far far from one of them.

***

At 19, Brody didn't believe in family. Didn't believe in love. Didn't believe in law and order and anything dogmatic. He wondered about God because Don and Emma were gone from his life. They were all he ever believed in when it came to anything pure or good. Had it not been for that single moment when the strange woman offered to kill the school bully all those years ago, Rex would have written off God completely. Because of her, he believed in strength with no limits. In power that was never lenient. In control that was iron-fisted. Whether that came from God didn't mean a wit's lick, but he had to find out.

Emma was gone. Don was gone. And the only thing left in the world worth anything was the fight.

The rules were simple: if anyone wasn't breaking others, then the others would surely do the breaking. Because if you weren't the one breaking people, you were the one getting broken.

Rex Brody was finished with anything that related to broken.

***

By his junior year in college, he was already a ghost to most people; a figure who moved through the hallways and dorm areas with silent precision, unapproachable and unknowable. Exactly how he designed it.

There were two elements that came to Rex with ease. One was computer science and technology. Coding and the main coding languages at the time—C++, Java, Visual Basic—came easy for him. One day after he'd seen the film, Good Will Hunting, when hearing Mat Damon's character talk about how he could see advanced math and science and could just "play," was exactly how Rex felt about computer programming.

The other—the one he would take to the level where he could get even with the world—combat sports. Wrestling, boxing, martial arts, all became his outlet, his way to channel the rage and confusion that never left him. On the mat or in the ring, there were no lies. Especially with wrestling. There was only strength and submission, a brutal honesty that made sense in a world where everything else felt like a deception. But even that wasn't enough. Combat sports taught him how to fight anyone regardless of size or strength, but it didn't teach him how to truly cause pain and hurt. And that was what the world deserved.

When he learned Brazilian Jiu Jitsu, all through the 90s, and the Gracie family's philosophy, it was like finding a new language for the war he had been waging in his mind. He wasn't content to just win; Rex wanted to destroy. To humiliate. He tracked down an MMA gym and threw himself into Judo and Jiu Jitsu with the same relentless intensity that had once fueled his childhood need to protect Emma and Don. On the mat, there were no family court hearings or state-issued warrants, only survival. He spent countless hours, seven days a week in such intense training it didn't take long before his natural abilities fused into highly skilled professional ones.

By the time he entered his first amateur MMA tournament, he had advanced to black belt in record time, faster than any pro-level coach had ever seen in the sport; a predator learning to kill. His first opponent, a self-proclaimed street fighter, learned that lesson in less than sixty seconds. Rex closed the distance with surgical precision, wrapped his arms around the man's throat, and squeezed until the fight dissolved into unconsciousness. But that fight was far from satisfying: it awakened something deep and ugly inside.

His second opponent, a wrestler like himself, had more grit, more experience. The match dragged into brutal rounds, each second sharpening Rex's endurance. When he finally won by split decision, he felt no relief, only hunger for more. Starvation, in fact. His third opponent, a Muay Thai specialist, lashed out with kicks that left Rex's legs bruised and his ribs tenderized. But such pain became fuel, and he took on pro-fight after pro-fight to keep feeding the fuel that eventually turned into an addiction as fierce as any addict in the corner of an abandoned street with a dirty needle stuck deep in the arm.

Fight after fight, month after month, year after year, Brody absorbed every hit from every level of fighter who was matched with him. He would end fights in clinches and submissions, and chokes, until fighters all over the country wanted a piece of him.

Brody's only defeat was delivered by a professional boxer, Neil Kramer, a boxer with fists like concrete and a kicking game that was unmatched. Brody had pulled Kramer into an armbar and felt the man's tendons snap under the pressure. But Kramer didn't quit. He fought through the agony, broke free, and pummeled Rex until the referee stepped in. Rex left bloodied but not broken. That loss wasn't an ending; it was a revelation. He couldn't be untouchable if he only excelled in grappling. To be feared, he had to master every weapon available.

Later that same year of the Kramer fight, driven for perfection, Rex left the country and moved into a Muay Thai gym in Cambodia. He traded comfort for brutal simplicity: waking at dawn to train under the blistering sun, practicing strikes until his bones felt splintered. In the sweltering heat, he learned the language of elbows, knees, and fists, the art of eight limbs. Every sparring session was a symphony of violence, every fight another scar added to the map of his journey.

During his time in Southeast Asia, Rex's fascination with Kun Khmer—the Cambodian form of kickboxing—took root. Cambodia wasn't just a country to him; it was a mirror to the lawlessness he felt inside. Phnom Penh's streets were wild, its fight circuits raw and merciless. Fights spilled into alleys, debts were paid in blood, and survival meant knowing when to fight and when to disappear. Here, Rex was no longer an outsider; he was home.

Phnom Penh didn't forgive weakness. It didn't care about rules, morals, or the thin membrane of law that barely held the city together. It was a place where violence bled into every street corner, where men killed for a debt smaller than the price of a meal, where a whisper in the wrong ear could get you dumped in the Mekong River with your hands zip-tied behind your back and your throat cut so deep they'd never find your voice again. Rex thrived in it. Yet all the while thriving in such fierce danger, he still sought the confidence of the strange woman from his childhood, a confidence that he knew now as a trained professional was overpowering.

The city was a perfect reflection of the lawlessness inside him. It was anarchy, a controlled brutality, the need to always be one step ahead of the predator lurking behind you. The fights weren't just in rings or cages; they spilled into alleys, into bars reeking of sweat and spilled whiskey sours, into back rooms where men settled disputes with fists, knives, or guns.

This was the real deal, not the padded gloves and controlled environments of the West. Rex wanted the feeling of bones breaking beneath his knuckles, the sound of a man gasping for breath after having his ribs crushed, the raw, ugly honesty of violence without safety nets; that's exactly what he got.

He started in underground rings, fighting locals who had been training since they could walk. There were hard, trained men, conditioned by years of street brawls and blood feuds. Kun Khmer fighters were different from the soft, weight-cutting athletes in the U.S. These were killers in the truest sense. Every fight was war. Every strike was meant to cripple, to erase the opponent from existence. Rex learned it all at lightning speed; he ate it up as easily as the 1s and 0s in computer code.

His first few fights were brutal. He took beatings that would have broken lesser men. His ribs cracked, his face swelled, and he woke up more than once on the floor of a filthy gym, blood crusting his mouth, with nothing but a bucket of water to rinse himself off.

The longer he stayed, the more he adapted. He learned how to absorb punishment, how to turn pain into precision, how to see every opening before his opponent even made a move. He studied their rhythm, their footwork, how they breathed. He let them kick him, let them elbow him, let them feel like they had control, until he found their weakness and broke them, systematically, piece by piece.

By his twentieth fight, the locals started betting on him. By his thirtieth, they started fearing him. By his fortieth, they called him something else.

"Piset Sâmas," one of the trainers whispered after Rex finished a man in under a minute. "The Specter." The name spread fast. Any visiting Americans who wandered into the fights saw something else in him, something they couldn't explain but could feel crawling under their skin.

"He's not normal," they'd mutter over their cigarettes and shitty shots. "He doesn't blink. He doesn't stop. He fights with something inside that doesn't care if it dies."

All of it, true.

It was in a back-alley fight late one night, a real one, where Rex's inner psycho demon was turned loose for the first time. No ref, no rules, just two men in a circle of drunks and gamblers waiting to see who would still be breathing by the end of it.

His opponent was a beast. Far more size and mass than Rex; far more experienced. A seasoned killer with dead eyes and a mouth full of loose, broken teeth.

The fight was over in two minutes. Rex dismantled and humiliated him.

He caught a kick and snapped the man's shin like a piece of cheap wood. He drove an elbow into his temple, and the sound it made was like a hammer hitting a wet stone. But Rex didn't stop when the man hit the ground. He kept hitting him, over and over, until his hands were drenched in blood, until the crowd wasn't cheering anymore, until he realized he had been smiling the entire time.

That night something inside him snapped completely. The control he had always held, the leash he had kept on his worst impulse, gone. He was coming full circle as a trained killer. Or at least well on his way.

After that night, Rex started fighting differently. Not to win, not to survive, but to break people, to see how far he could push them before they begged for their lives. If they were able.

He stopped fighting with restraint and began to experiment. How much pain could a man take before he stopped trying? Before he died? How much blood could someone lose before they collapsed? How long could he keep someone conscious while choking them out, keeping them on the edge just long enough to see horror in their eyes?

The underground world of Phnom Penh didn't just make him a lethal fighter, it turned him inside out as a human being, stripping away what little humanity he had left. He stopped feeling anything when he fought. No nerves, no adrenaline rush, no sense of victory. Just the mechanical process of destruction. Hit. Break. Kill. Walk away.

Men who once sought him out as a challenger began avoiding him. Trainers who once took pride in his progress stopped making eye contact. Even in a world of killers, Rex became something different. Something that no longer feared anything, that never hesitated, that never cared for consequence.

Something that had been waiting to be born since the day he was taken from his father's house where he saw himself ramming a hot poker down his Aunt Anna's yakking throat. Phnom Penh didn't just shape him. It finished him. The man who boarded the plane back to the U.S. in the spring of 2001 was darker, colder, more patient. More wicked, but with a purpose he had to discover what it was and where to start it.

A few house cleaning tasks were first: finding those who tried to destroy him and his siblings and yes, his pathetic father, Sam Brody.

***

That spring of 2001, back from Cambodia, Rex had a brief stint in New York. He was a weapon, forged by abandonment, sharpened by defeat, and polished in the blood trenches of Phnom Penh. The monster that had stirred awake in that police car so many years ago was now fully formed. Mostly physical, that is.

The world had always tried to name men like him monsters, madmen, psychos. But Rex knew what he was. He was no longer invisible, and he was far from just another fighter.

Fighters had rules and limits. Brody wanted neither.

New York was a test. A pressure chamber of vice, filth, and unrelenting movement, a city that endlessly pulsed, driven by greed and violence. He fit right in. The underground fight circuits were nothing compared to Cambodia. Too much theater, too many soft men looking for a payday rather than a real fight. So Brody still found other ways to entertain himself.

One night, after a fight in a sweat-drenched, whiskey-soaked basement, he stepped out into the dimly-lit alleyways of the Lower East Side. The night smelled of trash and rain; the pavement was slick with the filth of the city. That's when he heard it, the shuffle of feet, the quiet whisper of breath trying to stay hidden.

A man was stalking him.

Brody smirked as he kept walking, letting whoever it was believe he was unaware, allowing the would-be predator to sink deeper into his own mistake. He turned a corner into a dead-end alley, pausing as if confused, as if lost, waiting.

The man lunged with a knife flashing in the dim light. Brody didn't blink or hesitate as he instantly sidestepped, grabbed the man's wrist mid-strike, and twisted with just enough force to make the bones creak. The man yelped. His other hand swung wildly, but Rex blocked that blow with ease, spun him around, and slammed him face-first into the brick wall.

"Bad fucking plan."

The man whimpered, his body trembling beneath Brody's grip. Fear seeped out of him like sweat.

Brody didn't need to kill him. He didn't even need to maim him. He just needed him to know. Know that he had made a mistake and that he had indeed picked the wrong victim. Knew that, if Brody wanted, he wouldn't leave this alley alive. He released him and watched him stumble away, his legs jelly.

Standing there, breathing in the night air, Brody felt nothing. Not anger. Not satisfaction. Just the cold realization that he had changed. Who he was just a few months ago might have beaten the man to pulp, may have acted out of rage, out of impulse. But this Rex was patient. Controlled... And becoming someone else.

New York offered no shortage of lessons. Rex watched people, the way a predator studies prey. He sat in bars, in diners, in crowded subway cars, watching how people moved, how they avoided eye contact when they sensed danger, how they carried themselves when they thought they were alone.

He started testing things as he did before in Cambodia. Walking too close to people just to see if they flinched. Staring at them a second too long just to watch the unease set in. Positioning himself in ways that forced them to notice him, to feel him before they even saw him. Rex was also starting to understand something crucial: people didn't fear violence itself. They feared what they couldn't understand.

A mugger, a gangster, a junkie with a knife were predictable. Most people could never wrap their heads around such a threat. But someone like Brody who didn't look unhinged, who didn't act erratic, but carried something dark and unknowable beneath the surface, was a true harbinger of fear, and its personification fascinated him. It was the fear the strange woman put inside of him as a child, a child who couldn't protect his brother.

New York was teaching him a new kind of violence. Not the kind that came from fists and blades, but the kind that came from presence alone. He was learning how to haunt people like a ghost while he was still alive.

Brody spent months drifting through the city, absorbing its lessons, feeling himself become something new...but he didn't know what. He was smart enough to know it would take years of practice to unleash the psycho beast inside of him to become altogether different. He had no idea how to do it but knew it would happen when the right trigger was pulled.

A trigger he found on September 10th, 2001.

2: 09-10-2001

Houston that night was more pleasant than the city's normal summer when heavy thickness in the air overstayed its welcome. The normal sweltering grip was considerably loosened as the sun dipped below the horizon, but the humidity still lingered like dying fumes from a charcoal grill.

The city unfolded before Rex Brody, a sprawling labyrinth of lights and shadows, each turn of one freeway system leading to another one, offering another opportunity, another potential prey. He was dressed for the night to impress anyone with a decent set of eyes: sand-blasted fashion jeans that hung low on his waist with a fitted silk t-shirt that showcased a perfectly sculpted body. He'd spent hours each day lifting weights, running laps, and fiercely training in mixed martial arts, skills he had honed since childhood, and boxing. His boots were black alligator, and the overshirt hung just loose enough to not stick to his skin in Houston's perpetual sauna. He had slicked back his jet-black hair with gel that was more like glue than anything fashionable.

The downtown streets were busy as always, a steady stream of cars moving in and out of the heart of the monster town. But he wasn't looking for the hustle and bustle of downtown; he was searching for something meaningful, more isolated. His fingers drummed on the leather-wrapped steering wheel of his 2000 metallic-blue Porsche Boxster S, a chop-shop car he'd driven from New York. Everything about it was illegal and untraceable. The rhythm of his tapping matched the pounding of his heart as he cruised down one of the main arteries of the city, Commerce Street, his eyes scanning the sidewalks for...what? He wasn't sure. He just knew that he needed to find something, or someone, that would finally release the pent-up violence coiled within him. A raging lunatic lived inside Rex, and he had to unleash it so he could understand just what the hell it was he was dealing with.

After a stop at the bank, he decided on Fitzgerald's and whoever was there to practice all his latest moves on. Moves he'd been honing for many years.

In the dim corridors of Houston's rusted history, Fitzgerald's stood as a spectral monolith, a mansion first raised in 1918. For over half a century, the building pulsed with the haunting hum of life as *Dom Polski's*, a Polish hall where holdovers from the old world twirled beneath chandeliers that glowed with perpetual energy. Then came 1977, the year of its metamorphosis, a new soul fused to its foundation. G.B. FitzGerald, a visionary or perhaps a madman, seized the property and breathed new life into its aging frame. Thus, Fitzgerald's was born with a lowercase "g," not merely as a venue, but as a crucible where dreams would ignite or crumble into ash.

It pulsed with a dual heartbeat: two sprawling event spaces stacked one over the other. The upstairs lounge was infamous for its grit and sweat-drenched nights, while the downstairs, dubbed "Zelda's" by those in the know, felt like stepping into a subterranean den of chaos. Both rooms boasted stages primed for war, armed with towering speakers and spotlights that cut through the haze. The bars, stocked with top-shelf liquor and enough beer to drown the world, kept the masses fueled and reckless.

The stages of Fitzgerald's were hallowed, cursed, and blessed in equal measure. Thousands of fledgling musicians stood beneath the cruel gaze of stage lights, their fates sealed in chords and lyrics.

Legends rose and fell there. Kayote, ZZ Top, and David

Allan Coe had thundered across the venue's marquees like titans. James Brown and Etta James conjured spells of rhythm and blues that lingered long after the music ceased. Soon after, the music scene ran hotter: R.E.M., The Ramones, and Sonic Youth left their fingerprints on its decaying brickwork.

The upstairs lounge was always ripe with a frenetic energy, a heartbeat of muffled bass and the low hum of conversations. The place had once been a stately two-story home, its skeleton still visible beneath layers of reinvention. Dark wood paneling lined the walls, worn smooth by decades of sweat-soaked hands and half-forgotten memories. The ceiling beams loomed overhead, splintered and sagging in places, lending the room the weight of something ancient. Maybe something haunted.

The floor groaned under the shifting feet of the overstuffed crowd: college kids, drunk regulars, and late-night wanderers drawn to the gritty music scene that clung to the club walls like a second skin. The venue's signature scent lingered: a pungent mix of stale beer and whiskey, cigarette smoke that hung in the air, and sweat. It soaked into every surface, refusing to fade no matter how many times the floors were mopped or the tables wiped down.

The sound system was notorious. Superb twin speakers perched above the stage blasted music that reverberated off the walls in distorted waves, sharp enough to rattle ribs. It was raw, gritty, made for survival. Onstage, the guitars growled and snarled through the amps, and the drumbeats came down like hammer strikes. Reverb filled the room like static electricity, charging the air until even conversations felt like shouted confessions.

The lighting was minimalist and deliberate. Strings of colored bulbs flickered along the beams, throwing splashes of red, green, and purple across the crowded room. Overhead, rusted metal fans spun lazily, their shadows slicing through the dim light in slow revolutions. Most of the stage was illuminated by two ancient floodlights, their yellow glow fading at the edges. The rest of the room was cast in twilight, a space where faces appeared and disappeared in the haze of cigarette smoke.

Brody stood at the end of the bar, barely noticed among the shifting bodies. But that would soon change. Chaos swirled around him—drunken laughter, clinking glasses, the screech of microphone feedback—but he was silent, motionless. His gaze cut through the dimness, locked on a single figure. The woman moved with an unconscious grace, unaware of the nutcases lurking just around the corner.

***

An hour before Brody decided Fitzgerald's would be the place to find his first real trophy, he was in line at the Wells Fargo Bank in Downtown Houston, Wells Fargo Plaza, to be exact. He went to make a simple deposit to his checking account only to get behind a portly woman in her early 20s, wearing a filthy pair of sweatpants with matching hoodie. She, too, was making a deposit, but it was far from simple.

During the woman's deliberately slow transaction, a few others in line behind him began to lose patience. "My God, what the hell is she doing?" "For God Sake, you've gotta be kidding." An older lady directly behind him was really getting heated while the sweat-hooded fat woman kept at it. "There are other people in line here, missy, really?"

Brody slowly turned around, smiled at the old woman, winked, then faced the counter again, his own patience having lost its way long before the others in line breathed a word. When the young fatso with no care on the earth finally wrapped things up, she shuffled away without not so much an eye toward the others in line.

He paid special attention to exactly where she was walking when she exited the bank. His deposit took a minute, tops. With stealth grace and speed, he left the bank quickly enough to follow the woman with a subdued cadence; she would never suspect she was being followed.

She lumbered down to Lamar St. After a hundred feet or so, Brody could see she was heading toward the Houston Public Library. He extended his lag a few more strides as his heart picked up its pace. Inside the library, he would have ample opportunity to make sure the woman would never delay another fellow bank patron again.

He'd always been different. Even as a child, there had been a quiet intensity in him, a storm brewing behind his eyes that others could sense but not understand. The martial arts and combat sports had given that storm form and focus, molding him into a high-powered weapon. But all that training, all those years spent honing his body and mind, had never seen the light of real combat. At least in his mind. Regardless of how many competitions he'd won, they were all in controlled environments, tucked away in the safety of dojos and arenas with referees and coaches. Out in the real world, he felt like a caged animal, waiting for the right moment to bust out and rip something to pieces.

He followed the sweatpants and hoodie as the fat woman waddled into Houston's massive library. He followed her up the escalators to the 4th floor where she made a stop in the ladies' restroom. Brody took a small drink from the water fountain that was between the men's and ladies' restrooms, then stalked into the ladies' room and broke the woman's right arm, buckled her left knee, shattered several ribs on both sides of her chest, grabbed her by her hair and hoodie, slammed her face into one of the toilets, and held her underwater until her fat body stopped jerking and convulsing.

With ease, Brody finished the deed by lifting the woman—easily 200 pounds—up to prop her body on the toilet and lean it against the wall until he was satisfied it wouldn't topple over. He completed the murder within a few seconds, quickly and efficiently enough to avoid anyone outside the restroom from suspecting anything was afoul. All was fine and dandy in Brody's mind, which is all that mattered.

He took a few more sips of water from the fountain, wiped his lips, and took the escalators down to the lobby, and proceeded back to the Wells Fargo Plaza where he'd parked his Boxster. It was time to plan his evening, time to keep practicing various moves he'd been working on over the past several months that he wanted to use as a test-run later that night. He opened the sunroof and turned the car's fabulous stereo high enough for nearby drivers to be forced to hear. Soundgarden's "Super Unknown" blasted into Houston's searing night, Chris Cornell's raging voice crying out about stolen souls. That's when he decided to spend the evening at Fitzgerald's.

***

When Chelsey Bingham heard Rex Brody tell her that it wasn't possible for her to have a better time that night, it was a line she'd heard countless times. Or similar ones that were always delivered with the same end-result: getting her panties off. Chelsey was gorgeous and knew it. Loved to dress in tops and skirts that highlighted every perfect curve. She also knew her raspy voice was one that men found more than enticing. Everything about her breathed sex, and she knew that, too.

It was late on September 10th, 2001, and she was on a mission to enrage her boyfriend. Why not? He was rarely decent to her, at least lately. She also knew he had been sneaking around far too often for her liking. Far too many lies that were becoming easier to spot when knowing what to look for, and she knew where and how to look in every corner no matter how small or carefully hidden. Most men were never careful enough.

Every time she had gone out over the past few months, she went out alone. She'd been working with "Mr. Clean" (the nickname she picked the moment she first laid eyes on him) for over a year, but since the past summer it felt more like a decade. The "Mr. Clean" came from the doctor's uncanny resemblance to the iconic image of Mr. Clean cleaning products: shiny bald head, six-nine frame of solid muscle, 250 pounds or more. He called her his recruiter, which was fine by Chelsey. She enjoyed the work, as every potential candidate was always different, always something specific to his thinking. Tonight's assignment was no different. Her work with him was a part-time gig, but one she knew one day would make her famous. She knew her boss's full-time gig was a surgeon of some kind. That's all he ever wanted her to know, which was also fine. She never bothered to do any background check on him. She wouldn't dare. Mr. Clean was rich, powerful, and scary.

So, why not entertain Rex's stupid line? He was far different than anyone she'd ever met. For one, it was refreshing to really look at a man who was in such perfect condition who had hair and wasn't a giant, like her boss, or a loser like her boyfriend, who she was done with. Rex looked sculpted, jet-black hair and all. Even his clothes looked sculpted: fitted black t-shirt, low-waisted fashion jeans and black leather boots.

Second, Rex had a voice that was sophisticated and polished. Not like a car salesman or some talking head on Houston's Channel 13 Live Weekend Nights. Rex's sound was one of pure confidence that landed on even purer authenticity. Chesley had been hit on by a thousand men, every one of them with the same tired agenda, especially when seeing her in a braless top and mini skirt, which she made sure, that for this night, she wore the skimpiest one in her wardrobe.

But not Rex, which was also far different from most men, including her boss. Rex's eyes never roamed—not for a second—over any part of her body. Eyes that remained locked on hers regardless of any move she intentionally made. Most men's eyes wandered, but not this guy's.

Last but far from least was Rex's smell. It wasn't just the fine cologne he faintly wore. She knew all the finest brands; his was a natural smell that was powerful...deeply masculine; not at all the base animalism of Mr. Clean, nor the cheap Old Spice her boyfriend wore to mask showering only once a week, if she was lucky.

Perhaps Rex knew it, perhaps not. Didn't matter; how he carried himself, how he took care of himself, how he presented himself when he said, "it's not possible for you to have a better time tonight than with me." It sounded like the most original and flattering opening she'd ever heard. As he spoke, the fabulous sound system lit into Korn's "Freak On A Leash," Jonathan Davis's wicked voice wailing on about cheap sex that took pieces of his soul away.

Maybe she would recruit him, she was thinking, as she moved her body to the heavy rhythmic pulse of Korn while doing her damnedest to keep eye contact with Rex's, which, of course, were yet one more showcase item. Where she'd seen so many leering eyes roam all over her, including Mr. Clean's near perpetual pitch-black ones, Rex's were a glassy hazel, nearly green, she could get lost in. His chiseled frame seemed to move with more grace than her own.

"Is that right? Not being 'possible' to have a better night?" As much as she wanted to sound sexy, she knew that having to yell over the music always stripped away what she intended.

"Absolutely. Let's find a nice sit down, shall we? Place looks like it has hundreds of them." Rex moved his head and eyes around the ceiling and walls.

Chelsey thought he was looking for something more than just a place to sit, which kept the intrigue even more tight.

"You've never been here?" Chelsey stopped dancing

and placed both hands on her hips genuinely puzzled. Fitzgerald's in Houston was one of the hottest night venues in Texas, so it was clearly one of the hottest in the world.

"No, first time. But...heard a lot about it. I've been in New York but originally from Lake City, so I thought—"

"You a Mormon? Is that why you're the best time here? I hear you Mormon boys are so pent up with gospel living that most are hooked on porn and pain killers. But you don't really look the—"

Rex stopped his dance movements and held both hands out toward her, his index fingers up in a clear message he didn't appreciate being interrupted.

Chelsey had the distinct feeling that keeping quiet was the better option with this one. Maybe he was the exact thing she needed, maybe he was the perfect recruit.

"I wasn't finished." Brody's voice cut through the music like icy wire.

Chelsey nodded quickly. "I didn't mean to interrupt."

"Of course not."

She sensed that Rex quickly softened with her apology and moved closer in. "The upstairs area is a little quieter. Not much, but a little."

Brody moved his eyes only to look up at Fitzgerald's second tier, his eyes roaming a few seconds before moving back to Chelsey's where they locked in place again. "I'll follow you up. I'm Rex Brody." He held out his right hand.

Chelsey took it in her own, thought it felt like a piece of boned oak; easily as strong as Mr. Clean's and far more muscled. Where Mr. Clean had a natural strength that matched his size, what she felt in Rex's handshake was something that had taken years to produce.

"You work out a lot?" She giggled at her own stupid question as Rex gave a slow nod. "Sorry. I'm Chelsey. Bingham."

"After you, Miss Bingham."

"Ohhh. So polite."

Brody raised his right hand slightly with his index finger up, moving it slowly side to side. "Not what I'm saying at all. You can trust me when I tell you I'm a far cry from polite, little honeypot. Let's find a spot and continue this, yes? And I've changed my mind. Follow me." Rex said it in a perfect Al Pacino voice but doubted she caught on. He was in one of those moods when everything he could whimsically come up with would be the only way to mentally cancel out the blows he'd just given to the fatso bank customer who would never make another deposit again. Whimsical would do.

"Lead the way then, Mister Brody."

Rex liked the sound of it. Had a ring he liked...but it wasn't perfect. Reminded him of something he heard long ago as a child listening to his father tell the world he couldn't be a father, that he never intended on being a father and that he, Rex, his sister, Emma, and brother, Don, were in the way of everything he wanted to do.

Brody had been looking for a perfect nickname for a while. None of the ones other fighters came up ever caught on. He needed something that sounded perfect. His lips curved slightly at the sound of "Mister Brody," but the smile didn't quite reach his eyes. He turned from Chelsey and began to ascend the stairs, his movements deliberate, precise. Chelsey followed him in perfect sync. The old wooden steps groaned under their weight, the sound swallowed by the thrum of the music below.

The second-floor lounge at Fitzgerald's was darker, more intimate, filled with white noise that softened the noise from below to a lower, more steady pulse, accompanied by the distant clatter of glassware and bursts of laughter. Fewer people lingered here, but still, plenty gathered in small groups around battered tables or slouched in corner booths. Mismatched couches and chairs added to the room's cobbled-together charm, upholstery frayed from years of restless use.

Chelsey remained close behind, brushing her hair away from her face as she took in the dim surroundings. A string of blue fairy lights wound along the ceiling beams, casting an eerie glow that made the shadows come to life.

Rex led her to a booth in the far corner, one that was tucked just enough out of sight. He slid in smoothly, resting his arms on the table as he watched her take the seat across from him.

Chelsey crossed her legs and leaned forward slightly, her eyes glinting with curiosity. "So, Mister Brody..." she began, her raspy voice honeyed and lower, "what's a New York-to-Lake City boy like you doing so far south? Got an itch to be a cowboy?"

He paused, as though weighing his response, rested his fingertips lightly against the table's edge, tapping once. Twice. "I'm no boy." His tone was measured, charged with an undertone that caused her discomfort.

She tilted her head. "I didn't mean anything by it."

Rex stared.

Chelsey shifted her body on the padded bench seat, trying to adjust. She cleared her throat. "Just curious why Houston, then again, it's as good a place as any. I mean I love this town, best food you'll ever eat, New York included."

"I needed a change."

Rex's gaze locked onto hers with an intensity that sent a shiver down her spine. She shifted her body again for a different position.

"Houston's a lot like Cambodia. I also spent a lot of time there, five years or so, maybe six, before coming back to the states and making a go at New York for a few months before saying enough was enough. At least for now. I'll get back there again one day, but here...it's a lot like Cambodia. At least the climate is."

Chelsey shook her head side to side slowly as she drank his words. "What in God's name were you doing in *there*?"

***

The Houston Police Department's downtown headquarters was a hive of hyper chaos, a fortress of brick and glass that pulsed with relentless energy. The hum of dispatch radios blended with the clatter of keyboards and the steady ring of phones, creating a discordant symphony of urgency. Constant urgency. The fluorescents overhead cast a cold, sterile glow, buzzing faintly like the city's heartbeat, tireless and unyielding. Unforgiving. Printed in large black sans serif lettering, the HPD codes were posted for everyone's constant viewing pleasure:

Houston Police Department Codes	
261 - Rape	217 - Assault w intent to murder
261A - Attempted Rape	245 - Assault w Deadly Weapon
314 - Indecent Exposure	419 - Dead Human Body
240 - Assault	417 - Person w a Gun
187 - Homicide	417K - Person w a Knife
218 - Sexual Activity with a minor	444 - Officer Involved Shooting
214 - Kidnapping and Murder	999 - All officers respond/ city wide emergency
211 - Robbery	

Detectives in wrinkled suits hurried down the hallways, files tucked under their arms or coffee cups clutched like lifelines. Uniformed officers moved with practiced efficiency, their expressions a mixture of exhaustion and readiness. Each face told a story: some etched with the weariness of double shifts, others hardened by the ghosts of unsolved cases. Yet there was a rhythm to the chaos, a strange order beneath the frenetic disarray, as though everyone was locked into the same unspoken tempo. It was as though hysteria was the norm.

In the bullpen, desks were crammed together in uneven rows, cluttered with stacks of reports, half-empty Styrofoam cups, and framed photos of distant family moments. The air carried the faint, stale scent of burnt coffee and stress. Shitloads of stress. Overhead, old ceiling fans creaked with every slow rotation, fighting a losing battle against the thick humidity that seeped in through the building's aging windows.

The noise in the bullpen ebbed and flowed with the night's crises; there were many:

An arrest brought in from a robbery gone awry in Sunnyside, a hood of crucible desperation, its streets burdened by a reputation carved from staggering crime rates and fear. With a reported 92 incidents per 1,000 residents, the odds of becoming a victim weren't distant probabilities, they were grim certainties etched into daily life. Here, one in eleven people would feel the cold grip of crime firsthand. Robberies, brutal assaults, and the consistent murder punctuated the rhythm of Sunnyside's nights like discordant notes in a requiem. Despite its name, there was no warmth in its shadows, only the suffocating sense that danger could strike at any corner, without warning, and without mercy.

A domestic disturbance that escalated into something more brutal and violent in the 5th Ward, an area in Houston that was a wound that refused to heal. Crumbling houses lined the streets like broken teeth, their windows darkened and hollow. Graffiti-marked walls bore the stories of despair, while streetlights flickered weakly or lay shattered altogether. The air hung in perpetual oppression, thick with the metallic tang of rust and decay. Gunfire constantly echoed sporadically in the distance, punctuating every night like a heartbeat out of rhythm. Violence in the 5th Ward wasn't just an occurrence, it was a way of life, woven into the fabric of the neighborhood.

There was always the possible rape in the Sharpstown area as well as drive-by shooting. Sharpstown bore the scars of decades of decline, its streets worn down by poverty and unchecked violence. Once a thriving neighborhood, it had become synonymous with crime, a place where locked doors and wary glances were as common as the cracked sidewalks and boarded-up storefronts. Drug trade and gang conflicts surged through it like a wicked current, feeding a cycle of hopelessness. Residents struggled to carve out a sense of normalcy amid the chaos, but hope was fragile, easily shattered by the echo of gunshots or the siren's mournful wail. Sharpstown was a neighborhood caught in a cruel chokehold, where survival itself often felt like a victory.

Every update crackled across the dispatch speakers, each new incident another thread in the tangled web of the night.

"Code 45, suspicious activity near Fifth and Lamar." "Code 187, possible homicide near Liberty and Jensen." "Code 261 on Greens Road near Imperial Valley, rape in progress." And on and on it went. Night after fucking night.

The dispatcher's voices cut through the din, met with a chorus of shuffling papers and officers grabbing their radios. In the corner, a young patrolman, a rookie, scribbled notes while juggling the phone on his shoulder, his voice low but tense.

At the center of it all, sitting at a desk surrounded by a bunker of case files, was Detective Heath Spade, a veteran, an HPD fixture for over twenty years. His reputation had been built on hard work, a sharp mind, and an almost pathological refusal to let a case go cold. His presence commanded respect, not because he demanded it, but because he had earned it with his own blood.

Spade had the broad shoulders and weathered hands and face of a man who had lived through countless long nights and hard truths. His suit jacket hung off the back of his chair, revealing a sweat-stained dress shirt rolled up at the sleeves. The tie around his neck was loose, as though strangled by the weight of another night gone south.

Photographs were pinned to the corkboard near his desk, as were crime scene notes—pieces of a puzzle that no one wanted to solve but everyone feared. Known to the public as The Bone Break Killer (no one official had any clue to his real name) he was a serial killer who'd been paving a bloody path across Houston for what Spade believed to be at least eighteen months. Spade suspected longer. The nickname came from his brutal signature: broken bones, even shattered bones, before death, as though his victims had been sculptures he wanted to dismantle piece by piece but leaving the fragments inside the victims' skin.

Spade's eyes flicked over the photos of the killer's victims. Young women and men, completely random, zero pattern, nothing obvious except for the violence inflicted upon them. Spade leaned back in his chair; the old wood creaked under his weight. He rubbed his chin, feeling the stubble scrape against his palm, exhaled slowly. He was sure another body would soon show up, left behind in a parking garage or inside a trash dumpster, unthinkably twisted and unrecognizable.

The body-count to the night of September 10th, 2001, was at fourteen. Who knew what September 11th would bring?

Detective Carmen Hayes, his partner on the case and partner of ten years plus a few months, appeared at his side with a clipboard.

Without looking up: "Any word on the evidence I'd sent to you the past few days? Any thoughts you'd care to share?" Spade felt tired, irritated, ready for combat.

Her face was drawn tight with exhaustion, but her eyes were sharp. "I haven't had time, Spade, and I'm just as goddamned irritable as you are, for that matter. I take it you've not heard yet. A preliminary report just came in." Carmen tossed him a new file folder without a care in the world if it would land on the floor all sprawled and messy. "Same type of shit. Femur, tibia, and radius, snapped clean. Looks like he used some kind of vice or brace, but with some kind of padding between the metal and skin. Again, skin intact. No fingerprints, no fibers."

Spade slammed his palm on the folder before it could slide off the pile, then looked up to Hayes with a deep frown. "Really?"

"Look for yourself."

He flipped through the pages, his brow furrowing deeper with each line. "Jesus Fucking Christ. He's getting better."

"Or bolder."

Spade's jaw tightened. "Let me ask you this...it's been hammering at me and won't let up. Do you think he's got an accomplice?"

Hayes scowled. "Sure, it's possible."

"I didn't ask you if it's possible. I asked you what you think."

"Christ, Spade. I'm as overworked as you. We can't say shit to the press because we don't know shit. I can't sleep. I'm drinking almost non-stop. I've got no life, just like you, so—"

"Stop." Spade stood quickly with his hand up before Hayes could rattle on about her endless woes. "Sorry. I got it. You're right. I'm asking because I don't think it's an angle anyone's considered. Maybe someone has but no one's told me different. Let's take a look back, if I may. Bundy. Gacy.

Slasher Eugene Watts. The Railroad Killer, Angel Reséndiz. Anthony Shore, The Tourniquet Killer. Jeffrey Fucking Dahmer, for that matter. They all worked alone. In fact, every one of these pieces of shit over the years has worked alone... Except one."

Hayes put her hands on her hips. "I give up. Who are you talking about?"

Spade shook his head in irritation. "Really, partner? Manson. Man. Son. The Manson family? You remember that lovely hippie and the Sharon Tate fucking Helter-Skelter case?"

She got in his face. "Don't patronize me, Spade. And don't try and tell me that what's going on with The Bone Break Killer is some kind of modern Manson Family Special."

Spade sat, shut the folder with a sharp snap, and leaned forward, his hands clasped on the folder. "I'm not saying that exactly," he growled. "Not yet. But think about it, Hayes. Every serial killer back to Jack the Ripper has worked alone. We're still in the dark with The Ripper; no one really knows jack shit. No pun. I'm just saying, 'what if?' What if this motherfucker has someone helping him? Why does that sound so Goddamn crazy? Plus, I'm not giving him the satisfaction of knowing we're scrambling."

"I don't know, Detective. It just feels like we're reaching."

"*We're* reaching. Then I'm not so far off base. There's nothing wrong with reaching, Detective."

"I didn't say that. Heath, I know what this case has been doing to you because it's done the same thing to me. Have you thought about that? But it's the nature of these murders. I have to think there's only one of this guy because there's no one else on earth who'd want to be part of it."

Spade made sure to pay special attention, as Hayes rarely called him by his first name. Unless it was something beyond stress she kept it last name only, regardless of how much time they had been together.

"You're giving humanity a bit too much credit. Tell you what, why don't we get a fresh set of eyes on this for a sec. We've got yet another prelim report, and that's all that matters right now. Let's ask that rookie over there. What's his name? Doesn't look like any rookie I've ever seen."

Hayes looked across the room to the rookie, hands on her hips in thought. "Paul. Marion Paul. Lue's got him on a Beat near Greenspoint. Smart one. Masters in Criminal Justice and shit."

"Fancy. Looks too old and wise to be a rookie."

"Yeah. Also took a two-year stint out of the country for religion or some damn thing. Fluent in French. The works, this one."

"Mercy. Well, nothing wrong with doing time for The Lord Thy God, Hayes, but I wonder what the hell he's doing here. Whatever. He's got street-smarts, a moral compass, educated, and bilingual. Could come in handy."

"Learn something new about you every day, partner. What do you mean street-smarts?"

"Anyone who leaves the country for a few years to teach The Word will do a lot more learning than teaching. Bank on it. Bring him over here."

***

Marion Paul heard the woman detective call over to his workstation. He was familiar with her, Detective Carmen Hayes, worked homicide for some ten years—which was a lifetime in any police department—and was considered one of the Houston streets' most effective weapons. As he walked over to her, he couldn't, at first, recognize Heath Spade but when close enough, there he was. The legend himself. One of Houston's most famous detectives. One of the most feared. He looked just like his pics pinned all over HPD corkboards. Lean, weathered and shredded. Maybe

5'9" tops, 150 pounds, who could easily bench 275, maybe 300, several times clean. He'd also taken down some of Houston's ugliest players.

When Marion reached the two partners, he extended his hand to both. "Marion Paul, ma'am." Hayes looked at him with a light smile as he then extended to Spade. "Marion Paul, detective."

"Christ, Paul, got some stout on you. What do you bench? Three-fifty?"

Marion took a step back after shaking hands with confidence, a slow grin on his face, proud that Spade had noticed him as much as he noticed Spade. "Just cleaned 405 a few weeks back. Four plates."

"Why the fuck are you not competing somewhere? And Hayes tells me you're quite the scholar. That true, too?"

Marion nodded to both experienced detectives. "I don't know if I'm a scholar, but I've done plenty of homework, sure."

"Graduate degree in Criminal Justice and bilingual, English and French. You're a mite over qualified to be a beat cop. Trying to figure out why you're here, to be honest, trying to make the connection. Family?"

Marion thought before saying anything. He and his wife had just become proud parents, and he wondered if being a cop was a serious mistake. "Houston native. Married. We just had a baby girl. Named her Casey. I've got a brother here, too. Steven Paul. Been in and out of jail a lot, Drinking, drugs. The works."

"Good Christ, Paul." Hayes shook her head, an echo to Spade's surprised expression. "Why the fuck are you here? Good God. Why Houston PD?"

It was Spade's turn to shake his head in agreement to her reprimand of rookie Marion Paul. He rubbed his chin slowly in thought. Of course, he'd wondered the same thing many times. Went round and round with his wife about it. But this guy...

"It's fairly simple, detectives. I've always wanted to be a cop. Nothing else really appealed to me. I did a stint in the military, didn't really work out. This will. I've always been one for action."

Spade looked Marion up and down. "I see. I'm sure I don't have to tell you this, but you're gonna hear it anyway. Action will get you killed, rookie. I've seen it far too many times. Tried to revive a few. Do you want to leave your wife a widow to raise that little one all by her lonesome?"

Marion knew it was best to keep from arguing but also knew it was best to hold his ground, especially in front of two of Houston's finest. He took in a deep breath and let it out slowly. "You guys called me over here. I appreciate your concern, but as you can see, I'm no spring chicken. I've thought this through plenty. So, please, what is it you want? I've got a Beat to get to."

Spade slowly grinned and lowered his head, moving his gaze back and forth between Marion and Carmen. "Assertive. I like that. I'll tell you what. Your Beat can wait. I'll cover for you. Besides, I think you're gonna find this case a lot more up your alley. If you want in on this, let's see what you got. Follow me down the hall."

Marion followed them to another more raucous bullpen area. There, he saw hundreds of photos pinned up and down massive corkboards with colored pins stuck in a hundred places or more, which represented different sections and ghettos and apartment complexes in the Greater Houston Area.

"Take a good look, Paul. You recognize any of this? Take your time."

Marion scanned all the hopeful connections carefully before saying a word. It was something he had done all through his undergraduate and graduate work, always making sure to focus on one thing: the matter at hand. In this case, what Detectives Spade and Hayes were showing him was a matter at hand that could have him off the Beat and into this playing field in no time. Spade and Hayes were tracking someone, and they needed someone fresh to take a crack at it. Had to be the newest serial killer case. “You’re after The Bone Break Killer.”

Both detectives nodded. Spade’s nod urged Marion to keep talking.

“What do you want to know?”

Spade scoffed. “You say that like you have an opinion on the matter. Do you, rookie?”

Marion rubbed his scuffed face with both hands. “Yeah, I do.”

“Nice. See, Hayes. I had a feeling about this rookie.” Spade turned to Hayes then back to Marion. “Let’s hear it, Paul. What do you want to share? And please don’t waste my time with shit I’ve heard a hundred times over. Time is running out on this motherfucker. I can feel he’s about to make a mistake.”

Marion took in another deep breath and held it, knowing this could be his first real shot at the big leagues, knowing that such an opportunity took years for cops to find. Many never would. What he said next could catapult his brand-new career on a fast path that most cops only dreamed about.

“The Bone Break Killer, I think he has an accomplice, luring his victims, someone who can attract men and women. And I think he’s using a big rig for cover. They can move around this town without any suspicion. Plenty of space in the trailer, too, for all the shit he’s been doing. Sick bastard.”

“You know of a serial killer who isn’t? Please fill me in.”

Marion could tell that Spade was growing impatient. “Touché.”

Hayes rolled her eyes the second Marion mentioned an accomplice. “Paul? Why does a beast like him need anyone to coax the victims? And why would anyone want to be part of something this bent?”

Marion paused. He was a thinker and spoke only when thinking things completely through, which drove a lot of people into interrupting him, but he saw that Spade and Hayes were patient. They would have to be on such a hunt.

"This guy can break bones so precisely and so brutally without causing any skin lesions. So that means he's both incredibly strong and knows exactly what he's doing."

"Yeah, yeah, yeah." Irritated, Spade put up his hand. "We know all this, Paul, Jesus. Son-of-a-bitch could be an anatomy specialist or pre-med or was pre-med and got himself a real itch for the barbaric. Could be some wacko nerd who has a photographic memory and has watched a shitload of surgery videos, or any—"

"Doctor?" Spade quickly locked eyes with his partner then back to Marion. You think this killer's a doctor. Is that what you're saying?"

"Why not? Look at Jack the Ripper. Lots of folks believe he was a surgeon. Plenty of journals and theories written back in the day with solid evidence that suggested the possibility. Of course, there were, and are, plenty of other theories, but what's the difference here? I'm surprised you guys haven't considered that possibility."

Hayes shook her head slowly.

Spade huffed. "Not exactly... So, enlighten us."

Marion paced the few steps to stand beside Hayes. "Ever heard of Occam's Razor?"

"Christ." Spade's irritation cranked up a notch.

"Just go with me here, Detective Spade. The simplest explanation is usually the correct one."

Hayes elbowed him. "Go on."

"This is Houston." He indicated the map. "We've got the Medical Center here." He finger-traced a circle around a multitude of pushpins. "A city-sized complex with more doctors than anywhere in the country, the perfect environment for a sicko who wants to take his orthopedic skillset to the streets and run unchecked. It's the perfect setup for Occam's Razor. The killer puts something right in front of your face, knowing it's going to go undetected."

Both Spade and Hayes eyeballed the rookie cop. "Not bad," Spade said. "You're right about The Medical Center. Fuck if I know, or anyone else here, how many doctors we're talking about. Could be thousands. Where would we start, got a plan on that?"

"No, not yet, but...and it's a big but...from everything I've read that he's done, I would think he's a big fella. Like Shaquille O'Neal big."

"Point?" Spade had a hand under his chin as if holding his head up in thought.

Carmen signaled with her hand to keep it moving.

"The point is a turd like that is not gonna to be approachable. Not even by his patients. And if he had approached any one of the victims so far, they would have run off or moved away quickly enough to avoid him. So, he's got someone else doing the approaching. Not someone in the medical field, either. Someone he's paid off or knows about who would be into such sick shit. Occam's Razor again. It's just a thought."

"Turd" was the standard term a lot of Houston cops used for their worst hard cases, though it was clearly a bit tame for someone who was destroying people's skeletal structure. Not piece of shit. Not motherfucker. Not son-of-a-bitch followed by multiple expletives. Turd.

Carmen stepped closer to Marion. "Let's talk about the truck. And before you interrupt me...come to think of it, you're not the interrupting type I've noticed, so scratch that. But I don't want to hear Occam's Razor again. I get it. We get it. If he's a doctor, why the semi-truck? Why not some rigged out Dodge or Ford with a long bed? Better yet, why not some private dungeon playground in a place he could afford, and to have such a place to go on with the bone breaking to his sick-as-fuck heart's desire?"

Marion frowned. "Sure, those are all possible, too. Not

ruling them out. I'm sure he does have some kind of 'dungeon' as you say. Doctors, good ones, have that kind of money. It's just a theory. But a semi-truck feels like something this one would use. Think about it. A doctor who owns a semi-truck to do this kind of shit? He's thinking, *No one's ever going to put two and two together. No way.*"

Spade shook his head slowly, clearly impressed. "Feels like? Already getting hunches, rookie? I like that. In fact, I like all of it." Detective Spade slapped both his hands together as if a light would come on. "Alright, Hayes, let's start working this angle. We've got nothing to lose except the time we're wasting. Let's start shaking down the whole fucking Medical Center with the focus on who's the biggest doc in town. Good work, Paul. I won't forget this, believe me. Hit your Beat, and I'll stay in touch. Anyone gives you any shit for being late, have them page me."

Marion Paul felt elated as he walked off, trying to not show it.

The bullpen door swung open, and a uniformed officer hurried in, out of breath. "Detective Spade. Another call. Downtown garage on Westheimer. Security found something. Something terrible."

Spade exchanged a glance with Hayes, his gut already twisting with a grim certainty. He grabbed his jacket and slid it on in one smooth motion. "Let's roll."

The bullpen swirled behind them as they strode toward the door, the noise and chaos resuming its relentless pulse. But for Spade, the world had narrowed to a single point: the specter of The Bone Break Killer looming just beyond the edge of reason, daring him to step closer.

***

Rex Brody chose Houston as the place to live for however long was needed to fulfill his destiny. Or at least start it. It had all the excitement of The Big Apple at half the cost and a climate that matched Cambodia: hot and humid. The best climate for skin, and Brody was in love with his own. He also chose Houston because it would be the last place his ex-girlfriend, Collette, would ever go. He met her in New York and, within the first few days of dating her, found out she hated the South. That he ended up being with her during the entire time he was in New York was nothing short of parting the Red Sea. Before her, the longest relationship he endured was just over three weeks. Three and a half, tops.

The breakup had come only hours before his run-in with Mrs. Fat Hoodie Sweats at the Wells Fargo Plaza in downtown, a scene that kept replaying in his head repeatedly, along with replaying, in jagged flashes, what went down with Colette. He imagined her tear-streaked face, the way her voice trembled in horror on the telephone as she said, "You're not the same man, Rex. You're...dangerous. Fucking crazy is what you are. Probably always were and I just never saw it. Psycho fuck, I never want to hear your name again."

Dangerous. Crazy. Psycho fuck. Words that stung like the backhanded compliments they were. Reminded him of childhood memories of his endless trauma from his dad, Sam Brody, and his sleaze girlfriend—Kathy something or other—fighting to the point of exhaustion. More exhausting for his sister, Emma, and himself than Sam Brody's lack for any life.

Brody had things brewing inside him much deeper.

His hate for humanity wasn't born from a single event years ago in the empty halls of a caseworker's conference room; it was a slow, relentless build, fueled by years of stifling monotony and forced conformity. When he was older and finally out of his last foster home disaster, he turned to reading scriptures, spending countless hours digging through *The Bible* in multiple languages—English, Spanish, even French. But instead of finding enlightenment and some form of release from the anguish of being tossed from one foster fuckshow to the next, he found only exhaustion. The same exhaustion he and Emma felt in their childhood wreckage of Sam Brody's making.

The scriptural words became jagged lead anchors hooked deep on his mind, their meaning diluted by repetition. His church leaders had insisted he read daily, hammering home the same doctrine until it all blurred into a mind-numbing haze. It didn't take long before scripture became synonymous with resentment. The act of reading itself, something once noble and expansive, was twisted into a tedious chore that left a bitter taste and never healed the open wounds of his father's betrayal.

It wasn't just the reading, it was the ritual, the sermons, the same hollow lessons repeated until his spirit felt caged. He tried to go to church every Sunday, but it quickly began to feel like a prison sentence, the same rote answers and reverent nods from the same obedient faces. To Rex, the church wasn't a sanctuary, it was a machine built to grind people into submission. He broke free of it in eight months, severing his ties to the congregation. He never found peace; he found exile.

He found the tribalism of the community cut deeper than any doctrine. To leave meant becoming an outsider, a pariah in the eyes of those who once smiled at him during hymnals. The warmth of fellowship turned ice-cold, replaced with hollow pity and whispered condemnation. He was no longer invited to gatherings or treated as one of their own unless he repented...unless he returned to the boredom, the sameness, the slow suffocation of spirit.

He was done with all of it.

The isolation carved a permanent scar just as ugly as the ones left in childhood. Rex saw humanity not as individuals, but as herds –blind, clinging to routine, too afraid to question their place. He viewed any faith as fragile, an illusion that disintegrated under scrutiny. His hatred festered in the shadow of that betrayal, not just of church, but of the deeper truth he'd discovered: that most people preferred the prison of routine to the terrifying freedom of standing alone.

For Rex, the world became a stage of hypocrisy, a stage he would no longer watch in silence. His disdain became a furnace, fueling his desire to strip away the masks and reveal humanity's hollow core, one agonizing piece at a time. He knew the raging lunatic inside of him was the answer, he just had no idea why or how. Or what, for that matter.

His hatred for humanity wasn't just born of betrayal and isolation, it was a slow, ugly build, as though inherited from something far older and far more sinister. The more he examined the threads of his existence, the more convinced he became that he was a part of something vast, something that had been whispered through history like a cursed refrain.

He began to dig deep into his past. Genealogy of all things, and the one thing that church had shown him that made any sense. Finding that sense of history and his own place in it.

He began to find stories that began as shadows in his family's history, fragments of strange tales told in quiet, shameful voices. On his mother's side, there had always been rumors of a dark connection—a name spoken with a bitter, trembling reverence: Jack.

Brody had dismissed it as the kind of grotesque family myth designed to make the mundane seem extraordinary. But the deeper he dug, the stranger the possibility of the trail became.

One late night, after paying a visit to his broken father, Sam Brody told him a story where letters hidden in a tin box could be found at the back of a crumbling ancestral home north of Odessa in a town called Williams. It was where his great grandparents had grown up. Sam told him of letters that reeked of time and rot, most likely were faded in ink but perhaps their meaning sharp as ever. Sam said the letters spoke of legacy and obsession, of nights spent in the fog-choked streets of Whitechapel, searching for meaning through chaos and death. Sam said that one name appeared repeatedly: Conrad Ellington.

That same late night, Rex made the drive out to Williams and found the tin box just as his father had said. One of the only truths the poor son-of-a-bitch ever told.

Who was Ellington? Why was there so little history of him? Brody discovered his ancestors had kept the name alive like a secret talisman, though no one dared to speak it aloud.

Ellington's journals—buried in the depths of history—were filled with the kind of reflections that chilled Brody, and that was saying something. They didn't berate madness as much as they embraced it, wrapping themselves in a belief that humanity was a sickness in need of a purge. In the final letter that Brody read, Ellington made the claim that he, in fact, was Jack, that he wanted to carry out a new philosophy of murder like a sacred torch that could be passed through generations. But how could such a thing be generational? There was no known bloodline of The Ripper.

Rex read the last letter. He read it repeatedly only to read it once more out loud as he paced back and forth. He read that same letter out loud again just before his deposit at the Wells Fargo Plaza.

To my descendant—blood of my blood,

If these words have found you, it means the shadows of our shared legacy have finally drawn back their velvet curtains to reveal the stage you now stand upon. Or at least could stand upon. You are not here by accident, nor by the fickle machinations of fate. You are here because you were always meant to be here. To fulfill a destiny. Our destiny.

I have no illusions about who or what I am. Or what I was if I am no longer here. The world called me monstrous. Let them. They saw only fragments of what I was capable of, pale reflections of a grander design they could never understand. My acts, unbridled and precise, were orchestrated. My nature is not a perversion. It is a talent given. A talent that was honed to perfection.

Whitechapel was where I learned the depth of such a talent, an awakening that came not from steel alone, but from an encounter—one that haunts me even as I pen these words. I met her in the Ten Bells, seated at the corner of the bar when she walked in. She was unlike anyone I had ever seen—draped in shadows and crowned with an unmatched beauty. Her eyes—violet flames that seemed to pierce through the marrow of my being—held the weight of centuries.

She called herself Lillian. I knew, even as I introduced myself, that she was something metaphysical yet as real as the paper I write upon. She spoke of fear as though it were a language she had invented, and I, in that moment, became her pupil. She did not merely teach me how to command terror—she showed me how it could be wielded like a scalpel, cutting into the very essence of whores who walked blindly through their lives.

Lillian told me I would be remembered as the first—the harbinger of an entirely new breed. She whispered how history would be rewritten in the wake of my actions. "You will be the one," she told me, her voice like smoke, "the one who strikes fear so deeply that others will mimic your work but never surpass it." She described the precise details of the murders long before I committed them: where the incisions must be made, how terror could be heightened with silence, and how to make the world gasp in bewildered horror. When the fog of London swirled thick in the alleyways, I did not walk alone. Her words, her laughter, her whispers, all guided my hand.

Perhaps you, like I once did, wonder why you feel so deeply out of step with humanity. Why humanity sickens you. Why the very sight of their empty eyes, their listless wandering, fills you with... hatred. I assure you, it is not madness—it is clarity. Before Lillian, I sought it in the halls of knowledge, in the pages of sacred texts. Yet it was not until I peered into the abyss and saw it reflected in her eyes that I understood my purpose.

In Whitechapel, I found my calling—not just in the act of severing life but in the mastery of fear. There is beauty in the primal gasp of terror, in the way it reveals the soul's trembling core. But I tell you this: mastery is not savagery. Power must be wielded with artistry, with precision.

Do you feel it now, that deep hum beneath your skin, that unrelenting call to reshape the world on your terms? Do you crave the mastery of your own domain—the dominion that is your birthright?

My heir, beware the seductive lie of weakness disguised as virtue. The masses will try to drown you in their self-righteous pity. Resist their clamoring. They will brand you with names meant to shame you into submission: monster, killer, fiend. But remember this—they feared Prometheus for stealing fire from the gods, and yet they warmed themselves by the gift of his defiance.

I write these words not to offer absolution, but as a pact between you and me. We are not bound by the laws of lesser men; we are sculptors of destiny. You have the will to carve your legacy into the flesh of history.

But remember: true power demands sacrifice. You will lose pieces of yourself to the hunger, but what remains will be something eternal. Embrace it. Let your shadow grow long, and let your name be whispered in awe and dread.

And if you ever doubt yourself, if you ever feel the weight of the abyss pressing upon you, know this—you are never alone. You carry *my blood, my vision, and my strength. And somewhere, her voice still echoes.*

Take your place in the lineage of blackness.

—Conrad

"Fear is a crown for those brave enough to wear it."

Brody remembered reading the letter late that night when discovering what his father told him as he read it out loud before killing the fat white trash in the Houston Public Library. Every time he read it, he wondered if it was possible he was related to Ellington. Related to The Ripper, if in fact The Ripper was Ellington.

Though it felt like an impossibility, it also felt...right. Related somehow to the bigger picture. He never told a soul about any of it. But he knew his purpose could be in that letter. It was the "could be" that would just take time for all to come to fruition.

Brody held on to the possibility it wasn't merely philosophical; it was blood-deep, like an ancestral whisper that cut through time. There was something uncanny about the way the pieces fit together: the precise, clinical cruelty that marked the unsolved killings stretching across decades, the same obsession with dissection and domination. The letters described not just violence but an almost reverent approach to death, where each kill was not an act of destruction, but a twisted kind of communion. Brody understood such thinking. In fact, he embraced it.

He had always seen the world as an endless cocktail of lies and ruin, and men like Ellington had toasted to the fall of civility with blood. Brody had stood at the edge of that abyss, tasting the same bitterness. He saw now that the hatred he felt, the pulse of disgust when he watched people in their daily routines, blind to their own insignificance, wasn't his alone. It had always been there, passed down like an inheritance carved from bone.

The idea that he might be the Ripper's heir wasn't just a grotesque fantasy. Maybe it was a calling. Conrad Ellington's name had disappeared into history, swallowed by the fog of time, but men like that didn't die; they simply found new forms, new masks. Brody welcomed the legacy and was in deep search for the mask. He also knew there was no recorded death of Ellington. Why?

More importantly than all of it, who was Lillian? What exactly did she teach Conrad Ellington? What kind of power did she have over him? These were questions that kept Brody up many nights and early into many next mornings. Though he had no answers, what he did know was that he was part of it, and whoever she was would come to him one way or another. Maybe Ellington was with her. For all Brody knew it made as much sense as any other goddamn thing in his tormented life.

In his quieter moments, he would find places of solace and imagine Jack standing beside him in the shadows, unseen but undeniable. The haunting echo of the letter was a gift. The Ripper had carved his message into the world with steel and precision, and now, decades after decades later, Rex Brody felt a similar hunger begin to sharpen. Where Ellington had spilled secrets beneath the London fog with images of Lillian the night creature with the power to teach death, Brody would paint the streets of Houston with a new symphony of terror, steeped in purpose. And unlike those who had come before him, he didn't need the shroud of fog or shadow in which to hide. Nor Lillian, for that matter.

He was ready to be seen.

He was working on the how, what, and why.

***

The more Chelsey Bingham listened to the man who told her she would never have a better time than with him, the more she was drawn into him. The night at Fitzgerald's was growing late, and she was getting warmed up to him. She thought...hoped that he was feeling the same way when he answered her thoughts directly.

"How long do you normally stay out, Miss Lovely Bingham?" Brody tossed back his fourth or fifth shot, Chelsey had lost count. But his mind never seemed to alter in any way as the shots kept coming from his consistent signaling to the barkeeper.

"Normally? I usually do a lot of barhopping around this time...what time is it, by the way, I've lost track." What she did notice was that Brody wore a watch that was clearly as high fashioned and classy as everything else about the new love interest. She kept wondering if she wanted to keep him all to herself.

Brody's precision eyes scanned Chelsey's face and body. She was clearly toned from hours of weight training and running, had a small tattoo on the left side of her neck, one on her right wrist and who knows where else. He scanned her eyes again to see how hardened they could be. "Somewhere else you need to be?"

"Of course not, silly, just thinking about what place we could hit next or what's next to do."

Rex moved his eyes to his Urwerk UR-101 wristwatch, a fine new timepiece that's design was inspired by the Soviet satellite Sputnik. "It's almost one. We haven't even danced yet."

He had a point. Chelsey loved dancing, but with Rex, all she wanted to do was learn more about the man. He was so different in every way from any of the others who had approached her over the past year for their own purposes. Hers too, but that wasn't the point. With Rex, she hadn't once felt in control to catch his interest in leaving with her. Dancing hadn't crossed her mind until he mentioned it.

Maybe that would do the trick. But before she agreed she thought suggesting a few more places where they could go could turn to getting him to her place. She needed to check in with her boss, but that, too, was losing its luster.

Chelsey leaned in, resting her elbows on the table as the soft glow of the overhead string-lights caught in her amber hair. She traced the rim of her glass with her fingertip, a thoughtful smile playing at her lips. “You know,” she began slowly, her voice carrying a different tone, one more somber and stranger. She wanted to sound strange to him. She knew he was the type who craved...demanded the strange. So, why not open to him with a story?

“I’ve seen some crazy shit in this town, but there’s one memory that still freaks me the fuck out.”

Rex’s hazel eyes locked onto hers, unblinking. “Tell me.”

She hesitated to glance over her shoulder at the crowd, then back at Rex. “There’s this place near the outskirts of downtown. Hidden, almost impossible to find unless someone takes you there, or if you’ve been there half a dozen times or more. It doesn’t even have a real name, at least I don’t think it does. I’ve never heard of one. But locals call it The Serpent’s Veil. On the outskirts of Harris County.

“A few years ago, some friends dragged me there after a night of barhopping. They said it was unforgettable. And it was...but not for the reasons I first thought.”

She paused as Rex remained silent, his gaze sharpening as he read the subtle tremor in her voice. “It’s okay. Keep going, you can tell me.”

“The place was packed with all kinds of people. I mean every fuckin’ kind, if you know what I mean. It felt like stepping into another world. Low, low lights...lights that didn’t seem like...I don’t know, like they came from another source. Incense was heavy in the air. I know that doesn’t sound like another world or anything, but it was. It just was. Some walls were completely mirrored. Others were deep blue stone. Place had a stage in the middle of the floor, surrounded by a railing, and all night, performers would come out and do things that...weren't exactly normal." She swallowed hard. "There was one act I'll never forget."

She leaned in closer, her voice trying to whisper but remaining loud enough to hear over the music. "A woman came out. Tall, elegant...terrifying. Her skin was pale as bone, but her eyes..." Chelsey's brow furrowed as if trying to summon the exact memory. "They were lavender. Or violet. Never seen anything like them. She had this giant python...had to be fifteen feet long with a girth thicker than her body, and she moved with it on the stage floor like they were one creature.

"She didn't just move, she slithered. The way her body undulated, the way the snake wrapped around her. It wasn't a performance. It was...something else. Something...sexually wrong."

Rex's jaw tightened as he thought about Ellington's description of Lillian's eyes. He jolted his head away from the letter as another memory stirred within him, unbidden. It was far too much coincidence for Rex to wrap his head around all the pieces. He shook his head again quickly and tossed back his whisky shot. Chelsey's description had also conjured someone he had seen once, long ago.

She noticed the story hit a nerve, something she'd never suspected with him. "What? What is it?"

Rex leaned back, uneasy. "Several things. Some ancestral history my dad gave me. He told me about it, and I found it but... Never mind. It's impossible."

"Impossible? What are you talking about, Rex?"

"I said never mind that. But your story also stirred up something I remembered when I was a child. I was about ten." His voice lowered, roughened.

Chelsey blinked, caught off guard by the abrupt shift.

"I was walking home with my brother and a friend. My sister wasn't with us. Emma. She was at another foster fuckhole. Longer story. Anyway, we were walking home after having just gone through a bullying situation. School bully who fucked with everyone. That's when I saw her."

Chelsey tilted her head, her breath caught. "Who?"

Rex's eyes became distant, shadowed. "She had a similar look to the woman in your story. Same skin, same eyes...only I couldn't see them completely through her sunglasses. She was wearing a black bikini, lying on a towel in an open backyard. She spoke to me while ignoring my brother and friend, signaling for me to come over to her. When I did, she offered to kill the bully who had just humiliated me in front of the others. I remember being frozen...remember that she was far more terrifying than the school bully."

Chelsey shivered as they both said nothing for a minute; the loud music sounded stuck in an echo chamber. She reached her hands across the table, but when Rex remained stoic, she leaned back. "You're not thinking she's the same person I saw on stage with the giant snake, right? I mean, that's not possible. You were just a boy, Rex. I saw this bitch just a few months ago."

Rex stared at her and signaled for another round.

"Okay...So, what did you do?"

"I backed away from her. Carefully backed away one slow step after the next until I was with my brother and friend, then we kept walking." Rex held his whiskey shot the moment his order arrived and stared at it. "I've never spoken of it. You're the first person I've ever told."

A heavy silence settled between them, the distant thrum of music and laughter fading deeper into the echo chamber.

Chelsey finally cleared her throat, trying to shake off the unease that she thought would never end if she didn't do something. "I guess that's a pretty high compliment. Thank you, Rex, really, for sharing it. It's just a coincidence, Rex. Just some eccentric performer or—"

Rex put his hand up.

She fell silent again, unsettled as Rex slowly rotated his wrist, shot glass circling and gently swishing the whiskey. "Let me say this about it, and I'll leave it alone. I don't believe in coincidences, for one thing. Especially with the day I've had. Not sure what to think, lovely Chelsey, but after that happened...what I told you...I've done nothing but train to fight. Martial arts, boxing, wrestling. All of it. The years in Cambodia...nothing but training and competing and teaching. Judo. Tae Kwon Do. Jujitsu. Karate. Aikido. Aced 'em all. I lived and breathed fighting. Yet there's a deep part of me that believes whoever she was, or is, has protected me in some way my entire life...given me strength far more than most men. Maybe any man."

Chelsey wondered at that moment if Rex Brody really was who he said he was. So many men had lied to her, made themselves into things they could never be, much less were. But maybe Rex was the one who could change her life. She would have to see as she kept slowly nodding, listening to him tell her about his early life bouncing around from one foster home to the next with his brother and sister, his hatred for just about everything. Though in many ways he scared her, she understood him on a fundamental level, as her own life had gone through her mother divorcing and remarrying three times, to a rape that had nearly ruined her just a few years back, to working for Mr. Clean as his recruiter for things she thought she'd never see.

Maybe Rex could take her away from all of it. He would be a tough one to handle, but one way or another she was up for the challenge and had to break through the ice. "Awfully young to have so many miles on you."

Rex nodded once and finished his shot. "Few years shy of thirty."

Abruptly, Rex's expression shifted. Chelsey thanked God as the tension in his shoulders loosened, and a sly grin tugged at the corner of his mouth. He stood and extended his hand to her. A techno version of Kiss's "War Machine" roared from the dance floor below to Gene Simmons bellowing about demons taking over humanity.

"I like this song. Especially this version. Enough of the ghosts," he said, his voice smooth and even once more. "We're not here to relive the past. Dance with me."

***

Detectives Spade and Hayes arrived on scene to find the latest victim of what they both knew in their guts was notch number 15 on The Bone Break Killer's belt. They arrived at a Westheimer parking garage just past 3 a.m. The crime scene was already cordoned off, red and blue lights flickering against the cold concrete like pulses of mechanical blood. The air carried the stale stink of motor oil and exhaust fumes, but beneath it was something far worse: the unmistakable copper tang of blood and decay.

Spade took a long drag from his cigarette before flicking it to the ground and crushing it under his heel. "Tell me this is something different." He rubbed the stubble on his chin.

Hayes adjusted her blazer, her lips pressed into a tight line. "No way. It's him. Same M.O."

The body was found near the farthest corner of the garage, a place where the security cameras conveniently didn't reach. The victim—a young man, mid-twenties—was contorted into a shape that no human body should ever be in. Limbs grotesquely snapped at impossible angles; arms bent backward; shoulders dislocated as though they had been pried apart with the hands of something inhumanly strong.

The skin was, once again, freakishly intact. No visible lacerations, no excessive bruising beyond the catastrophic breaks. It was as if the killer had found a way to disassemble the body from the inside out.

"Jesus fuck," Spade muttered under his breath as he crouched down beside the corpse, his eyes scanning every brutalized inch. "I don't know how the hell this guy does it. Unless the rookie was right about this fuck being a doctor. There are no signs of a struggle, no hesitation. Just calculated fuckery."

Hayes exhaled through her nose, arms crossed. "Still think he's got help?"

Spade didn't answer right away. Instead, he reached out with his gloved hand and tilted the victim's head slightly, exposing the neck. There was something new. A thin, dark line barely visible against the skin, like a precise incision made with something impossibly sharp. No blood.

"And what the hell is this?" Spade looked up to Hayes as he crouched down lower to see the neck closer. "Makes no fucking sense."

Hayes's face hardened. "Maybe he's getting bored."

The forensic team worked in silence, snapping photos, taking measurements, documenting every inch of the horror before them. Spade stood, jaw tight, thoughts swirling in ways he didn't like. "Something's changed," he murmured. "I don't like it. And we're all waiting for his next goddamn move."

Hayes looked out over the city, its lights glittering against the dark horizon. "Then we better start thinking more like him," she said quietly. "Before he decides to break something else we can't ever—"

Spade put up his hand and let out a breath and turned toward the garage entrance when something caught his eye. Down at the far end of the service road, a pair of glowing red taillights burned in the darkness. A semi-truck rumbled at a slow crawl before picking up speed and disappearing into the night.

A chill slid down his spine.

"You see that shit?" He motioned to Hayes.

She frowned. "What?"

"That semi." Spade stared blankly into the night, pointing to the truck.

Hayes followed his gaze and took in a quick breath. "Jesus."

Spade's own breath quickened, his heart raced. Like a slow-moving revelation, rookie cop Marion Paul's theories were quickly coming alive.

It's just a theory. But a semi-truck just feels like something this one would use. Think about it. A doctor who owns a semi-truck to do this kind of shit in? He's thinking, No one's ever going to put two and two together on this one. No way.

Spade hadn't dismissed the rookie's theory about the truck but also didn't expect it to just drop into the case's lap like manna from the heavens.

"Come on. We're tailing that fucking truck." Spade was already walking to the Crown Vic before he said it. Hayes was right behind him.

***

Chelsey hesitated for a second before slipping her hand into his. His grip was warm, strong—scary strong—unyielding. He moved down the steps with the grace and power of a panther, Chelsey feeling the confidence from a man she never knew could exist. Not even her boss, but this was her night now, her time.

The crowd parted slightly as Rex led Chelsey onto the dance floor. At least that's what her eyes saw.

His first few dance moves were normal enough. Strong, confident movements where his body moved as much with grace as with athleticism while the bassline thundered around them. Chelsey moved in rhythm to Rex's body, but she could feel something different in the way he began to move midway through the song. It wasn't just dancing; it was becoming a performance.

Then things really changed.

Rex's body began to dip low in quick and jolting

movements, his legs bending at odd angles as he slid across the floor with a fluidity that shouldn't have been possible. His arms moved like the limbs of a spider, precise and unnerving, stretching and contracting as though each joint had a mind of its own. He was able to arch his back and torso in ways that looked violent, almost insect-like. He took control over the dance floor as the final chords of "War Machine" blended into a fierce crescendo of house tech music. His circling movements kept him not more than Chelsey's waist level, her head and neck turning with her body as her eyes followed Brody at first in awe, but the longer he moved in such ways, awe turned to fear.

Her eyes stretched as if being pulled open as she moved carefully away from Rex's pulsing dance moves that began to freak her out. By the time he began to violently twitch and dodge, most of the patrons on the floor looked on in the same stunned way as Chelsey.

Everyone around them stopped, their conversations died mid-sentence as they turned wide-eyed to watch. Rex's movements grew more intricate and violent, his feet tapping out patterns faster than the beat itself. His spine arched, and his head rolled back, a grin splitting his face as he twisted and contorted with terrifying grace, even as he completely dropped his chest to the ground, arms and legs outward and bent to support powerful movements that looked obscener than anything else.

The crowd was spellbound. A few gasps rippled through the onlookers as Rex launched into a sudden spin, his arms slicing the air like blades. He dropped low again, his fingers skittering across the floor like claws before snapping upright in a single, terrifying motion.

Chelsey's next breath caught in her throat. Rex was transforming. His body looked like something alien, a predator weaving through the thrum of the music. With as much coke and whiskey she'd taken during the night, that is what her eyes made out as well as mind could figure out.

A young man near the edge of the floor muttered, "What the fuck?" before falling silent.

The room felt charged with static. Every eye locked on Rex Brody. He moved with a precision that was weird and distant, his shadow stretching long beneath the swirling lights like a creature born of some crazed ordeal people weren't meant to deal with.

Chelsey could feel her heart pounding in her chest. Despite the fear that had overcome her, she couldn't take her eyes off him. No one could; he was mesmerizing, a dark force suddenly let loose in the middle of Fitzgerald's normal and controlled chaos.

The house tech number reached its climax, the bassline dropping into a final, resonant pulse. Rex stilled for a moment, his chest rising and falling, his eyes glowing as if being lit too frequently. And then, slowly, he reached out his hand to Chelsey.

She was stunned and hesitated before stepping forward, slipping her fingers into his. Though the crowd had become unnerved and leery, they slowly began clapping in a way that felt they were needing permission to do so before finally breaking into scattered applause, unsure whether they had witnessed brilliance or something else entirely. Within a few minutes, everyone seemed to comfortably move alone with the night but with caution.

Rex pulled Chelsey close, his strength far more than she originally imagined when she felt his handshake. Every bit of him felt like wood. He brushed his lips against her ear. "Told you."

Her voice was barely a whisper as she attempted to move a few inches apart for the slimmest of breathing room. Her breath was still shallow. "Told me what?"

"That you'd never have a better night."

She closed her eyes, letting herself sink into the strange, electric energy that surrounded him. Somewhere, in the back of her mind, the memory of the violet-eyed woman lingered, like a warning she couldn't quite decipher. What she'd just seen on the dance floor seemed every bit the strangeness of the woman and the python snake.

But for the time being, she chose to ignore it. She had to, with so much work to still do, and she was in terrible shape to continue. She also didn't have a choice, knowing that if she didn't come through, then whatever it was about Rex Brody would seem like child's play.

So, she thought.

To keep things as safe as possible she asked Rex to drive; she could get a ride later, back to the club and pick up her car. Her boss would certainly owe her that. The night belonged to Brody. At least for the meantime. After he settled the bill, Chelsey led him out to the parking lot, and he put Chelsey in the passenger seat, as she would direct him to the place she was staying for the night. No retort from Rex; hardly a word spoken to Chelsey as she tried to put aside the vivid images of the man who had just visually worn her down, and she wondered how exponentially more he could do on a physical level.

***

The drive to Houston's old-money estates of River Oaks felt surreal, the cool night still thick with humidity as the streetlamps flickered in and out of focus through the Porsche's windows. Chelsey leaned back in her seat, her hair loose and wild, the night air brushing her cheek through the open window. She continued to say as little as possible after they left Fitzgerald's. Her lips curved in a half-smile that spoke of secrets untold. Rex's grip on the wheel was firm but relaxed, his mind wandering through the tangled discussions and events of the night. He had had as much to drink as she had or more, but he drove as if completely sober.

"What's on your mind? Not the performance back there, I hope. Or my tormented childhood memories."

Chesley turned to him. "Maybe some of it. The dancing I mean. Never seen that kind of shit before. But something else comes to mind as I was watching you, checkin' you the fuck out."

"Go on."

"Have you heard about this latest serial killer out here, still loose in Houston? Read anything about him or see any news spots?"

Rex's face suddenly frowned in thought but remained focused on the wheel, knowing his BAC level was several digits past the 0.8 limit for driving. Regardless of his skillset and how he felt to drive, keeping a perfect balance while driving at such levels was a challenge, but mandatory. Cops could do several things if he were pulled over, so behind the wheel in this shape needed to remain dangerously cautious. "Odd question out of the goddamn blue."

"It's been quite an odd night. Sorry."

"No doubt. I've read some things, seen some news, details about a perp breaking people's bones before the kill. Apparently leaves no trace of blood...which means he's skilled. And strong. Real strong. Still, do you always ask such weird shit out of the blue? Into that kind of thing, are you?"

Chelsey scoffed while opening her mouth wide to catch some of the hot humid night breeze. "Maybe, I don't know, but how you moved out there on the floor...well, you seem the type who might find the dark side of life more to your liking. Not that I have a problem with it. I mean, I'm still taking you to my place."

Brody cleared his throat. He'd never been asked such a question and hearing it out loud suddenly gave him as much caution as his driving. He had murdered someone with his bare hands before meeting Chelsey, then proceeded to dance a lunatic fringe right in her personal space, so why not wonder about the girl's wondering about his behavior. Behavior he had practiced for years. He was ready for the perfect time and perfect choice to begin his own rituals for his first real trophy. At first, he thought Chelsey was the perfect choice; the longer he was with her the more he began to feel things go a tad off from the original plan.

"You have a fetish about that kind of thing, breaking bones to kill people. This guy seems to be getting away with. Weird shit."

Chelsey laughed. "Maybe I'm a little kinkier than you think." With that she gave Brody exact directions, at least for the rest of the late night.

When they finally pulled into the circular driveway of a massive estate, Rex's brow furrowed. No way the place was hers unless she inherited it. The mansion loomed like a shadowed colossus beneath the Houston moonlight. Its sprawling, two-story facade of limestone and wrought iron was elegant and imposing, drenched in the kind of old money grandeur that could buy silence and erase sins. The fountain at the center of the driveway trickled softly, the stone sculpture at its heart shaped like a coiled scorpion with jeweled eyes that caught the low light.

Rex killed the engine, the rumble of the car dissipating into the heated stillness. He stepped out, eyes tracing the fine craftsmanship of the double doors ahead, arched and adorned with iron flourishes that spiraled like thick black veins. He opened the car door for Chesley and followed her to the entrance, but something gnawed at the back of his mind. She never mentioned any kind of serious money, and here she was leading him into a palace.

The door swung open with a soft creak; they stepped into an atrium vast enough to echo their footsteps. The floor was polished marble, so pristine that it mirrored the ornate chandelier hanging above, a towering production of brass and crystal, glimmering like shattered starlight. To the left, a grand staircase swept upward in a perfect curve, its banister wrapped in intricately carved mahogany.

Rex's eyes flicked from the staircase to the room

beyond, his pulse slow and steady but sharpened by suspicion. He had to keep going with her, just to see how it would end. He took in the furniture: deep leather armchairs with brass-studded edges, an obsidian coffee table topped with a collection of strange curios encased in glass domes. One held a butterfly pinned to black velvet, its wings a haunting shade of deep violet. Another displayed an antique pocket watch, its face cracked but the hands still ticking.

Chelsey's heels clicked against the floor as she wandered toward a decanter set on a glass-topped sideboard. She tossed her light-tan leather jacket across the room, not caring where it landed. She poured two fingers of something amber and potent into a crystal tumbler, her movements casual. She turned and offered him a smile as she extended the glass toward him. Brody saw she had several more tattoos on her shoulders and wondered how many adorned her fully naked body. Though he wanted to be inside her, he wanted to destroy her even more.

"Welcome to my humble abode. After such a performance on the dance floor, this place could be perfect for you." There was a strange edge to her voice only professionally trained ears such as Brody's wouldn't miss.

He accepted the glass but didn't drink. His gaze roamed the room. The walls were lined with built-in bookcases brimming with first editions and leather-bound tomes, their spines gleaming gold in the dim light. Above the shelves, framed portraits stared down; a procession of solemn faces caught in the amber light, each figure draped in finery from a bygone era. On one of the shelves was a collection of classic top hats, another a different assortment of white gloves, some leather, some silver-speckled. Brody looked at both sets of odd attire with more than curiosity. On the wall was a massive plasma television, world class. The antique elegance surrounded by modern technology was a fabulous design ensemble.

It was the next item that really caught his eye: a framed

photograph positioned on the mantle above the fireplace. It was larger than the others, housed in an elaborate frame of dark wood and tarnished brass. A black and white photo, the image slightly faded with time. It showed a massive man standing in front of an old theater, dressed in a long coat and top hat. His build was enormous, his shoulders broad enough to fill the frame; his face sharp and angular, marked by a cruel jawline and eyes that burned, even in monochrome. He was bald.

Rex frowned quizzically. “Who’s this?” He turned to Chelsey, tapping the glass lightly with his middle finger.

Chelsey’s posture stiffened for a split second before she forced a laugh. “My grandfather.”

Rex scoffed and raised an eyebrow. The man in the photograph looked nothing like Chelsey, no shared features between them. The eyes were too harsh, too knowing. The weight of the photograph pressed down on the room like a heavy secret not ready to be known.

“Right. Such an uncanny resemblance.”

Rex’s disbelief muttered with an unease growing in his chest. This was supposed to be his first real trophy hunt. The first one where all the planning and all the practicing would take place, and yet here he was in an environment that created a sense of awkwardness, his control losing its grip. Maybe he never had control. Maybe that was the lesson: regardless of extensive covert training or professionally trained martial arts, suddenly all the applied practice seemed far out of reach. He realized he was out of his element and needed to quickly get back in the game.

Chelsey crossed the room and placed her hand over his, gently pulling him away from the mantle and shelving units. “You’re overthinking things. I know you want me.” She then quickly backed up a step. “Right?”

Rex winked and pulled her back tightly to his body.

“Sure.”

He released his arms, stepped back a few steps and

finally took a sip of the whiskey, the burn trailing down his throat. He allowed himself a brief, bitter smile. Had to remain detached.

“Fascinating place.” He moved his head and gaze up and down the fabulous walls, high ceilings, the various entrances to different hallways, then back to her. “It’s not yours of course.” He knew he was right and had to regain control. The home had plenty of palace-sized areas where he could practice his moves on her.

Chelsey eased over to Rex as she finished the shot. “No. It’s a friend’s. My boss’s to be honest. You can see this is old money. Place has probably been in his family for who knows how long. I’m sorry I lied to you about my grandfather. About everything. Surely you knew when we pulled up.”

He turned toward the massive living room window that stretched from the floor to the ceiling, its glass flawless and reflecting faint distortions of the room’s interior. The moment he began to focus his eyes he knew he’d been drugged with something overwhelming. He instantly hated himself for being so stupid. He instantly hated Chelsey even deeper and needed to get the fuck on with it but while his body was ready his mind felt as if it had been hit with a hypodermic needle filled with sleep juice. He had to keep playing things out and rely on his skills to keep pushing through. If he could find them.

He turned back to Chelsey afraid to speak because he knew he’d slur and perhaps even sound unintelligible. He hoped the look in his eyes would be enough for her to know he knew, then slowly turned back and looked beyond the glass. The night shifted as headlights cut through the darkness. A low, rumbling engine hummed through the silence.

Rex stepped closer to the window, his eyes narrowing as a semi-truck with a full trailer slowed and pulled into the impressive estate’s driveway service entrance. The headlights dimmed, and the truck's massive frame settled into place like a beast at rest and groaning as the diesel engine shuttered off.

Though the drug was hitting on all cylinders, Rex's pulse quickened and hair stood on his arms. Just like that, on a dime, things were off and his reaction time seemed to just as instantly hit a slow-motion button. A semi in River Oaks wasn't just strange; it was an anomaly.

Chelsey appeared beside him; her expression filled with more deceit. "It's probably a delivery." She chuckled.

Rex craned his neck in clear irritation. "Cut the shit." His voice was low, calculated, but as slow as he expected. He didn't know if he slurred.

Chelsey shrugged off her lie but didn't meet his gaze. Rex felt the tension coil in his gut, that familiar, predatory instinct whispering that something was wrong. Very wrong, as his normal light speed reactions were feeling increasingly hindered as each second ticked away.

The driver's side door of the semi opened, but the figure stepping out was obscured by the thick Houston night. Rex exhaled slowly, watching the unfolding scene with the quiet focus of a hunter waiting for a tell, but one with no weapons. The night was far from over as Rex's hatred toward his mistake was now thumping him like a rubber mallet.

***

Spade stayed behind the semi, easily four car-lengths back. Hayes leaned in close to the dash. Both detectives were working on fumes.

"How the fuck did Paul get all this shit right?" Spade's exhaustion was showing more than usual.

"We don't know for sure that he's right, partner. We havc no idca who's in that fuckin' rig."

"But I know you're feeling what I'm feeling. How did

we miss it? Did we miss it? I mean, Jesus H—"

"Whoa, whoa, whoa, Heath. You're tired, please. Focus on the rig. Let's just stay with it."

Spade turned his gaze to Hayes, his fuse at its last end. "Goddamn it, Carmen. Get off my—"

Bang!

Spade had taken his eyes off the road one second too long. A small pickup truck slammed into the driver's side rear of the Crown Vic, spinning the large cop car several times. Spade's athletic reflexes fought the steering wheel and kept the car from flipping as it screeched to a tire-smoking stop.

Hayes's body slammed into her passenger door then slammed into Spade's right shoulder, her seat belt keeping her anchored. The airbag had burst, knocking Spade in the chest and face, but he was plenty conscious.

"Fuck! Fuck! Carmen, you okay? Tell me you're okay. Christ, please."

Hayes had both her hands to her head making sure she could still think and that nothing was broken. "I'm good. I'm good. Call it in quick. Get someone else on that rig, we can't lose it."

Hayes's plea fell on deaf ears as Spade busted out of his seat, his Glock pulled, his body low as he shuffled toward the pickup truck that had broadsided the Crown Vic and nearly killed him and his partner.

"Get out of the fucking vehicle, motherfucker, with your hands up. Slowly. Get the fuck out." Spade's previous exhaustion had disappeared with a shot of adrenaline that sent him into the stratosphere. He screamed at the driver of the pickup repeatedly. When the passenger door creaked open, Spade could see that the damage would prevent it from fully opening. He fired a round into the destroyed door.

"On the fucking ground. Move!"

Detective Hayes saw her partner in her peripheral vision as she shouted into the cop radio that backup was needed on a semi-truck heading East on Westheimer toward the Hardy Toll Road. But she couldn't remember if the truck was blue or red or black or yellow.

"Calling all units, calling all units, requesting backup on a full rig semi. Don't know the color. New model semi probably heading toward Hardy Toll. Requesting backup. Also, need backup on Westheimer. Officer's hit, possible DUI. Get help now."

Hayes clicked the handset back in its cradle and kicked her door open. Upon getting out of the wrecked car, she was checking her ribs and hips when she heard Spade fire off a round toward the pickup. She watched him in action, knowing that, regardless of the situation, there was no one better under duress. "Backup is on the way."

"You got the rig covered?" Spade's call out to Hayes didn't take his eyes off the pickup, not for a split second. He kept low and inched his way forward, as the pickup driver hadn't exited yet. Maybe he was dead. Spade couldn't care less.

"I couldn't remember the color."

Spade let out a deep breath. He couldn't remember the color of the rig, either, but he knew someone would get on it asap.

***

The moment Rex saw him stepping out of the semi-truck, he knew his instincts were failing. It was the last thing Brody expected. His shoulders filled the doorway of the truck's cab, then he descended with deliberate, measured steps. Even from this distance, under the dim light of the estate, Rex recognized the cruel features of the giant man from the black and white photograph on the fireplace mantel, the one Chelsey had lied about, which had to be the giant's grandfather or uncle. No relation to Chelsey, of course. Maybe it was a photo of the giant himself.

Rex turned to Chelsey who stood at the doorway with a glass of fresh whiskey in her hand. Her expression was unreadable, but the glint in her eyes spoke volumes.

"Who is he?" Rex's voice was low and now heavily slurred.

Chelsey sipped her drink, her lips curving into a faint smile. "A friend. And my boss, to be honest, and there's no reason to lie at this point."

Before Rex could respond, the man entered the house, his boots heavy on the marble floor. His presence filled the room like a suffocating fog. Rex's pulse quickened as the man's icy gaze locked onto him. He wore a large white doctor's coat with shirt and loosened tie underneath.

Brody suddenly recognized the giant man from a recent notorious medical court case that he'd taken a keen interest in, a case involving a severely abused woman who was herself a doctor. A colleague. Story that was all over Houston's local channels and newspapers. The first time Brody had seen the doctor on television during a press conference, he thought the doctor was the splitting image of Mr. Clean on floor-cleaning products. Same bull-sized body, same bald head with sky blue eyes. It freaked him out.

"You're Doctor Kelly Manson," Rex muttered under his breath. "The fuck you're doing here?" Of course, he already knew what the doctor was doing there, though the shot of laced whiskey was doing quite a number on him, so he wondered what kind of drug, with such a small dosage, could cause such rapid physical decline.

Chelsey moved closer, her movements languid. "You should relax, Rex, you're all wound up." She held out another deep glass of single-malt whiskey. "Have another drink."

The edge in her voice and the sudden tightness in her smile made Rex want to immediately reach forward and break her neck. Though he knew he could still do it with whatever drug was crippling him, he also knew he probably couldn't take Dr. Kelly Manson with such ease. He had to play this out, regardless of how far south it was going. He glanced at the glass in disgust. "You've done your damage."

Chelsey's smile faltered, but she quickly recovered. "We'll soon see."

Manson stepped forward; his frame dominated the room. Yet his voice and demeanor were shockingly warm. "Please, don't mind me. You're more than welcome to be with us. Though you do seem a little over your limit, if I may be so bold. Chelsey brought you here, so of course, you're our special guest now. Closely vetted I would say."

Rex's muscles tensed, ready for anything by default, but his world further tilted. His vision went double, and his legs buckled beneath him. The last thing he saw before the darkness swallowed him was Chelsey's satisfied smirk and Manson's massive shadow looming over him.

***

When Rex came to, he was bound to a chair, his arms zip-tied behind him, ankles zip-tied to the chair legs. He had no idea what time it was. He'd been moved from the living area to a grand room of some kind, dimly lit by a single overhead bulb from extensive track lighting that cast stark, unforgiving shadows, long and deep. He scanned every inch of the room as best he could.

To his left was a long table of medical instruments and devices, none of them appealing. Plastic sheeting hung from ceiling to floor. Though his head throbbed and his wrists and ankles felt cut up, his brutal training in Cambodia kicked in. He'd trained countless times in such predicaments, training his joints and to break free, and his skin and muscles to tolerate intense pain. He'd even done such training under the influence of drugs and alcohol, but nothing like what Chelsey had slipped in his whiskey.

Still, he gaged an immediate assessment while, at the

same time, forcing his mind to cope with the drug as well as the pain in his head and zip-tied extremities. His professional eyes scanned for any possible advantage, knowing he would have one hell of a fight in front him, especially if the two psycho fucks had similar murderous intentions that he himself had planned for Chelsey.

Across from Brody stood Dr. Kelly Manson, as if he'd stepped from the shadows. His face was a mask of brutal confidence. He had taken off the doctor's coat and rolled up the sleeves of his pristine white shirt, exposing forearms crisscrossed with faint scars. Chelsey leaned casually against a nearby wall, her expression cool and detached, but eyes beginning to wig out.

"Well, well." Manson's voice dripped with mockery. "Looks like you're coming around. Wakey, wakey. I'll tell you, Mister Rex Brody, from your expression when I walked in...you seemed to recognize who I am. I, on the other hand, have no idea who you are, only that you've been carefully vetted by my...Chelsey. She's done some nice work since we've been together, but it's come to me that she's done her finest work with you. You've lasted this long. She's curious to see how much further you can make it."

Rex's lips twisted into a faint smirk despite the pain, a pain he began to realize had come from being hit, though he couldn't remember how long ago it happened or how many times he'd been hit. More than enough, he was certain of that. His mind was a cloud, his tongue far too heavy and knotted in his mouth, but he had to say something. Begin asking questions. Anything to find a way out and stall long enough for the drug to finally wear off.

"I'm not sure what this twit has told you, Doc, but I'm not the one you want to test." Brody nodded his head toward Chelsey.

Manson chuckled, stepping closer. "Hmm. But we've been testing you, and yes, she mentioned a few things. Quite the dancer I hear. You're certainly the most...how should I put it...the sturdiest we've had, but I trust who Chelsey brings to me. Have had all types and she's vetted them perfectly. You've got spunk, I'll give you that. A lot more than many of my patients I've had under the knife...in surgery."

Rex didn't respond. He was already testing the zip-ties as well as the strength in his wrists and what it would take to snap out, searching for a weak point. The drug in his system was still strong, but his adrenaline burned through the haze. He feigned sluggishness, drawing Manson in closer.

"How long has this been going on?" Brody spoke to keep Manson from getting right in his face. Buy more time. Even just a few seconds could make the difference.

Manson stopped and cocked his head. "You mean tonight? Or generally, overall?"

Brody stayed focused. "Now that you put it that way...both. This is quite the setup you have here." Brody moved his gaze in an arc up the room's walls, across the church-like ceiling then down to the table and focused on the medical instruments.

"It is a nice setup tonight, that's for sure. First time we've done this here at my place. Normally we use the rig's trailer out front, but Chelsey thought, in your case, this would be a better option. I agree with her. In fact, I'd like to ask you about it. Didn't you sense something way out in left fucking field when you saw that monster of a truck pull up to such a home, in such a neighborhood?" Mason's voice changed from his medical professional tone to one that could have boiled up from a cauldron in his stomach.

"Fair point. We'd both had a bit to drink, so...touché, it was certainly an over—"

"Horseshit. You felt something and yet...did nothing. That's how I see it." Manson's voice was filled with slight mockery.

Rex blinked slowly a few times to wet his eyes. "I was going to say it was an oversight."

When Manson leaned in, Rex could see the powerful build on Dr. Kelly Manson, how strong he was. How careful and patient. The next blow that Manson landed on Brody's jaw would have taken most people entirely off guard, and possibly knocked them dead. Brody sensed it coming before Manson even threw it, so he prepared himself for the strike, same as he would in any professional match. It didn't ease the pain much, but it did wonders for more adrenaline release. Any further pain Manson and Chelsey would inflict would provide Brody enough spark to make a move, at least up to a point.

Manson slowly circled him like a massive wolf.

The more Rex began to feel his body the more he knew he'd been taken for quite a ride so far. He knew his ribs were bruised, possibly a few broken. He felt deep, icy pains in the lower back and kidney area; the tailbone ache was becoming more intense than he'd ever known, but depending on how long he'd been tied to the chair, he couldn't determine the actual damage. Then there was Manson's latest: the immediate pain in his jaw that was moving quickly to his entire face. Everything in him hurt.

Brody certainly never planned his first hunting kill to be a double whammy of a psychotic giant doctor and his trusted lunatic female scout, but so be it. He had to find some kind of goddamn edge that would give him a chance to prevail.

It was Chelsey who stepped into Brody's immediate space next. She signaled to Manson that it was her turn. "Would you mind, fine Doctor, turning on some of our favorites? Haven't heard them in ages on your system."

Dr. Manson nodded, letting Chelsey take the reins.

She turned back to Rex, looking down at him. "You didn't see this one coming down the halls at Fitzgerald's, did you? I must say, I was falling for you, Rex. I mean it. Even had this fantasy going that you'd be the one who could take me away from all of this. But here we are."

Brody locked his head up to focus on Chelsey's eyes. Keeping eye contact would also buy some time. He rocked his body slightly back and forth, feeling the chair and how much it would take to break something free. In his peripheral, he saw Manson click a remote-control device. KC and the Sunshine Band came to life in a crisp and echoed surround-sound that instantly filled the grand room. Chelsey began moving her body to the rhythm of "Get Down to Tonight."

"They didn't play any of this at Fitzgerald's. I'd have loved to see you dance to this the way you did to that Kiss song."

Brody nodded slowly as he mouthed the words "War Machine," his own body beginning to feel the rhythm of KC's ragged voice, the synthesizers and drums in perfect disco harmony. Though his movements were extremely limited, he could feel the pain and damage that his body had gone through, and knew that could be a problem when he broke free. He had to rely on his adrenaline supply to ramp up several notches.

He continued feeling the rhythm of the music, following Chelsey's body but keeping his eyes locked on hers. He took in deep breaths, let them out slowly, thanking the God he'd stopped believing in years ago for the exact moment when it was now or never.

Using his mind far more than his body's ability, Rex twisted violently, giving every effort of power and skill to pop his wrists free, movements he had trained countless times in Cambodia, Lake City, and New York, when training in the fiercest hand-to-hand combat. His adrenaline fully kicked in. Though the pain was instant and searing, he didn't falter as one hand broke free, the zip-tie cutting deep enough into both wrists to bloody both his hands. He shot his freed hand straight up and rocked the chair backward, landing on his back. He knew he'd taken Chelsey off guard with the move, but he had to maneuver with precision, speed and power as Manson dropped the remote and shoved Chelsey out of his way, knocking her to the floor like a large pin-up doll.

Just before Manson was upon him, Brody was able to quickly use his free hand to break the other away, more blood but free, nonetheless. Manson was quick for his size and quick enough to be right on Brody, driving a forward kick into the grounded Brody who was frantically digging his hand into the first ankle zip-tie. While Manson's kick landed, Brody was able to inch enough away to where the kick caused no permanent damage.

Still, Manson was able to grab Brody with his massive hands, lifted him forward and sat him upright on the chair again. What Manson didn't see were Brody's free hands and just how fabulously talented they were. Adrenaline at full potency now, Rex easily blocked and dodged Manson's grabs and strikes, then grabbed the chair's sides, stood upright with the chair legs now facing perfectly outward and parallel to the floor. He used the core muscles of his abs and hamstrings to twist his body and the chair legs in a solid, circling motion that struck Manson hard enough to knock him to the ground.

In an almost simultaneous movement, Rex reached with both hands to dig under the zip-ties that were strapped around his ankles and the two chair legs. In one explosive upward movement, with every source of power from hands and forearms and shoulders to his hamstrings and glutes, every piston firing on every cylinder in unison, Brody was able to snap his powerful legs and feet free of the final straps. He grabbed the chair by its back to use as a shield from another Manson onslaught.

But he wasn't fast enough to escape Doctor Kelly Manson's full charge into him, driving his shoulders deep into the chair Brody was using as a shield, and thus Brody's chest, knocking him to the ground again. The lunge was violent and filled with rage, the weight and strength of the doctor being more than he'd taken in years.

When the doctor had drilled into Brody, it felt like he'd rammed a vault door, not a man. He felt his shoulder pop out of place and hoped it wasn't broken. The doctor easily had 100 pounds over Brody, yet it was Brody who felt twice the density.

"Get me more of that fucking serum, goddamn it. Can't you see we've got a situation here?" Doctor Manson's booming voice caught Chelsey's attention immediately, as she had been watching from the floor the entire fight in as much awe as in horror. She scrambled to her feet, her legs trembling and unstable.

Rex surged back to his feet, still holding the chair in front of him, his movements still sluggish from the drug, but still precise enough despite his injuries. Knowing the chair was now only in his way he tossed it to the side and delivered a lightning-fast spinning back kick into Manson's chest, sending the larger man staggering backward. Chelsey screamed, grabbed a heavy vase from a nearby table, and threw it at Rex's head.

With an effortless dodge, he knew he had to take out Chelsey immediately in order to focus on Mr. Clean. Rex lunged forward and quickly drove Chelsey to the ground with a deep one-leg takedown. His injured body slammed into Chelsey's ribs as he landed on top of her. The move was one of Brody's signature take downs he'd executed countless times. From there he moved to the knee-on-belly position to shift his body into perfect position so his knee broke several of her ribs instantly. He grabbed Chelsey's arm and snapped it at the elbow with a simple arm bar. The pain was so severe and the damage so great that she didn't have the wind to even whisper.

Just as he performed the attack, and as luck was then on Manson's side, the doctor was on him again, this time landing a sloppy front kick into Brody's shoulder, knocking him off Chelsey's ruined body and to the ground. But the doctor's kick lacked any staying power.

Brody could feel the tide turn, knowing that Chelsey was out of the match. In another signature move with pure adrenaline fueling every effort, he lifted his hips and legs to immediately pop them into the air to flip back to his feet in a single move, his body now facing Manson.

Manson screamed in rage while charging at Rex like a bulldozer on steroids. A second before impact, Rex stepped aside, grabbed Manson's arm, and used his momentum to flip the larger man over Rex's shoulder: a perfectly executed Judo throw.

The doctor hit the floor with a thunderous crash but recovered fairly quickly for his sheer size and strength, allowing him to shrug off the impact. He lunged at Rex again, swinging his massive fists with brutal force. Brody dodged and weaved, like a boxer, and countered with a series of rapid strikes to Manson's ribs, pelvis, and jaw.

Each punch was calculated, exploiting the weaknesses Rex had learned to identify in countless opponents. But Manson was relentless, absorbing the blows and pressing forward. He grabbed Rex by the throat and lifted him off the ground with terrifying ease.

Rex's vision blurred as Manson's grip tightened. He wrapped his legs around Manson's waist, locked his feet together, and pulled him into his guard position with all his strength, clinching Manson like a massive spider, which brought them both to the ground. Now Rex had a far superior position over Manson. It was clear to Brody that the doctor, while overly strong, had little to no skillset for a ground fight.

To Brody's surprise, and before he could sweep Manson into a finishing move, the doctor was still strong enough to stand with Brody locked onto him, and then slammed him on his back to the floor, breaking Rex's guard and knocking out his breath. Instantly, Brody shrimped his way to a position where he was able to scissor his legs into

Manson's chest and stomach and move away from the massive doctor.

In an astonishing act that Rex caught in his peripheral, Chelsey tried to struggle to her feet before she fell again to all fours. She then crawled to a leather sofa where she left her purse to pull out a small handgun, snub nosed .38 and fired off three rounds in Brody's and Manson's direction, missing them both.

"You almost fucking shot me!" Manson's screaming distraction came at the perfect second Rex needed. With a quick three-point get up, he then threw a perfect low sidekick into the doctor's knee, breaking it instantly as Chelsey fired another round, this one grazing Brody's shoulder. With the doctor down Rex's only move was to somersault toward the room's doorway that led to one of the hallways of the estate. He heard Chelsey screaming like a maniac that she would kill him, but Brody knew she had only one round left.

He found refuge in the mansion's fabulous kitchen where he took precious seconds to clear his head and focus on an endless display of knives, pots, pans lavishly hanging from custom knives and pot racks, a dream setup for any fine chef. Brody picked out a large carving knife and a cleaver, made one somersault back into the room, threw a perfect strike into Manson's belly with the carving knife, and watched both Manson and Chelsey stare at the fatal attack in utter disbelief. Manson dropped to his knees, hands cupped around the knife handle.

Brody took the moment in stride as he watched the doctor put his hands on the knife's handle. The blade looked to be all the way in. Satisfied, he took several deep breaths to regain some of his senses. Rex continued to feel his adrenaline pumping. He slowly walked past Dr. Manson, eyeballing him to make sure no sudden moves of desperation were made.

When he stood directly in front of Chelsey, he could see the terror in her eyes was more than she'd ever known.

He had no idea how much Chelsey had seen while doing all she'd done with Dr. Manson for however long she'd been his accomplice. But he knew the terror in her eyes at that moment was her peak fear.

"Bet you didn't see that coming." Brody's mockery of Chelsey's earlier taunt kept the tension far too high for her to do anything other than stare at him open-mouthed, eyes so wide they looked pried open. She held the .38 at waist level as she looked at Dr. Manson, her entire broken body quivering.

"You're in shock." Brody was in her immediate space with movements still catlike regardless of what he'd been through, relying on as much adrenaline as was Chelsey.

She glared at him, her hands trembling barely able to hold the .38, her chest heaving. "You don't understand," she spat. "Doctor Manson—"

"I understand perfectly." Rex held the cleaver in one hand as he took the gun from Chelsey in the other. He tossed the gun to the floor and turned back to Manson, who was struggling to rise, his breathing slow and labored. Both his massive hands clasped the handle of the carving knife.

Rex didn't give him any chance to recover. With his forearm and leg he scissor-swept Chelsey, laying her out flat on her back and tailbone, a drop that would further the damage he'd already inflicted on her. If left alone she would surely die, a plan far removed from Brody's mind.

"I'll deal with you in just a moment."

The tunes from KC and the Sunshine Band Dr. Manson had turned on at Chelsey's request, cut to "Get Down Tonight." Brody closed his eyes and slowly tilted his head back, arching his neck as far back as possible. He outstretched his arms slowly to the rhythm of the song, keeping the cleaver tight in his right hand. He began to move his body to the song's addictive third-beat drum and remembered, suddenly, of the weird nostalgia that Dr. Manson had been collecting for who knows how long. He remembered the shelf of white gloves and opened his eyes wide at a thought he knew was brilliant.

Knowing that neither Chelsey or the doctor could do any further harm, he left the room and shuffled down the hallway he remembered that connected to the mansion's grand living room. Though he had been drugged he was still able to remember the bits and pieces that mattered most. He went to the shelf of white gloves and picked out a thin white leather glove and slipped it on his right hand. It was thin enough where he could pull it tightly down his fingers and roll up at the cuff. A little big but would do just fine.

Before heading back to his trophies, his eyes scanned the shelf of top hats where one fancied him. A taller top hat that he imagined Lincoln would wear. Or Jack the Ripper. He put it on and, although a little big, it fit well enough.

Back to the room he went to see Manson still holding the handle of the knife blade that was buried completely into his gut. Chelsey's body was slightly twitching, but he knew she was just about finished. He walked over to the remote-control Manson had dropped, picked it up, and turned up the volume as high as his ears could stand. He turned back to Dr. Manson and strutted over to him with the cleaver now tightly held with the white leather glove.

It wasn't at all like anything he'd planned when he first laid eyes on Chelsey, but it turned out to be a far better ceremony. He stood above Dr. Manson and reached down to grasp the carving knife handle. Brody did a quick step back while pulling the knife from Manson's stomach. A gush of blood and stench spewed forth.

Manson teetered on his knees, wide-eyed in disbelief as the KC music cut to "I'm Your Boogie Man." Brody paused for just a second as he remembered the song playing in the background those years ago when his family was torn apart.

He raised the cleaver high and came down with a brutal slash to the doctor's neck. Normally, Brody would have been easily strong enough to cut the man's head completely off, but where the cleaver stopped midway would have to do. He pulled it out. Jugular flow jetted into the air. He kicked the doctor's body to the floor where it sprawled in a bloody heap. Satisfied, he strutted back to Chelsey, the top hat tilted and loose.

When standing above Chelsey's broken body, her eyes wide in horror, she still had a whisper of fight left in her. "Who the fuck are you?"

Brody stared into her eyes, the meat cleaver in the white-gloved hand, the bloodied carving knife in his left, arms stretched out, his head tilted with the top hat nearly falling off. "Let me introduce myself. I'm Mister Boogie."

Mister Boogie wanted to savor everything that had taken place. Much of the details were fuzzy but he could play catch up more quickly than most. The routine that he had planned when dancing at Fitzgerald's with Chelsey hadn't come to anything resembling what he'd just now concocted, but he knew there would be plenty of time to refine the bloody mess he'd left in the grand room where the good doctor and his assistant thought they had another one in the bag for The Bone Break Killer.

With a quick downward movement and flick of the wrist, he threw the meat cleaver down to stick perfectly into the wooded floor, no more than an inch from Chelsey's head. Her eyes widened to the point where they looked like they would pop out of her skull. Mister Boogie then crouched low to a deep squat position, straddling Chelsey's body. He tossed the carving knife from his left hand to his gloved hand, and with four quick slashing movements, he cut into both Chelsey's wrists and both sides of her neck, his body moving left to right in a smooth shifting movement with each slash.

Mister Boogie stood upright after the deed, took in a deep breath and let it out as slowly as he could. He felt the internal damage that had taken place, but he relished in the pain's ability to create intense focus. KC's mantra ended, and the room fell silent, the metallic scent of blood thick in the air. Rex stood over Chelsey's body, his chest moving in and out with slow controlled breaths as hot adrenaline cooled in his veins. He wiped the knife clean on his shirt and dropped it with a perfect stick next to the cleaver, his mind racing but also controlled.

He couldn't stay. The mansion, the bodies...everything about the night would lead back to Rex Brody if he didn't disappear and cover his tracks with precision thinking. Inside the great living room once again, he saw the morning of September 11th, 2001, was getting on. Time had flown by.

He used one of the remote controls that were on one of the large cedar coffee tables, clicked on the giant plasma television, bolted to the front living room wall, to get a quick catchup on the news, wondering if Miss Fat Hoodie's body had been discovered at the library.

He watched in deep captivation and bafflement as every news channel he clicked to showed over and over again the billowing smoke and endless debris of The World Trade Center Towers crumbling to oblivion from being hit by two hijacked Boeing 767's. Jet planes that were purposely flown into the towers to wreak hell on earth, to bring forth the coming of a new world order that arrived with the call of rage, death, and a permanent reshaping of terror for all the world to see.

Mister Boogie's new world.

3: THE SERPENT'S VEIL, THE ORB, AND THE WEIRD SISTERS OF MACBETH

Rex Brody stood in the savaged madness of Kelly Manson's estate, his pulse steady, his breathing slow. He was doing everything possible to get it together; ready for whatever was next. He kept the massive plasma television on one of the major cable networks as the unfolding of the 9/11 Terrorist Attacks that annihilated New York's Twin Towers dominated every news cycle. He wanted to be part of every word and moment as best he could.

The ghouls of violence, now silenced by Mister Boogie, along with the backdrop of the Twin Towers being blown to hell, felt like the perfect cocktail. Blood clung to the air like it had been sprayed from a flocking machine, a metallic tang that mixed with the sharp scent of antiseptic from Dr. Kelly Manson's sterile world. The bodies were cooling. The morning stretched on and on as Brody ransacked the fabulous estate. He had a few hours tops. Maybe three, maybe more but he had to move quickly, regardless.

Had it not been for the terrorist's Boeing 767s, Brody knew the Houston Police could have already been here. Or at least it was possible, but an attack on the entire country would keep things in chaos nation-wide, which included Houston. Mister Boogie banked on the extra time and squeezed out every half-second of it.

Now came the most crucial part: eliminating every

trace of himself.

His mind raced through the options.

Fire. The most effective method. If he torched the place, the flames would swallow DNA, fingerprints, blood, fibers—everything. A house fire—especially one the size it would take to consume the doctor's mansion—could burn hot enough to degrade all human remains, incinerate bone, and make bodies unrecognizable.

But fire was also unpredictable. Investigators would pick it apart, and in a neighborhood like this, the blaze would be noticed before it did enough damage. Rex shook his head and kept thinking, taking the white glove on and off his right hand. The top hat he'd tossed onto one of the estate's leather sofas. He enjoyed his newfound gimmicks. Plenty of time later to get new ones.

He thought about bleach and ammonia. Combined, they could destroy biological evidence beyond forensic retrieval, but the smell was powerful, could be too attention-grabbing. Plus, he'd have to scrub every inch of the place, which had to be ten thousand square feet; he felt he had some extra time, but not that kind of time.

What about superglue fuming? Brody learned of this trick forensic techs used in a recent article he found fascinating. Heated superglue in an enclosed space would coat surfaces, revealing latent fingerprints. The problem was that it only worked in controlled environments, so the practicality was not viable.

His eyes swept over the open shelves in Manson's private study. There had to be close to a thousand books that lined the walled-in hickory shelves. Despite the urgent time frame, Brody took pause to at least browse over many of them on shelves stacked with Dante, Shakespeare, Mark, Lenin, Stalin, Plato. Plenty of what looked like the finest in medical texts and procedures.

Brody could see the good doctor was a fine surgeon, one obsessed with knowledge. Which meant control. There was no doubt in Rex's mind that the house would have industrial-grade solvents somewhere. Hydrochloric acid. Acetone. Muriatic acid. Chemicals meant to dissolve tissue, wipe away residue, burn through organic material at a molecular level. He just had to find them.

He moved swiftly with full purpose, searching the estate's rooms, the library, the cinema room, game room, pool rooms and lockers, any place he thought the doctor's personal stockpile was stored. The moment he found it in the utility closet, he bit his lower lip in irritation, thinking it should have been the first place to start. But stress was high, so Mister Boogie gave himself a break and cracked a smile when finding a collection of heavy-duty cleaning solutions inside the closet. They were likely meant for sterilization, but more than enough was there to suit his needs. He pulled on a pair of surgical gloves from the doctor's stash and went to work.

He wiped down every surface he remembered not only touching but could have touched when he was drugged; doorknobs, whisky shot glasses, the decanter of whiskey that Chelsey poured from, wooden banisters, even the leather chair he had leaned against while watching Manson take his last breath. Every inch that could hold an impression of his fingers, he treated with acid-soaked rags, ensuring nothing would be left behind.

Next came the sinks in the downstairs bathrooms. Though he had no memory of being there or touching anything, who the hell knew what took place when his mind fell out. Brody ran hot water, mixing in bleach and ammonia in precise amounts to produce a controlled chemical burn.

Finally, there was all the blood plus the bodies of the doctor and Chelsey which presented, of course, a much different and bigger problem.

Dr. Kelly Manson lay on the floor, broken and bled out. Brody could see his skull was probably cracked from the few strikes he'd landed. It was the knife strikes that were far more admirable. He took a moment to study the grotesque display of his handiwork. It wasn't nearly as efficient as what he'd done to the fat sweatsuit banking patron, but then again, he wasn't fighting for his life with that bitch.

He straddled Manson's body, looking at the doctor's peeled-open, vacant eyes where no one would ever be home again. The quiet horror of a man who had met something far worse than himself. Lights out, motherfucker.

Mister Boogie walked over to Chelsey to study her broken, lifeless body with the slashes in her wrists and neck, her once-sultry smirk permanently frozen. Her dead eyes still in shock. Watching her dance at Fitzgerald's seemed like a lifetime ago. Her betrayal had been swift, but her choices sealed her fate. He wasn't about to leave her like a piece of tossed evidence. She was far too special for that. The doctor meant nothing, but Chelsey needed something more special, a place for safekeeping. Preservation of some kind as well as something to show the police the thinking of a true mastermind.

He scanned every room, analyzing every option. Dr. Manson had a 4-car garage connected to the house by a single door. In here, there were endless possibilities, but no cars. A workbench, tools, rags, red gas cans on a shelf. A deep freezer sat at the far end, large enough for medical-grade storage or a ton of food. He strode to the chest and opened the lid. Empty. Freezing cold. Perfect for Chelsey.

He moved more quickly knowing time was against him. Still, through it all, he stopped every now and again to watch the news replay the towers come crumbling down, repeatedly, and the president promising quick vengeance. A new world order where Mister Boogie and his glove fit in, skintight.

Brody set Chelsey's bloody body on a thick plastic sheet he'd pulled down from the ceiling. His every movement was precise, controlled, filling him with satisfaction as his mind absorbed a skillset he knew the world needed. While terrorists had attacked the country's pinnacle city, Mister Boogie believed the country needed more. Everything was coming together in perfectly orchestrated chaos.

He carried Chelsey's body as if it weighed nothing into the garage, then maneuvered her into the deep freezer with care. He crossed her slit wrists and turned her head chin-up to reveal the meaty and oozing gashes to her neck. Once so pretty in life, now so macabre in death. The plastic sheet he wadded up and stuffed in on top of her. He let the heavy lid slam shut with a dull thud, tucking her away from prying eyes. At least for now.

Brody then raced back as quickly as he could to the coagulating pools of Chelsey's blood, the knives, and her handgun. He took the knives out of the wooden floor where he'd thrown them to stick next to her head and placed them and the gun in a way that the blades and gun-barrel pointed to the garage. If he did everything as perfectly as planned in his mind, then the police would see the knives and gun and wonder what their placement meant. If they were skilled enough or experienced enough, they would recognize the clue.

Now for the mess he'd made of himself. In the kitchen, he washed the blood from his hands, his face, his neck...some was from Manson, some was Chelsey's, some was his own. He ran his head under the sink tap to wash out as much blood as possible from his hair. Then he scrubbed his clothes, shirt, pants, boots, anywhere a forensic team might swab. It seemed an impossible task. Murder was a messy business. Plan A: get rid of these clothes.

He gave the kitchen a scrubbing same as he'd done for the bathrooms.

Now for the estate.

Dr. Manson had security cameras everywhere, but exactly how many there were, Brody had no idea. He had spotted them on the way in. This time he checked the master bedroom first and smiled when he found the recording system, which he disabled before making his next move. Curiously, there was only the footage of him somersaulting into the kitchen and choosing the knives, which meant the kill room didn't have a camera. Zero real evidence of his entry or exit, although there was the shot of him throwing the carving knife. He was going to destroy it anyway, so none of it mattered unless the system was hooked into another system for backup copies.

Still, no time to worry about it. Then it came to him that most of the footage of Kelly Manson's gruesome serial murder reign would most likely be outside in the semi-truck, which Brody would have to be prep last if at all.

Brody couldn't leave anything to chance, so he doused some of the chemicals all over the recording devices.

Next, he took more plastic and spread it across the blood-soaked areas, ensuring no footprints, no blood patterns could be traced. He scrubbed everything down best that he could with the acid solution, then carefully rearranged the living room to look as if a struggle had taken place between Manson and an unknown intruder.

Finally, he made his way upstairs, his boots barely making a sound against the rich mahogany flooring. There was something else here. Something he felt.

The second-floor hallway smelled of old books, leather, and something darker, something that didn't belong in a doctor's house. He opened a door at the end of the hall and stepped into a medical sanctuary of horror. The walls were lined with preserved human remains, meticulously arranged behind glass cases. Skeletal hands, fragmented skulls, entire sections of flayed human skin stretched taut like canvas. Some were labeled, cataloged, as if Manson had been keeping records of his own private collection.

Brody remembered his first year in college when one of the pre-med students befriended him. His name was Arch Pearce, someone striking enough that Rex could never forget him. One day Pearce invited Rex to the medical school's basement cadaver room. What he saw now was so much like where Pearce had taken him that he wondered (just briefly) if Pearce himself was somehow involved in all this shit.

At the center of the room sat a massive wooden desk, and behind it, an ornate cabinet with locked compartments. Rex cracked it open with a careful twist of his knife and found bottles of corrosive agents, scalpels still coated in dried blood, and a leather-bound book detailing procedures that Manson had undoubtedly performed.

He exhaled slowly. He had met monsters before, had known killers, but Kelly Manson had been something else. There was an artistry to his depravity, a commitment that Rex could almost respect. Almost.

He gathered the chemicals he needed and pocketed a few scalpels as twisted souvenirs. He had an idea for his future as he handled them.

Satisfied, he approached the back door. The Houston weather that morning remained pleasant from the cool front that had come through, unusual for Houston in September. The sky was northern blue, the air electric in the storm of 9/11, but not ideal for Brody's immediate needs. Nice days could bring about unneeded attention.

He took one last glance around his work thus far; it was nearly complete. Every surface he had touched had been wiped down, Manson's body moved ever so slightly to showcase his work, Chesley's body in the freezer to tell his own silent story, and the last loose ends had been hopefully wiped down good enough.

But what about the house itself. It couldn't simply be abandoned. If there were any stray fibers, any overlooked trace of his presence, it needed to be erased. He had seconds, minutes at the most, to rig up something convincing and catastrophic without a lingering gasoline stench that could raise suspicion. It didn't have to be the entire estate, either, the first floor would be fine.

Harried and somewhat frantic, he finally saw it. Near the back of the kitchen pantry, lined up like an obsessive collector's pride, were several large oxygen cylinders, the kind used in surgical operations and emergency cases. Medical-grade and pressurized. Capable of feeding an inferno hotter and faster than gasoline ever could. Next to them, stored on a lower shelf, were several tightly sealed bottles of hydrogen peroxide, isopropyl alcohol, and industrial cleaning solvents.

Brody had read about it once. A fireman's story from years back, describing a "blast house" scenario. Oxygen-fed fires burned hotter than jet fuel, and if contained properly, they could turn a mansion like this into an instant crematorium. Not perfect, but good enough.

He moved faster, now dragging a few of the oxygen tanks out into the living room, setting them against the main support beams. He cracked the valves just enough to release an almost inaudible hiss into the air, allowing the pure oxygen to saturate the space. It wouldn't take long—five minutes, maybe less—before the room became a highly combustible death trap. He then tossed some of the many blankets the doctor had draped all around the living room sofas and chairs over the tanks hoping it would be just enough for coverage. Mister Boogie moved the blankets more carefully as to not make them obvious.

Next, he quickly soaked a few areas in the hydrogen peroxide and alcohol mixture, focusing on wooden beams, carpeted floors, and curtains. He slashed open the cushions on the doctor's pristine leather couch, stuffing them with the chemical-soaked rags he had prepared, then quickly flipped the cushions to hide the damage.

Now for the trigger. Brody knew it was one more damn thing that needed to be quick but inconspicuous. A delayed detonation, something that would keep police inside long enough to investigate the doctor's body, the table of surgical tools and the pools of blood all over the killing field, the strategically placed weapons; every-fucking-thing. Just long enough when things could go boom.

The plasma television was the best bet as it had been on looping the continuing news coverage of 9/11. The country was in a blind panic, absorbed in chaos. He left the television running, letting its blue glow flicker across one of the coffee tables. Then, he crouched near the power strip behind the couch when he found a lamp that he unplugged and plugged back in, just barely.

The loose prongs inside the socket would cause tiny electrical arcs, too small to notice but hot enough to grow.

It wouldn't happen immediately. Not in five or even ten minutes, but as time moved on, eventually, the connection would fail. It would have to. The plan had to work and when it did, one tiny, invisible spark could meet the pure, heavy oxygen filling the house. Mister Boogie knew the key word was "could." His hope was that the time police or EMS or whoever, were deep inside, standing over Manson's body, or looking into the freezer where Chelsey waited...BOOM! Lights out.

Brody took one last glance at the television, still playing footage of the twin towers being hit. By the time any explosion happened here, it would just be one more disaster to pile on the country.

He walked outside and stood at the edge of the massive driveway, his eyes locked on his vehicle, the final loose end. In front of him, the house sat in pristine, artificial silence, a crime scene meticulously stripped of all but the dead. At least that was Mister Boogie's hope.

But the Porsche was a problem. He couldn't be caught dead in it, not now, not if the cops get wind that the last time Chelsey was seen alive was when she was getting into that car at the club. There'd be an APB and a BOLO put out for the Porsche. Every cop in Houston would be looking for it.

Not a moment to spare, he went into action wiping down the interior, ensuring no hair, no skin cells, nothing traceable remained. But still, the mere presence of the car was enough to create a trail. The entire interior had to be destroyed.

His gaze drifted to the semi-truck parked at the front of the driveway, Kelly Manson's personal monster. The Bone Break Killer's traveling mobile slaughterhouse.

The trailer itself was just an empty husk now, a steel coffin that had carried death in its belly. He thought about rigging the semi but immediately dismissed the idea. He wanted the evidence of the doctor's criminal activity to remain.

Brody decided to set the fucking car on fire, not in a simple way, but something spectacular.

He moved faster. The wealthy neighborhood still looked asleep as the morning had moved toward noon. He looked up and down Dr. Manson's street to see if anyone would see what was going on. He knew the best way to keep things as inconspicuous as possible was to carry on normally, whatever the case. Like erasing the evidence of who butchered the doctor and his assistant. There were a few of Dr. Manson's neighbors strolling around, one walking a small dog, another toddling around for no apparent reason. No one Brody thought would cause any trouble. Everyone else was probably at work or watching the news coverage of the world burning down.

He stood in a near trance, arms folded, right hand under his chin as if holding his head in place, going over the best plan. While he was packing Chelsey's body, he knew he'd seen plenty of neatly placed gas containers on one of the shelves. Plenty of clean rags, too, as well as—

"It's such a tragedy. You know, I was in New York just a week ago. A week ago. Can you imagine that? Now the city's been blown to pieces. At least from the news cameras it looks that way. My god. No one expected this, surely not."

Rex flinched. He must have been pondering everything in a trance longer than he thought. Whoever it was who just came on him was lucky. Brody practiced restraint; Mister Boogie wanted to act immediately. Brody's body was feeling the damage and pain from the injuries sustained during the Manson ordeal; he wondered how many vials of adrenalin he had left to keep him sharp enough for escape, strong enough to push through whatever was next. At that moment it was one of the elites from River Oaks. He turned around to face the nosey neighbor.

The man looked to be in his early 60s, lean and wiry. He wore a light robe over a silk shirt and dress slacks, leather sandals. His expression morphed from casual to horrified. "Jesus, mister. What happened to you...your face?"

Brody was instantly aware of how he looked to the neighbor, beat up, and all. Regardless of his exhaustion, Mister Boogie knew it wouldn't take much to handle Mr. Fancy Robe and Sandals. Brody pointed to his face. "Bar fight," and followed up with a look that could kill.

"Have you seen the news?"

"What news?"

"Are you a friend of Doctor Manson's? I've not seen you around."

Mr. Fancy was making Brody think fast on his feet. "Doc's gonna patch me up," he lied. "I hate needles."

"A guy built like you?" He laughed.

Brody's eyes narrowed into a stare that pierced the wealthy neighbor, taking him off guard. He cleared his throat and stepped back. "Sorry. That was a little insensitive of me, my apologies. None of my business who Doctor Manson treats. I beg your pardon."

Brody stepped forward and put his hand on the neighbor's shoulder, gripping it hard enough to let Mr. Fancy Pants know he could break it at will. "But now it is your business, isn't it." Brody's grip felt like a vice as the man winced in pain and fear. "What's your name, Nosey Nelly?"

The man attempted to take another step away but felt

Brody's grip tighten unmercifully. He grimaced in pain. "Francis." His voice trembled. "I never meant to pry. I'm just shocked at what has happened in New York, probably shaken. I mean, we all are. Not thinking right."

Brody continued to tighten his grip to the point it caused tears to form in Francis's eyes. "Frank. You're right. I'm sure everyone is shocked. Including me. But with the night I've had... Let's just say it was one of those nights I will never forget."

Francis's heartrate and breathing increased until he felt faint. "Please. You're hurting me."

The adrenaline levels Brody was concerned about moments ago had suddenly surged in supply. He released his grip instantly, pulled his hand back in mockery. "I didn't realize I was hurting you. Looks like I need to apologize, Frank. Where do you live? Which home is yours?"

Francis slowly shook his head and grabbed his shoulder to feel if anything was torn or dislocated. The man in front of Dr. Manson's was like no one he'd ever seen. He had the look of someone who wasn't rode hard and put away wet, but the one who did the riding and putting away. The man's clothes were soiled and splotched with reddish-brown muck, his hair wet and slicked back, as if recently washed, with strands dangling down his chiseled face. His strength terrified Francis. He really wanted to be back in his luxury studio room, watching more of the Twin Tower scenes. He took a gamble instead of answering the bizarre man outright. "Listen...Mister...?"

Rex cocked his head, keeping deep eye contact with the neighbor. "Boogie."

The answer created more alarm in Francis. More fear. What kind of last name was Boogie, for Christ's sake? Francis nodded carefully and slowly, understanding whoever he was dealing with now was clearly on the level of those who had just torn New York City apart.

"I see, Mister Boogie. I'm just a block over..."

Brody stepped in close enough to where it would be overly simple to head butt Francis, killing him on the spot. But doing that would take more time to fiddlefuck with the body.

"Then move along, Frank. Move right along down these charming streets to wherever it is you live and do not come back here. Not anytime soon, understood?" Brody flipped his hands and fingers out as if to shoo away a pest. "Leave, Frank. I'll not say it again."

Francis nodded, knowing it was best to keep quiet and listen to the doctor's patient.

Brody watched every step Francis took until he was far enough away to where things felt back to normal while, at the same time, knowing nothing would ever be normal again. He turned back to his Porsche and popped the hood. Everything now was a gamble. He would have to attend to Francis later. But Francis who? Brody ground his teeth in more frustration. There was no time to get sloppy, and forgetting to ask Francis his last name was sloppy. Not disastrous, but certainly not polished, something that Mister Boogie would have to continue practicing and correct if things were to move forward for him to change the world as much as the terrorist-hijacked planes had done just hours ago. Brody thought about the letter from Conrad Ellington, thought about his possible ancestry, then slapped himself hard enough to regain focus.

The next crucial item was removing the license plate. A missing plate often complicated an investigation, slowed down the identification process, not that it'd do them any good.

The car needed to be destroyed, same as the house, to wipeout any remaining DNA and fingerprints he may have missed. He remembered the red gas cans stored in the garage. Moments later, he found them on a shelf near Manson's workbench, full and waiting.

Brody grabbed one of the cans and unscrewed the cap.

The raw scent of gasoline punched into his lungs, sharp and biting. Almost refreshing for Mister Boogie. He found a screwdriver, grabbed a handful of rags, rummaged through a drawer for some wire, then returned to the Porsche.

After removing the license plate, he tossed it and the screwdriver into the car. Both would melt in the coming inferno. He looked more carefully under the dash, moving fast. Time, ticking, ticking away. Brody heard Pink Floyd's anthem in his head from Dark Side of the Moon with hundreds of different alarm clocks going off in the background before Roger Waters' voice yelled about time ticking away moments of dull days.

The fuse box was easy to access, just behind the driver's side dash panel. Porsche's early 2000s models still had simple wiring—nothing complicated, no digital anti-theft barriers. He pulled a copper wire from his pocket and ran it across a power circuit to an exposed metal contact near the fuse box.

He leaned back, exhaling slowly. It was set.

Then he poured gas onto the rags, soaking them enough to release fumes quickly and steadily

He tossed the fuel-drenched rags onto the driver's seat and the floorboards. The vapors would fill the cabin in minutes. Then he took the half-full gas can and set it in the passenger seat, lid slightly open, just enough to keep the air saturated with gasoline fumes. A perfect confined blast chamber.

Finally, Brody rolled up the windows, locking in the vapor; closed the air vents, checked that nothing leaked out; taped over the door latch sensor, keeping the car in a state where the circuit would only complete when the door was physically opened.

All that was left to do now was to leave.

The moment a cop opened the door, the sequence would trigger: The circuit would complete. An arcing electrical spark would ignite the gasoline fumes. Instant fireball. Every miniscule trace of him and Chelsey, gone in a heartbeat. At least in theory.

Mister Boogie took one last look at his work. If all ended well, a masterpiece of controlled chaos.

He wiped his hands on his pants and brushed hair back again, stepping back to survey his work one last time, thinking it was clean enough, he'd be untraceable. By the time anyone realized what had happened, hopefully the Porsche would be nothing but ash and ruin. He knew that when police saw everything that had taken place, they would wonder what kind of new monster was on the loose. Whatever police detail was on the case of Dr. Kelly Manson and his lovely associate, Chelsey Bingham, would now be onto something in perfect alignment to the new chaos that came roaring to life as New York City's Achilles heels had been slashed.

He took one long last look at Kelly Manson's estate, up and down the street, up into the clear Houston sky. He knew he'd be on foot for the time being, but he knew the area well enough to find quick transportation and regroup. Though injured and exhausted, his fabulous conditioning allowed him to take off at a strong pace, leaving behind nothing but death and mystery. One thought cemented itself in his mind as he was doing the cleanup and watching and hearing the Twin Towers fall to terrorists. The world either belonged to those who wanted the world to bathe in blood or to those who could erase themselves.

Mister Boogie wanted both.

***

The air around Kelly Manson's estate was dense with the stillness of a crime scene untouched by frantic responders. The smell of blood had settled into the air like a permanent aerosol.

Detective Spade stepped out of the black unmarked

cruiser, then ran a tired hand through his wired hair. Detective Hayes moved stiffly beside him, wincing as she adjusted the makeshift brace on her arm. The drunk driver that had nearly killed them in the middle of the night had delayed any kind of swift arrival because Hayes wasn't even sure if the big rig patrol had found was the one she had called in.

When the call came back to Spade, as the lead on the case, they were both chilled with surprise when they finally arrived on scene, set inside the wealth and protection of River Oaks where a nice big shiny blue semi parked out front of one the finer illustrious estates in the area; the home of Dr. Kelly Manson, a surgeon who practiced in Houston's Medical Center, Memorial Hermann-Texas Medical Center, to be exact.

No one had answered the door, so the first responders were unable to ask the homeowner about the truck. On specific, shouted instructions from Spade, they remained parked in front of the estate with their emergency lights flashing. Several of them had begun to cordon off the area around the truck with standard crime scene yellow tape.

"One fucking hell of a rig, partner. Even for around here." Spade shut the police car's driver's door and looked over the semi-truck. "It's looking more like the rookie Paul's instincts are starting to unfold one fucking page at a time. What did he call it? Razor something?"

"Occam's Razor." Carmen Hayes shuffled over to stand next to her partner while he looked at the rig in awe. "And he didn't coin the phrase, Spade. It's old. Some philosophy way back in the fourteen hund—"

"Yeah, yeah, yeah. Whatever. Simplest explanation is the best one. Got it. Let's get inside, Hayes, and see what in God's name is right in front our faces."

Hayes was clearly irritated for being interrupted but walked alongside her partner as she looked over to see a metallic-blue Porsche, the perfect car for any hotshot surgeon. "No one said shit about the Boxster. No plate, either." Hayes looked to the uniforms who were now walking around the estate's manicured lawn. "Officer, let's get some intel on this car, pronto." The officer who believed he was being called out didn't even look at Hayes and Spade, though he knew them both well enough that taking orders from them would be a step in the right direction toward a promotion.

The estate was eerily silent. The kind of silence that made the hairs on the back of Spade's neck stiffen, and that was a rarity. They crossed the property line cautiously, boots crunching gravel of the fabulous circular driveway. The front door was unlocked. Spade swung it open. The first thing that hit them was the coppery smell of death. Second, the acrid sting of chemicals. Instantly, both detectives sensed the chaos and violence that had taken place inside.

Hayes pulled a handkerchief from her pocket and held it to her nose. "What the hell?"

A large, private room just to the left of the living room with a connecting hallway to a kitchen area was nothing short of a slaughterhouse, and yet, it had the distinct feeling of controlled chaos. Dr. Kelly Manson's enormous body was lying center stage, where it was meant to be. Plastic sheeting had been placed all over the blood pools to compromise any blood patterns. Though there was evidence of some desperation and frenzy, whoever had done the killing was someone highly skilled in hand-to-hand and weapons combat.

"Christ. Clever fucker," Spade whispered.

Dr. Manson lay on his back, his massive legs sprawled out, arms just as massive, one hand over his stomach where he was either shot or stabbed, the other limp and posed outward as if trying to survive the bleed-out.

There were pools of blood covered by more plastic sheeting, two large kitchen knives, and a small handgun a few feet from Dr. Manson's body. On first glimpse, the weapons looked like they had been placed oddly.

Hayes crouched to get a better look at Manson's hands and arms. "Look at this. No defensive wounds. This wasn't a fight. This was an execution."

Spade stood a few feet from his partner and the body while looking over the other murder area. "Stabbed or shot?"

"Definitely stabbed but not close range. Whoever did this knew how to throw a knife perfectly." Hayes didn't move the doctor's hand or touch anything, but she'd seen enough knife wounds to know this one was done with expertise.

Spade exhaled sharply, took a slow walk through the bloodied area while paying attention to the table with medical instruments set in neat lines. He and Hayes then walked around the first floor to see and smell that every surface had been wiped down, every potential piece of forensic evidence methodically erased. They would wait to investigate the second floor and went back into the kill zone.

"Take a look at that." Spade stopped and looked around the room, the hallway attached to the room that led to the kitchen which then opened into the massive living room. The impressive plasma wall television was on one of the news stations airing non-stop, minute-to-minute coverage of the twin towers' destruction.

"Who would leave the goddamn television on with this shit going down? Good Christ and His soda crackers."

Carmen nodded, unease settling in. "I noticed it when we entered. This isn't just another psycho killer. Well...maybe he is Bates-psycho, but whoever did this was...methodical. Someone who knows his shit...a lot of shit."

Spade turned to her, jaw tightening. "Let me retort that a bit. This was something way fucking worse. Knowledge part... You're spot on. But look at the chair in the middle of the room and the table over there with all the tools on it. All those surgical tools. Take a good look at both these pieces,

Hayes, and tell me what you see. Or what you missed that's right here in front of us."

Hayes nodded slowly in irritation, still holding her injured arm. "You think I need that, Spade? Really? We were nearly killed in the middle of the fucking night, and I was a lot closer to that situation than you were, so my apologies if I'm not as quick on the draw right now."

Spade took in a breath before saying anything. "I hear you, partner. Do you need some rest? I'm not patronizing you. I just need to know what you've got left in the tank, because if it ain't there, get some rest and I'll handle this until you're ready."

"Fuck off. I'm here, ain't I?"

"Okay. Then *be* here, because we are going to need every bit of gas in our tank with this one. Tell me about that chair and the surgical tools table."

"Clearly it was their M.O. Whoever was here, whoever they brought here, they had plans to do it here, in this room. So why this particular room, is that what you're getting to?"

"Yeah, why not in the truck trailer? The fucking semi-truck that's parked out front of this monster house. Why is it out there, and the deed was done here?"

Hayes stepped closer toward Spade. "The deed was attempted here. It wasn't done here. Whoever was supposed to be Number Fifteen on The Bone Break Killer's list turned the dial on him, or them, and that was entirely unexpected. For whatever reason, the next victim was supposed to be something special...until it wasn't." Carmen turned her gaze to the doctor's enormous dead body. "Assuming he's The Bone Break Killer, of course. Now, I'm curious about the weapons lying on the floor placed over there like a goddamn sign."

Spade walked over the heavy pools of coagulated blood where a large carving knife and a cleaver were placed in front of each other and a .38 handgun in front of them both. He stopped to examine a broken zip tie. Not cut. Jagged.

Broken.

Hayes crouched to get a closer look at the weapons.

"You know how hard it is break one of these?" Spade said. "I mean, these are the standard ones you'd buy at any Walmart, nothing industrial, but still tough as fuck."

Hayes nodded but kept her eyes on the weapons and all the blood covered by the plastic, enough blood that looked like it had come from several parts of a body all at once. "So, the doc's killer, if that's what this is from, is not only wildly strong, but also has a high tolerance for pain. I'm sure the ties cut into his wrists. But he's also able to take out the doctor...who looks like a goddamn giant and would not be easy to take out...then wipe this place down as clean as any clean-room technician, and place these weapons as a clear sign that we need to head in this direction, to that door." She stood.

"Garage." Spade was one step ahead, already leading to the inside entry door to the garage.

Spade pressed his palm against the door, hesitating for only a second before pushing it open. The house had already given them plenty to process, a slaughter so methodical it felt like a challenge, an invitation. What the hell were they going to find in here?

As they stepped inside, the air thickened. Not the heavy, cloying scent of fresh death, but something colder. Something sealed away and pristine.

The garage was immaculate; walls painted a clean, modern white, spotless and polished concrete floor. The air smelled of almost nothing. A little gas, but faint. Not a tool out of place.

It was too perfect, it seemed, before they saw it, at the far end of the garage, nestled against the wall like an intentional fixture, a luxury stainless steel chest freezer. A sleek, high-end model for the wealthy to show off in their well-organized garages, stocked with expensive meats and whatnot.

But in Dr. Manson's garage its presence felt wrong, as it was too far from the door for quick access. A small bead of condensation ran down the lid's side. The kind that came from a sudden temperature shift. Spade moved first, stepping toward it with measured purpose. Hayes stayed just behind him, her breath steady but controlled.

He ran his hand along the edge of the freezer. There was no lock. He gripped the handle and lifted the lid. A rush of cold air billowed out, thick and slow, the icy mist curling around him.

Inside, a huge wad of plastic sheeting and...

"Blood." Spade stepped back. *What kind of sick shit is this?* He knew better than to touch anything barehanded. Forensic evidence could be compromised, but he had to find out what was under the bloody plastic. Driven by morbid curiosity, he pulled on a black glove, and with a cursory glance to Hayes and a nod, he returned his attention to the freezer. Careful as a surgeon, with Hayes looking over his shoulder, he lifted the frozen-stiff plastic, slowly...revealing blood-soaked hair...wide-open eyes staring up at him, frozen in terror. His instinctual reaction was to lurch backwards, get as far away from her as humanly possible, but he held steady on course, removed the plastic, set it on the floor, and swore he'd find out who she was and bring her sadistic killer to justice.

The woman's body appeared to have been carefully placed. Both detectives saw that right away. They also looked over the nasty wounds on the sides of her neck, a butcher's work, her wrists crossed over her stomach, damn near detached. Her legs weren't bent at awkward angles, the bones not broken, but folded at the knees and tucked together gently. Whoever did this had cared. Or at least, he wanted it to look that way.

Hayes's stomach twisted. This wasn't just another body in a long line of murders; it was deliberately posed.

Neither of them spoke for a moment.

Then, Hayes murmured, “Could be our accomplice.” Her voice was barely above a whisper.

Spade’s grip on the freezer lid tightened. “Yeah.”

“A real beauty queen, too.” Hayes pulled out her camera flip phone and took a quick shot.

Spade had seen enough. Finally, he let the lid ease shut with a quiet, final thud.

They turned back toward the house, toward the wreckage of Kelly Manson’s final moments.

Just as they stepped over the threshold, Hayes muttered, “Whoever did this wanted us to find her, but not easily. And it took a lot of extra time, too. Distracted us from something else...in fact...fuck.”

“What is it Hayes? Spit it out, Jesus.”

“The Porsche. Outside. What if it doesn’t belong to one of these two? Did they come here in the semi? And why is there no plate on the Porsche? We should have vetted it more closely. Oh my god, Heath. It’s the killer’s car!”

Spade’s eyes popped wide open. “Boobytrapped?”

Hayes grabbed his arm, then both started racing through the living room to the estate’s front entry door.

Just as they rushed out to the front drive, “Get back!” Hayes screamed at the uniformed officer who was about to open the Porsche’s door. “Get away from the car!”

The door latch clicked.

Officer Bernard Sampson, two years on the force, never smelled the gas fumes inside the sports car. He never heard the explosion that left his wife, Lena, without a husband of three years, and their new baby boy, Christopher, without a father, for the rest of their lives.

“Fucking Christ!” Detective Spade’s voice was nearly as loud as the explosion. Expensive Porsche parts flew in every direction. Fire raged. Smoke billowed. He frantically turned to Hayes. “Get everyone here, Hayes. Call every-fucking-one, now!”

Only one time in her career was Hayes ordered to call

in everyone. Which meant the HFD, EMS, FBI, ATF, the whole goddamn HPD ecosystem. It happened with Spade while working the first case of The Bone Break Killer: the victim, 17, track runner by the name of Leo Campton, from the Aldine District, had every toe, every finger, every rib, every bone in both feet, the spine, and the neck, not only broken, but shattered. Spade thought it was such a freakish ordeal it warranted everyone and their dogs brought in.

A low whump echoed through the house, a sound that blasted every survival instinct in Heath Spade's body into overdrive. Carmen Hayes's, too. And the other uniforms who had just seen their brother in blue blown to hell. Time stopped.

***

The city swallowed him whole.

Rex Brody moved as fast as his bruised body could take him through the tangled veins of Houston's backstreets. Houston was one of the few massive cities worthy of being called a megapolitan. It was also one where zoning didn't apply or had ever been accepted. Which meant estates the size of Dr. Manson's could be close enough to poverty shacks that it was relatively easy to slip in and out of the shadows, as would a ghost in a world that had just birthed yet one more monster to join ranks with the ones who'd just crippled New York City.

The Houston air clung to him like old blood, thick and invasive. He walked quickly in some areas, and in others, he would sprint until it became too painful to continue at that pace. Easy movement was deliberate. There was no panic, no fear. He was simply moving into what he knew he had become back at Manson's place.

He needed transportation.

A stolen car would be too traceable. A bus, too slow, maybe not if he could get to one quickly enough and far away enough from River Oaks. Taxis were out because drivers remembered faces. Taxi drivers remembered a lot of things, and they loved to chat. He needed something immediate and unnoticed.

It didn't take long before he spotted a homeless man slumped outside a liquor store—Barrels and Bottles on Kirby—an old bicycle lying beside him. Brody noticed the chain had been recently oiled. It was the little things that made Mister Boogie smile.

The man's eyes were bleary, hands shaking from the withdrawal that gnawed at his bones.

Brody approached, slow and measured as a predator. "Trade you." Brody reached into his pocket. He pulled out a wad of crumpled bills soaked in Kelly Manson's blood. Maybe it was Chelsey's. Didn't matter. The old man's eyes flickered toward them, the hunger outweighing any reason. Like most vagrants in any big city, Houston's were filled with doubt.

"For this bike? What's the catch besides that blood money?"

"Afraid it won't spend, old sparky?"

"Afraid of what it's been spent on, young hipster."

"Touché." Brody chuckled and twitched his upper lip. The vagrant was right. The bloodied money could end up anywhere, not that the man knew two shits—or gave them—about anything other than his next drink.

"Here's the white-knuckle truth, Mister Ask-A-Lot. I could just take the bike and there wouldn't be a thing you could do about it. But it's been one heck of a twenty-four-hour shift; I don't need to leave behind anymore large breadcrumbs. Stand up. I'm not going to hurt you, just stand up. We can help each other out."

The man said he was Roger Denison, that he'd been homeless going on nearly three years, and this was the first time anyone of such caliber as the young hipster had ever so much as offered him a lousy 7-11 slag of coffee or sandwich.

Suddenly some hotshot—clearly one who'd been in the thick of it not long ago— hotshot, nonetheless, was offering him a wad of cash. Bloodied, but cash. Roger hadn't had such an interesting moment in any day the past three years since the night he was fired for drinking on the job by a boss who drank even more.

Roger did as the hipster asked, not just because he asked him to, because, for some reason, Roger felt a thread of dignity come back to him, threads that were lost long ago.

When he stood, Brody looked him up and down. Late 30s, sandy blond hair that hadn't been washed in months, wiry but big-boned frame; decent suit jacket and shirt that were now ragged and stained with whatever the Houston mean streets could piss on them. All items that Brody could work with. Ideal, in fact. "How much you want for the bike?"

"A grand."

"A grand?"

"There's an ATM inside, and I'm sure you've got plenty in it. Looks like you've been in it, this twenty-four-hour stint you just mentioned. You need the bike bad enough, you'll pay it."

Brody nodded, his mouth slightly open as he processed what to say next. "You've got a point, Roger Dodger. I could use your clothes, too, come to think of it. We're close enough in size, not that it matters. Throw those in?"

"I might. Why?"

"Ever hear of the Serpent's Veil?"

"You into kinky shit?"

"I'm sure you can put the pieces together. It's heavy enough shit."

Roger extended his hand, another first in many years. "Who am I doin' business with?"

Brody looked at Roger's hand that was caked in grime and silt from Christ knows where. "I'll pass on the handshake, Roger. You can call me Rex. Well... Mister—"

"Rex? Mister Rex, is that it?"

Brody slowly shook his head in irritation. “Boogie. But you interrupted me and screwed my thinking sideways, so never mind. Stay put, Roger. I’ll go to the ATM. Anything else you need in there. Fresh Tallboy? Wine cooler? Couple of fat boy dogs with cheese and peppers?”

“Funny. No, just the cash. I’ll get what I need.”

“Doesn’t look like you have anything you need.”

Brody put his hand up to silence Roger from any more last moments of sudden bravery. He walked into the liquor store—Barrels and Bottles on Kirby—and mulled over things several times before hitting the ATM. He had plenty in it, as Roger had alluded to. His last two tech gigs—a final one in New York and the one he just wrapped up a week ago here in Houston—had paid him a cool 50k each. But using the ATM would leave a paper trail. He 86’d that idea.

The loss of the Porsche was no big deal, as it was untraceable. His only real assets were his fine choices in clothing, 25k in a wall safe, and the rest in a money market account he could pull from as often as he wanted. But now on the run, he’d have to be far more careful about withdrawals. His best option was the cash at his condo, but that would have to wait. He wanted to go back out and tell Roger the whole deal was off. Take the bloodied money or get lost. Then again, bloodied money could end up in anyone’s hands, even the cops’. He needed to launder the money, literally.

In the restroom, he pulled the bloody wad of cash out of his pocket, tossed it in the sink, and turned on the water, let it get hot, threw in some hand soap from the dispenser, and made like a washing machine with his hands. The blood dissolved and swirled down the drain.

He draped the cleaned bills over the sink and across the counter, padded them with paper towels, took inventory. Twenties, ones, a couple hundreds. Not a grand.

He clicked his tongue at the next idea: the watch. Brody looked at his Urwerk UR-101 wristwatch, realizing it wasn’t lost during all the perks of the wild night at Dr. Kelly Manson's pad. Roger the vagrant would have to settle for the timepiece, or Mister Boogie would have to take over.

Why Mister Boogie hadn't taken this vagrant out and moved on was still something Rex Brody was learning. Could have killed the poor son-of-a-bitch before he knew what was going on while trying to spurt out one more phrase of Tomfoolery. Brody knew this was all going to take skilled planning from here on out, including the ins and outs of Mister Boogie. Every move would be crucial, and homeless vagrant men were not on his agenda. What was on the agenda moving forward were the lovelies of the world—the Chelsey Bingham's of the world—the seductive temptresses that gnawed and ate at the insides of Conrad Ellington back in the days of Whitechapel, and who were now quickly doing the same goddamn thing several centuries later. Brody thought about the letter and how it was relating to everything that had just happened.

What would The Ripper do in such a situation?

He purchased a burner phone, a few sticks of beef jerky, and a high-protein shake.

The clerk tallied the sale. "Forty-eight fifty."

Brody laid out the soggy cash.

"Hey, mister. This money's wet."

"It'll dry."

The clerk shrugged and activated the phone.

Back outside, he gave Roger the burner phone and kept the food for himself. "Change of plans." Rex took off the Urwerk. "Take this phone and watch. The phone is for me to call you. The watch for the bike. I'm not able to get any cash out of the ATM right now, and if you're as clever as I think you are, then you know this watch is worth more money than you've seen since the cows came home. Am I right?"

Roger took the watch and admired it. He looked at the two items far longer than Brody wanted him to take. It was a stunning timepiece. Could easily pawn it for several grand just a few blocks away.

"Everything understood, Roger?"

"I was just thinking. Connecting the dots 'cause there sure are a lot of 'em I'm seeing just around the corner, am I right, young hipster? On the dots? Lotta shit connecting if I take enough time on it."

Brody remained patient regardless that his body was now screaming in places he'd not had scream in years. He reached out his hand to Roger's and gripped it hard enough to send a signal.

"I'm sure you could work the dots, old sparky, but time's not your break today. I am. Give me your jacket and shirt and we'll switch. Keep your pants and shoes, those would be a tougher fit. Take the burner phone and don't lose it, don't sell it, don't pawn it. Pawn the watch. This area yours? Your own loitering and begging spot?" Brody turned his head and swept his arm across his body.

"Not necessarily, and not all of it."

"For the next few days, make it all of it and make it necessary. I'll find you, don't worry about how. You up for doing a job later in the week when I get some shit sorted?"

Roger shook his head slowly, as he mostly thought about how much money the hipster's watch would bring in, and then what next drink he'd buy, as well as what meal he'd enjoy for the first time in ages.

"Hey. Roger. Focus, goddamn it. I may need your help later this week. Stay around here. Understood? And keep that phone with you."

Roger's mouth was open, his head shaking. "What's all this? Why you helping me?"

"Because you're helping me. That's all it needs to be. Two people helping each other for the greater cause. Just stay around here so I can find you."

Brody took the bike before Roger could say anything further. Brody was betting that the exchange that went down would not be forgotten by a mind too far gone, but one that still had hope. It was an untraceable move for Brody if Roger stuck to the plan. "We've never met, you hear?"

It became much more than that in Mister Boogie's mind. He had just found the perfect alibi for the future. No one cared for the homeless. The homeless were uninterested in belonging to something, if it temporarily removed them from their dire situation of having nothing. The homeless were the key. Set up whatever elaborate murder trophy Mister Boogie knew should be his, plan it, find the right homeless vagrant with nothing to lose, leave the scene with the vagrant stuck smack in the middle of every move. Police arrive and what do they see other than some sicko whack job who killed simply for the chance to find one last thrill before he died.

It was almost too fucking perfect.

He rode south, cutting through alleyways, past flickering neon signs and the skeletal remains of a city still reeling from 9/11. The paranoia was thick. He doubted that anyone was looking for him yet, but everyone was looking for someone.

He knew the bike couldn't take him as far as the outskirts, where The Serpent's Veil was located. He would need a bus, after all. But exactly where on the outskirts, Chelsey hadn't told him, only that it was hidden and didn't have a real name, only known by locals who knew it well.

He'd have to venture out, find people who would know. He remembered Chelsey talking about The Serpent's Veil and the strange woman who danced with a python. As good as place as any.

Texas liquor laws allowed bars to serve until 2 a.m.—the witching hour for the desperate and the damned. Any joint still pouring drinks that late wasn't just open; it was feeding off the last clinging dregs of human weakness. River Oaks wasn't a sprawling bar district, but its proximity to Westheimer and Shepherd made it a perfect hunting ground for the lost and the reckless. Spots like Marfella's and

Blanco's still pulsed with life in those hours, dimly lit refuges where bad decisions took root in the bottom of a glass. Brody knew about Blanco's; it was ten minutes tops on the shitty bike.

Blanco's, a gritty honky-tonk at 3406 W Alabama St. near River Oaks, roared to life in 1982 and was a full-on Texas scene by the time the terrorists had destroyed The World Trade Centers: cowboy boots scuffing the dance floor, neon buzzing over cheap beers and whiskey. Open late, it drew a rough mix of locals and strays from the upscale neighborhood, all chasing the twang of live country or jukebox riffs in a barn-like dive that didn't care who you were. Once inside the bar, Mister Boogie fit right in.

Within thirty minutes, Rex had been able to ask all the right questions to get a dial-in on The Serpent's Veil. Honky-tonk bar or not, frequent bar patrons anywhere knew what was what and where shit was. A few young hotties even wanted to tag along, but Brody was running on empty. Back outside, he ditched the bike in favor of a bus ride.

Houston's bus system had been running for decades, threading through the city like veins feeding something restless. By 2001, METRO ran over 100 routes, its buses crawling past the edges of River Oaks, connecting it to downtown's sleepless underbelly. Westheimer was the key artery, a corridor dragging the lost and the wandering from the city's black heart beyond Route 8 to the outskirts. Routes like the 82 (Westheimer) and 27 (Shepherd) ran close enough for anyone to disappear into the night, a five-minute walk to the bus stop, a $10 ticket to anywhere in or out of the city, a city that never stopped moving, and neither did its ghosts.

Mister Boogie's ticket would take him to The Serpent's Veil.

By the time he reached it, his body had taken quite the pounding over the last 36 hours, thanks to Chelsey and her bad choice of friends. Brody's clothes were damp with sweat, thanks to Houston's soggy air, and his body thrummed with exhaustion. His mind seemed sharper than ever since the drug had worn off. The club loomed ahead, a blackened maw in the city's rotten underbelly. The red bulb above the steel door flickered like a dying star, casting a sickly glow across the pavement. He straightened the shitty jacket and shirt he'd bartered from Roger, bushed dried blood off his pants, and walked through the door.

Straight into hell.

***

The moment Spade and Carmen and the other uniforms heard the thumping sound that came from the ground up, he had just a heartbeat to look at his partner to see if she had heard the same thing. They were able to make eye contact as Dr. Kelly Manson's front door blew apart, followed by a blast of flames that roared outward as if a dragon was inside the home, bellowing in rage.

Everything flashed to slow motion. The shockwave hit like a sledgehammer, the heat so sudden and violent that Spade felt the moisture in his mouth evaporate.

Both detectives dropped instinctively, hitting the pavement hard, palms scraping against loose gravel as the explosion swallowed everything in a cyclone of hellfire.

The sound was beyond deafening, an all-consuming roar, a pressure wave that punched into their bodies and stole the air from their lungs.

Then came the debris. A wall of shattered glass, splintered wood, and flaming lumber tore through the air. Shards peppered the police cruisers, punched spiderweb cracks into the windshields. A piece of smoldering banister cartwheeled through the air like a flaming javelin and slammed into the semi-truck trailer, leaving a big dent.

Spade covered his head with his arms. Something sharp sliced across his forearm. The pain barely registered in the chaos. He forced himself to look toward Hayes. “Carmen!”

Yelling her name came so naturally to Spade, he suddenly realized how important she was to him. In the flash and thunder of the explosion, he realized that Carmen Hayes was his most trusted and loved friend. In that same moment, he wondered what his life would be like without her. She had ridden with him on some of the ugliest and most grueling cases Houston had to offer: rapes, murders, sicko torture chambers. He had grown to need her far more than he ever intended.

Hayes couldn’t hear Spade, but she felt him, their eyes locking in the chaos. She thanked God they were both alive, then prayed to God—a quick prayer—for the ability to find whatever new monster was riding the coattails of similar monsters who had just ravaged New York City.

Spade crawled toward her, his body screaming in protest. The stench of burning fuel, seared flesh, and smoldering wood twisted in his nostrils and sank deep into his lungs.

Then, yet another terrible sound. A sickening, warbling scream from Officer James Terry, the uniformed cop who had been closest to the Porsche, behind his partner, Bernard, was now rolling on the ground, engulfed in flame, his bare hands beating his burning uniform, trying to smother the fire that had already eaten into his skin.

The stench of burning human flesh hit Spade like a brick wall. He moved without thinking, instinct taking over.

Spade knew that Bernard was gone the moment the car blew, but there was a chance for Terry to survive. He lunged toward him while yanking off his coat. He intended to smother the flames, but the gasoline-fed flames ballooned into a fireball. The inferno gnawed through the fabric, turned flesh into something grotesque, something bubbling and blackening as the fire ate deeper. It was too late for James Terry.

Spade’s stomach twisted. He had seen people shot;

people butchered, but burning was something different. “Fuck!” Spade gritted his teeth, trying to move forward, trying to help, but the heat drove him back.

Hayes grabbed his wrist, yanked him back farther with all the strength she had left. “He’s done,” she said, her voice a harsh rasp, like she had inhaled half the explosion into her lungs.

Spade looked at the burning body, at the way the flames had already fused fabric to flesh, muscle to bone. Nothing left to save. But he could still see Officer Terry’s face. The horror frozen in the last moment of realization before the fire consumed everything. “Motherfucker.” Spade turned his gaze back to the house, or what was left of it. Two cops now dead.

The house fire had spread fast, far too fast for a natural burn. It had to have been rigged different than the Porsche, which further affirmed this killer had far more skills than Dr. Manson had used on his victims. This was designed as a controlled demolition, and whoever had done it had timed it so the cops would be inside the house, and not for just a few minutes. Spade knew it wouldn’t have taken much, especially with someone as talented as they were now hunting. Could have been sparked by several things: frayed wire, loose plug from something...anything that could have been easily jolted by the car’s blast.

Hayes was furious. “Whoever the fuck he is, he wanted us to see his handywork before it was destroyed. He wanted to impress us with his artwork. Fucking choke on the horror of it.”

Spade wiped soot from his mouth and spat into the dust. “I believe you, Hayes. Otherwise he’d have burned the place down before he left.”

As if to punctuate his logic, a second detonation ripped through the estate. The roof collapsed, the walls fell inward, and a towering pillar of fire curled skyward, chasing black smoke like something alive, something feeding. A firestorm.

Spade and Hayes took one last look at the inferno that used to be Kelly Manson's house, then turned toward their cruiser.

They weren't just hunting a killer anymore.

They were hunting a hunter of killers.

***

The air inside The Serpent's Veil was all wrong. Not thick with cigarette smoke, not stale with spilled liquor, just wrong.

The moment Rex Brody moved to the bar area and dance floor, he could sense a shift but couldn't place his finger on it. Not exactly. The world seemed to compress. The temperature dropped just enough to raise the hairs on his arms. The walls, black as coal and slick with unseemly moisture absorbed sounds and echoes. Conversations—if there were any—had died in the corners, swallowed by the abyssal hush.

The lighting shifted without a source, pulsing from deep crimson to sickly gold, casting shadows that seemed to crawl like living things. The bar itself stretched longer than it should have, a twisted relic of polished wood and charred edges, lined with bottles that lacked labels, filled with dark liquids that caught the light in unnatural hues.

In the corners, only a few patrons barely moved, their faces indistinct, their features blurred, as if time had forgotten to define them, as if they had forgotten time. Somewhere in the distance, music lurched from a slow, crawling dirge into something discordant, notes clashing as if the song itself were unraveling.

Rex exhaled. It wasn't just a bar. It was a threshold to something on the other side that was waiting...for him.

The Serpent's Veil unsettled even Brody, its darkness pressing on him like an invisible weight. The air hung sickly, a cloying mix of stale incense, charred wood, and something sweeter, something that rotted beneath the surface, unseen but present. It resembled what Chelsey had first told him back at Fitzgerald's: strange but fascinating mirrored walls, others that were created in chunks of stone. And the incense she mentioned was certainly one of the odors that danced around with the others.

He stood alone in the dimly lit room, his eyes scanning the bar's decrepit splendor. The ceiling loomed far above, lost in shadow, while the art-fashioned walls seemed to close in, adorned with ancient tapestries that depicted scenes of torment and ecstasy intertwined. The flickering light from hidden sconces cast distorted shapes that slithered across the floor, moving with a serpentine grace that made the room feel alive.

Without warning, everything shifted again.

A low hum resonated through the floor, vibrating through Brody's boots and into his bones. The lights dimmed further until darkness claimed everything. For a moment, there was nothing but the sound of his own breath, steady and unafraid. He saw the other miserable patrons had simply vanished, but why?

The room's illumination was all adrift; a fractured spectrum that bled crimson and violet into the blackness. A stage materialized, as if from the shadows, a skeletal structure of weathered wood and velvet curtains that fluttered, though there was no wind. The stage was empty.

Brody's pulse quickened, not from fear, but from the primal awareness that something unnatural was unfurling before him. A spotlight flashed on, beaming down to centerstage. From the far recesses backstage, where shadows clung like sentinels, a figure emerged. A massive, towering man moved with a deliberate slowness, each step measured, each movement captured in the spotlight, crawling forward. He was monstrous, clad in a black trench coat that fit him like a shroud. His face was obscured by the shadowed brim of his hat, but his presence alone was suffocating. His skin was like weathered wood, deeply chiseled.

In his arms, cradled like a macabre offering, lay a woman. Dead or alive, Brody didn't know.

She was ethereal, breathtaking in her beauty, but disturbingly still in a black negligee. Her long jet-black hair cascaded over his arms like rivers of midnight, draping down and nearly touching the floor. Her porcelain skin glowed faintly under the fractured light, her sculpted arms dangling, taloned black nails glinting; her shapely legs dangled, as well, seemingly useless. Her eyes were closed, lips parted slightly, giving her the appearance of a broken doll, fragile and lifeless.

Rex felt his breath hitch. She looked exactly as the woman Chelsey had described when she saw such a woman dance around with a python. "Slithered" is what Chelsey had said. At least how he remembered talking about it back at Fitzgerald's.

It wasn't just that, either. The memory clawed its way from the depths of his own mind...that sunlit day from his childhood, a moment seared into his psyche. The woman lying in the sun, ivory under its intense glare, whispering an offer he never forgot.

"Would you like me to slit that boy's throat open with my straight razor."

He felt a chill.

The giant reached the center of the stage and halted. Silence devoured the room, thick and absolute. Brody had to do a double take, several times. The man looked like Adrian Kane, one of the premier IT venture capitalists whose offices were out of New York and Houston and spreading world-wide. What he was doing at such a strange club, holding such a strange woman was beyond Brody's understanding, but he had met plenty of jetsetters, high-end sophisticates who gossiped about Kane, that he was getting ramped up in more pre-IPO gigs that were flourishing with as much aggression as the NYC terrorists. The more power and influence, the deeper the strange and the bizarre.

Brody also knew about him from whispers in the dark corners of the fancy weirdo internet underworld that was rising as fast as the online porn industry. The hush-hush online discussions on Kane came from twisted legends carried in hushed tones through the sickest crevices of every major city where he funded ventures on the race to the fastest IPO. Maybe such a freakish club was exactly the place for Adrian Kane. But doing what? And who was the woman he carried?

Maybe some kind of performance art.

The giant's head lifted slowly, revealing eyes that burned with a timeless malice. They locked onto Brody, pinning him with a gaze that felt metaphysical.

The woman in his arms remained motionless, but Brody could feel her presence, too, like a phantasm brushing past the hairs on his skin. A slow, disquieting smile curved from the giant's lip. Then, as suddenly as it had begun, the spotlight shut off, as if cut by a blade. Darkness reclaimed the stage. When the room lights sputtered to life, the stage was empty. No more giant; no more dead woman, though Mister Boogie knew she was far from dead.

The entrance to the stage was placed perfectly centered on the room's floor, an open drain that suddenly sucked Rex Brody into the bowels of something primordial. The air changed the moment he stepped onto it: thick, wet slabs of steam that nestled against the back of his neck. A slow, crawling house number began to hum and thump in the background, pulsing the club to life. The walls were still black, the ceiling lost to shadow, as before, but his boots stuck to the floor, on the residue of a hundred nights soaked in spilled liquor and filth.

No one was at the bar. It was simply a strange backdrop to a presence Brody had never felt. It was right in line with Mister Boogie. The long, crooked counter stretched across the room, warped and blackened as if the wood had been pulled from a shipwreck, a complete contrast to the bar's walls and overall design. The bottles on the shelves were unmarked, the labels long peeled away, leaving only glass containers filled with things that shimmered in colors that didn't belong in the natural world.

A handful of figures lurked in the corners of the bar area, silent, unmoving, watching with empty eyes.

Brody knew the feeling of being observed as a familiar weight, far more familiar than he had realized when he met Chelsey and Dr. Kelly Manson. A predator recognizing another in its midst. But this was different, like someone was expecting him.

He walked to the bar and took a seat on one of the cracked leather stools. The barkeep was nowhere to be seen, and yet, a drink waited for him. A heavy tumbler filled with something deep red, thick as blood. The glass sweated in the dim light.

Brody stared at it, didn't touch it as he thought about the drink Chelsey had given him that nearly got him killed.

His eyes drifted to the three figures who were seated in the center of the stage in three high-back chairs that looked designed from the Middle Ages. Where they came from and when they had come out was yet one more piece of chaos that was fitting right in with Mister Boogie's new world.

They were time-worn women with skin like parchment stretched too thin over brittle bones. Their fingernails were long, curved, painted in metallic crimson that captured the faint lighting and shadows on the walls. Their clothes were black, not the sleek darkness of modern fashion, but the heavy folds of something older. Cloaks with layers of silk and decay.

They sat in perfect stillness, their faces sharp with knowing.

"Lo," they suddenly spoke in unison. "What specter steps from fire's breath, a wraith unshorn by time or death?" Their voices braided into a single thread, layered, echoed, stretched beyond the confines of the room.

Brody stared for a moment before their voices irritated Mister Boogie as his face cringed. It wasn't speech, it was prophetic. How did they know anything? He stood from the barstool and slowly walked toward them on the stage, his curiosity peaking.

The one in the middle, eyes sunken in cracked sockets but alive with red wires that surrounded their cornea, leaned forward. "Dost thou seek what thou cannot hold? Dost thou hunger for secrets old?" Her breath smelled like rot that had been rotting forever.

Mister Boogie kept staring.

Brody had seen monsters in men while in Cambodia; Mister Boogie had just killed one who had plans to kill him. He had met death and left him wanting for more. But these women looked beyond age or reason. In fact, they had little-to-no resemblance of any woman.

The second one, her fingers tapping against her bony knees, grinned with blackened teeth that were broken and sharp. "A traveler lost in tangled fate, knows not what waits beyond the gate."

Mister Boogie kept staring and listening in fascination. There was something here. Something real. For the first time in years, Rex Brody felt this could be the next step.

The third one, silent until now, walked to the bar and took the drink Brody had ignored, then brought it back to him, her fingers so bony and white he wondered if they'd been bleached.

"A draught to steal, a draught to see, the door unlocked, the soul set free." Her eyes lifted, and in them, he saw something shifting, swirling and endless. Hollow, yet in their emptiness Mister Boogie thought he could see small black holes where his light at the end of their awful tunnels could be his own fate. Something that had always waited for him.

He breathed slowly as he took the glass and tossed it back.

The air inside The Serpent's Veil thickened, the dim lighting pulsed like the slow, rhythmic heartbeat of something foreign. The three hags, their faces carved by time and all the horror that time dished out, moved with a slow, deliberate grace as they gathered around a small, unassuming table at the back of the bar. The background music volume increased just enough to keep the tension increasing right along with everything.

Brody followed them and held out his hand, becoming more fearless in a needed approach. "Okay, ladies. Just who the hell are you, and where did the big fella with Sleeping Beauty go?"

"Aye," again, in unison, "a tale as thick as time from the days of MacBeth and his frightful cunt, the Lady of Lore. We are his Weird Sisters, filled with spite and gore."

Brody nodded slowly, his eyes moving just as slowly to each of the three, one by one, wondering exactly what was happening and why. "I see. The Weird Sisters. Nice touch."

All three burst out in cackles that pierced Brody's ears. He wondered if they would ever stop, and when they finally did, from beneath the folds of a tattered velvet cloth, one of them produced something that did not belong in this world, and held it out toward him. It was a spherical object like he'd never seen. Mister Boogie wondered if it belonged in any world, but he knew he needed it. Instantly he knew he must have it.

"I am Elspeth, the cunning and sly one." She was the one with the shocking breath.

"I am Alisa, harsh and unyielding." Alisa was the one who held the orb. She took a single step forward and then back as if in a dance, her graceful movement such a contrast to her brittle body.

Brody leered back in curiosity, never taking his eyes off her or the other two.

"And I..." The final one spoke in a voice that was just above a whisper. "Am Mairi, the deceptive one."

The Weird Sisters: crone-thin, black eyes that were tunnels to nowhere, lips that looked more torn than cracked, carefully watched Brody in knowing silence. Then, in unison again. "Lo, thou dost stare upon the abyss, a wanderer bound by tethered fate. Hast thou not dreamt of crown and kiss, yet known thy throne be built on hate?"

Brody said nothing as Alisa stepped forward again, now handing the orb to Brody. He looked down at it as it pulsed in his hand.

Alisa grinned, her yellowed teeth jagged and caked with so much tarter that the buildup itself looked like extra chunks of teeth.

"A king we named, a king was made, a blade in hand, a world unmade. He heard our words, his path was writ, yet folly's fire consumed his wit."

Elspeth leaned closer, her odor reeked of damp earth and rotting fruit. "Macbeth did walk with fate-bound tread, by whispers spun, by omens fed. But thou, dark specter, art not he—no pawn of fate, but death set free."

Mairi lifted a single gnarled finger and pointed directly at Brody's chest. "Thy crown is blood, thy kingdom fire thy rule not built on vain desire. Not wretched fear nor weakened will, but darkest night, and blackest thrill."

Brody's breathing tightened as did his fingers around the orb. He began to feel the truth behind their rhyme and riddle, their creeping knowledge wrapping around him like a noose.

They weren't warning him; they were welcoming him.

The orb was flawless yet unnerving, a perfect sphere that seemed not to reflect light but to absorb it. The surface was blacker than space, but within its core, there swirled something deeper, something living. Tendrils of crimson and molten gold slithered beneath the obsidian shell, coiling and shifting as if the very soul of the object pulsed with its own dark will. It was the perfect size for Brody's palm. It had a power that was pulling at his mind, his emotions, and even his physical nerves.

He felt the air tighten even more around him as he stared into its depths. The longer he looked, the more powerful he felt. His reflection did not appear upon its surface. Instead, he saw flashes, visions of things long past and things yet to come: Blood soaking into cracked earth; A face contorted in beauty and power; A great beast writhing in fire. When he thought he saw Conrad Ellington writing the lost letter, Brody popped back a few steps as if in a sparring match.

The Weird Sisters spoke again in unison, their voices a layered murmur, whispering from places beyond time. "Once, in the Garden of Eden, before the world knew sin, the devil himself held this in his grasp. The Great Beast, Cain. It is said that before the serpent whispered his lies, he held dominion over all things...power unchallenged, unshaken. And when the garden was lost, the orb was cast from Eden with him, carried through the ages by those who sought its gift, and by those who feared its price. Carried and owned by Her, The Beast's own Harlot."

Alisa reached forward with gnarled fingers, tracing the surface as the orb pulsed, its glow intensifying in response to her touch. "It is power, bound and raw. It will reveal paths unseen. It will turn death's gaze. But power is never without price."

Mairi leaned forward, her lips slowly curling back and forth from grin to frown. "It will grant you passage when there is none. A key when the doors are closed. A whisper when the world turns deaf. But once claimed, it is yours forever."

Elspeth took the orb from Brody's palm and extended it toward the ceiling.

Rex Brody was not a man easily shaken, but something in the depth of that abyssal sphere called to him, a force that pulled from within his very spirit. Having it snatched out of his hand without him noticing was something he never expected. He reached out for it, but Elspeth kept it from him with stunning agility as the other two stepped in his way.

"Swear to us. Swear to Cain. Swear to Her your unbridled service and worship. Swear it." Mairi's quiet voice was now filled with authority.

Brody felt shaken. Who were they talking about? He knew about Cain, about The Weird Sisters, and he needed to pay some kind of allegiance to have the orb, then Mister Boogie had no issue. But who the hell was the "Her"?

He stepped a few feet back, both arms at waist level, hands out. Brody needed to gain back control. Any appearance of weakness he knew would be a mistake. "Who are you talking about? Who is 'Her' or she, that is. You know what I'm saying."

The Weird Sisters looked back and forth at each other and then held hands. Mairi spoke again as she stepped forward, clasping the other two with the edges of her long-curled nails. "You know full well who she is."

The moment she said it he did know. It's not that he knew her personally, of course. But, as he'd told Chelsey when reliving the childhood bullying experience, when he saw the woman in the black bikini who "summoned" him when he and his brother and friend were walking home so completely defeated that day. He remembered telling Chelsey that he'd felt protected by the woman his entire life. That was only a day and night ago but suddenly felt like it was ages. It had to be the same woman Conrad Ellington had written about that frightening rainy night when at the Ten Bells Pub, when Jack the Ripper was born. Mister Boogie wondered about the possibilities. Impossible or not, he knew the orb was what he needed most.

Brody put his hands to his sides then cupped his hands across his belt line. He slightly bowed his head. "I swear it. To you, to Cain, to Her."

With that, Elspeth handed the orb back. Brody's fingertips grazed the cold surface. The moment his palm closed around it again, the air around him shifted, the entire room felt as if it had tilted, the weight of something massive pressing down.

For a fraction of a second, he swore he heard a distant, guttural laugh, something old, something waiting, something filled with power. Then the feeling was gone and the hags only smiled.

"Now, it is yours, Mister Boogie." They whispered it in unison, all three bowing their heads with their clawed hands coming together as if in prayer. "And with it, you shall never be caught."

He felt his entire body chill deep within, knowing he had never said the name of Mister Boogie.

***

The fire chewed through Dr. Kelly Manson's estate like a starving beast, leaving nothing but a blackened skeleton clawing at the Houston sky. The air was thick with ash, a gray haze that stung the lungs and coated the tongue with the taste of ruin. Detective Heath Spade stood at the edge of the wreckage, his boots sinking into the soggy mulch of the once-manicured lawn, now a churned mess of mud and cinders.

The heat still pulsed from the debris, a dying heartbeat radiating from parts of the roof that had collapsed, destroyed walls and shattered windows. Detective Hayes coughed into her elbow, her arm still cradled in that makeshift brace, her face streaked with soot and sweat. They'd been there for hours—that felt like days—watching the flames give way to smoke, the smoke give way to silence, and the silence give way to something worse: the gnawing certainty that they had lost any forensic evidence to begin searching for whoever the fuck it was who did this.

"Jesus H Christ." Spade kicked a chunk of charred wood that might've been a piece of doorframe once. It crumbled under his heel like brittle bone. “This ain’t a crime scene anymore. It’s a goddamn disaster site. Seems the whole world is becoming one over-fucking-night.” His voice was raw, shredded by the smoke he’d sucked down when the second blast hit. His wired hair stuck to his scalp, matted with grime, and his eyes burned red, not just from the haze but from the fury boiling behind them.

He turned to Hayes, jaw tight. “You smell that? That’s not just wood and plaster. That’s all the flesh that has gone up in smoke. That bastard’s laughing at us. I can hear him.”

Hayes didn’t answer right away. She was staring at the Porsche. What was left of it. The metallic blue shell was a twisted husk, its frame melted into the pavement like candle wax, the explosion so fierce it’d blown out every window within fifty yards. Officer Sampson’s body remains were gone, hauled off by the coroner in a bag that barely held together. Officer Terry’s crisped body was hauled off in another, his screams still echoing in her skull. She could still see his face, that split-second of knowing before the fire swallowed him whole. Her good hand clenched into a fist, nails biting into her palm.

“He didn’t just rig the car, partner. He rigged us all. Everything. We missed it. And two of our own are torched.”

Spade spat into the mud, a thick gob of black phlegm. “Yeah. We did. We’ve got ourselves a real fuckshow with this one. This is a goddamn declaration. Christ.” He swept his arm across the scene: uniforms scrambling, fire crews dousing the last embers, EMS hauling stretchers with nothing left to save. Everyone talking about The Twin Towers while having to deal with their own personal cauldron right here in Houston.

“He turned Manson’s palace into a kill box, and we walked right into it. The woman’s body in the freezer. Fuck. That evidence is ash. And we’ve got jack squat to show for it except a semi-truck that don’t mean shit.”

“Well, I happened to get a pic of it, partner, so all is not entirely lost. Benefits of a camera phone."

Spade chuckled. Any piece of good luck he would take. "I didn't even see you do it. Nice work, partner."

Hayes nodded and turned her attention to the rig. "He could have blown this, too."

"Agreed, but he wasn't taking his time. Maybe he thought about it, maybe not. Maybe things were just too harried. Doesn't matter. The Bone Break Killer is dead and gone."

Spade paced, boots crunching glass and splintered wood, his shadow cutting through the floodlights the crews had set up as dusk bled into the horizon. "Let's get that photo checked on immediately. We need to know who she was. First things first, let's get this area scrubbed, the whole fucking neighborhood, see who could have seen something. See if there are any camera systems in the lights. River Oaks spares nothing, so we could get lucky there, too."

Hayes limped after him, her brace creaking, pain shooting up her arm like a live wire. "You think that truck's empty?" Hayes nodded toward the rig, still curious of the doctor's leftovers.

Spade shook his head as if in brief disbelief. "Doesn't really matter, Hayes, we can have the uniforms dig into it if they haven't already, been too buried here to notice or care. Paul called it. Rookie genius. Occam's Razor of all things. Simplest answer right here. Kelly Manson's The Bone Break Killer, no doubt about that. And the girl was in it with him from the beginning. Got to find out who the fuck she was, if that's possible, but Manson's got a big name for a lot of intel. Yep, that's his slaughterhouse on wheels. But this other guy..." He jabbed a finger at the wreckage. "Whoever flipped this script is going to be a real issue."

"A big one." Hayes kept staring at the truck.

Spade stopped pacing, hands on his hips, staring at the semi like it was a coiled snake. "If that truck's got clues, they'll have nothing to do with this cat. But I'll bet my left nut it's clean as a whistle. Manson was too smart for sloppy. And if this new killer torched the house, blew his own car, what's to say he probably wiped his ass with Manson's silk sheets before he lit the match. We're several steps behind him, Hayes. We're nowhere."

The weight of nowhere hit them both like a fist to the gut. The estate was a void now, a black hole swallowing every lead they might've had. The security system was slag, the bodies, of course, of Manson and the girl were torched to ashes, and the Porsche blast had turned half the driveway into a crater. There was always the chance of dental records, but Spade had looked the woman over with thorough eyes. A beauty, yes, but very young and very hard; a combo that usually didn't do the dentist thing.

As night was breaking, a stroke of luck happened upon the crew when a neighbor had called in earlier during the middle of the action. A man called Francis Hollister said he had a strange conversation with one of Dr. Manson's visitors, someone he had never seen. Said he knew the doctor well enough and that the visitor "scared him." Exact words.

Spade's gut churned when he heard the news. He'd seen killers before—psychos, gangbangers, husbands with too much bourbon and a kitchen knife. But this was something entirely different, and Spade had learned to trust his gut years ago. This was a phantom with a plan, and every second they stood here, he was slipping deeper into the city's veins.

Later that evening, Hayes rubbed her temples. The two detectives and various officers were still at it. She was exhausted, and the pain in her arm was screaming. "We need forensics to find something. Anything. A hair, a fiber, a goddamn gum wrapper. And have we heard anything back on the fuckin' photo?" Her voice cracked, desperation seeping through the cracks. She'd called in the whole HPD circus—fire, EMS, narcotics, the works. She kept reliving the fire and explosion. The first crews had barely unrolled their hoses when the second blast took the roof, and now the arson team was picking through ash with tweezers, shaking their heads.

"He's now got a full day on us, Spade. Full day. And with 9/11 clogging every channel, no one's coming fast enough. Hey, are you hearing me, partner?"

Spade snorted a bitter laugh that died in his throat. "Sorry. Yes, I am. Just had a call about a neighbor who apparently talked to this sick fuck." He kicked another chunk of debris, sending it skittering into the dark. "This 9/11 is his cloak. Towers fall, nations fucked up, and he's waltzing through the chaos like it's his personal playground. HPD's stretched thin, feds are chasing hijackers, and we're here sifting through a Texas barbecue."

"Excuse me, Detective Spade."

Spade quickly turned to see the voice of one of the overworked uniforms. Next to him stood an older gentleman dressed in a 3-piece silk suit. Cream colored with alligator loafers. No socks.

"What is it, officer?"

"This is Francis Hollister. He called in earlier."

Hayes moved right beside her partner, more than curious. Spade looked Francis up and down a few times.

"Thanks, officer. We'll take it from here."

The officer nodded and headed back to the team.

Spade and Hayes took a deep breath and let it out slowly, as if sharing body and soul.

"I'm Detective Spade. This is my partner, Detective Hayes. I hear you had some kind of conversation with this..." Spade turned to get a long purview of the entirety of the destruction, then back to Francis. "Whoever did all this. That right?"

Francis cleared his throat and put his manicured hands in the pockets of his silk trousers while looking at the ground.

Carmen watched his every move as Spade led on.

"It's okay, Mr. Hollister. I know this doesn't look it with everything blown to hell and beyond, but you're safe here talking to us. As stupid as that sounds right now. Want to tell us what happened? Who was this guy?"

Francis perked up immediately, clearly anxious, worry hanging over his face and shoulders like invisible anchors attached to his ears. "I have no idea who he was. Never seen him, never seen anything like him, and all I was doing was being friendly. I'd been watching the news and everything going on and had to get out for a little walk, think about the mess the world was in, and I saw him standing here. I wondered if he'd heard the news...wasn't trying to pry into Manson's business or anything like—"

"Whoa there, Mister Hollister. Slow down. Just take it one piece at a time, there's no hurry."

"That's right," Hayes said, "and we appreciate you coming over here instead of having us set up a time for you to come down to the station. Thoughtful of you." Carmen reached her hand out and gently touched Francis on his shoulder. She had the touch of instant calm and trust that Spade never had and never wanted to have. But her *good-cop* way always made the interrogations run much smoother.

Francis took his hands out of his pockets, reached for Carmen's hand and held on to it for a few seconds. "Thank you, detective." He looked up into the deep Houston night sky and took a few deep breaths. "Like I said, I was just being friendly. But this fella...he was having none of it. I knew immediately there was something off about him. For one thing he looked injured. I asked him what happened to his face. Barfight was all he said. Now, I'm not an expert on those kinds of things, but his clothes were wet, his hair slicked back. Like he'd just washed himself off with a hose or something, but even through the wet clothes it looked like he had blood on his shirt. Blood is easy enough to see on a white shirt even it's wet, but he also had on an overshirt that was just as wet, so hard to tell. I didn't know what to think."

Spade put his hand up. "Whoa, whoa. Wait just a minute, Francis. Why did you approach him if he looked so banged up? I mean, wasn't that a signal to go the other way?"

"I didn't notice 'til he turned around to look at me."

"Possible blood stains, soaking wet, slicked back hair, just standing here doin' nothin? You expect me to believe that shit?"

Carmen cleared her throat.

Spade shot her a glance. "What? He sees someone soaking wet and wants to have a chat with him in the middle of the day." Spade focused again on Francis. "What gives, Mister Hollister?"

Francis saw the detective's point and shook his head slowly in embarrassment. He looked at the woman detective for solace.

.Carmen looked him in the eyes with reassurance, motioning him to continue.

"I was probably in shock from seeing the towers fall. I was supposed to go to New York just a week ago or so to see some friends. I was thinking about what could have happened if I were there...and so on."

Spade and Hayes nodded in understanding as Francis suddenly paused. He had tears in his eyes which was something they had both seen thousands of times, but rarely so genuine.

Francis went on to tell them the man had grabbed his shoulder, squeezed until it hurt, until he begged him not to hurt him anymore. The man let go, apologized, and told him to leave and not come back. "He didn't have to ask me twice. The man was terrifying, scared me like I'd never been scared before."

Spade folded his arms across his chest, tapping his foot, thinking things over. "Okay, Mister Hollister, please, if I can press a bit more. What exactly...was it about him that was so scary? I understand feeling afraid of someone's strength or their demeanor, especially under the circumstances. But there's something else. Am I right?"

Francis kept eye contact with the detective. "His black eyes, detective. He'd taken a beating, but there was nothing in his stare. Empty of anything. No soul. Inhuman is the best way to say it. I think he wanted to kill me where I stood. I wet myself, detective, but he was too focused on what he was saying to notice. I got the hell out of there."

Hayes cleared her throat. "Understood, Mister Hollister, just a few last items. Besides his eyes, what did he look like? Tall? Short? What kind of build?"

Hollister stared blankly for a second before answering. "Medium height. Black hair. Jeans, fitted shirt, fancy watch. He was built like chiseled granite."

That was it for Spade. He called back to the uniform who had introduced them to Francis. "Take him home."

Hayes shook her head slowly, needing a drink more than life itself. "We need an APB out on this guy."

Spade shook his head quickly. "You're not thinking, Hayes. I get it. But we can't do that, and you know it. What do we send one out on? Somebody who has shark eyes and is super strong? Mister Hollister just described half this city's gym dwellers. Think this cat is still wearing the same clothes? Think he looks anything like he did when he scared the shit out of ol' Francis? This is ours and ours alone right now. We must do the digging. Let's find out who the girl was and go from there."

"Right...right. If we can find her."

"Hayes, here's the positive. We have a lot more to work with than we did just an hour ago, but we also don't need a goddamn taskforce until we have more to go on. Deal?"

Carmen nodded. "Deal."

The night pressed in, the floodlights dimming as a generator sputtered somewhere in the chaos. Hayes felt it, the clock ticking, the city sprawling out beyond them, swallowing their killer in its concrete jaws. "He's planning his next move. And we're standing in his ashes." Her voice trembled, not with fear, but with a fury she couldn't choke down. "We've got to move faster. Smarter. Or the next body we find won't be in a freezer. It'll be on our doorstep."

Spade nodded, slow and deliberate, his mind racing through the fragments they had. Francis's story. A killer who out-smarted The Bone Break Killer. The photo of the girl. A puzzle with too many pieces burned away. "Then we don't sleep." He locked eyes with her. "We don't stop. He wants chaos. We give him chaos right back. He met that girl somewhere. We check out every bar, every alley, every shithole in this city. It's on, Carmen."

Hayes grabbed his arm, her grip fierce despite the pain shooting through her. "I'm with you, Spade."

They slogged through the muck, knowing the hunt was on, and the desperation clawing at their throats was the only thing pushing them on.

***

The Serpent's Veil felt different now. The air was thicker, pressing against Rex Brody's skin, the weight of The Weird Sisters' eyes still crawling over him like worms on a freshly hoed garden bed. The bar's shadows seemed deeper, the red glow of the overhead bulbs flickering as if they were breathing, casting jagged shapes along the walls that moved when they should have been dead still.

The orb lay heavy in Brody's palm, its smooth, obsidian surface absorbing the light. It was a remarkable object, vibrating with an energy from unknown depths. After breaking its hypnotic spell, he realized he had missed the departure of The Weird Sisters. Their ghostly comings and goings and strange talks of MacBeth predicting his fate lingered in his mind.

They had clearly lost their minds long ago, but Mister Boogie's mind was far from lost, trying to fit the pieces into his own plan when he caught a slow shift of movement.

From the farthest corner of the bar, where the light barely reached, the giant stepped out of the shadows, the one who had left with Sleeping Beauty. Brody adjusted his eyes to see it was in fact, Adrian Kane. This time there was no mistaking it.

He moved slowly, deliberately, like something heavy was shifting on his shoulders, but also with a grace that reminded Brody of how the Weird Sisters moved. His presence filled the space, swallowing up the dim light, casting a long shadow that reached across the floor. His appearance had also changed. He looked more plastic and manufactured, his hair manicured and slick in a light-blue coloring. His lips painted in a gloss. Dark pink makeup applied to his face in perfectly blended patches.

Brody didn't flinch. He simply tilted his head, fingers still running over the orb's impossibly smooth surface.

Kane stopped just a few feet in front of him. Though his appearance had changed, he had the same unreadable expression on his face, the same calmness that didn't belong in a man his size, in a place like this.

"You are holding something dangerous. Something precious." Kane's voice was so overly effeminate it took Brody off guard.

He looked straight into Kane's sky-blue eyes, so light they looked a glow of powder, his lips barely moving.

"Am I?"

Kane's eyes flicked down to the orb, then back up to Brody. His gaze was unreadable, but his presence felt like a weight pressing against the air itself. "You don't feel it? The power it brings, resting in your palm. Far more than sexual, yes? Like it's speaking to you...seducing you." Kane's voice went to a higher pitch.

"Like you're trying to do to me?" Brody turned the orb in his hands, watching as the swirling blackness inside pulsed, shifting into something almost like shapes—faces, bodies, things twisting in. "I know who you are, Mister

Kane, and I'm not the one. Trust me on this. And if you don't believe me maybe you'd better check out what's been going on..."

Brody caught himself before finishing what he wanted to say about his night with the good doctor. Getting arrested was not in the cards. Besides, regardless of his skillset, he wasn't quite sure he could take Kane. At least not injured.

Kane exhaled slowly. His breath smelled more rotted than Elspeth's. "And what if I do...trust you, that is?" Kane was silent for a long moment. Then he stepped forward, lowering himself just enough so that his towering presence leaned into Brody's space.

Mister Boogie allowed it, but he was also on high alert, ready to put it on as he did to the good doctor.

"What you have now, it belongs to the first deceiver." Kane's effeminate voice lowered just above a whisper. "The First Wife, in case you're wondering. You don't know her yet. But you have seen her. Long long ago. She knows you as deeply as she has known them all."

Brody nodded quickly in irritation. "Known them all? Known who all? Fuck are you talking about?" Mister Boogie put up his hand to stop Kane from interrupting. Kane titled his neck in amusement but kept silent. "You know...Mister Kane, Adrian. Okay that I use your first name?"

Kane tilted his head with a simple nod, a smirk across his face that Mister Boogie wanted to cut off.

"Listen, don't think I'm in the dark about all your whacko bullshit, okay? So, whatever this is..." Mister Boogie spread his arms as if to embrace the club's ambiance. "And the orb, I guess it is, and the whole witchcraft gig? It's okay. I'm down. How about a few more rounds of whatever shit it was the witches gave me. Or...Weird Sisters."

Kane kept his neck tilted and smiled a smile that Mister Boogie didn't like. Kane picked off right where he left as if Brody hadn't said a word.

"That's correct. The Weird Sisters, so pleased they told

you."

"Right. I've read the play. Even thought of playing MacBeth once in college—"

"Shut up and listen." Kane lifted his hand. "Before there was death, before there was sin. The first hands to hold that orb twisted the world into what it is now. And now, it's been given to you."

Brody smirked. "Should I be honored?"

Kane's expression didn't change. "I think honor is a tad beneath this one, dear boy."

The air in The Serpent's Veil grew colder. Or maybe it was Brody's injured body finally catching up without much food. In fact, he couldn't remember the last time he'd eaten. With Chelsey at Fitzgerald's, they only drank. Maybe a bag of peanuts if he remembered. Then there was the Kelly Manson Funhouse where no food was offered.

For the first time since he had walked into The Serpent's Veil, since he had sat across from the sisters and heard their prophecy, something in Brody's gut twisted. But it wasn't fear. It was more like recognition. But that seemed odd, then again not any odder than every other goddamn thing that had happened the past 24 hours. Or had it been longer. Brody wondered, suddenly not knowing exactly how long he'd been in there with Kane and his gang of witchery.

Even more suddenly, the orb's surface rippled, the swirling darkness inside reacting as if it had heard Brody's thoughts. A whisper slithered through the bar, low and inhuman, curling around his ears. "The door is open."

The voice came from nowhere. From everywhere. Certainly not Kane's voice, either. It was a woman's voice. Deep, velvety. Terrifying.

Kane's eyes never left Brody's. "Things are just getting heated, dear boy. Best you remain cool."

The orb grew warm in Brody's hands.

The Serpent's Veil, once just a den of the damned—at least that's how Chelsey spoke about it—now felt like a cathedral for something much older. The air smelled faintly of charred wood and something metallic.

The television above the bar suddenly flickered to life.

Kane straightened, exhaling slowly. "And there it is."

No one had touched any remote; in fact, there was no remote as far as Brody could see as he scanned the entire bar area. And yet, the screen blazed, static crackling before a familiar voice broke through.

"Breaking news. This is the Emily Casey Report."

Brody lifted his gaze to watch the stylish news anchor appear, her lips moving, the words sinking into the air like a final nail driven into a coffin lid.

"The notorious Bone Break Killer has been identified as Dr. Kelly Manson, the infamous Houston surgeon, after a grizzly discovery at his estate."

The screen flashed on, showing the ruins of Manson's estate, the twisted remains of Brody's Porsche, the faces of the detectives, Heath Spade and Carmen Hayes, staring into the wreckage with something close to awe, something close to fear.

Rex Brody leaned back in his chair, the weight of the orb pressing against his fingertips. A slow, knowing smile curled at the corner of Mister Boogie's lips.

Kane let out a low, nauseating breath, something between amusement and something else. "Now...let's see what you do next. I'll be in touch when the time is right." Kane stepped back into the darkness, his voice fading with him. Gone.

Emily Casey continued her report:

"In a shocking development, Houston authorities have confirmed that the elusive serial killer case has been solved. Detectives Heath Spade and Carmen Hayes, the lead investigators, announced late this afternoon that Manson's River Oaks estate had been transformed into a house of horrors, an operating theater for gruesome murders, as was a semi-truck trailer parked in front.

"The blast, which investigators say was set to erase crucial evidence, left nothing of the home intact. However, forensic teams have confirmed the presence of two human remains within the wreckage, along with disturbing traces of surgical experimentation. A deep freeze unit contained the frozen body of an unidentified young woman. Though the circumstances surrounding her death remain unclear, police are investigating her connection to Dr. Manson. She may have been a victim or an accomplice."

"The investigation had been ongoing for months, following a pattern of disappearances tied to individuals frequenting Houston's underground social scene. But it was an APB on a semi-truck that led Spade and Hayes to Manson's doorstep. Our on-site reporter spoke with Spade."

Detective Spade spoke into the reporter's microphone. "We were tracking a semi when we got broadsided by a drunk driver. Patrol located the truck, and when we arrived, we weren't expecting to find the kind of carnage that was waiting inside that house. Then it exploded."

Brody grinned at the news. Mister Boogie was delighted their plan had worked.

Casey added, "According to police reports, victims were subjected to extreme skeletal mutilation."

The reporter aimed the mic at Detective Hayes. "Is it true that every bone in the victims' bodies were shattered, one by one, before they were killed?"

"According to the coroner, yes."

"Do you know why Dr. Manson was so violently angry?"

"This was not about rage," Detective Hayes said. "This was not impulsive or sloppy. Manson had a level of surgical precision and psychological control over his victims that we rarely see...even among the most prolific serial killers."

Photos of two uniformed officers appeared on the screen. "Patrolmen Bernard Sampson and James Terry were killed in the explosion. Houston mourns their loss."

Mister Boogie grinned.

"Perhaps the most disturbing revelation of all is that Dr. Kelly Manson's killer has proven to be clever, resourceful, and more lethal than any HPD has seen in recent history. In fact this new killer on the scene is reminiscent of Jack the Ripper from the 19th century."

Detective Hayes again: "We're not dealing with a simple crime of passion killing. This was a calculated execution. Whoever did this was efficient, organized, and left behind no forensic evidence. That's not a coincidence."

Emily Casey now: "Further complicating the case is the absence of clear leads on the suspect. Surveillance footage was wiped from Manson's security system. No witnesses. The killer erased himself completely. No prints, no DNA, nothing that ties a suspect to the crime scene. It's like he never existed.

"As news of Manson's secret life spreads, shockwaves are rippling through the Houston medical community. Once regarded as a brilliant, albeit eccentric, surgeon, Manson was known for his research into bone regeneration and orthopedic trauma surgery. He had worked with some of the city's most prestigious hospitals and had even been a guest lecturer at medical conferences across the country.

"For residents of River Oaks, the truth is no less horrifying. Many expressed horror at the thought that a monster had been living among them, masquerading as a respected member of high society. This is the stuff of horror movies."

The scene of the crumpled Manson estate faded out, replaced by a replay of the burning twin towers. Then the television snapped off; the glow of the screen died like the last ember of a fire.

Brody had watched the story as if in a trance. Silence settled over The Serpent's Veil, thick and knowing. The bar remained empty. In fact, Brody didn't see a single patron come or go the entire time during the unraveling freak show.

It was as if the place itself had been watching alongside him, waiting for him to absorb the truth before spitting him back into the world.

He leaned back in his bar stool, the weight of the orb still heavy in his hand.

He'd always been far too clever. Something his cunt Aunt Anna used to say a lot when she thought her word meant shit to his life. He chuckled out loud, wondering what she would think of him now. And yet, soon enough, she would know, as would his grandpa, if still alive. But Anna was plenty alive, and Mister Boogie would soon be on his way to her. She was an important piece of his past to remove in his own special way.

But first things first. The news story was not an ending; it was only a beginning.

The world now knew that The Bone Break Killer had been unmasked, burned to ash in his house of horrors. But what they didn't know—and what Spade and Hayes now certainly knew—was that another monster had stepped forward in his place. Then again, as Brody had watched the detectives in action, how they spoke, how they reacted, maybe they knew exactly what was coming around the corner.

Brody turned the orb over in his palm, watching the blackness inside pulse, twist, breathe. Its warmth was remarkable. The Weird Sisters had said it would give him power, that it would guide him through situations too dangerous to survive otherwise. That it would free him when he least expected it.

Was that why he was still here? Had it already saved him? The thoughts were legitimate.

He rose from his seat. Weird Sisters gone. Kane gone. Not a single trace of them anywhere. No empty glasses, no lingering scent of perfume or decay. Just a vacant booth and a large spacious and strange empty bar, the ghost of their voices still simmering in his head.

Suddenly—too suddenly—a barkeep came. He glanced around and then looked at Brody, eyes dull, uninterested. He didn't ask if Brody wanted a drink, didn't ask if he was leaving. It was as if he had always known Brody was there for something specific and then would be on his way. No big loss, one way or the other. A lot like social workers would act when a new foster home popped into play.

Still, Brody didn't like the silence and wanted answers. "You been here while?"

The barkeep turned his head to each side as if Brody was talking to someone else.

Fine. Brody didn't mind taking the bait. "Yes, you. How long have you been working here?"

The barkeep took in a deep breath. His lips curled down in a deep sneer. "Well...now let's see..." He looked up to the ceiling and around the bar until he found the remote, then clicked the television back on. "I think it's going on nearly five years or so."

"And how long has Adrian Kane been coming here?"

The barkeep stopped as if his shoes suddenly stuck to the floor. He rubbed his face with his soft, fat hands. "Since he bought the joint. That was a few years back. Who's asking?"

"I am." Brody leaned in closer on the bar.

The barkeep took a small step back; he'd been in the business long enough to know the real hard cases and the ones who pretended.

"How 'bout muting the television and turning on some music. I've had my share of destruction for today."

The barkeep kept his frown and moved his head in agreement. Though he had no idea what the crazed-looking man really meant, he knew the man was dangerous. The sound system kicked on with "Highwayman," the voices of Willy Nelson, Waylon Jennings, and Johnny Cash humming the melancholy of weathered warriors going out in flames.

"Let me get you a drink...on the house."

"That's fine by me. Make it a double whiskey, neat. I'm not sure what it was I had with the sisters a la weirdos, but a double whiskey sounds like a goddamn miracle right now. How long they been around this gig, the witches? Kane bring them along with his weird shit circle?"

The barkeep had his back turned, looking over the whiskeys. He didn't want to ask the man what brand, so he chose Maker's Mark, as it was a popular choice. He pulled out a shot glass, filled it to the rim, turned around, and served the double. "Listen...mister..."

Brody cleared his throat before taking the drink. As much as he wanted to use his new persona, he needed real answers. The less crazy sounding the better.

"Rex Brody. I can see you don't want to talk about Kane. He's into some heavy shit. I know this. Forget about the ragged hags. I want to know who the woman is. You know exactly who I'm talking about, too."

Brody saw the truth all over the barkeep's face, but also saw *the woman* struck a deep nerve. He tossed back the entire double with a single swallow, shook his head a few times quickly, and leaned back in while slamming the shot glass down, causing the barkeep to flinch.

"When I came in here, I saw Adriane fucking Kane carry her across the stage and disappear Exit Stage Right. She dangled in his arms like she was dead, but of course she wasn't, and you know that. Dead or not, she had the look to strike anyone—"

"Dead? Is that what you wanted to say? Don't. Just don't."

Brody tapped the shot glass gently. "Interesting, barkeep. The plot around here just keeps getting—"

Grabbing Brody's hand as quickly and urgently as the barkeep did was more than enough to interrupt him. In a lightning move Brody cupped and trapped the barkeep's hand and wrist and torqued it just enough to not break it but to drop him to his knees while maintaining complete balance while leaning over the bar enough to keep the barkeep in the wrist lock. Yet the barkeep kept his resistance despite the severe pain.

"I don't care...you kill me right here right now whoever-the-fuck you are, but I cannot and will not talk about her. You best do the same, let me go, and walk out of here while you have all the cards you've been given."

The barkeep's refusal to break was refreshing as well as fascinating, which fit right in with every fucked off event that Mister Boogie was now privy to. Brody released the triangle grip while simultaneously grabbing the barkeep's wrist to pull him back up to his feet, as well as straighten himself up against the bar.

There was a truth to the barkeep's words that were absolute. It would be pointless to keep pushing him. Mister Boogie could see into the barkeep's eyes that he would rather give his life than go against whoever the woman was. Whatever she was.

That was good enough for Brody. He slid the orb into the filthy jacket pocket, feeling its presence against his ribs like a second heartbeat. He turned toward the exit, his boots grinding softly against the warped wooden floor. He was spent from top to bottom.

When he pushed open the door, the deep Houston night greeted him like an old friend. The muggy air clung to his skin, thick with the weight of his secrets. He exhaled slowly, tasting the damp scent of the monster city's outskirts grime, gasoline, and rot. The city stretched out before him in every direction, waiting, pulsing.

Kelly Manson's time had ended in fire and blood. In Mister Boogie's time, he was ready to dance.

4: REUNITED

BREAKING NEWS
Front Page Exclusive – The Houston Post
September 24th 2001
SERIAL KILLER LINKED TO SURGEON'S MURDER; NEW DETAILS EMERGE IN GRISLY HOUSTON INVESTIGATION
By Houston Post Editorial Staff

HOUSTON — The investigation into one of Houston's most shocking crimes took a dramatic turn today, as detectives officially connected the recent murder of Houston surgeon Dr. Kelly Manson—revealed last week as the notorious "Bone Break Killer", to the violent death of 24-year-old Jennifer Armstrong, whose body was discovered in the women's restroom of the downtown branch of the Houston Public Library on September 10th.

The discovery, confirmed in a joint press conference by Houston Police Department Lead Detective Heath Spade and his partner, Detective Carmen Hayes, has intensified efforts to track down a suspect authorities describe as "meticulous, intelligent, and exceedingly dangerous."

Spade stated, "After rigorous forensic analysis, we have conclusively determined that the murder of Jennifer Armstrong and the events at Dr. Manson's estate are linked. The way evidence was eliminated at the Manson crime scene demonstrates a high level of forensic awareness and suggests a sophisticated killer operating with an alarming degree of planning and execution. But evidence at the Armstrong scene is far more erratic and brutal. The striking differences suggest someone highly unstable and extremely dangerous."

Jennifer Armstrong, described by friends and family as quiet and reserved, was previously considered a victim of random violence. Armstrong had no known criminal record or discernible connection to Dr. Manson, whose hidden life as a serial killer sent shockwaves through Houston's River Oaks neighborhood. Armstrong's murder initially perplexed investigators due to its violent nature and the disregard for human life from the crime scene.

The Armstrong investigation was stagnant until police started piecing it together with the horrifying discovery at Dr. Manson's estate. Manson's mansion, located in the exclusive River Oaks community, was rocked by a devastating explosion shortly after police arrived to investigate the surgeon's murder.

Detectives Spade and Hayes discovered Manson's body inside, brutally killed and surrounded by what Hayes described as "a scene of gruesome horror, but also one of survival." She went on to explain that whoever killed Manson had survived being tortured but had turned the tables on the Bone Break Killer and his accomplice, Chelsey Bingham.

Police now believe the explosion was intentionally set to erase any forensic evidence linking the killer to the estate.

Adding further complexity, Bingham was positively identified as the woman found dead and hidden inside a deep freezer in Dr. Manson's garage. Bingham frequented several popular nightclubs around Houston. Authorities speculate that she played a significant role in Manson's criminal activities, though details are under investigation.

In another striking development, police confirmed they have interviewed a River Oaks resident, Francis Hollister, who witnessed an unsettling interaction near Manson's property on the morning of the murder. Hollister described the man he spoke with as "intense, physically imposing, and deeply unnerving," raising immediate concerns among authorities that this individual is a likely suspect of the Manson crimes.

Additionally, a critical eyewitness account surfaced earlier today. Roger Denison, a homeless man living downtown, came forward after recognizing details of the case in local media. Denison informed detectives that early on September 11th—a day after Armstrong's murder and just hours before the terrorist attack on New York's Twin Towers—he encountered an unknown male who urgently requested Denison's bicycle and clothing, offering a burner phone, cash, and a luxury watch in exchange. Detectives believe this encounter might have been directly related to the suspect's movements following Armstrong's murder, potentially indicating efforts to alter his appearance and obscure his trail.

"We believe this suspect is one in the same as the man Frank Hollister spoke to," said Spade. "His meticulous planning indicates he has likely taken extensive steps to conceal his identity and cover his tracks. Anyone who interacted with or witnessed suspicious behavior from an individual matching this description on or after September 11th should contact authorities immediately."

The Houston Police Department has not yet identified specific forensic details or potential motives behind the crimes but emphasized that the suspect poses a severe threat to public safety. Local and federal law enforcement agencies are pooling resources to apprehend the suspect swiftly and prevent further violence.

Houston Mayor Vic DeAngelo issued a public

statement urging calm but caution. "Our police department is diligently working around the clock. We ask all Houstonians to remain vigilant, report any suspicious activity immediately, and trust that justice will be swiftly served."

The community, especially in the usually peaceful River Oaks district, remains shaken. Residents have expressed fear and uncertainty, while city leaders and law enforcement promise exhaustive efforts to ensure public safety.

This developing story continues to unfold as the city waits anxiously for answers—and justice.

The Houston Post will update readers immediately as new information becomes available.

It was weeks after the world trade center towers had fallen, the country still in as much shock as outrage. Emma Madalin sat alone in a quiet booth toward the back of Houston's Bar and Grille, one of the city's most elegant such establishments, where the soft lighting, rich mahogany, and polished brass fixtures whispered refinement rather than shouting wealth. The low hum of classic and modern rock muted conversations that drifted through the air, mingling enthusiastically with the clink of crystal glassware and the subtle aroma of oak-grilled steaks and fine bourbon.

She chose this classy place deliberately. Somewhere sophisticated, somewhere anonymous, somewhere worlds away from the grimy chaos of the Houston streets she knew so intimately. Here, under the warm glow of designer sconces, she was just another beautiful woman sipping a dirty martini, unnoticed and unremarkable to the affluent crowd that filled the restaurant. It was one of the spots Emma treasured for some solace and personal time.

Her eyes moved slowly over the front-page story in *The*

Houston Post, absorbing every chilling detail of the brutal murders and the meticulous cleanup. Her pulse quickened. Something cold and certain twisted inside her chest—a realization sharper than the vodka and olive juice sliding warmly down her throat.

Rex. It had to be him.

For many years, she quietly traced her brother's shadowy steps, never daring to draw too close but always close enough to where she hoped he could feel her. But now, reading about the connection between Jennifer Armstrong's brutal and reckless murder, a young woman's body, apparently Dr. Kelly Manson's co-serial killer, stuffed into a freezer after a ritual killing and the explosive end of Dr. Kelly Manson himself, Emma felt a deep tremor inside her soul, something between dread and admiration. Her brother had finally emerged, stepping boldly out of obscurity into the glaring, unforgiving spotlight. At least she believed it was him who had taken out The Bone Break Killer and in ways only he could. Detective Hayes mentioned "survival." If anyone could survive anything from such a monster and end up on top, it was her brother.

She carefully folded the newspaper and set it aside just as her server—a polished young man with impeccable manners—appeared beside her booth.

"Another drink, Ms. Madalin?" He was practiced with an unobtrusive smile on his lips.

"Yes, please." Emma forced her voice steady. "Another dirty martini. Make it a double."

He nodded discreetly then disappeared as smoothly as he'd arrived.

As Emma waited, she glanced toward one of the large flatscreen televisions mounted high on the wall just before the entrance to the bar. The muted images flashing across the screen shifted suddenly to the familiar scene she just read from The Post: a solemn press conference, microphones clustered around Detectives Heath Spade and Carmen

Hayes. Emma's heartbeat spiked, her eyes narrowing sharply.

"Can you turn that up, please?" she called out to the server, her tone urgent yet measured. Moments later, Detective Spade's voice filled the bar, authoritative yet tinged with tension.

"We are dealing with a highly skilled and extremely dangerous individual. Anyone who witnessed these interactions or has any relevant information should contact the police immediately. We believe he remains in the Houston area."

Emma leaned back into the plush leather seating, her expression unreadable. She lifted the fresh martini glass the moment the waiter set it down and walked off, fingers cool and steady around the stem, and took a slow, measured sip.

She knew more than anyone else in the elegant bar—as well as Houston itself—exactly who the dangerous individual was; she had no intention of letting anyone else find him first. As he had always done everything in his power during their childhood to protect her and their brother, Don, Emma felt it was—or at least could be—her time to repay those early favors.

Suddenly, things changed from the bar area. Emma had seen a thousand predators in her time. But this one was different. From her booth—the dark alcove tucked beneath the golden sconces—Emma had a clear view of what was going on. As she was reading over the news article again while comparing notes from the press conference, she noticed a particularly striking woman strut into one of Houston's finest restaurants, wearing a fitted gold and green dress and matching heels. Emma always took notice of beauty to capture new ideas for herself, but just as quickly she turned her interest back to the Kelly Manson Murder Story.

The woman at the bar was the same woman Emma noticed when she first walked in. She wasn't trying to seduce or charm. She wasn't trying, at all. She moved like something that had shed the burden of pretending to be human. She was built for elegance as much as raw sex and dressed for all things wicked in that golden green shimmer.

It wasn't just Emma who noticed, as the whole of the restaurant's energy shifted.

People didn't see it outright. They laughed and drank and forked overpriced appetizers into their mouths. But under the surface, their posture adjusted. Breaths shortened. Nerves were being tested. A few glanced up without knowing why, their eyes flicking to the bar before quickly turning away.

The woman's dress captured all the bar lighting, made it look alive, tight as a nylon. Her hair, black and lacquered, was pulled tight against her skull like a crown of thorns. Her skin was flawless. Too flawless—at least that's what Emma thought—like it had never known daylight or time. Her lavender eyes caught light in the strangest way. Not reflective—refractive, as if they bent reality around them. She took her seat at the bar.

Emma stopped reading and watching the television...to watch the woman. She had a calculated detachment of someone who'd spent years learning how to see without being seen while at the same time wanting to be seen. It was also one of Emma's best skills she'd learned while moving up the ranks from the underbelly drug world of Lake City to digging her hooks deep into Houston's heavier players and hitters.

The woman placed a single finger on the bar and nodded once. The bartender came quickly. She didn't ask for a menu and clearly didn't need one. "Green Fairy."

Emma could see that she wanted the request loud enough for everyone in the restaurant to hear. Striking and aggressive, not quite shouting, a voice of authority.

The barkeep nodded, already setting up the absinthe fountain.

Emma's jaw tightened. As the ritual unfolded, the woman shifted in her stool. A man had just taken the seat beside her—mid-50s, Rolex tan, the kind of guy who asked if you were "a real blonde." His sense of wealth and entitlement permeated the barroom. Emma pegged him in a second: empty confidence wrapped in fine linens and mediocre ability.

What took place was something Emma had never seen. The woman turned toward the man and inhaled. Not subtly or sensually. She bent slightly, tilting her head and moving it directly in the space just beneath his jaw, and drew in a long breath through her nose. Like a wolf inhaling the scent of its prey.

Emma's stomach rolled. She felt disturbed and fascinated at the same time. She was far enough away, thinking no one else had noticed, yet the longer she watched the more she saw the deep discomfort of all the bar patrons. Many who were seated at tables and booths soon took notice.

The woman caught the tension in the man's shoulders, the way his eyes darted, then settled back into his drink with a shaken stillness. But she continued inhaling and exhaling with exaggeration around the man's neck and chest, breathing him in. When he moved his seat back, she leaned in even closer with her mouth slightly open, her tongue reaching out to lick him. Nirvana's rendition of "Love Buzz" filled the area. The speed of Cobain's guitar and Novoselic's bass matched the intensity of the woman's aggression.

When she spoke, Emma couldn't hear all the words, but she didn't need to. Whatever was said made the man flinch and jerk back in his seat, nearly falling out of the bar stool. Emma couldn't tell if he was afraid or repulsed. Probably both. He stood seconds later and left, his drink unfinished.

The woman sat alone again and turned her gaze right to Emma's booth.

Emma froze as the woman's violet eyes landed on her and held. Not curious. Not flirtatious. Targeted.

Nirvana still at it, she stood and began to walk across the restaurant directly toward Emma. Each step was as precise and poised as a panther, her hips in sync with Nirvana's escalating love buzz crescendo.

Emma didn't move or even blink. Her fingers lightly grazed the steak knife beside her plate, a reflex more than a decision and one she had learned to use over the years.

The woman stopped at the edge of the booth and tilted her head with a thin smile. "Is this taken?"

Emma studied her, saying nothing.

She slid into the booth without waiting for an answer. Across the table now, up close, she looked even more wrong. Her beauty was striking but...architectural; as if deliberately designed, symmetrical in a way nature wouldn't create. "I saw you watching me. I like being watched." Her voice was thick and velvety.

Emma was far from one who could be taken over with intimidation, regardless that the woman seemed the type who could do that to anyone or anything, for that matter. "I see a lot of things and...the whole place was watching you." Emma folded her arms slowly.

The woman's smile widened. "Hopefully. I think it's best to catch attention in unique ways when the mood strikes. Like this song, for example. You like Nirvana?"

Emma nodded but didn't respond. She was waiting. Listening with curiosity.

The woman nodded back, moving her body in perfect sync to the music. "There's something...old on you. Like ash and flames and blood and secrets. I could smell it from across the barroom and had to come by for a visit."

Emma's expression didn't flicker, but her pulse was hammering in her ears. It was all she could do to prevent an instant shock reaction as her accident that left her splayed out all over the Lake City freeway concrete rushed in on her as if the woman had struck her in the chest. The accident where she had rolled her pickup truck three times, where she was violently thrown from the truck and knocked completely out of her body.

Still, she had to remain as calm as possible; focused. “Seems you like to smell a lot of things. What was that all about? Was there something about that guy that made you cause such a scene?”

The woman chuckled, leaned forward, and rested her head in the palms of her hands, her nails touching her sculpted cheeks. “Something tells me you didn’t mind it one bit. Maybe even enjoyed it?”

Emma smiled. Even though she’d never seen such a thing, there was, in fact, something about it that was enjoyable to watch while the other patrons were clearly unnerved. “You’re not from around here, that’s for sure. That was as far from southern hospitality as this place has ever seen.”

The woman slowly nodded. “I’m from beneath here.”

A beat passed as the music shifted from Nirvana to Charlie Sexton’s “Beat’s So Lonely,” Sexton’s voice a wail drawn-out over the machinegun rhythm of the guitars and drums.

Emma took in a deep breath and slowly released it. “I’ve known people like you...women who come in dressed to kill, acting like they own the air. I’ve seen all types and dealt with all types. But...you’re certainly something I’ve never seen or felt.”

The woman leaned in closer. “You’ve met no one like me. That’s a promise.” Her voice was an icy whisper, her eyes gleaming and coming more to life, if that were possible. She sat back rather abruptly, slightly scratching her chiseled ivory chin. “Someone very close to you...left behind a wake. It’s still rippling through this city. Through you. Through the streets. He’s made a rather fine mess of things. Perfect timing, too, wouldn’t you say? With the whole country burning to the ground?”

Emma’s mouth went dry. The front-page news article.

The murders. The fire.

She's talking about Rex, but how was that possible.

"By now I'm sure everyone's looking for him. Well, police that is. Some good ones, too. Hunting him. Most of them fools, but not the ones assigned to his case."

Emma held the stare. "What the hell are you talking about? Who are you?"

The woman smiled. "I'm the part that comes after."

Emma looked down at her empty glass, then up again. "What does that even mean? After what?"

The woman leaned in closer. "Everything."

Emma chuckled in irritation. "Again...no idea what the hell that means. Do you realize how that sounds? Never mind. You know him, don't you?"

The woman tilted her head and clicked her tongue, obtuse, almost bored. "I know what he's becoming. In fact, at this very moment he's just beginning to get into his groove...doing his groove thing. He's picking out his next trophy while we speak and drink. Trophies, to be exact."

Emma exhaled slowly and leaned in much as the woman had done. She had to keep her composure, play the game as polished as the strange woman's. The more she watched and listened to her, the more she knew she was in over her heard. Still, she was Emma Madalin and didn't take shit from anyone.

"I'm sure he is. I've been following him a long time, but something tells me you already know that. If you hurt him—"

The woman quickly lifted her hand, her nails like talons. "Hurt him? I am here to see him grow to his fullest potential. The potential where his long-lost bloodline left off." She tapped her nails on the table. "Yours, too."

Silence settled between them. Emma signaled the barkeeper for another round for both. "Green Fairy, is it?"

The woman smirked as Emma ordered another double martini and the Green Fairy.

When served, they looked at their drinks, both women swirling the alcohol around as if in the same thought on the same page. Emma had no idea how the woman knew so much but also didn't find the need to question her, as everything about her—sinister and inappropriate as everything about her was wrong—felt right.

With no more words said while finishing, the woman stood and slid smoothly from the booth. "You'll see me again." Her voice was barely above a whisper but just as velvety thick.

Emma's voice emulated it. "I never caught your name."

The woman put up one hand, her back now to her while walking away, her body swaying more than walking, in perfect sync with the music. "I never offered it."

She was gone, walking out the way she came, without sound, without trace. Just the echo of absinthe as something ancient burned into the air she left behind.

Emma sat still for a long time, her thoughts unraveling like thread being pulled from a large messy spool.

Now she knew this wasn't just about Rex. It was everything that had become of him, everything that he was becoming. All the years she had been following him, her love for him longing and deep, was finally coming to fray. It was about everything beneath him. Whatever that meant, Emma didn't know, but she was thrilled to find out.

***

Rex Brody was playing a Billy Squire Greatest Hits CD; "My Kind of Lover" on full throttle. His body in the car seat moved in sync to Squire's rhythmic, power-cord seduction. Brody had always loved Squire's music because his own voice sounded so similar to the singer's, seductive and throaty, yet always more than sophisticated enough to hold his own with the best of them. He also purchased a KC And the Sunshine Band's Essentials CD, but Squire was more the mood for now.

When he pulled the rented burgundy 4-door Chrysler Concorde (managing to convince the Hertz rental associate to pay for it fully in cash) into the lot of the Houston's Sports Outlet, he turned the stereo up as loud as it could go as he shuffled the CD to "In the Dark," sat in the car with the windows rolled down to see if anyone would approach and tell him to turn it down.

Anyone would do. He briefly thought of the scene in Hunter S. Thompson's *Fear and Loathing In Las Vegas* when Thompson was so whacked out on hard drugs that he felt like shooting anything, even a lizard would do. Also, like Thompson, Brody knew he would need drugs sooner or later and a lot of them. There would be no way to sustain the journey Mister Boogie was on without them. Which was fine with Brody.

In the weeks that followed his ordeal with Dr. Kelly Manson and his trusted assistant, Chelsey Bingham; the exchange of his Urwerk UR-101 watch for the vagrant's bicycle; the ultra-bizarre visit to The Serpent's Veil with Adrian Kane and the haunting woman's body he was carrying; meeting the implausible witches, Brody focused on the one thing that made it all make sense: the orb.

Whatever power it held, Brody knew he was only scratching the object's impossible surface. Though it fit perfectly in his palm, he never carried it on his person over the weeks since he offed Dr. Manson, aka, The Bone Break Killer. Holding it and tossing it back and forth from one hand to the other was always enough to provide an edge over anything that he would face.

He juggled it a few more times while watching around the parking lot as shoppers here and there gave pause to glance over, wondering why he had the music so loud, but just as quickly looked away.

Satisfied no one would approach, he put the orb in the glove box, killed the Chrysler's heavy 3.2 L V-6, locked the car, and strutted into the massive sports outlet.

The reason for the visit was to shop around for knives and .22 pistols. He always wanted a Randall hunting knife, as they made the best money could buy. All hand-made blades and handles. Brody also wanted a Ruger octagon barreled .22 target pistol, the most accurate on the market. Over the years of training, he'd mastered weapons, as well as his martial arts and boxing skills. It was time now to begin using them, too.

He stepped through the sliding doors of the outlet, the cool artificial air hitting him like a sudden exhale. The interior lights, stark and sterile, gleamed across endless aisles of tactical gear, fishing rods, and ammunition stacked with clinical precision. He moved fluidly through the store, his pulse thrumming gently beneath his skin, eyes calmly scanning the glass display cases ahead.

Knives. Pistols. Power.

As he drew nearer, a few women's voices pulled him from his internal monologue, a conversation unfolding near the knife counter. Brody's gaze sharpened as he slowed, observing quietly from the shadow of a nearby display of hunting optics.

Two sales associates—both women in their mid-twenties, uniforms pristine and freshly pressed, bodies tight, which Brody noticed instantly—were speaking earnestly to a mother and her daughter. Both their bodies just as tight. Daughter looked 20 or so, the mother in her late 30s but looked better than the daughter. One of the associates, tall and fit with glossy dark hair tied back tightly, pulled a small folding knife from beneath the glass. She pried it open awkwardly, clearly uncomfortable while she attempted an explanation that reeked of incompetence.

"So, this one would be good for you. It's small, easy to carry." Her voice was thin, uncertain. "If someone grabs you, you just...um, stab toward the neck. Or face, I guess. Something like that could work."

The other one, a little shorter, just as fit, with pale, nervous eyes behind fashionable horn-rimmed glasses, nodded vigorously. "Right! And don't forget, just like aim for something soft." She laughed nervously, so far out of her element Brody wondered how in God's name either of them made it past the application phase of the hiring process. "You know, soft spots. Places that are vulnerable."

The mother's expression darkened, frustration tightening the corners of her mouth. "This isn't helping. We need something effective, not random stabbing. How are you even talking this way, honestly?"

Brody could no longer contain himself. It wasn't just their incompetence—though that grated deeply—it was the absurdity of two clueless saleswomen peddling violence they never tasted, danger they never brushed against, talking about it as if they'd never read about it or at least seen a crime thriller and tried to fake it. They were so utterly clueless he had to check himself before losing it all together. They talked about knives like accessories, about defense like some 101-Self-Defense class taught to those who wanted to learn some new stretching routines. It was insulting.

He moved closer, positioning himself within earshot, feigning casual interest in a nearby display of tactical flashlights, flint items, and other cheap outdoor camping gadgets.

The mother leaned forward, lowering her voice, the words still clear enough to carry to Brody's ears. "My daughter has a stalker. He's dangerous. Follows her after work, sends her threats. We need real protection, true, but do you have any idea what you're talking about? Is there someone else here who can help us? Someone with a lot more experience?"

Brody felt a quiet thrill crawl up his spine, his irritation dissolving into something darker, something familiar and sweetly dangerous. His eyes drifted to the daughter: stunning brunette with hair pulled hastily into a ponytail, eyes wide with discomfort and poorly concealed fear. Her body perfect at every curve.

Her mother glanced again at the associates, becoming increasingly disgusted.

That was Mister Boogie's moment. He moved toward them slowly, footsteps deliberate, expression open and calm. The associates glanced up, startled. Brody acknowledged them with a brief, dismissive nod before turning gently toward the mother and daughter, but his eyes focused on the mother. She was dressed in jeans that look painted on, a short top that showcased perfect abs, hair pulled back like her daughter's, but looser, more casual. She wore red lipstick with a sheen that was lit.

"I don't think that's going to be necessary. Sorry to interrupt...but I couldn't help overhearing all this. If your daughter truly has someone threatening her, this isn't the approach you'd want to take. I can assure you."

The tall associate frowned. "Sir, we're handling this."

"Handling? Jesus Christ." Brody's voice tightened subtly, just enough ice to send the girl recoiling slightly. "This lady's question was spot on: do you have any idea what you're talking about?"

Silence fell swiftly, dense and awkward. The associates exchanged quick glances, their discomfort palpable.

Mister Boogie quickly softened, pivoting smoothly back toward the mother. "These knives won't help your daughter. In untrained hands they're as useless as toys. And toys won't stop a predator. You need experience. Tactics. You need help."

The mother hesitated, wary, but drawn in by the commanding clarity of the man's voice. He was rugged with an iron hard body and enough confidence for the entire outlet. "Are you a cop?"

Brody shook his head, offering a slight, sympathetic smile. "No, no, no. Just someone who knows how these things play out. Someone who's seen it all. Someone who can help."

The daughter's voice emerged suddenly, anxious and strained. "Mom, please. I don't know about him. This feels wrong. I don't know about—"

Brody slowly held out his hand and looked directly at the young woman. Her gaze was soft and warm, only an illusion of safety. "I understand your fear...understand every level of fear your lovely little head could imagine. You have every reason to feel such things. But I can help you."

The mother glanced sharply at her daughter, then back to Mister Boogie, clearly torn but desperate. "How? How can you help?"

He was about to pull out his own folding Spyderco Police knife for a demonstration but thought better of it. He stepped into the mother's and daughter's immediate space, completely ignoring the saleswomen. Mister Boogie would deal with them later, that was a guarantee. Brody's voice was measured and calm. "I know exactly how to deal with men like him."

The mother nodded. The man had an aura about him that she sensed could deal with her daughter's stalker and then some. She was more than convinced he was speaking the truth, and she had nothing to lose. The stalker had terrorized his daughter, and it was time to do something about it. "I believe you, Mister..."

"Boog...ah...Brody. Rex Brody."

"Nice to meet you, Mister Brody. I'm Dana Sutherland. My daughter, Samantha."

Samantha folded her arms in irritation as well as protection. She was plenty sharp enough to know when a man's eyes were undressing her, though this man had scarcely paid her a moment's notice. Which was rare.

Brody eyeballed Dana and Samantha back and forth, a few fingers on the side of his chin, sizing them up and down in a memorizing scan.

Before stepping back, he asked one more question,

carefully modulated to sound casual yet purposeful. "Please. Call me Rex. This stalker...do you know him personally?" He spoke directly to Dana, but Samantha's eyes darted to her mother then back to Brody.

Samantha had enough of being ignored. She cleared her throat and took a step closer. "James Corbin. He's been harassing me nonstop. Police won't do shit, and it's a lot more than just harassment."

Mister Boogie grinned slowly unphased by Samantha's growing irritation.

James Corbin. He let the name settle in, absorbing it like a promise. "He's really upset you. Understandably."

Dana thought the sincerity in his voice was like silk over steel.

"Truth is, people like James rarely stop on their own. The James Corbins of the world. Most of the time...come to think of it, all the time, the Corbins of the world always need to be handled. Not like these two have been yakking about without a lick of understanding." He turned his entire body toward the sales ladies then pivoted back toward Dana and Samantha all in a single move.

He spoke to Dana and Samantha without so much as a glance back to Associates One and Two. "I've never heard such stupidity, trying to talk to someone about how to kill with a knife without the slightest idea of a single word that popped out of their mouths. Reminds me a lot of my Aunt Anna, stupid stupid woman that she was. Still is, for all I know, but I'll find out, one of the next boxes on my check list. But that's another story." He slowly turned back to them, this time walking to the glass showcase to rest both hands on the top. He looked at their name tags from his peripheral while moving his eyes one to the other.

Leslie Ames and Tina Parker.

"Ms. Sutherland asked you if there was someone else to talk to. I should talk to your manager about this, but that's no longer needed. I think you both understand the situation here. If you don't, you will."

Leslie and Tina looked at each other with their mouths open, speechless. Rex Brody scared them more than they expected. They could not make eye contact with him as they fidgeted with their shirts and hands. But they noticed his eyes more than anything else. Regardless of his good looks, he had the eyes of something soulless. Their faces flushed with embarrassment, confusion, and fear.

Mister Boogie turned back to Dana and Samantha, already feeling the dark threads of intention forming in his mind for lovely Leslie and Tina.

"Come walk with me for a minute. I still have some shopping to do but wanted to get a few more details, if I may."

Samantha looked to her mother. Dana kept focus on Brody. "It's fine, Sam. Let's at least listen to him. I'm sure it'll be better than what those dimwits were telling us."

The women followed Brody toward the ammunition where he stopped and looked around not bothering to speak. It was always best to have others make the first move.

Dana gently cleared her throat. "Mister...sorry, Rex. You wanted to talk more, so...can you just tell us what you wanted to say, please? This whole thing has been nothing but an ordeal."

Brody nodded and sighed with a mock frown. "I like that, Dana. Coming right at a thing. You're right. Police have bigger issues than your James Corbin. Much bigger. So...I'll come right at this with you." He turned to Samantha. "He harasses you at work? Your workplace, after hours? Before? What exactly?"

Samantha nodded gradually gaining some trust. "All the above. Has been for months. At work is where I met him. Kept coming on to me. Put his hands on me. Many times. It's why he was fired. Fuckin' creep."

"I see. Where do you work?" Brody's arms were folded as he listened carefully.

"Landon's Accounting, out on the Katy Freeway. He has a mouth on him, too. Openly telling me he wanted to screw me. Among other things. Lot of people heard it, but it took pulling teeth to get anything done. That's when the harassment started after work, only he's always been sly enough to keep enough distance, so nothing sticks."

Brody nodded while thinking things over. Landon's Accounting. Check. He had established trust, now he needed to move on it.

"What are some of Corbin's hangouts?"

"Hey, you said you weren't a cop." Dana's voice was cautious but assertive.

"I'm not. I'd have to tell you if I were. But if I'm going to help you, you've got to give me something. Anything."

"My God, mother, this was your idea to hear him out, so let's hear him out." Samantha faced Brody with direct eye contact after her brief scolding. "Numbers. He loves Numbers. You know it?"

Brody nodded. "Of course." Brody hadn't been in Houston long enough to make Numbers a personal spot, but certainly knew of its fame for its dance floors and house tech music, where throngs of Houston's weirdest would come in for long nights of hedonism.

Samantha looked at her mother then back to Brody. "What are you going to do?"

He turned his head slowly from side to side with one hand up, index finger pointing side to side. "It doesn't matter what I'm going to do, Samantha. What matters is you don't want him in your life. So that's where we are. Both of you...stay safe. Stay alert." He pulled out the burner flip phone from his back pocket. What's your number, I'll call you when things are...let's call it, 'settled.'"

Dana reluctantly gave Brody her cell phone number, still believing he was as good of help as anything she tried so far, and she needed to do something to gain her daughter's trust back.

As Brody left with his purchases, each step felt lighter, his irritation had transformed into Mister Boogie's quiet exhilaration. James Corbin's name echoed from within, a new mark etched into the blade of his mind.

Corbin would be first, then the Sales Associates One and Two, Leslie and Tina. Mister Boogie was formulating a plan that could emulate what he'd done at the good doctor's palace. One that he wanted refined once he found Brody's Aunt Anna.

This time, he would take more than just lives; they would be trophies, mementos, perhaps continuing with a white glove and top hat from the Kelly Manson Estate, a symbolic gesture whispered by the witches of The Serpent's Veil, guided by something older and darker than he could fully comprehend. He would rely on the orb for clarity through the madness.

Mister Boogie smiled to himself as he walked back to the Chrysler, anticipation blossoming into a quiet, potent hunger.

***

At the same time, in line at the Coffee Hut kiosk across the parking lot from the sports outlet, Detective Carmen Hayes's eyes opened wide, and her skin hairs stood straight up. She was looking at the man who could have murdered Dr. Kelly Manson and blew his home to hell.

"Spade...Spade." Hayes's urgency was always the signal to Detective Heath Spade that shit was about to go down.

"What is it?"

"Look over there. The Chrysler. Four-door."

Spade looked to see what Hayes was talking about.

"Doesn't that look a lot like the description we have on the Kelly Manson killer?"

Spade whistled under his breath. "Could be, partner.

Could be."

***

Heath Spade stared blankly at the pile of photographs scattered across his desk, each image an unanswered question: Jennifer Armstrong's body at the library, Chelsey Bingham's corpse, frozen and staged with horrific precision, but then destroyed along with Dr. Kelly Manson's mansion and the metallic blue Porsche with two dead cops. Weeks of sleepless nights and bitter coffee had drawn shadows beneath his eyes, deepening like bruises.

Spade felt the dull ache of exhaustion behind his temples. The Houston PD bullpen was quieter than usual, the fluorescent lights overhead buzzing softly, adding a white-noise soundtrack to their dead-end frustration. Weeks of chasing shadows, leads unraveling faster than they could pull them in. The horror at Kelly Manson's estate, Jennifer Armstrong's brutalized murder, Bingham's frozen body, cops dying, it all felt like a dark, endless labyrinth.

Hayes approached swiftly, slamming a stack of files onto his desk, startlingly loud. "Heath, we need to revisit some shit. We've missed some things."

Spade rubbed his jaw, rough stubble scratching beneath tired fingertips. "What. What now? We've gone through it so many times my eyes are dizzy. Christ, Carmen."

Hayes pulled out a thin folder and flipped it open. "You don't think I know that? Never mind. Just listen. It's Denison's interview. Listen to what he said again: he mentioned something about The Serpent's Veil club and about the guy's eyes being wrong. Wrong is what he said. But he also hinted toward other shit if you listen closely enough to what wasn't said."

"Yeah, yeah, yeah, yeah, Carmen, so what about it?"

"It's something about that club, Heath, and everything being off, so I did some digging while your ornery ass was sucking coffee after coffee. Get this. Adrian Kane is involved with that club. Not directly, but he has ownership in the goddamn place."

Spade's mouth opened as he nodded quickly. His gaze sharpened. "Interesting...The Veil...Adrian Kane. Okay, detective. Are you thinking this is one of that sick fuck's playgrounds?"

Hayes nodded, tension pulling her features tight. "More probable than possible. Maybe this isn't random madness. Maybe Kane's influence is deep into this shit. For all we know, what if it's Kane pulling the strings? We've assumed our guy's working alone. What if he's not? What if he's got an accomplice just like Manson."

The thought chilled them both. Adrian Kane was one of those ghost stories whispered among Houston cops: someone untouchable, dangerous, the unseen hand that seemed to pull every string under Houston's ugliest sores: kiddie porn, human trafficking, witchcraft. The list went on.

"Okay. But let me play The Devil's Advocate here for a sec. Let's say Kane is involved somehow. Let's go back to Manson and the girl."

"Chelsey."

"You saw what went down in that torture room, as well as I did. Whoever killed Manson was tortured, no doubt, and he kicks into survival mode. Chelsey baited the wrong guy. Manson had no idea what the fuck he had gotten into."

Hayes put her head down and shook it slowly while taking a few deep breaths. "Yeah, I know that, Spade. I get that part. All of it. All I'm suggesting is that our killer could have ended up at The Serpent's Veil and hooked up with Adrian Kane for a reason. I mean, we have no proof that Kane was even there that night, but it just feels like he could have been, and we've got nothing to lose by checking it out. Until we do, we won't know how deep this rabbit hole goes."

"But let's also look at Jennifer Armstrong. If, and it's a big fucking if, our guy killed her and the doctor and Chelsey, how is all this related? If you're thinking Kane is the answer it seems pretty fuckin' thin, partner. Our suspect is a killer, no question, with a bullet-proof skillset. But if he's the same guy who killed Armstrong, then he's more unstable than the doctor ever was. Killing her was an act of pure rage."

"Or pleasure." Hayes shook her head. "I doubt he's more unstable than the doctor's killer, Christ, Spade, please. Maybe he's psychotic, dual personality or some such shit. Maybe he was just irritated with Armstrong and killed her for the fun of it. Have you considered that?"

Spade slowly nodded, his eyes opening wider. "Nice, Carmen. Nice."

"Right. So, my gut, Spade. We've got to check out Kane, and you goddamn know it."

Spade gave up on that one. Hayes's thinking about their new killer was most likely the correct route. And she was right about Kane being a mandatory check. "Fine. Let's run Kane's known associates. Cross-reference every goddamn thing we have on Kelly Manson and Chelsey Bingham being possible connections, too. Look for overlaps. We need to also check every angle on Armstrong. What was she doing? Where did she come from? Was she in involved with Kane, the whole fucking nine yards."

They dug through the files, sifting desperately through any hidden crevice. Minutes had bled into hours had bled into days, which had turned to weeks. One late night deep into it, Hayes surfaced from the paperwork, her voice tense.

"Check this out. I found something else." She carefully placed down on Spade's desk a faded report.

"What is it?" Spade pulled his tie through and tossed it over his shoulder not giving a shit less where it landed.

"Years ago, in Lake City, Utah, CPS took a teenage girl into custody. Abuse case, real ugly. The father went down hard, did some time."

Spade narrowed his eyes. "Utah? And? What the fuck are you getting at?"

Hayes raised her hand immediately. “Please. Stop. Her brothers were taken separately. The records on them are spotty, lots of redactions and name changes. Seems the brothers vanished into the system and stayed off grid.”

Spade felt a cold prickle at the back of his neck. “So, what about the CPS case? Hayes, spit it out. Christ.”

A tense silence settled between them, broken suddenly when Hayes leaned forward and pulled one of the photographs from the old file. A snapshot of a woman, young and beautiful, caught candidly by a news camera outside one of Houston’s elegant restaurants, scenes from back in the early 90s. A file marked with question marks, half-built theories, uncertain leads.

“What is this, Hayes?”

Carmen tapped the photograph a few times as she put it in front of him.

“This isn’t the only photograph of her. Look at this one.” Hayes had another file with dozens of shots all around the press conference she and Spade led just a few days ago. Hayes slapped the photo down on top of the older one. “She’s in this photo with the crowd that was gathered that day. She’s been a person of interest for Narcotics for quite some time, but they’ve never been able to pin anything on her. Probably why we’ve never heard of her. A drug taskforce agent by the name of Kerry Ellis tied the older photo to this one. Same woman.”

Spade tossed his hands up. “Okay...great. Who is she?”

“Emma Madalin.”

Spade tapped his desk, growing more impatient by the second. “Who the hell is she?”

“I’m getting there, Heath. Here’s my theory so far. The more I dug around, the more I think that Emma Madalin is one of the three siblings in the Lake City CPS case.”

Spade started clapping slowly in frustration. “Big whoopie fuck. We’re looking for a killer, not a lost little girl.”

"Stop. I think she could be related to our killer. His sister. We know nothing of the brother, with all these goddamn redactions and shit from the sloppy file. But what if, Spade, what if she is our killer's sister? Is that such a stretch? I mean we don't know anything about this guy. This is a piece that could tell us a whole lot more about this puzzle. I've done a lot of digging on our Missy Madalin. There's not much on her that's solid from her Lake City days, except a serious auto accident. Rolled her truck and was tossed out on the freeway. Flight for Life gave her a ride to save her life. There were a few notes I accessed on microfiche from one of the surgeons on her case. She needed a lot of reconstructive surgery. He gave her a body every woman dreams to have, as you can see in some of these pics. She was in a coma for several weeks, and when she came out of it, she was like..."

"Like what, Hayes?"

"She was a completely different person. Surgeon said she had the 'inner appearance of something strangely dark, something that seemed completely opposite from the people in her life who knew her.' 'Strangely dark,' exact quote."

Spade shook his head with an over-compensated sigh. "Terrific. Just terrific. What does that even mean, Hayes?"

"No idea, but this is my thinking, and it's my gut again, and I know I'm on to something. While she was in that coma... maybe she made some kind of deal with..."

"Christ, Hayes, are you saying what the fu—"

"You got anything better, Spade?"

"Alright. Don't yell at me. We'll check it out along with every other goddamn thing. Let's get hold of Officer Ellis immediately on this bitch. Maybe she's hiding from her brother."

Hayes shook her head. "Really, Heath? She's following her brother. That's more like it."

"Right. I'm tired is all."

"Oh god—"

"We'll go with your gut here, let's just get on it. Get everything you can on her."

Hayes stood abruptly, adrenaline sparking. "Also, *The Houston Post* article. The murders, the doctor, Chelsey, Jennifer Armstrong. It mentioned nothing about a family, but Emma Madalin keeps popping up in places she shouldn't."

Spaded kept following his partner, nodding slowly, eyes intense.

"Brothers are gone. Vanished like I said, and Emma's trail shows her moving around, dodging law enforcement, disappearing into and resurfacing from every dark corner imaginable. Lake City and here. Spade, we are talking about strip clubs, drug dens, even suspected ties to human trafficking down in Juarez and Tijuana. But it's all whispers, nothing solid."

Spade felt a deep chill spread through his chest. "Are you thinking she's also tied to Adrian Fucking Kane?"

Hayes quickly shook her head. "Doubtful. She's not that level, but who knows."

"That's why we need to talk to Ellis like yesterday. How reliable are the trafficking suspicions?"

"Reliable enough for Lake City PD to flag her as a person of interest multiple times." Hayes sounded grim.

Spade leaned back, a heaviness settling over him as he wrapped his head around all of it. "She survives an accident that should have killer her. Doctors rebuild her but she comes back all fucked up mentally, stays low-key, resurfaces only to be spotted around Houston's high-end nightlife, suddenly refined and watching over this investigation. That about nail it, Hayes?"

"Think about it," she pressed, her intensity growing. "Three siblings split apart in Utah. We have what we have on Emma, but what if one of the brothers who dropped into darkness suddenly emerges decades later to end up killing The Bone Break Killer and is now possibly hunting down people tied to Kelly Manson and the Houston underworld.

But I don't think that's it. I'm with you that he survived the doctor, and the doctor was in over his head. I think our killer is now learning as he goes because he's got a beef with what happened as a child with his sister and brother. That's my hunch."

Spade exhaled sharply, hands clenched on the edge of the desk. "Maybe she's been waiting all along. Either way, we can't ignore it."

He rubbed his face, feeling the case twisting into something deeper and uglier by the minute. "So, keeping this going, our killer grows up in darkness, turns violent, crosses paths with Adrian Kane and his Serpent's Veil club, learns or creates some bizarre symbolic ritual with Manson's murders and Bingham's frozen corpse. Meanwhile, Emma walks a parallel line in the shadows. All roads leading back here in our back-fucking-yard. Not bad, detective."

His tense oration was broken suddenly by Hayes's phone buzzing violently on the desk. She snatched it up, eyes blinking as she read the brief text.

"Hey, we got something," she said. "Anonymous tip claims there's someone who fits the killer's description hanging around the sports outlet off I-10. He's sitting in a Chrysler Concorde, burgundy, blasting the stereo."

***

The elevator in The Mark moved with a smoothness that almost felt unnatural, as if the air were holding its breath. Emma Madalin stood barefoot in the center of the chrome-paneled lift, her long black robe clinging to her skin in damp folds from the shower she had taken. She didn't bother toweling off as she'd left her purse in her car, which was parked in The Mark's covered garage. The heat of her own breath was the only warmth in the steel womb enclosing her. Her arms were folded tightly across her chest. Her spine was straight, and her strange eyes that had never been quite the same since the coma, remained fixed on the mirrored wall in front of her, where her reflection glared back like a corpse caught mid-blink.

There was something about the lighting in The Mark that always made her look embalmed. The pale fluorescence above was calculated, precise, and sterile, casting her features in that mortuary palette of rich bone and distant warmth. No shadows softened the edges of her cheekbones. Her lips, freshly painted in oxblood red, looked like a knife wound against the monochrome of her face. The elevator's mirrored walls fractured her reflection, giving her seven Emma Madalin's to look over; none of them blinked.

Floor 21. Floor 22. Floor 23.

She could count every breath she took between the chimes. Her heart didn't race. Her body was loose and coiled, ready but not tense. Beneath the robe, she held the obsidian blade flat against skin that hadn't felt another person's touch in over a year. She always fastened it instinctively, part of her dressing ritual. For Emma, the act of preparing for Houston's underbelly was more of a ritual. Every movement measured. Every breath loaded.

The elevator stopped with a soft chime and the doors peeled back like theater curtains. The foyer was empty, bathed in amber light and silence. No neighbors. No voices. No signs of life except for the light fixtures humming faintly above. The Mark was luxury stacked on top of apathy. It was built for the elites who wanted their deeds hidden in prosperity, deeds too dangerous to be named, the private lives of the wealthy's sickest shit. She walked barefoot across the marble floor of her private entryway, Penthouse 2312, her footsteps echoing faintly as if even the walls were reluctant to listen.

The door to her penthouse was already open; she never bothered locking it.

Inside, the air was cold and sharp. The open space beyond the threshold was perfectly curated for solitude. No personal touches, no sentimental clutter. A single low couch, black leather, untouched for months. Floor-to-ceiling windows overlooking the Houston skyline, currently fogged by the haze of stormy humidity. A liquor shelf with a half-empty bottle of mezcal and a tumbler beside it, the glass still stained with the ghost of her lipstick from earlier that afternoon. And on the wall, tilted slightly to the right, hung the only photograph she had ever carried with her since Lake City.

Her eyes locked on the photograph. A young Rex, his arm around her and Don, his gaze hard, a boy who'd learned to bleed for them. She'd tracked him for years, never close enough to touch but close enough to feel his rage. Close enough to see him grow over the years.

It had been a little over a week since her strange encounter at Houston's Bar and Grille when visiting with the woman who had smelled a bar patron up and down like a wild animal. *The Houston Post* article, folded on the couch, screamed his crimes: Jennifer Armstrong's brutal murder in the library restroom, the precision kills at Dr. Kelly Manson's estate, which he blasted to rubble. She had been closely following Detective's Spade and Hayes on their hunt for The Bone Break Killer. Emma's pulse thrummed, not with doubt but with certainty. She didn't know if Rex had done the killing, but she knew it was possible. Her brother, the boy who'd taken their father's perpetual neglect to provide her and Don's only shred of comfort, could have easily turned into the force who could do anyone in. Her goal of finding him before the cops, or that lavender-eyed woman from Houston's, was the only thing that mattered. Her street thug connections had given her the edge she needed to succeed.

Specifically, Chain Willis.

Chain was older than Emma, mid-thirties, and he had grown up much like Emma. His emotions and mind as hardened as his sleeved-up tattooed body, his world inside the madness of state care all from Houston to Dallas, to San Antonio—all in city ghettos—made Emma's childhood in Lake City seem a little soft. Once out of middle school, Chain ran away from his final foster home after the foster dad had raped him for the last time. When police found Edgar Blume gutted from his balls to his ribcage, it didn't take long for them to put things together that Chain was the culprit. Police who were on the case couldn't give a shit's last care about the grisly murder. Blume deserved everything he got.

It was Emma who found Chain when he had taken a trip to Lake City for his first heavy drug and human trafficking gig. They hit it off immediately. Chain knew Emma had the streets as well as the wits to give him a life he always wanted: one with power and control. He would kill for Emma on a moment's notice. So, when he called her with intel on her brother's possible next moves, she knew the intel was righteous.

Chain had managed to follow Rex just enough to know that Rex had taken interest in a mother and daughter who were dealing with a possible stalker. Rex had also taken interest in two sales associates who worked at one of Houston's sports outlets. Chain had tried to link things together, but none of it made any sense to him, but it's what Emma wanted, so that's what he gave her.

Emma's mind reeled back to the restaurant, to the woman who'd slid into her booth like a refined Boa Constrictor. Her eyes that bent light like a prism had pierced Emma, seeing past her sculpted flesh to the fractures beneath. Her voice, velvet thick, had coiled around Emma's thoughts: "I'm the part that comes after." The woman's absinthe ritual, the "Green Fairy" she'd ordered loud enough for the entire room to hear, had been a performance, a taunt. Her gold-and-green shimmering dress, her black hair pulled so tightly back. She'd spoken of Rex "picking out his next trophy," and their bloodline, hers and Emma's, something ancient. What it all meant, and how it was all connected, Emma had no idea.

She crossed to the custom black-lacquered liquor shelf, her bare feet silent on the marble. She popped the frosted crystal topper from one of the many crystal whisky flasks and poured herself a healthy golden drink of Southern Comfort. Steadying herself, her dizzying reflection in the window unyielding, her mind drifted to when she rolled her truck. The accident crashed through her mind, raw as the day it happened. Lake City, so many years ago, but it still felt like last night.

She was running product for a dealer, her pickup truck roaring down the freeway, the night thick with Utah dust. A tire blew, the truck swerved, and the world turned to chaos. Metal screamed, glass shattered, and Emma was thrown, her body splayed across the concrete, blood flung about like a drunk painter's paint. She felt herself rise, weightless, watching her own ruin below, her soul untethered. The darkness had swallowed her, but she heard whispers of promised power that ricocheted endlessly in a world she couldn't believe was possible. She clawed her way back, not for herself, but for Rex, for Don, for the family torn apart by their father's neglect and ambivalence. The CPS's iron hands and their fucking fraud Aunt Anna.

The hospital was a haze of shattering light and antiseptic. She'd awakened from the coma after weeks, her body rebuilt with plates and screws, her face and breasts sculpted into flawless beauty. But her eyes scared the nurses: too sharp, too knowing. They'd seen beyond anything anyone ever knew. The surgeon's notes, stolen later, called her "strangely dark," a presence that unnerved him. Emma had felt it, too, waking to a world that tasted sharper, more bitter...but clearer.

Her instincts were predatory now, senses honed. She'd tested them in Lake City's drug and prostitute culture, cutting through dealers and pimps with a precision that felt preternatural. Her mind bounced from the accident back to her childhood, remembering how much she and Rex loved knives, how they loved to torture lizards, the faint moments of their love for each other that they grasped onto, all the while knowing it was only a matter of time before the pathetic Sam Brody would get rid of them forever.

Emma remembered their last moments of hope ripped apart that fateful day in the sterile room with Lake City CPS, her grandparents and their partners. Her Aunt Anna Stannis and the surgical façade she put on with the real agenda to eliminate any chance of staying together with her brothers and father. Regardless of Sam Brody's impotence as a father, she knew as well as Rex that state custody would be far worse.

She drained the whiskey and poured another while shaking her head quickly to snap to, holding her treasured obsidian blade that was given to her after her first major drug score, not so long ago. It was a knife she held as dear to her as the aged photo of her with her brothers. She learned to strap it to her thigh beneath skirts, or a robe when not wearing slacks or jeans where she wore it on belts. It was a relic that hummed when she held it. A weapon she knew from where approval would matter most: Rex's.

She cut on her stereo system, firing up Peter Gabriel's "Red Rain," from his *So* album, Gabriel's haunting, wailing voice crying out about life's cold cruel ground, how the world pours its horror down on the earth like great drops of blood.

Emma put down the drink and began to move around her penthouse living room floor with dance moves that were slow and precise, every part of her feeling all the pain the world had given her and all the pain she knew that Rex would give right back.

With her help, of course.

Her lips curled, oxblood-red against her sharp face. She'd been tracking Rex since the moment she was able to discover his whereabouts after she began her journey into Lake City's drug world, staying in his wake, never close enough to be seen. She'd built a network in Lake City's and Houston's most elite dealers and consumers, her hooks deep in both city's heavy players.

It was the first Tuesday in October when Chain called, his voice was low and urgent. "He'll be at Numbers, Emma. He's been sniffing around someone named James Corbin. Stalker type. Creepy, but simple enough to handle. Your boy's got that look...like he's hunting."

"What do you know about Corbin?"

Chain's voice was tight, sharp. "Like I said, creepy predator type. Numbers is his thing. He'll be there tonight, late. No exact time. It's as hot a lead as I've had on this one since you first asked about it."

"Anything else?" Emma focused on the photograph.

"What do you mean, exactly? About Corbin or your boy?"

"Not my *boy*, Chain, my brother."

"Emma...we've not established that he's your brother yet, right? Don't you think it's—"

"Right. You're right, Chain. But you know me well enough to know that... Never mind that now. Just let me think this way, okay? I don't need you jinxing shit."

"Okay, Emma. You're the boss. If you're asking about him, no, there's not much. He's been impossible to tail. Like he owns everything around him, if that makes any sense."

Emma's breath caught; her brother hadn't changed. "Stay on him, Chain. Don't get too close. Call me when it's all green lit."

She hung up, her mind racing. Rex was hunting, his transformation mirroring hers, a darkness born in Lake City's CPS ruins. The woman from Houston's Bar and Grille knew, but how was another story.

Emma had pressed and pressed Chain for details on Corbin. Why was Rex on him? What was the purpose? Etc.,

etc. She paid him double to find out everything possible. As soon as she heard everything from Chain, she was fully committed to find her brother at the nightclub any night, any time.

She moved to the photograph, lifting it from the wall. The frame was heavy, the glass cold. Rex's young eyes stared back, hard but protective, a boy who'd kill for her. Don was a phantom, lost in the system forever. She never found out what happened to Don, regardless of how much she offered her connections and her connection's connections. Emma's own face, soft and unscarred, mocked her. She'd been weak then, a girl who needed saving. Not anymore. The strange woman's words about their bloodline echoed, a promise of ruin and power. Emma felt it too, in the dreams where Rex's shadow loomed, his hands certainly blood-stained.

Emma also knew that the detectives she watched at the press conference, Spade and Hayes, were closing in. She dealt with some of the most bull-headed and talented cops from Lake City and Houston over the years, but when she watched and listened to Detective Heath Spade, she knew he would never stop, that he was an opponent neither she nor her brother needed huffing and puffing with the only goal to blow their house in.

She set down the photograph, the siblings' faces a silent vow. She gently traced her fingers over the obsidian blade, its black edge gleaming, then dressed quickly: black spandex under a fitted leather skirt, leather jacket, boots that wouldn't slip on oil, the blade strapped on a biker's belt that double-wrapped her waist.

She stepped back into the foyer, the amber light swallowing her. The elevator doors closed, the chime a war signal. Houston waited below, its streets raw with fear and anxiety, a city on the edge of something ancient. Emma Madalin was ready, blade in hand, her brother's shadow her only guide.

***

The Houston PD bullpen was a war zone of paper and despair, its fluorescent lights buzzing like a swarm of dying wasps. Desks drowned under stacks of files, crumpled coffee cups, and cigarette butts, the air heavy with stale ambition and the acrid bite of burnt Maxwell House. Outside, Houston's skyline flickered through smudged windows, the city's post-9/11 paranoia a constant hum, sharper now, first week of October, weeks after Detectives Spade and Hayes had locked eyes on their suspect in the sports outlet's parking lot. That burgundy Chrysler Concorde, its driver with a predator's gait, had seared itself into their minds; they couldn't shake it.

Spade slumped in his chair, his tie a noose, his face perpetual sandpaper stubble that scratched like regret. The photographs on his desk related to their newest killer glared up at him, each a taunt. Over a month of relentless digging had left him hollow, his eyes shadowed deeper than the bruises from his last case, a rapist who'd walked free. He wouldn't let this killer slip, not with Houston bleeding on the coattails of 9/11.

Hayes stormed in, her boots pounding the linoleum, a manila folder clutched like a weapon. Her dark eyes blazed. She slapped the folder onto Spade's desk, the sound like a gunshot in the quiet bullpen. A rookie flinched, but the veterans didn't look up; they knew Hayes's urgency meant that she was onto something that could break open the case...or at least move the needle.

"James Corbin." Her voice low and sharp. "I think our guy's after him, and it's going down at Numbers. Most likely tonight."

Spade straightened, his exhaustion shoved aside by a jolt of focus, but his hand straight up to interrupt.

"Whoa, whoa, slow it down." He flipped open the folder, revealing a rap sheet. Charges: stalking, harassment, possible assault, always dodging any kind of time. Below the rap sheet, a surveillance still from Numbers' parking lot showed the Chrysler, its driver a blurred figure, but the posture was unmistakable. Spade's gut clenched.

"How'd we get here? We'd followed him that day at the sports outlet, but lost him in traffic." His voice was gravelly as he scanned the file.

Hayes leaned against the desk, her arms crossed, her intensity a live wire. "We've been working the tip. Our beat cop, Ramirez, tailed the Chrysler late one-night last week and few nights back, catching it at Numbers both times. Each time it was there, so was Corbin. Get this: Ramirez knows Corbin, says he's a fixture there, always preying on women. Men, too. Ramirez has seen our guy inside, not drinking, not dancing, just watching. Watching and waiting as if to memorize everything Corbin's doing. This is it. No idea the hows or whys yet, but this is it."

Spade's mind flashed to the parking lot when Hayes's voice was so urgent. "Look over there. The Chrysler." The man had strutted out of the sports outlet with razor-blade confidence. Spade had felt it the moment Hayes alerted him. Though their tailing him that day went nowhere, the pieces now locking in were confusing.

"Why's he following Corbin?"

"I don't know. Possibly something to do with this." Hayes pulled a witness statement from the folder, her nail tapping the paper. "This is from Dana Sutherland. Her daughter is Samantha. Apparently, she and Samantha were shopping for knives that day. According to Dana and Samantha, Corbin's been stalking Samantha for quite some time. She worked with him at Landon's Accounting where he was fired for groping her. Stalking escalated to threats. Dana said a man intervened, called himself Rex something or other. Said he could help them, for Christ's sake. Description matches our suspect to a T: shredded...with eyes like a fucking void. But, and here's the kicker, she said she trusted the guy."

Spade's chest tightened. Rex. Rex who?

"Alright, so we have a first name...which means jack shit, could be Johnny Boy for all we know. Still, the description is spot on. Maybe he's hunting now. For whatever reason we have no clue other than what we've gone over fifty-thousand fuckin' times."

Hayes nodded, her jaw tight. "There's a few more things to go over." She could feel her partner's irritation; it was thick enough to smell it. "I know, I know, but we've got to think of everything. Two sales associates, women, were working the knife counter that day. They also gave a statement about this fella. Said he was more than just rude. Could be nothing, but they sounded..."

"Sounded what?"

"Scared. Disturbed is more accurate but never mind that for now. Let's race back to Chelsey Bingham at Fitzgerald's the night she was killed."

Spade stood from his desk. "Self-defense from our guy, Hayes, and you goddamn well know it. She was a co-conspirator serial killer accomplice with Doctor-Fucking-Kelly Manson."

Hayes nodded in agreement while raising her hands in objection. "Wait a minute, I didn't suggest anything other than the night she was killed. Really, Heath. I know she was in on it, and I'm not giving her any leniency. She got what was coming to her, but please, just hear me out. I'm talking about Fitzgerald's right now."

"Then get to the point."

She took in a deep breath, then: "Stages, Spade, stages. We don't have anything or anyone at this point who knows who Chelsey was with that night at Fitzgerald's. Haven't had much time yet to begin that dig, but of course, we both know it had to be her killer. Let's call him X for now since it's close enough to Rex, and we don't really know shit about the name."

Spade nodded, softening his approach.

"What if Fitzgerald's was a stage for him. This is the kind of guy who wants an audience, at least for now. Numbers could be his next stage. Ramirez says Corbin's there a few nights a week and at least one night every weekend, always looking for someone or something. Our guy knows it. He's been casing the place, mapping Corbin's routine. Sutherland's statement also says X asked for Corbin's hangouts, where she mentioned Numbers. That's plenty to go on, Heath, and you know it as well as I do."

Spade picked up Corbin's rap sheet and studied the smug face. Corbin was a bottom-feeder, but maybe Hayes was right. Whoever this X was had an interest in him. From what Spade's own gut told him, it was blood. The murders thus far had been wildly random from Armstrong's brutality to the precise theatrics of killing Manson and Bingham to blowing up Manson's estate and the Porsche, a middle finger to forensics. Spade's mind churned, the Lake City CPS case was also nagging at him. Emma Madalin's file—her accident, coma, the surgeon's "strangely dark" note—was some kind of weird connection to everything.

"What about Madalin?"

Hayes's expression hardened, her fingers twitching like she wanted to punch something. "She could be part of it. Remember, Ellis has flagged Madalin's involvement in Houston's drug scene. High-end shit, untouchable so far. Well, check this shit out. Ellis says she's connected to Chain Willis, a street urchin with a rap sheet longer than I-10. Chain works for Madalin. Word is, Willis has been tailing someone for her, someone possibly matching our Mister X's description. The bitch has an interest in our X."

Spade nodded. "Lake City relationship, for all the fuck we know."

His stomach kept twisting, a chill deepening. Spade knew that Ellis was one of HPD's true hard cases. One of the department's finest or not, Ellis was as raw as Spade had ever been. But Ellis was corrupt through and through. Spade knew firsthand that every heavy scene that Ellis had been on over the past several years, something went missing. Cash. Jewelry. Whores. Whatever. Hayes was also right about Emma Madalin being no bystander. Her press conference photo, her strange eyes, the CPS case—three siblings torn apart with the brothers vanishing, Emma reborn after a crash that should've killed her—all of it felt like the root of this nightmare.

"If Chain Willis has been tailing X to Numbers—"

"Exactly." Hayes's voice approved. "She's not just watching. She's making a move. Ellis says Willis was spotted near Numbers a few nights back, scoping the place. Madalin's closing in, same as us, and Numbers is the goddamn showcase."

Spade leaned back, the chair groaning. His mind raced, stitching together X's kills, Corbin's rap sheet, Madalin's hovering. Ellis. Willis. A Venn diagram was needed at this point. His mind then switched to The Serpent's Veil and Adrian Kane. Hayes had dug up Kane's ties to the club, a hint of ownership, a nexus for Houston's darkest and ugliest players. His protected ownership was also traced to another silent partner. An unknown woman. But that's all they knew other than she was one finger tapping on the growing migraine. He thought about Denison's ramblings about the suspect's "wrong" eyes and the Veil echoed, a sliver of something unnatural Spade couldn't shake.

"Let's go back to Kane before I've got nothing left in the tank. We know he's got ownership in The Veil even though we can't prove shit. He's got endless pockets with bookkeepers and accountants who can give him Fort Knox protection. What about this woman who turned up as a possible silent partner to Kane. Anything on her?"

Hayes's eyes flashed, her frustration raw, shaking her head. "Not a clue on that one. Whoever she is she's far deeper in the shadows than Kane, and that's some weird shit.

We know The Veil's a goddamn abyss, and X was there after he blew Manson's place, per Denison. Maybe it explains some of this ritualistic shit. Bingham's body and the slashes across her neck and wrists. What X was going through before he was able to kill the doctor and Chelsey, we have no idea. But his revenge was a goddamn performance. We need to keep checking deeper into Kane's inner circle, if possible. Maybe something will turn up on the unknown woman, but Heath, Numbers is our best chance right now."

Spade's fingers clenched, the desk's edge biting his palms as he squeezed. For now, Kane would remain untouchable as always. Whoever the woman was, fuck her. But X was real. Corbin a possible hit, and Numbers the trap. "Alright." His voice was hard. "Let's stake out Numbers tonight. Ramirez is our eyes. Chain Fucking Willis for that matter, though he's rarely around at any crime scene. We ID X, grab him before he gets to Corbin. Letter perfect."

Hayes scoffed and grabbed her jacket, already moving. Her partner's direction sounded simple, but she knew, with this X fella, it would be anything but.

They crossed through the bullpen and passed a group of cops too drained to notice. The air outside was a humid fist, thick with asphalt and fear. Houston was a city on a razor's edge, the towers' fall a fresh scar, every odd movement a possible threat. Spade's Crown Vic growled to life, Hayes behind the wheel, her hands steady, her eyes locked on the road.

"Carmen...you think this shit will all go down tonight?"

Hayes stopped and shrugged. "Probably."

"Thought so. We'll get there early. See what is what. Numbers is a fuckshow. Pure chaos."

Hayes nodded, waiting for him to say something she didn't know.

"Drunks. Junkies. Pimps. Whores. Dealers. Every freak nutcase all gathered as a single neon mob scene. Believe this, partner: X will use that chaos. He breathes it as normal air, I feel it."

Hayes felt it, too. She never wanted to show any weakness to Spade. During all the years they had been together, one awful scene after the other, Carmen Hayes always held herself together, and she would do the same with this case. But for her, this was a new feeling she never had with other cases: whoever X was, he scared the hell out of her.

***

On that first Tuesday of October, the burgundy Chrysler Concorde idled in a shadowed alley off Montrose, its engine a low growl under Houston's humid night—though cooler—the air thick with asphalt, stale whiskey, and the sour rot of uncollected trash. The city's post-9/11 paranoia was a fever, pulsing beneath the flickering neon of Numbers' sign nearby.

Rex Brody sat motionless, carefully thinking through everything that had happened in a month's time and where he was now.

He had purchased a new black leather jacket that fitted as a second skin. His hands on the wheel, fingers steady, itching for the steel he didn't yet own. He had the Spyderco folder, a police folding knife, but he knew it wouldn't be enough down the long road now laid out before him. He now owned a Randall hunting knife, hand-forged, razor-sharp, $400 at the sports outlet, its steel a killer's promise, and the Ruger .22 target pistol, octagon-barreled, $350, for precision shots when things would get heated.

Both weapons he'd purchased a few days after he knew he was being tailed by police, the day he met Dana and Samantha Sutherland. It was easy enough to lose the cops' interest that day as he kept things simple and calm. He knew it was Spade and Hayes on his tail, as he'd seen them following him. They probably knew it, too, so the dance had begun. The day he purchased the weapons was also the day Mister Boogie decided on the fate of Leslie Ames and Tina Parker.

The orb, locked in the glove box, hummed. At least Brody thought it did. Mister Boogie knew it was a dark current surging through his veins, a hymn of blood and purpose. Alice in Chains was playing low, "Man in the Box," Layne Staley's ragged voice grumbling about being buried in shit, raw and restless, vibrating through the car's steel frame.

Brody and Mister Boogie's eyes were blackened, staring inward, dual minds a labyrinth of kills but not trophies. The mayhem thus far replayed: Dr. Manson's estate, a cathedral of fire and shattered glass; Bingham's stuffed corpse, her neck slashed with Manson's kitchen blade; Armstrong's battered body, broken in the library's sterile hush. Now it was James Corbin who needed removal from Samatha Sutherland and her mother's worries. Maybe doing it as Mister Boogie on Numbers' dance floor. Or something. Brody hadn't figured it out completely.

Each kill was a step toward a new ritual he felt in his bones, a bloodline's awakening, guided by the orb's pulse and the witches' rhymes at The Serpent's Veil. Leslie Ames and Tina Parker with their toxic beauty and clownish stupidity would be the first real trophies, the first he'd claim for the orb's altar. He would pull from their fear a nectar to feed his legacy.

Killing Kelly Manson was survival, a monster undone by Brody's rage and skill. The surgeon's torture room, its walls slick with despair, was a crucible in sheeted plastic where Brody's kitchen knife trick ripped through Manson's arrogance. Chelsey Bingham was collateral damage, her wrists and neck opened, her body staged in the freezer as a taunt to the cops. She was also the catalyst for Mister Boogie's grand entrance.

The explosion that razed the estate was Mister Boogie's

cleansing fire. Armstrong's death was simply an annoyance but her body a scream against Utah CPS that tore him from Emma and Don.

Corbin was a predator like Manson, a stalker who dared touch Samantha. Brody took Corbin's name the moment Dana said it, promptly following him. Just as Samantha said, the stalker's sweet spot was Club Numbers. In just a few short follows, Brody learned the stalker's habits: the way he swayed drunk, hands groping, cheap cologne masking his filth, eyes darting when searching for who or whatever it was he needed. Corbin's fear would be exquisite, his life almost a trophy, his death a vow on the dance floor. It was planned for the first Tuesday night in October, when the club's chaos would hide Rex's blade. He would use the Spyderco. The Randall knife and Ruger .22 he'd locked in the hotel's safe for future use. Whatever went down at Numbers, he was perfectly confident he would get out with his hands and the Spyderco folder.

Brody exhaled, tapping his fingers on the steering wheel, the car's air heavy with leather and his own fine musk. Mister Boogie stirred, not a separate self but a fused essence, born in Dr. Kelly Manson's personal hell with a single purpose: to hunt, to kill, to claim trophies for a legacy that Brody wondered was all linked back to Conrad Ellison's letter of claim to Jack the Ripper and their bloodline. The orb was his guide, its living surface reflecting truths: his father's abandonment; Aunt Anna's agenda of betrayal; CPS's cold hands; Emma's and Don's fractured faces in that sterile room; the years of training in Cambodia; The Serpent's Veil and its witchery.

Brody began to feel a new power growing from within, a bloodline older than Houston's decay, surging with every kill, urging him toward Leslie and Tina, their beauty a canvas for his ritual. But what would the ritual become and how was he to get away with it? He thought about Conrad Ellison again and the historical letter, wondered what he would do in such a situation. What would Jack the Ripper do? Mister Boogie smiled; he knew he had to pin such kills on someone the cops would never suspect.

In the immediate aftermath of 9/11, along with his Urwerk, Brody gave the vagrant Denison a burner phone just in case he needed to find him. Spade and Hayes had spoken to Denison, and God knows what was actually said. It was the perfect setup. If Brody setup Denison, Spade and Hayes would have no idea what in Christ's name was going on. At least long enough for Brody's next move. He took out a small notepad from one of the hotels he'd been staying at and made note to call Denison after the Corbin affair was finished. Everything was a work in progress.

Brody's money fueled his hunt, the healthy stacks of cash (on top of the $25k he had in the wall safe) from the recent Houston tech contracts, cybersecurity gigs for some of Houston's pre-IPO startups. He purchased a nice briefcase for the cash he kept locked away at the various ritzy Houston spots, the St. Regis, Four Seasons, etc.

Since the Kelly Manson dance, Brody drifted between the hotel life but remained rigid in his daily routine, treating each room like a sterile cocoon, marble floors and silk sheets a contrast to the blood he would continue spilling. The money was freedom: the Chrysler, rented in cash; burner phones; tailored jackets; whatever was needed.

His daily rituals kept him lethal, a predator's discipline learned from his broken childhood to his martial arts mastery in Cambodia. Each morning began at 4:30 a.m. with the orb placed on the bed. He would stare into the bathroom mirror to admire his hardened and chiseled physique. He started with push-ups, squats, ab crunches—200 each, no rest—keeping muscles lean and coiled. Then, shadowboxing, quick, yet perfect shots placed exactly where needed, followed by weights and conditioning. Next were 2-minute sprints as fast as he could handle, 8 to 12 sprints with 30 second rests in between. He would finish with knife drills, his Spyderco blade flashing, then practicing with the Randall's weight, its balance, preparing for its steel.

Breakfast was black coffee and raw eggs, ordered to the room, fuel for the hunt. He'd sit at a glass table, the orb before him, rolling it between his palms, its hum clarifying his thoughts. Lunch was sushi or chicken. Dinners were steak and eggs. Over the past weeks he also connected with plenty of Houston's seedy types for coke and pills that became as much a part of his routine as shadowboxing. Mister Boogie loved them.

Most mornings, he split the time between studying Numbers' layout and what specials the nightclub offered each night, then memorizing the routines of Leslie Ames and Tina Parker. Within a week, he knew the dance floor's chaos, the bar's shadows, all the exits for escape. Corbin was there like clockwork on Tuesdays, Thursdays, and Fridays, drunk on arrival, groping men and women, his arrogance a beacon. On the night planned, the first Tuesday of October, Mister Boogie believed Corbin would slip in somewhere around 11:00 p.m. Brody would blend into the techno haze, find Corbin on the dance floor and go from there. By this time, Brody was also quite familiar with Leslie and Tina. Though their lifestyles were far more unpredictable than Corbin's, learning their routines had become one of his daily pleasures.

Afternoons consisted of more training. Running down Houston's humid streets, shoes pounding, senses drinking the city's flamboyance of graffiti, hookers' eyes, sirens. At times when he felt no eyes on him, he would climb abandoned buildings, fingers gripping rusted fire escapes, agility honed for the hunt. In a Fifth Ward gym one late night he even sparred with ex-cons, toying with them, his void-like eyes unnerving even the hardest men.

Evenings were for reconnaissance, cruising in the Chrysler, music blasting, casing Numbers, watching for Corbin; casing Leslie and Tina, deciding who was first and which one reminded him of his Aunt Anna most. Probably Leslie. But that was for later.

One after-hours night he went back to The Serpent's Veil, its memory a fever. The club was a labyrinth of incense and sin, Adrian Kane's shadow a weight on Brody's chest. Kane wasn't there that night, nor the witches or the woman Kane was carrying that first night, but he knew they were part of club's wholeness and would be there when the time was right.

The orb began to feel somewhat like a 360-degree map. Staring into it became as much habitual as the coke and speed, its surface reflecting his kills: Manson's screams, Bingham's gasps, the crack of Armstrong's bones, Corbin's future whimpers. It sometimes whispered of Emma and Don, though he had no idea what became of them. He knew he failed them, the CPS tearing them apart, Aunt Anna's smile a slit across his throat. The kills were for them, a reckoning for the system, for their father's neglect. Leslie and Tina and their tight asses were more atonement, their beauty a mirror to Emma's, their fear trophies to honor her. Don's, too.

Brody kept idling that night, planning Corbin's takedown, with the Chrysler's stereo shifting to Rage Against the Machine's "Killing in the Name," Zack de la Rocha's voice a war cry. Mister Boogie's lips curled, a smile not human. He stirred with a thirst for murder that felt insatiable.

The more Brody thought about Leslie Ames and Tina Parker and their incompetence that masked a hidden agenda, the less Mister Boogie regarded their life as anything meaningful. The sarcastic tones of their voices, the false giggles, the pretense of knowing the answers to everything of which they knew nothing. Dual reflections of Aunt Anna; all three reflections to soon be shattered.

Brody opened the glove box; the orb's hum spiked. He rolled it in his palm, its surface reflecting his empty eyes. He could feel Detectives Spade and Hayes hunting him, their

Crown Vic always on the prowl, but Brody knew he could shake them. He did it before, no doubt he could do it again.

It was game time. He took a few deep breaths, put the orb back in the glove box, killed the stereo then the engine, stepped out, boots hitting pavement, jacket catching the streetlamp's glare. Rex Brody walked towards the entrance of Numbers with a steady pace. Mister Boogie smiled within, a vow of blood and rituals.

***

Emma Madalin slipped into Numbers as comfortably as she did her fitted leather skirt, the matching leather jacket just as tight against her sculpted tits, obsidian blade strapped sideways to her belt. Numbers' chaos hit her like a fist: techno pounding, lights slashing, the air thick with sweat, decadence, and the faint metallic tang of blood. Her eyes, sharpened since the coma, cut through the haze, scanning for Rex. Chain Willis's call had been urgent, his voice low, tight. "Corbin's there now. It's going down." Emma knew it was the night she'd find him, after years of following his shadow.

She moved along the wall, her boots smack-clicking on the sticky floor, her gaze fully alert with a preternatural edge, a gift from the accident that had shattered her and remade her. The crowd was a blur of writhing bodies, their faces smeared by the strobe's flicker, but her eyes locked on a figure slumped against the wall near the bar. From everything Chain had told her, it looked like Corbin. Her breath caught, her pulse spiked, a raw jolt of recognition. She thought she could see blood seeping through his shirt, Corbin's eyes glassy, dying. Had to be Rex's work, a signature of his rage and skill. But whatever happened had to have just happened. She scanned the dance floor, her heart a storm.

He was moving through the crowd when she saw him.

Part of him was dancing while the other part was looking around to make sure he wasn't spotted. No one else could have detected it, his moves too polished. Perhaps the police, but she doubted they were there, Chain would have known something and given her the heads up. At least that was part of what she was paying him to do.

She slowly swallowed the sudden lump in her throat. Following her brother all these years had forced distance between them that became so normalized that the reality of being with him again seemed too much. But there he was, lean and strong, broad shouldered, his leather jacket a second skin, his eyes cavities that drank the light.

Emma's chest ached, a raw, visceral thing, love and pain braided tight, a wound that had never healed. Of course he was different. Hard. Sharp. He looked like a weapon, but he was still Rex, the boy who'd bled for her and Don, who'd shielded them from the wreck of their father, from the CPS's cold grip. Until he couldn't.

His face was weathered for so young, carved by years of rage, his jaw a hard line, but those eyes, those voids, were the same, haunted and protective, mirrors of her own. She moved toward him, through the crowd, moving to the music's pulsing instrumentals, matching her feet to the movements of the strobe lights, drawn to him, entirely unsure what to say or how to say it. If she could just reach him. She pushed herself to move more quickly, more urgently, her mind racing back to the what-if-the-police-were-watching paranoia. She moved fast enough to reach out to his shoulder, grabbing it. Of course, he instantly reacted, and she feared he would break her wrist and elbow as his hand cupped hers in a pivoted moved. But he was easily fast enough to change reactions as his eyes locked onto hers.

"Rex." At first, she thought she lip synced it.

The club's chaos pressed in, the techno music pounding the walls and floors mercilessly, the crowd a mindless tide, their shouts and laughter drowning her voice. Emma's mind flashed to the woman at Houston's Bar and Grille, her striking eyes bending light, her velvet voice coiling around her thoughts. *He's picking out his next trophy. Or trophies.* The woman had known Rex, had seen the darkness in him, in herself, their bloodline a thread of ancient power, a legacy of blood and secrets. Emma felt it now, a pull stronger than blood, a promise of ruin and reunion as her boots had cut through the crowd and her eyes now locked on her brother.

The crowd was too drugged to resist or feel irritation, thousands of eyes glassy, unseeing, but Emma had made it through to find her brother. A cascade of thoughts from her raw and bloody truck rollover in Lake City to the CPS room with their Aunt Anna's cold smile from the day she and Rex and Don were torn apart to this very moment fused together at once. She felt simultaneously unsure and thrilled, weightless, and watching her own ruin, as those moments she saw her own body in the hospital bed where the whispers of power echoed in the dark, reading the surgeon's notes calling her "strangely dark."

After years of cutting into Lake City and Houston's underbellies, through dealers and pimps to rapes and syringes, here she was now in Numbers looking into her brother's haunted eyes.

Both of their instincts screamed. Brody was here for a fresh kill and her only thought was to shield him from anything that would want to catch him. He couldn't take his eyes off her, nor would she think to let him. Her feelings moved to hyper speed, *The Houston Post* article, the murders, Detectives Spade and Hayes's press conference, their voices tight with urgency. Rex was being hunted, but Emma found him first to protect him, as he'd protected her. She grabbed his hand, which felt like a block of wood, but when he held hers back, she knew he wouldn't hurt her. His mouth was barely open. When she thought he wouldn't speak, his hand tightened.

"We need to get out of here." His voice was filled with

authority and purpose. As soon as he said it, she saw his eyes suddenly dart toward the far side of the dance floor. Something inside of him instantly changed into someone she'd never seen. Nor ever wanted to.

***

When Brody walked into the Numbers that first Tuesday in October of 2001, it was no different than the other times he'd been to scope out James Corbin. A writhing string of neon lights that slashed through Houston's inner core, its sign spitting red and violet into the humid night. The club's techno beat was a living beast, a relentless pulse that shook the walls, the floor, the souls of everyone inside, rattling teeth and bones. Strobe lights hacked through the darkness, slashing across sweat-drenched bodies in jagged bursts—blue, red, white—turning the writhing crowd into a fevered mosaic of desperation and lust. The air was a swamp, thick with cheap perfume, spilled whiskey, and a sour, metallic tang, like fear gone septic.

Houston's freaks and lost souls flocked here to drown with the country on the verge of ripping apart at the seams. Houston's underbelly was a slaughterhouse primed for its new butcher.

Brody moved through the chaos with laser focus, the collar turned up on the leather jacket that caught the strobe's flicker. His normally ice-blue eyes were black saucers that swallowed light, reflecting nothing but hunger. Coiled, his movements were too precise, too deliberate for the drunken haze around him, each step calculated and polished.

The dance floor was a sea of flesh, bodies grinding to the pulsing house tech music that was part of the club's notorious trance-like qualities: endless instrumentals that fused together as a single sound that was alive enough to see.

Mister Boogie spotted Corbin dead center on the spacious downstairs dance floor, a skinny, sharp-faced weasel, his white silk shirt unbuttoned to his navel under a powder-blue silk suit jacket, sweat shimmering on his pale chest. He swayed with a blonde, his hands groping her ass, his grin a predator's leer, oblivious to the monster circling him. Corbin was sloppy drunk, his laughter a grating bark that Brody heard over the music. Mister Boogie could hear it as a sound that made his fingers twitch, itching for the Spyderco. He watched from the edge of one of Numbers' many long wood and metal railings, his lips ravenously curling.

He wove through the crowd, his boots clicking in rhythm to the music, the club's heat pressing against him like a lover's fever. The air was heavy, saturated with the sour stink of sweat, high-end umbrella drinks, and the faint chemical burn of hard liquors. Faces blurred past—painted lips, glassy eyes, bodies lost in MDMA zooms—but Brody never lost focus.

He stopped a few feet away, close enough to smell the stalker's cheap cologne, a cloying mask over the whiskey on his breath, making Brody's gut coil with disgust. As the music surged, Mister Boogie could feel his blood moving in perfect synchronicity to every pulse of the dance floor to the strobe lights. His heart became a dark rhythm that drowned out the world.

Brody knew Corbin's awareness was gone; Mister Boogie could strike him down deaf and dumb right then and there. But where would be the sport in such a strike? He continued watching. Patiently.

The air thickened, the reek of sweat and liquor even more so. Yet there was also something older, something primal that clung to the club's walls and dance floors, like the strobe lights were burning through it. Brody watched Corbin's eyes, hazed over with bravado, flicker with the first cracks of fear, his awareness eroded, a lamb too drunk to sense the wolf circling. Brody could snap his neck with a twist so effortless it would go unnoticed as a simple dance move amongst thousands, let his body crumple like a ragdoll in the strobe-lit chaos.

No, Mister Boogie needed to savor it, to peel back Corbin's soul layer by layer until the man's fear was a raw, bleeding thing. He continued his circling, his body feeling the power of the house tech music.

Before preying on Corbin, Brody had slammed home several lines of coke in one of the club's upstairs men's rooms with fellow freaks. He remembered how he felt when he turned up the heat at Fitzgerald's as the crowd there had soon stopped what they were doing to fixate on him as he circled Chelsey Bingham. Now was not the time for such a dance he had blessed Chelsey with. Instead, he gracefully inched his way close enough to Corbin almost shoulder to shoulder, then slammed his shoulder into the stalker hard enough to dislocated it.

Corbin's pale face lost any last remaining trace of color as he stumbled, his grin twisting into one of sudden breathless pain, his breath a sour gust of whiskey and desperation. Clearly in shock, he managed to turn toward Brody, his mouth agape, speechless. The blonde at his side, all glitter and instinct, sensed the sudden shift, like a deer catching a whiff of blood, looked at Corbin's limpness, wondering what had just happened.

Brody's eyes burned into her, twin pits of black fire, unblinking, drinking the tremor in Corbin's stance, but focused on the blonde. He moved his body in a slower dance around her, close enough to smell her sweat. She couldn't take her eyes off him as he grasped her waist and pulled her to his body. Her head arched, her eyes locked onto his, she knew whoever was holding her felt like she was in a vice grip, fearing her ribs and spine would break.

"Time to dance away, little Blondie. Your heart of glass calls elsewhere." The blonde wanted to say something back, but the moment Brody released her she felt sudden relief she wasn't crushed. With her best effort, she gained composure and shifted away into the writhing crowd.

Brody shifted away from her and back to Corbin in a single move, smelling fear coming from his pours as much as drink, his breath a slow, scalding hiss against the man's ear. He could see that Corbin's injury was still something the stalker hadn't fully comprehended, other than it was severe.

"You love the chase, don't you, Jimmy?" Mister Boogie's voice was a metallic slash wrapped in silk, each syllable carving deeper, splitting skin, spilling dread. "You love her fear, the way it chokes her. Makes her yours. Young Samantha Sutherland. Hissing into her innocence the cunting of her you'd counted on." The words spewed with venom, and Corbin's bravado crumbled, his eyes darting like a trapped rat's.

He stammered, stepping back in winced pain, but the crowd surged, a suffocating wall of flesh and heat, their laughter a mindless drone, their bodies a prison of grinding limbs. The strobes bled purples and reds and deep slashing blues, painting Corbin's face in gore-light, his sweat like Brody had thrown hot oil all over him, his fear on hyper-speed with no drug to stop it.

Mister Boogie's smile split wide, a crescent of teeth, sharp and slow. He swayed, his body mocking the club's rhythm, each movement liquid, serpentine, a dance of coiled menace. "Samantha Sutherland, little ripe-for-the-taking-Sammy. Such a naughty boy." His tone purred, lips grazing Corbin's ear, close enough to taste the sour bloom of pure terror. "You thought your dipstick would be inside her, then someone like me tosses a wrench right into the gearshift."

The stalker's face collapsed, more color drained, if possible, his eyes hollow, searching for a gap in the crowd's cage, his breath shallow and ragged. The air grew heavier, the club's haze curling like smoke from a pyre, the crowd's pulse a heartbeat of oblivious chaos. He opened his mouth but couldn't speak, his face spilling the words of retreat. He felt like he had been hit with piece of steel pipe. Still, with a last thread of dignity, he mouthed something like, "I don't know what you're talking about," but knowing exactly the opposite. He raised his good arm and placed it on Brody's shoulder as a gesture of good will. The moment Brody felt it land, he used grace and dance laced with a Judo Master's pivot all at once, grabbing Corbin's wrist and elbow in a violent and instant twist that destroyed the bones and ligaments.

The move was so quick and effortless, everyone dancing around them thought it was nothing more than friendly bump and grind. Brody yanked Corbin close, forcing him into a grotesque waltz, their bodies pressed tight, Brody's breath a furnace on Corbin's neck. "Here I am, James, running over your lane, and all you can do is let all the wheels fall off the bus." The crowd didn't see, didn't care, their eyes glazed, their minds drowned in neon and noise, but Corbin's world shrank to Brody's grip, to an emptiness in his eyes that Corbin had never thought possible in another man.

His broken bones attempted a pathetic recoil, but the music devoured his plea, the crowd in utter meltdown mode, indifferent to his or any others' unraveling. Brody spun him, brutal and swift, wrenching Corbin's arm behind his back, his other hand clamping the man's throat, fingers digging into soft flesh, squeezing until Mister Boogie knew the Adam's Apple was crushed. The strobes flashed—red, black, red—fracturing Corbin's terror in jagged bursts, his sweat a slick sheen, his pulse dying under Brody's grip.

"No begging tonight." Brody's voice a vigilante's vow dipped in blood, each word a lethal slash. His hand slipped behind to his jeans back pocket fingers curling around the Spyderco, pulling it, opening it, moving it to Corbin's back and driving it deep through his spine in a single move. Everything was perfectly hidden by the crowd's chaos, the metal's plunge into the back and spine a promising hiss of ruin. Corbin froze, a sob breaking free, his body shaking, his bravado a distant memory, reduced to a mewling human slug; only Brody's strength kept it from dumping to the dance floor.

Mister Boogie's eyes flared, the strobe catching them, turning them into twin voids, endless, merciless, like gateways to a hell tunneled through just for Corbin. Brody drove the knife upward again, a single, fluid thrust deeper into the side of the ribcage. Corbin's body jerked, a puppet with cut strings, his eyes wide, a silent scream locked in his throat. Blood bloomed, hot and thick, soaking his shirt, but the club's shadows and the strobe's frenzy hid it, a secret shared only by hunter and hunted.

Mister Boogie held him, swaying, their bodies locked in a grotesque embrace, the crowd blind to the death in their midst. The blade slid free, clean and silent, wiped on Corbin's back with a surgeon's care, then back into Brody's jeans pocket. He leaned in, lips brushing Corbin's ear, his voice a final requiem. "For Samantha." With that, he moved Corbin's dying body, guiding it to slump against a wall near the bar, the shadows swallowing the husk. The crowd parted, mindless, their laughter a hollow echo, their eyes blind to the predator slipping back into their tide. No had noticed a thing.

Or so Brody thought.

***

Detectives Spade and Hayes pushed through Numbers' entrance, badges tucked away, handguns heavy under their jackets, steel anchors in the chaos. The club was a sensory assault, a techno-physical force with a writhing beast of a crowd that reeked of desperation and fear, a city fueled with rage. Spade's eyes scanned the chaos, his gut tight, the weight of the case: Jennifer Armstrong's precise murder, Chelsey Bingham's frozen corpse, Dr. Kelly Manson's estate blasted to rubble—all of it pressing harder than the Glock at his hip. Hayes was a step ahead, her jaw set, her intensity a live wire, her dark eyes burning with the hunt, her hands steady despite the ghosts that haunted her.

"Ramirez's at the upstairs bar. No sign of Willis, of course." Hayes's voice was as loud as possible over the house music, cutting through the noise like a blade, sharp and unyielding. "Our guy's close. I feel it."

Spade nodded, his hand brushing his holster, the steel grounding him, a cold reminder of the high stakes. The sports outlet's tip, the burgundy Chrysler, Dana Sutherland's statement, the small facets of detail surrounding Emma Madalin, Denison, Kelly Manson—all of it pointed here, Numbers, to X, their killer, a shadow from Lake City possibly tied to Madalin and the CPS case that haunted their files. This time the mark was Corbin, Numbers the trap, a powder keg ready to blow. There were also the ties to Chain Willis and The Serpent's Veil, a knot they couldn't untangle, a wildcard that chilled Spade's blood. "If Madalin's here, we've got a problem."

Hayes's eyes flashed, her frustration raw, a fire that burned through her fatigue. "We've got to find X first, and that starts with Corbin. Then we deal with her. Think we should split up?"

Spade hesitated as his eyes scanned everything in Numbers, doing an initial check for anything that seemed out of place in a sea of chaos. He adjusted his Motorola single-ear earpiece and signaled Hayes to do the same.

"Yeah-yeah, stay sharp and connected."

Hayes nodded and moved toward the upstairs bar area; Spade moved down the staircase to the lower level, their movements practiced, instinctive. Spade's gaze mapped the crowd, searching for the predator gait of their Suspect X, his void-like eyes, the man who'd left a trail of bodies and carnage. The strobe lights made things difficult, bodies a blur of motion, every club patron's face smeared by liquor and lust, but something drew his attention. A man dressed in a sweat-soaked silk suit was slumped against a wall near the bar.

He adjusted his earpiece to make sure it was tight.

"Hayes...Hayes..."

"Hear you loud and clear."

"I've got something down here. Can you see me?"

She moved toward the upstairs balcony, her trained eyes catching her partner moving in and out of the writhing bodies.

"Copy. I got you."

He didn't need to look up to find her; he knew she had his back regardless of what was going on and what could go down.

"Check the west wall of the bar area. Power blue suit, open shirt. Something's wrong with him."

His gut twisted the closer he approached the slumped man.

Corbin.

Spade pushed through the crowd more urgently; grinding bodies parted reluctantly, their eyes glassy, unseeing. When he knelt next to Corbin, he knew it was only his body. He pressed his fingers to the man's neck, searching for a pulse. Nothing. Blood had pooled from the sides Corbin's shirt and jacket, dark and viscous, having flowed from the fatal wounds in his back.

"Fuck."

Hand on his Glock, he looked up toward where Hayes was keeping eye on him; his eyes then darted around the crowd, heart pounding like a war drum. They were too late for Corbin, but what had happened to him had just happened; the likelihood was high that Suspect X was still in the club.

As soon as he stood, breath ragged, Spade's eye caught a possible glimpse of their suspect, a patron who was moving like a panther, fitted leather jacket a dark slash. The man had his eyes locked on something, someone, his posture coiled, lethal. Spade followed his gaze and froze, his blood icing over. Emma Madalin, her presence unmistakable, her eyes burning with something primal, raw, and dangerous, her face wet with tears, her lips moving, forming a name.

"Hayes. Get the fuck down here."

***

Hayes caught what her partner was focused on: Emma Madalin dressed to the nines with her own eyes locked on someone moving toward her with a striking contrast of grace and focus compared to the psychedelic dance floor. She couldn't tell who it was but saw that Spade's eyes were on him. She turned and moved swiftly through the upstairs crowd to Ramirez's place at the bar, in his plainclothes, broad frame hunched over a soda, his eyes scanning the crowd, jaw tight.

"Anything?" His voice was low but strong enough over the noise, hand hovering near his Smith & Wesson .357 revolver, Ramirez's handgun choice, deadly accurate with the stopping power to bring down grizzly.

"We gotta move. Now."

Ramirez knew Hayes's urgency and needed no further questioning but still shook his head in frustration. "I saw Corbin on the dance floor, groping some girl. Lost him in the crowd. No sign of the Chrysler guy."

Hayes's jaw clenched in equal frustration. "Yeah, well, he's down there, Ramirez, and I don't think he's groping or dancing any longer. Spade's with him and has eyes on the suspect as well as Emma Madalin. X is not so fucking invisible after all."

As she turned to lead Ramirez down the stairs toward Spade, her eyes caught more clarity of the figure in a fitted leather jacket, catching the strobe's flickers. She recognized his coiled-like posture from the sports outlet's tape, lethal, a predator in motion.

She moved faster, jolting her head for Ramirez to step up his game. Her boots cut through the crowd to the staircase, heart a steady rhythm despite the chaos. Then she saw Emma, stepping toward X, her face a mask of raw emotion, her eyes wet, her body locked in paralysis.

Hayes was seeing something deeper than fear from Madalin; it was more love mixed with anguish. A reunion. Her gut screamed danger, her hand tightening on her gun, but before she could react, Suspect X launched himself toward Ramirez in a series of moves that stunned Hayes and the immediate crowd into awe.

It was an eruption in the cacophony of shouts and dancing feet as the tension on the dance floor was peaking. Hayes could see Ramirez was struggling through the crowd, bodies locked in a chaotic dance of resistance and control.

From her periphery and under the harsh fluorescent lights, X charged forward with the precision of a predator. His approach was a blur of motion, his boots tapping a dance on the tiled floor.

As he closed the distance on Ramirez, X suddenly launched himself into the air with a burst of explosive energy. His body twisted and contorted in mid-flight, executing a series of aerial maneuvers that defied gravity. His legs scissor-crossed through the air, a symphony of motion that was both beautiful and terrifying, the first leg swinging high, arcing Ramirez's head, while the other leg snaked around, wrapping itself around Ramirez's neck and shoulder in a vice-like grip of a perfect Figure-4 submission hold.

X's momentum carried them both downward in a corkscrew yet controlled descent. Ramirez was yanked off balance, his feet leaving the ground as X's weight and leverage pulled them into a devastating takedown. Both men hit the ground with a thud that resonated through the dance space, X landing solid and upright with cat-like agility, his feet planted firmly on either side of Ramirez, now helpless on his back.

Without missing a beat, X delivered a series of precise

strikes to Ramirez's neck and face. Each blow calculated, a testament to years of lethal training, aimed to maim and kill the undercover cop.

The crowd froze in a mix of awe and terror, watching Suspect X's movements in a blur of efficiency and power, a ballet of violence and control that left the crowd and Hayes in shock.

But Hayes pushed on, snapping herself to, eyes on the acrobatic killer, slowly pulling her gun, pushing her mind to clear what had just taken place. For the first time since her rookie year as a Houston beat cop, she felt completely overwhelmed when she heard Spade's voice rage through the suddenly quieting chaos.

"Freeze motherfucker!"

Hayes thanked God Spade had seen their suspect's aerial assault. She knew Ramirez was either dead or would be in the hospital for the rest of his life.

The moment her eyes captured what Spade was doing, she focused back on Suspect X, both hands on the Glock with direct aim to his head, as in the next split second, X pulled Ramirez's .357, fired off a round toward Spade, hitting him dead in the chest, knocking her partner to the ground, then X had his sights on Hayes, all in a single move.

She could hear the stunned and frightened murmurs of the crowd over the house music, which seemed to hammer with even more intensity.

Hayes had no idea what to think other than everything was going south faster than Suspect X's sudden command over the entire stakeout. Her partner was down, though she knew Spade had on his body armor vest. Their supporting officer was most likely dead. She was alone and clearly outmatched but had to press on, her heart racing, her breathing erratic.

"You've made your point, get off him." It was the best she could muster as she held the Glock tight and steady.

Instead of obeying the command, Suspect X remained

on the mount position on top of Ramirez's body, placing the barrel of the .357 on Ramirez's forehead and pulled the hammer back. "How about I blow this copper's brains all over the dance floor."

Hayes tightened her grip on the Glock while moving her legs a few inches apart for a stronger stance. In her peripheral she saw Spade begin to recover, shifting his body to one elbow. In yet another of the evening's surprises, Emma Madalin—gripping some kind of knife—entered the picture with a move toward Spade to slash his neck.

Hayes took the risk of turning her gun to save Spade's life, fired off a round, aiming for Emma's body, then paid the price as Suspect X fired two rounds of the .357 into Hayes's chest and thigh. The crowd erupted, screams piercing the music, bodies shoving, panic spreading like a wildfire of fear. She knew her own body armor saved her life but also felt the leg shatter as she tumbled to the floor. Running on pure adrenalin she managed to brace herself on her elbows as she fell, keeping the Glock in one hand, though it was useless to attempt another shot.

X jumped to his feet and was with Emma in seconds, effortlessly lifting her and cradling her in his arms as he sprinted to the club's exit, bulldozing through the crowd while Hayes helplessly watched them escape, her exhausted eyes rolling toward her partner, praying he was still alive. Hayes's eyes then rolled back to Ramirez's body. Knowing he was dead, she wished she would have said something different to the killer when he'd placed the barrel to Ramirez's head, but what could she have said in a hopeful night that had turned catastrophic.

***

Brody loomed, Emma in his arms, his face a mask of feral intent, the orb's hum now a distant roar in his mind, urging blood, more blood, a ritual unfinished. He was a void, a force, the killer who'd blown to hell The Bone Break Killer's estate and Brody's own Porsche, killing a cop, who'd broken Armstrong's body and stuffed Bingham's slit corpse, who now had Emma in his arms.

***

When Emma first lip-synced his name, it was a silent scream that tore through the club, silencing the chaos, freezing time. She had pushed through the crowd, her leather jacket slick with sweat, her obsidian blade at her side, her eyes locked on him. Now she was in her brother's arms, still holding her knife, something that made Mister Boogie grin.

Ramirez was dead. Mister Boogie made certain of that. Brody knew his second shot at Spade landed as the first, striking home into a body armor vest, but no matter. The shots he placed into Hayes probably didn't kill her, but both detectives would be MIA for at least a few days, buying him some time.

The club was a riot, screams echoing, bodies fleeing, the strobe lights flashing red, blue, red, painting the carnage in fractured bursts.

Brody looked into his sister's eyes. "Emma." His voice a fracture, raw and broken, his mind drowned by the flood of memory—Lake City, their father's neglect, the CPS's cold hands tearing them apart, the sterile room, Aunt Anna's smile, the day they lost everything. She was here, real, her face sharp and fierce even through injury, her eyes mirrors of his own, haunted, changed, but still Emma, his flesh and blood.

She locked her eyes on his. "I've been chasing you." Her voice cracking, each word a confession. "All these years, Rex. I never stopped."

Brody's face twisted, pain and rage and love colliding, his breath ragged, his eyes swelling, a flicker of the boy he'd been. "You shouldn't be here." His voice was soft, a boy's voice, the one that had promised to protect her, to bleed for her, to keep her safe. "How did you find me here? Never mind that."

She kept her eyes locked on his. "You're not alone anymore. You never were. I've been with you, every step, in the shadows."

Brody looked up into the Houston night while slowly shaking his head.

The club had turned into a war zone, bodies shoving, lights flashing, screams echoing, but for them it was two broken pieces of a shattered family, standing in a pool of blood and chaos, the world reduced to their breath, their pulse.

The moment Brody had eyed Hayes and the undercover cop, he took action to finish them. Though he knew Spade was close, it was icing on a blood-lusted cake when Spade popped in at the wrong time.

Emma now clung to him, her tears hot against his chest, her body shaking with not only the pain of being shot, but the weight of years lost, years stolen. "I'm not losing you again, Rex. Not to them, not to anyone, not to anything."

Emma's mind flooded with memories: Rex bandaging her cuts, his voice promising they'd stay together, always; the CPS room, the cold walls, Aunt Anna's mock smile, the day they were torn apart; the accident, her truck rolling, her body broken, her soul rising, whispers of power in the dark. She saw Rex's childhood eyes, hard but protective, the boy who'd kill for her, who'd become the man before her, a killer, a force, her brother.

She felt her brother's iron physical strength as she searched his eyes. "You've changed."

He looked down to her again, the strange sharpness in her eyes, a mirror of his own. "Yeah. You're not the girl I left, either. It's time to move. My car's close...save your strength. Need to remove that bullet, but we can't go to a hospital."

Emma tightened her grip around Brody, her lips curled.

"I've got people here, let's get to your car and I can make some calls. I don't think the bullet broke anything. I've been through worse, believe me."

Rex's eyes burned, a flicker of pride, of recognition, a spark of the boy who'd loved her. "Okay. Hold on tight. I'm moving fast."

***

The air in Numbers was a choking haze, thick with the iron reek of blood, spilled cocktails, and the acrid sting of panic. The techno beat was still pounding, a relentless war drum, before Spade fired a few rounds of his Glock into the ceiling and lights before yelling at Hayes to keep from moving and stay where she lay; he had no idea how badly she was hurt nor the strength in himself, just yet, to manage her. The rounds fired off were a quick attempt to settle a crowd that had fractured into a screaming, shoving mass, bodies clawing for the exits like scurrying rats. Strobe lights slashed through the dark, painting the chaos in fractured bursts, turning the dance floor into a slaughterhouse tableau.

Spade signaled for one of the barkeeps and servers for some assistance as he called everything into dispatch, then looked over to James Corbin's corpse slumped against the west wall, his blood a dark pool seeping into the sticky floor, his glassy eyes staring at nothing. Ramirez's body lay sprawled out, lifeless, his .357 gone.

Numbers was a wound, raw and bleeding; X had made Heath Spade and Carmen Hayes its battered pulse.

Spade's chest was screaming where X's .357 round had slammed into his Kevlar vest. He knew his ribs were bruised, maybe cracked, each breath a knife twisting in his side. He kept the Glock steady in his hand, knuckles white, the steel an anchor against the vertigo threatening to pull him under. Blood roared in his ears, drowning the crowd's anxious muffles, the music's pulse, but his eyes burned, scanning past the chaos where X and Emma Madalin had exited, looking for anything that could claw back control.

As much in awe as was the crowd and in astonishment as was Ramírez and Hayes, Spade saw the killer's aerial moves that took down Ramirez. The killer moved with a precision of violence unlike Spade had ever seen. The takedown of Ramirez was something that belonged on a circus stage, not in a nightclub. Spade's gut kept churning over everything that had gone down. Ramirez was dead, his partner was hit, and X was gone, Emma in his arms, every planned step they carefully thought through had vanished into Houston's endless wet night.

He held his ribs, taking a few steps to continue surveying everything around him that had gone wrong. "Hayes." His voice was a raw bellow, cutting through the din. He staggered over to her with enormous relief seeing her hands reach around her bloodied thigh as if to rub away what had happened. She managed to prop herself on one elbow, free hand now directly applying as much pressure as she could on the gushing bullet wound. Blood was soaking through her pants, the .357 round having torn through muscle, shattered bone, but her vest had caught the chest shot, saving her life. Her dark eyes locked on Spade's, wild with adrenaline, her breath ragged but steady, a hunter refusing to break.

"I'm alive." Her voice trembling but focused despite possibly dying. "Fucker aced us, Spade. Ah, that didn't come out right, but you know what I'm saying. Emma, too." She forced herself up, leaning over her destroyed leg with an iron will. It looked like someone had dumped a gallon of blood on the dance floor, mixing it with the spilled liquor, a small crimson river under the strobes' flicker.

"Yeah, he did. And Ramirez's Dead." Spade spat the words like acid in his throat. He knelt beside her, his hand steadying her shoulder, his eyes darting to the chaos. "Try and ease down, Carmen. You're bleeding out." He yelled into his headset again, static crackling. "Dispatch, dispatch, Jesus Fucking Christ this is Detective Heath Fucking Spade, Numbers on Montrose. Officer down, suspect fled with female accomplice, Emma Madalin, both armed. Seal I-10 to Westheimer, every fuckin' nook and cranny. Burgundy Chrysler Concorde, likely vehicle. I need EMS and backup, now. Send every-fucking-body." His voice was a whip, but he knew Houston's main arteries in and out of Numbers needed clogging and pronto.

Hayes's fingers dug into his arm, her breath hitching. "Heath...we can't let them get away." Her voice was pain-laced and fierce, her eyes locked on his, burning to chase despite the blood soaking her leg. "Bastard played us...Corbin was nothing more than a goddamn stage prop. He's doing ritual shit—"

"Easy, easy, partner, save your strength."

Spade's jaw clenched, his mind racing. Corbin's precise kill, Ramirez's execution, the shots that dropped them. Hayes was right: it was all theater, X's middle finger to their hunt. The Lake City CPS case, Emma's coma, her "strangely dark" surgeon's note, the voided-eyes Denison rambled on about. The whole goddamn mess was a web of fuckery with its centerpiece a psychopathic acrobat.

Spade wanted to tear through Houston's alleys after the Chrysler, but the shape Hayes was in was quickly ticking from bad to worse with Ramirez's body now one more weight on his soul. "They'll still be there, Carmen, but you need a hospital, ASAP."

A glint caught his eye. A cracked flip phone on the floor glowed faintly, had to have been dropped in X's escape. Spade pointed, his voice snapping to a couple of uniformed cops who'd just arrived from the chaos. "Bag that, don't fucking put any prints on it. Forensics on Corbin, Ramirez, every inch. The phone could very well be X's or Madalin's, a lead to any next move, or another taunt." He turned back to Hayes, her face paling, her hand pressing the soaked towel to her thigh. “Hold on, partner. EMS is here.”

Hayes shook her head, teeth gritted, still very much in this fight. “Chain Willis...find him. Find him while I’m getting stitched back together again. He’s Emma’s little bitch. He’ll lead us to them.” Her voice faded, her eyes fluttering, but her grip on Spade’s arm remained firm as she pulled him closer.

“What is it, partner? I’m trying to get you to ease in, now.”

Hayes slowly moved her head side to side in irritation. “Did you see how that son-of-a-bitch took down Ramirez? Did you see that, Heath?”

Spade slowly nodded, holding his partner with more comfort. “Yeah.”

“Ever seen anything like—”

Spade gently put his index finger to Hayes’s lips. “No. Now let’s just focus on you.”

While sirens wailed outside, Spade and Hayes’s case went hemorrhaging into Houston’s endless pitch of night.

***

The distant wail of sirens clawed through the post-9/11 haze toward the fresh set of wounds Mister Boogie left behind at Numbers. Brody moved like a specter, Emma cradled in his arms, her leather jacket slick with sweat and blood, her obsidian blade still gripped in her hand, a dark mirror of his own hunger. Numbers’ neon sign flickered behind them, its red and violet spitting into the alley as screams and techno bled from the club’s fresh hell. Brody’s boots hit the pavement, each step a lion’s vow, his thin black leather jacket catching the streetlamp’s glare. The Concorde rental sat in the shadowed alley off Montrose like a beast waiting to flee.

When they reached the car, he yanked the door open

with one hand and placed Emma in the seat with the other while his eyes scanned the dark for cops. For a moment he even looked carefully for Spade and Hayes but, just as quickly, knew he'd put them down hard enough to buy some solid time. He could feel the orb's pulse and needed it like a new addiction, but Emma was first. Her breath was shallow, her face pale but fierce, her eyes—preternatural, like his, since Lake City—remained locked on him. "Rex." Her voice a whisper but tight. "Let's move. No need to be so careful."

Brody slammed the door, rounded the car, and dropped into the driver's seat. The Chrysler roared to life. He gunned it, tires screeching as the car tore out of the alley, weaving through Montrose's narrow streets, the city's skyline a jagged scar against the fog. He knew that Detective Spade would be shutting everything down around a ten-mile vicinity or so, knew this because that was exactly what he would do.

Emma clutched her thigh, blood seeping through her fingers, her leather skirt a mess. "Let me see." Brody eyes flicking between her and the road.

"Just drive, Rex. We can't go to my place. They know who I am by now. We've got to deal with that."

He pulled a small flashlight from the glove box, shutting it before Emma could see the orb. He clicked it on, more assertive. "Let me see it, Emma."

She instantly knew his tone was the change she saw take place at Numbers when he saw Hayes and Ramirez. Someone not Rex.

She lifted her hand, wincing, the wound a raw gash above her knee, torn by Hayes's Glock round. Brody leaned over, his fingers probing gently, his training sharp, martial arts, survival.

"Flesh wound. Nothing serious. No bone, no artery. You're fine." He shifted his body enough to remove the leather jacket, toss it to the backseat, then he ripped a strip from his shirt, all while keeping the steering wheel and car steady as she goes. "Take this and tighten it around your thigh. Tight as you can, anyway. We'll clean it at the hotel. No hospitals."

Emma nodded, her breath steadying, her grip on the blade loosening. "Good plan."

She leaned back, her eyes tracing his weathered face through years of rage and kills. Jennifer Armstrong, Chelsey Bingham, Kelly Manson, the cop blown to hell from the torched Porsche, now Corbin and the cop who was assisting Spade and Hayes. It was only by mercy that her brother didn't take them out. "I knew it was you...the murders. The Post article... Front page just a while back. I felt it was you, if that makes sense. I was sitting in Houston's Bar and Grille when reading it...feeling it when the strangest thing happened—"

"You need to save your strength." Brody's jaw tightened, his hands steady on the wheel as the Chrysler took back streets and blended into Houston's late-night pulse. "You shouldn't even be here." His voice remained assertive and in control. "How did you find me there, of all places?"

"Thought I need to save my strength."

Brody glanced over in quick reprimand.

"Like I said, when I was reading The Post article, knew it was you behind it all, then this bizarre woman ended up talking to me after she'd scared away some guy who came on to her...never mind that. You're not the only one since we were torn apart who has skills."

Brody eyeballed her but kept focused on the night road.

"Not like you do, Rex, but..."

"But what, Emma?"

"I've been following you, okay? As much as possible that is—"

"Following me? For how—"

"Doesn't matter. Point is, I've got connections and been around the block myself. More than I'd ever intended so when I read what has been going on around here with the murders...right when the twin towers were blown to shit, I might add...I had one of my people follow you around."

To Emma's relief, Brody chuckled at the thought.

"Of course you did. Seems there's a lot to talk about but you're in no shape to do it now, so let's put all this in the parking lot for later."

Emma nodded as she applied more pressure with one hand and feeling around her small handbag with the other, feeling around her for cell phone, which quickly irritated her brother.

"What do you need, what are you looking for?"

"I need to make a call and can't find my phone."

"Yeah, well, a lot of shit went down back there in case your memory's jogged from the cop's Glock."

"Christ, Rex, I need that phone. There's a lot on there that—"

"Phone's gone; we're not going back. Stay focused, we can go over all this when I get you cleaned up."

Emma stayed silent while keeping the pressure on her leg. Rex was right, she could catch him up later. What he didn't know is that her phone, if found and scoured by the police, had contacts on it that could do some real damage to her. Still, she was with her brother again and they were alive thanks to him. Everything else could be sorted out later.

She reached over to put her hand on his now sleeveless shoulder. "I'm not losing you again." Her eyes burned, mirrors of his own, haunted by Lake City, the CPS room, Aunt Anna's cold smile, the accident that remade her, what she just witnessed her brother doing to keep them both alive. "We're in this together now, whatever it is."

Brody nodded in silence. Mister Boogie had a sliver of a grin.

The Chrysler's tires screeched into the Four Seasons' underground garage, the city's sirens fading, the night swallowing their trail. Brody carried Emma through the service entrance, her arm over his shoulder, her blade tucked away, his steps eerily silent on the marble. The elevator to his suite chimed, reminded her of her own place.

Inside, the room was sterile luxury: silk sheets, marble floors that matched the lobby, a glass table with a massive black square vase. Brody set Emma on the couch, then grabbed a first-aid kit from his duffel, his movements precise, surgical. He cleaned the wound, stitched it with thread and needle, her hisses of pain a rhythm he matched with steady hands.

"That will hold." He taped gauze over the stitches, his eyes meeting hers, a flicker of pride, of recognition. Emma stood, testing her leg, the pain too sharp to bear, her leather jacket catching the suite's dim light. "We won't be safe here for long." Her voice was harder than Brody expected. "No matter how injured those cops are I can tell you that detective Spade will not go quietly."

"From what I saw, neither will his bitch partner. Hayes. How much do you know about them?"

"Enough to know he won't stop. Ever. I'm sure Hayes will follow suit."

Brody nodded, thinking things over while Mister Boogie replied, "Let them come. I've got more work to do. And a plan to throw off that copper's scent."

Emma noticed her brother's quick change of demeanor but didn't have the strength to try and figure everything out just yet. Maybe never. With all the options still available, she chose her brother's, wherever that would lead. Regardless of everything that had gone down or would go down soon, she needed to call Chain Willis, and her goddamn cell phone was probably on the dance floor of Numbers broken to pieces. Or worse, in the hands of the HPD.

"I really need to make a call, Rex, can I use your cell? Do you have a cell?"

Brody grimaced at her without a word.

"What? With everything I've seen from you, it's possible you don't have one."

Brody knew that whoever his sister needed to call was important. No way she could have tracked him to Numbers and Corbin without someone who was sharp. He also knew what she said about her own past wasn't something to brag about. Emma was clearly a hardcase. Something Mister Boogie could certainly use as an advantage for their next kill.

He nodded, but his mind was on Leslie and Tina, his first real trophies; Roger Denison, his patsy; the orb's rituals, the Veil's whispers. "We move tomorrow. New hotel, new plan. But tonight..." His eyes were drawn to the balcony, the Houston skyline glittering beyond the glass. The moon was nearly full. He stepped out on the balcony.

Emma was irritated that he ignored her and wouldn't even offer to help her up to join him. "I can't go out there on my own, Rex, Jesus."

Brody said nothing as he walked to her, picked her up as if she weighed no more than an empty duffle bag, and carried her out into the Houston night.

The humid air was a slap, the evening's bloody mayhem a distant roar. Emma leaned against the railing as her brother gently set her down, testing her leg ever so easy but using her hands for full weight, her breath steady, her eyes on the moon, its light carving her face in bone and shadow. Brody stood beside her, his torn shirt open, his void-like eyes drinking the night. The orb's hum was faint in his mind, but constant as he left it in the glove compartment, a thread in his blood, but something else stirred, a ripple in the air, a scent of blood's secrets.

Brody's eyes mapped the city streets below as Emma's focused on the moon. She shivered, reaching over to grab her brother's arm.

Brody kept scanning the streets below, unphased.

"Rex...Rex."

He turned to her in frustration. "Yeah, yeah, yeah, yeah, Emma, I'll let you use my cell, my God—"

"No, Rex. That. That. What is that?"

Brody looked up and over to the west and froze at what Emma was asking him. A silhouette hovered against the moon, sharp and impossible, its form cutting the silver light, its cloak trailing like smoke. The silhouette flew low on what looked like a metallic broom. Brody remained frozen; Mister Boogie thought he could hear faint laughter like a velvet hiss; he thought he saw pinpoints of lavender from its head but couldn't be sure. The air crackled.

Emma's hand tightened on his, her voice a whisper. "What. Is. It. Rex?"

Brody's lips curled, a predator's smile, Mister Boogie stirring, his mind racing back to The Serpent's Veil and MacBeth's Weird Sisters. Their rants and rhymes.

"Who is it? Not sure little sister. Seems we're just getting started."

The Houston night swallowed them, the silhouette's slash lingering, a promise of ruin and power, their shadows fused with the moon's icy portrait.

5: SHUT THE BOX

It was deep into the following night after the violence at Numbers, nearing 2 a.m. when Emma's penthouse felt diluted, weak against the residual darkness clinging to the edges of the room. Rex and Emma Brody had taken 24 hours to rest, but it wasn't nearly enough, and Brody knew his sister needed a hospital, but it was a luxury he also knew they could not afford. The floor-to-ceiling glass panes, usually a proud display of Houston's bustling cityscape, now seemed opaque, as if smudged by the restless gloaming of a world on the edge of madness.

Emma Madalin was slumped on her black leather sofa, her eyes deep wells of intensity stared at nothing visible, her wounded leg endlessly aching. The terror of what they saw the previous night clung to her skin like a sheet of ice: sharp, wet, impossible to shake. The woman on a broom for fuck-sake silhouetted in moonlight, a twisted mockery of every childhood story she ever heard, now made terrifyingly real. That haunted her more so than being shot by Detective Hayes and seeing Rex in action that didn't seem possible.

Her brother paced the room, every muscle taut beneath his black shirt, the fabric clinging to him like a second skin. His face a mask of restless energy, eyes thickened from lack of sleep the past many days, months. In fact, he couldn't remember the last time he slept. His fingers twitched occasionally, longing for something violent, something he could grip and break. Last night's event left him charged, on edge, his temper precariously balanced.

Emma watched him silently, her wounded leg feeling

more like it was ruined, tracking his movement as he prowled. This was the brother she'd searched years for, dreamed about, tracked relentlessly. But now, finally having him, brought a strange unease. There was danger in him she underestimated, a presence that filled her penthouse with a volatile edge.

She broke the silence, her voice quiet and steady. "I've seen her before."

Brody stopped abruptly, his pacing cut short by her words. He turned slowly, eyes narrowing, fixed on her face. Mister Boogie was only focused on the next move. "What? Seen who?"

"I can't be sure, but whoever was on that freakish broom. If that's in fact what we saw." Her voice wavered, betraying something rare. Fear. "At the bar...the woman who found me. She talked about bloodlines, Rex. Ours."

Brody moved closer, each step deliberate, controlled, nerves on edge. "Who did you see at a bar, Emma?"

"Whatever we saw last night on the balcony. I mean, it's possible. I didn't think she was...real. Still not sure."

Brody folded his arms, the knotted muscles in his forearms rippling under the strain of unspent tension. "I'm not following you."

Emma hugged herself tighter, as if trying to squeeze the memory out. "She knows about us. About you. She talked about trophies. She said you were hunting, said you were starting something."

His eyes darkened further, brow lowering in a concerned furrow. "What else did she fucking talk about?"

Emma hesitated to flick her eyes toward the city beyond the glass. "She said a lot of shit, and I thought it was just shit. But then said she was 'the part that comes after.' I have no idea what that meant, but she said things that aren't possible for anyone else to know but us."

Brody scratched his chin, thinking. "Go on." His voice had dropped to a harsh whisper.

Emma shuddered slightly as she gently felt around her wound. "Our childhood. Aunt Anna—"

His posture stiffened instantly at the mention, eyes blazing. "What about Anna?"

Emma leaned forward slightly, her composure fraying at the edges. "Forget about that for now."

Brody stared blankly at his sister.

"Listen to me, I know where she is, Rex. That's what I was trying to tell you before we saw that freaky silhouette of whatever the hell it was. Anna's still living in Lake City. Changed her name, hiding from her past just like me. But I found her."

A cold stillness overtook Brody. Every line of his body froze to the chilling words. Emma watched, pulse quickening, fear and fascination blending seamlessly. When he finally moved again, it was slow and methodical, every step meticulously weighed and calculated. This certainly changed the direction of things, as Brody thought all along that Anna had moved from Lake City years ago, that she'd taken a job down south right here in H-Town, but his sister was clearly on another page.

"You've known this?" His voice sounded dangerously even.

"Yes...I wanted to be sure before saying anything."

Brody crossed swiftly toward her, lowering himself onto the sofa beside her. Emma didn't move, didn't flinch, though every instinct screamed for her to pull away from the cold intensity he radiated. Instead, she met his gaze evenly, unblinking.

"Tell me everything." His harsh tone left no room for hesitation.

Emma felt breathless, the pain in her leg exhausting. "God Rex, my leg is really beginning to hit me. In the kitchen, top shelf, with the spare whiskey, there's a brass container. I need what's in there if you're keeping me up. You might want some yourself."

"Codeine?"

"Morphine."

Brody tilted his head. As much as he loved drugs, he had to remain sharp. No narcotics, not yet anyway. Nothing slowed down his skills more. "Morphine?"

"If you're keeping me from the hospital, it will keep me sane."

Rex found the brass container and brought it to his sister, looking over the leg himself and wondering just how fucked up it would get. Last thing he needed was to deal with gangrene.

"Go on."

She opened the brass container where Rex saw thin glass vials of deep green liquid. Mister Boogie grinned.

"After CPS took us, Anna disappeared into her own new life. I'm sure that's nothing new to you, but she left a trail. Lake City to Dallas, Dallas to Beaumont. Beaumont to Houston, then back to Lake City. She goes by Anna St. Claire now. Needed some fancy fuckin' alter ego. Married briefly, widowed mysteriously. She's been working as a volunteer counselor at a church. Hiding, Rex. She thinks she's untouchable. Protected by Christ Himself she must think."

Brody's lips curled slightly, a humorless, feral smile. "Let her keep thinking that. She'll need every goddamn prayer she can mutter."

Emma leaned slightly toward him, urgency in her eyes but said nothing. She watched his eyes glitter with a familiar hunger, but something darker. Something shaped from a hellscape she only partially recognized.

She reached hesitantly for his hand, gripped his iron fingers tightly. "God you've changed."

He studied her carefully, evaluating something fragile he might accidentally crush.

"Yeah. But I won't lose control, not yet."

Emma knew he could, which caused a small shutter.

His fingers tightened briefly around hers, a fleeting moment of shared strength before he stood abruptly, pacing again.

"So...this woman who seems to know so much. Feels like I know her, too."

Emma nodded. "Somewhere from the past, I'm sure."

Brody's mind briefly raced back to the woman in the black bikini in a time and place that seemed to have never happened. Yet what did happen seemed to be happening again, but in ways he couldn't wrap his head around, nor could Mister Boogie.

"We'll deal with Anna. Some others as well." Mister Boogie considered Leslie and Tina, but it was Anna first and foremost.

Emma's eyes widened slightly, realization settling coldly. "You're serious, aren't you?"

His hand fell away, leaving her skin tingling, charged with a promise of things still unspoken. She watched silently as he moved toward the window, staring out at the city beyond. In that moment, Emma understood clearly: Rex Brody was gone, consumed by someone else entirely, someone born from ruin.

***

She continued to enjoy the bathing glow of her Four Seasons penthouse bedroom, her body a vessel of unrelenting pain that pulsed with every heartbeat, the wound in her leg a raging fire that Hayes's bullet had ignited during the chaos at Numbers. Rex had done what he could to mend it, his hands iron steady as he threaded the fishing line through her flesh, but the fever had set in regardless, a slow-burning grill that made her skin slick with sweat and her thoughts fogged over.

Brody moved her to her bed but kept her propped up, telling her to not get comfortable. Their time in the penthouse was over. She shifted slightly, the sheets clinging to her like wet tissue paper, damp and uncomfortable, the air in the room thick with the scent of antiseptic and the metallic tang of her own blood. Outside the floor-to-ceiling windows, Houston stretched into the night, a labyrinth of lights and shadows under the grip of post-9/11 paranoia, where sirens wailed in the distance and National Guard checkpoints turned every corner into a potential arrest.

Rex stood at the window, his silhouette sharp against the neon haze of the city, needing the black orb in his palm as if it were a living thing, its surface to pulse faintly with an inner light that he now relied on. He had not let it out of his sight since the Veil, but now he turned to Emma with a look of reluctant determination. For the past 24 hours he never thought to leave his sister to fetch the orb. It was long enough. He would explain that he needed to retrieve something from the Chrysler parked down in the Penthouse garage.

He didn't know what to tell her: a spare magazine or cash or perhaps the burner phone he mentioned earlier. He hated leaving her even for a moment, his voice low and laced with the protective edge that was there since they were children, the boy who swore to shield her from the world's cruelties back in that sterile conference room in '83 just before they were torn apart for what they both thought would be forever.

"I need a few things from the car. Won't be long." He slid the Ruger into his waistband then pulled the leather jacket over it to conceal the bulge, his eyes meeting hers with a promise that cut through her haze. She tilted her head slowly as if her neck had no more strength to hold her head in place. Brody felt her reluctance.

"I'll lock the deadbolt behind me, and don't open the door for anyone, no matter what." He walked to her as she weakly held out her set of keys.

She managed a slight nod, her throat still raw from the

screaming during the escape from Numbers, watching as he stepped into the hallway and pulled the door shut with a soft click, the deadbolt turning into place with a reassuring thud. At least it sounded that way.

Silence descended upon the room as if a concert had suddenly gone mute, pressing in from all sides, the only sounds the distant hum of the city and the faint tick of the clock on the nightstand. Emma closed her eyes, willing the pain to recede just enough for her to briefly close her eyes, knowing that Rex would be gone for longer than he said. The elevator ride itself could take some time. However long he would be, she felt it would be an eternity of vulnerability.

Regardless of her state of slipping into a mental void, she suddenly heard a soft scrape of what a keycard in the lock could be. Maybe a thin strip of metal. God knows how many locks she mastered over the years. It was a sound that shattered the quiet, her eyes snapping open as adrenaline surged through her veins despite her body's ruthless signals to shut down. It could not be Rex—he had the only key, or did he? He had just left, his footsteps still an echo.

More shattering still came as the front door burst inward with a force that splintered the frame, wood cracking like bone under pressure as three men rushed through the opening like manikins given form and fury, their faces familiar in the worst way possible, remnants of Chain Willis's crew from the days when she had been their commodity, their plaything in the underworld of drugs and trafficking.

How the fuck they were now in her apartment was more fuel to stay alert as the morphine was going into high gear.

The biggest one, a meat slab named Rico whose tattoos crawled up his neck like an angry vine, crossed the living room and into her bedroom in long, sluggish strides, his hand clamping over her mouth before she could draw breath to scream, shoving a rag between her lips tasting of gasoline and old blood, muffling her cries into pathetic whimpers.

Emma bucked against him, her good leg kicking out with all the strength she could muster, her nails raking across his arm and drawing thin lines of blood that only made him laugh, a wet, guttural sound that filled the room.

The second man, a wiry fuck with a rat-like face she remembered as Tick was in her bedroom as if appearing out of nowhere, grabbed her arms and pinned them behind her back, zip-tying her wrists with plastic that cut deep into her skin, deep enough to leave open wounds, blood trickling warm down her forearms as she struggled. Tick quickly pulled out a pair of small shears and cut the excess plastic ends. She prayed to her uncaring God that Rex had changed his mind and decided to come back.

Of course, her God kept silent.

"Chain said the brother stepped out, or whoever the fuck he is." Rico's breath felt hot and foul against her ear as he hauled her off the bed, her ruined leg buckling under her weight and sending a white-hot shard of pain up her spine that made her vision blur. "Five-minute window. Maybe more, but we've got to fucking move."

They flipped her onto her back with casual cruelty, Tick kneeling between her legs and pressing his knee into her wounded thigh, grinding down with force that grated bone against any remaining bullet fragments, her muffled screams echoing in her own head as black spots danced across her vision. The pain was too much for any scream to come out, the violence keeping her from passing out.

The third man, a stocky brute with a shaved head and the eyes of a dead fish, stood watch at the bedroom door, his pistol drawn and sweeping the hallway, but he glanced back with a grin that turned her stomach, his voice far too eager. Emma had never seen him and never wanted to see him again.

"Look at her squirm. Bitch still got some fight left, even shot up like that. Chain's gonna have fun breaking what's left of her spirit."

Then it was Chain himself who entered her bedroom. He nodded to Tick and Rico but focused on the bald brute. "That's right, Squirrel. So, let's keep the fight alive in her."

Emma's eyes locked onto Chain's as he knelt and moved his face an inch from her own. "You didn't see this one coming, did you?" Chain moved his head side to side, his tongue out like a rabid dog as he pushed the rag deeper in her mouth. "Now you can't unsee it. We're out of time. Fuck outta here." Chain stood and led the way out.

The bald brute Squirrel tossed her body over his shoulder as if she were no more than a sack of laundry, carrying her out as Tick and Rico followed. Her good leg kicking futilely against his concrete body, the pain so intense that it felt like her wounded leg was being torn apart anew.

Emma fought with everything she knew, her nails raking Squirrel's skin, her teeth clamping on the rag in a desperate bid to scream louder, but Squirrel laughed as he slapped her hard across the face with his free hand, the impact splitting her lip and breaking her nose.

"You better calm yourself, little cuntling, before you're dead on arrival." It was Tick who was right behind them. "Your brother's gone, or whoever the fuck he was. Chain owns this city. You're going back where you belong."

Though the fight in her was on fumes, Emma did her best to calm her breathing, to remain hopeful her brother was wrapping things up in the parking garage, but also wondering how in the name of fuck did Chain manage everything that was happening. The morphine had startling little effect. She extinguished the thought as fast as it came. She had worked many crews with Chain over the years. Truth be told, he knew her as well as she knew herself. This was a case of her own doing. Sloppy thinking. Seeing her brother in action at Numbers the past night had given her mind a little luxury from the perpetual looking over her shoulder 24/7.

Bad mistake.

They were down the service corridor in no time, into the freight elevator. One more piece of detail that Chain must have been scoping for who knows how long. Emma never knew there was a service elevator. It reeked of stale food and cleaning chemicals—something that briefly shocked Emma, for as long she's lived there, she had no idea of a service elevator at The Four Seasons—the ride down feeling eternal as every bump and jolt sent fresh searing waves of fire through her leg. She prayed the stitches would hold.

Tick kept one hand on her thigh the whole way down, sadistically squeezing the wound, his breath acid on her neck as Squirrel kept her body tight on his shoulder, arm wrapped around her waist. Tick whispered things that made her broken mind begin to crumble, promises of what awaited her. Squirrel's shoulder dug into her stomach as he carried her, the pressure making her gag against the rag, bile rising in her throat as the elevator doors opened to the cool air of the parking garage.

Rex was nowhere to be seen; her God remained quiet.

A panel van waited, its back doors yawning open like the maw of a beast as Squirrel threw her inside like a bag of trash, her body landing hard on the bare metal floor with an impact that drove the air from her lungs and reopened the stitches in her leg, fresh blood pooling beneath her.

Tick and Rico climbed in after her, the doors slamming shut with a finality that echoed in the confined space, reminding her of the many times she heard jail house gates slam home with that same finality. Darkness closed in except for the red glow of the taillights. Rico zip-tied her ankles with the same brutal efficiency, the plastic cutting into her skin like wire, and then straddled her, his weight pinning her wounded leg to the floor, the pain so overwhelming that she thought only of death, but she forced herself to stay conscious, to remember every face, every word. Chain was at the wheel, Squirrel in the passenger scat.

Rico tapped his index finger into her neck and face a

few times, spit on her, slapped her, but it was Tick who spoke. "Keep that fight inside, little girly girl. Chain's been wanting this for a minute." Rico moved off her and shuffled back against the van wall.

It was also Tick's turn as he slid his hand under her shirt to dig into the soft skin of her stomach, his fingers like claws that left bruises in their wake as he grabbed her bra, pulling it down like a drunken pervert who'd never laid eyes on a woman. "We've got a long drive ahead, and you owe us for the trouble at Numbers."

"Shut it down, motherfucker. If it was the plan to do this, I'd be doin' it. Just simmer the fuck down. And take the fucking rag out of her mouth, you think I want that shit down my throat?" Chain's authority was immediate as Tick backed off, pulled out the rag and leaned against the side of the van next to Rico, Emma spitting out phlegm and blood.

His groping was a violation that burned deeper than Detective Hayes's bullet wound, a humiliation that stripped away the layers of strength she had built over the years, reducing her to the girl from the fosters who had learned to hide her body under baggy clothes. She moved as much as possible to simply regain a tad of dignity, her bound wrists scraping against the metal floor, the zip ties drawing more blood with every movement. She knew the fever was gaining strength, the pain sapping her of all strength.

Tick and Rico chuckled as the van tore out of the parking garage, Chain driving with reckless speed, twists and turns that threw her body around, each jolt a new agony that made her bite down and lock her jaw.

Her mind raced through the madness, piecing together how Chain had known, how he had timed it so perfectly, his thugs the insects on the city's walls tracking her every move. Every one of Rex's moves for that matter. Houston's nightscape blurred outside the tinted windows, the van speeding through backstreets to avoid checkpoints, the National Guard's presence a distant threat that offered her zero hope, zero salvation.

She felt the fever climbing higher, her skin hot as a poker, her thoughts fragmenting as the pain and humiliation merged into a single crushing weight. She thought of Rex returning to the penthouse, finding the door splintered, the place ransacked, and she hoped whatever the fuck it was he needed to get from his rental was worth the rage it caused inside of him...a rage that she desperately needed.

He must come. The hope of seeing him again was becoming as slim as her God speaking thunder to end the horror. The boy who had vowed to protect her in that clinical conference room so many ages ago; the man who had gutted James Corbin with a surgeon's precision at Numbers; the acrobat who flew into the air to take out the undercover cop as though it were a normal lunch date... He must come.

Even though her fate was destined for brutality at the sickening hands of Chain and his Tick and Squirrel, as the van sped deeper into the night, as the fever burned her from the inside out like a fresh case of Toxic Epidermal Necrolysis, she held onto the chance of Rex coming.

The van hit a pothole; her head cracked against the floor with a thud that sent stars exploding behind her eyes as darkness rushed in. As it rattled on, the men laughing in the front, their voices a distant cauldron as Emma floated in limbo between consciousness and oblivion, the pain a ruthless companion that reminded her she was still alive, still fighting in the only way she could.

It was an endless drive, the city giving way to industrial outskirts where warehouses loomed like forgotten tombs, the air growing thicker with the scent of oil and rust. She tried to track the turns, memorize the route, but the fever muddled her thoughts, turning time into a viscous sludge that dragged her down.

Tick kept at it, the whispering promises that there was no light at the end of tunnel, words that etched into her ears like spiders burrowing into sheetrock. She tried to block it out as Rico stared at her with gaping eyes, his mouth slightly open, stupid and dangerous. She thought of the fosters, the men who had looked at her too long, touching her hard when no one was watching, the body that had developed too early, too fast, making her a target in a world that preyed on vulnerability and craved sexual depravity.

But she survived that. She would survive this. Rex had taught her that much, his promise from the conference room echoing through the years, her final lifeline. The van slowed, turning onto gravel that crunched under the tires, a warehouse she'd never seen rising in the darkness like a monolith of despair, its doors creaking open as they pulled inside.

Tick hauled her out, his abrasive hands bruising her arms, her wounded leg dragging across the concrete as they threw her against a beam then walked around her looking curiously as if studying a dying zoo animal.

Chain Willis was the last to enter warehouse's belly, wearing a fitted sleeveless shirt to showcase tattoos from shoulder to wrist, his scarred face twisting into a grin that promised deeper humiliation, uglier degradation, his voice a rasp that cut through the air.

In the array of violence and shocking pain she did her best to look over the area then focused on Chain. "Why? I don't understand. I never went behind you, I never—"

Chain quickly put his hand up to silence her. "Stop. Don't go there, Emma. Don't fucking do it. Trying to tell me you never had me as some fucking sidekick? As someone who could never lead and take control over all of it? I've been planning this for a minute."

Emma's head slowly moved side to side, trying to see Chain's point of view before she knew her life would end. Trying to work something out at least for a moment that could change his mind or at least delay it. Before she could mutter a syllable, she knew everything was over with Chain's next command.

"Squirrel...you're up first."

She looked up at him through swollen eyes, the fever making the world swim. She refused to break at the terrifying words. But the words turned to action as Chain directed and provoked each of them to take turns. Every time it was Tick's he would howl out, "Welcome to the Chain Gang, welcome to the Chain." Just before she passed out others from Chain's gang arrived and took their turns. Emma lost count, her mind completely turned over into madness. Could have been four more Ticks and Squirrels...could have been forty. Nothing mattered. All life's meaning turned to pointless ruined flesh.

Maybe she didn't pass out. Maybe she died and it was Chain's demons that were raping her in a hell where she still believed Rex would break on through to the other side. Maybe it was Jim Morrison taking it to her just before he sung "The End."

***

Brody stepped out of the service elevator into the underground garage of the Four Seasons, fluorescent lights buzzed overhead with rattled insects circling around that cast dancing shadow dots across the concrete floor. The space held in the cool evening air of Houston's pleasant late October, as the night had long since descended upon Houston with its post-9/11 paranoia gripping every corner. He moved with the silence of a predator. The Ruger tucked into his waistband was a familiar weight that grounded him in the moment. His mind was already fixed on the orb left in the Chrysler's glove box. Its pulse was a distant echo in his chest that was calling him back. Almost yelling.

The car sat three rows over. He reached it in seconds and popped the glove box open with a click that echoed softly in the silent garage. The orb lay there. Black as midnight oil. Its surface smooth and cool to the touch at first.

As he lifted it into his palm, the heat began to build. A slow burn spread through his fingers and up his arm like a new vein filled with more power than blood.

He held it longer than he intended. The orb's pulse synced with his own heartbeat in a rhythm that felt ancient and inevitable. Visions flickered at the edges of his mind, whispers from a forgotten age. Images of lush gardens and stones raised in fratricide. Marks seared into flesh as scars he carried since '83. The power coursed through him, caused his muscles to tense and his breath catch. Time slipped away in the underground vault as if the orb had pulled him into a different time altogether. Seconds to minutes. The garage's hum faded into nothingness.

He shook his head to snap to. He had to get back to his sister. Though she was becoming a far heavier weight to deal with, she was his sister, nonetheless. How she found him didn't seem possible but the realization that she waited above in her fevered state forced him to jolt.

He pocketed the orb in the inside jacket pocket. Its pulse now a constant companion against his chest. He slammed the glove box shut and turned back toward the elevator. The brief lapse was a reminder that the darkness inside him grew stronger with every passing minute.

Fuck the elevator; he took the stairs two, three at a time. The Ruger heavy against his spine. The orb grew warmer with every step as if it sensed something brewing in the air above. When he reached the 22nd floor of the hallway on the penthouse floor, everything was silent except for the low hum of hallway vents.

Something felt wrong the moment he stepped into the hallway. The wrongness came rushing to reality as he saw Emma's front door was busted open; wood splintered around the frame like a gaping wound.

He stepped inside, stepping over the immediate mess. The world narrowed to a single blinding point of rage that exploded in his chest like a grenade. The living room was tossed, Emma's furniture overturned, her lamps shattered. Blood smeared across the marble in long frantic streaks that told a story of struggle and terror. The bedroom door hung crooked on its hinges. He crossed the space in three strides, stopping dead in the doorway as the full story unfolded before him.

Of course, the bed was empty, Emma's sheets were soaked crimson where her leg wound had probably reopened. Fishing-line stitches were scattered on the floor like dead worms discarded in haste from the cuts he had made when patching her up.

Emma was gone; the room a testament to violence that he alone let happen. The smell of sweat and fear and cheap cologne hung in the air like a shitty mist. The stench triggered memories of the underworld he had just pulled her from, back at Numbers. He knelt and touched the blood, just minutes old. Far too many minutes.

Brody's vision tunneled the rage that had simmered since the conference room moment where Aunt Anna's cold voice had sentenced them to life in prison. There were a few zip-tie pieces left on the carpet that caught his eye as he moved with stealth and precision, catching the boot prints leading out of the apartment to the service corridor.

He missed what happened by mere seconds. Then again, just how long was he in the car feeling the orb?

The penthouse was supposedly off the books. Completely safe, Emma said. But whoever the fuck it was who took his sister had waited and watched with the patience he would have practiced himself. Taken her the second his back was turned. The thought twisted in his gut like a knurled wire as he surveyed every inch toward the service elevator.

He moved before any thoughts could fully develop and raced down the twenty-two floors of steps in less than a minute, racing to thc Chrysler to fire up the engine like an awakening beast. Tires screaming against concrete, he tore out of the garage and into the locked-down streets of Houston. But where was he going? Who was he trying to find? As fast as he raced out of the garage, he slammed on the brakes in one of the back streets, then slammed the car into park.

"Think, think Goddamn it."

He wondered about the woman Emma talked about but had no fucking idea who she was and realized the thought was ridiculous the second he thought it, so he made the call to the exact people he had just tried to kill: The Houston Police Department. He hadn't killed Spade so maybe there was a chance to get him on cell. Nothing to lose. He knew HPD would ring Spade's phone directly regardless of what condition he was in.

Brody pulled the Chrysler over to Navigation Boulevard, cut the engine and noticed heat rising from the hood. Great, one more fucking problem. His hands were a bit uneasy as he thought about Emma and how much time was left. He knew Spade would have something. He also knew the cop would work with him. No other choice.

He dialed HPD with an answer after two rings.

"Houston Police Department. How may I direct your call?"

Brody swallowed hard. "I need a-ah detective—" His voice was low, cracked, murderous beneath the surface.

"Do you have the detective's name or a case number, sir?"

Brody stared out through his windshield at nothing, just the empty industrial street, the sodium lights humming.

"You gonna cut me off or wait for it?"

There was a slight pause, the kind where a civilian operator realized this wasn't a family member calling. It's someone else. Someone wrong. Brody heard faint clicks on a keyboard. "Sorry, sir. Go ahead."

"Give me Detective Heath Spade in Homicide."

"I'll transfer you to homicide. If we're disconnected,

the number is—"

"Just connect me, goddamn it."

The operator didn't push back; she'd heard the tone before. "Okay, sir. Please hold."

Brody listened to the dead air, not even music. Just the hum of fluorescent lights inside HPD Headquarters leaking through the line.

He rested his forehead on the steering wheel and whispered Emma's name under his breath, like it was the last thing tethering him to the earth.

Click.

A new voice answers, older, more guarded, a civilian clerk. "Homicide Division, this is Alvarez. How may I help you?"

Brody cleared his throat. It felt like gargling gravel. "I need Detective Heath Spade. Now."

Alvarez paused. The "now" carried weight; too sharp, too desperate.

"May I ask who's calling?"

He hated even saying his own name to a cop but knew he wouldn't get to the detective without it.

"Brody. Rex Brody."

Another pause. This time longer. Brody could feel her recognizing his name. She'd possibly seen it on internal memos, the kind detectives talked about when they thought no one else was listening.

"Let me check if he's available. Please hold."

Back to dead air.

Brody tapped his finger against the steering wheel, one tap per heartbeat. It's too slow. Too human. He wanted to rip the world open.

"Sir, Detective Spade is on another call. I can—"

"Tell him it's Brody, for fuck sake. I know good Goddamn well he's not talking to anyone. He's been injured. Tell him Emma Madalin has been taken, that I won't fucking wait."

Alvarez's voice shifted. Not fear, just understanding that this was not a normal call. Not a routine citizen looking for closure.

"Okay, sir, one moment, please."

"Christ."

Less than five seconds passed when: "Detective Heath Spade," came on the line. His voice was unmistakably dry, gravelly, yet deadly sharp.

Brody's breath caught. The silence stretched across the entire city. Then: "It's me."

"Brody." Spade's tone went cold.

Brody closed his eyes, as his spoken name sounded like a verdict. Not that he could give two shits. "Listen—"

"You killed a cop, motherfucker...and nearly killed my partner."

Now Brody didn't miss a beat. "Yeah, well, hey. It was a fun night all around, and you're still breathing, so you gonna listen, motherfucker?"

Another long pause as both Brody and Spade heard each other's breathing, waiting for the next move. Brody didn't blink, betting the detective would blink first.

"You called me, Brody. And I doubt you're calling to gloat."

"They took my sister. I don't know who. I don't know where. All I know is she won't have much time. So...are you in?"

Spade inhaled slow, quiet, controlled. "Sure. Why not? If it brings me one more step closer to nailing you, yeah, I'm in. But let me repeat that last bit: I am nailing you. If it puts me in the fucking grave, you copy that?"

Brody's own breathing slowed down, much more controlled, as Mister Boogie saw the power shift. "Yes, Detective, I copy you."

There was another long pause, not because Spade was scared or that Brody was too overconfident, but because the situation changed. For Spade, because the man who nearly killed him was now calling for help; for Brody it was the help he thought was needed; for Mister Boogie the game just became more fun.

"So, Brody, where are you?"

Brody looked up at the neon bleeding across the sky. The city felt infinite and empty all at once. Another lead suddenly struck him as vivid as the night sky, but he decided to keep that card in hand.

"Doesn't matter. I'm going somewhere else first. A lead, if you will, but you stay tight by your cell and stay tuned."

"What lead? Brody...listen to me."

Brody's grip tightened on the phone and steering wheel.

"Underground bar. That's where I'm starting. Well, after this call, that is, and that's as much as I'm saying for now."

Spade knew of a hundred or so such places spread all over Houston's underbelly, so he pushed to buy a little time with one more pry. "Listen, Brody...I told you I'm in. I won't be a fuck's lick good to you if I gotta go knocking on every fucking Houston—"

"That's enough, Detective, I've given you enough. If you're as good as everyone says you are, or what I've seen all over the Goddamn nightly news lately, then I doubt you'll disappoint."

Brody didn't hang up immediately as he listened to the silence between them, knowing that Spade's mind was racing as fast as his own, heavy, loaded, dangerous.

Before another word was spoken he ended the call without another thought, fired up the engine and pulled out, heading toward The Serpent's Veil, toward the witches who may know the whereabouts of his next lead, Adrian Kane.

Spade sat on the other end of the line, whispering to no one. "Fuck you, Brody. Game on, motherfucker."

***

Mister Boogie knew Brody had issues.

He thought the witch's silhouette in the last night after Numbers was no illusion. He was still unsure of her pinpoint eyes for some reason. But they were eyes that summoned, a challenge the orb understood. Saving Emma was his greatest act, not of mercy, but of power. He walked through the over-lit belly of the dancing beast, his Ruger singing, his hands shattering Detectives Spade and Hayes's crew to claim her. He thought about Emma's half-ass stitched leg, her eyes blazing with the same fire that burned in him. She was his, as much as the orb, as much as the kills. Leslie and Tina would fall, their bodies altars to the Brody's sigils. Anna would burn, her death the crescendo of his vengeance, a final reckoning for the boy who once screamed in the dark forever.

He stayed in the parked car for several seconds after the line with Spade went dead, and the silence inside the Chrysler felt heavier than the detective's last words. The phone lay on the passenger seat amid old maps, receipts, and a scattering of cartridge boxes, and it looked like another piece of wreckage from a life that was never in order. He stared through the windshield at Navigation Boulevard's sheen and understood that what he just did was something he swore he would never do: calling a cop for help. Heath Spade of all people who had been close enough to kill him. The only thing that mattered was finding Emma before she was dead. The world narrowed to the few places where answers lived, even if those places were worse than the questions.

He fired up the suffering engine in a low growl that vibrated through the steering column and into his hands. The city slid past on either side as he drove, its lights flattened by moisture on the windshield and stretched into tired stripes over the hood. Houston looked subdued in the late hour, but it was the subdued quality of a predator at rest rather than a harmless thing asleep. Police checkpoints glowed at intervals, their temporary floodlights throwing sharp cones over Humvees and armed silhouettes.

Brody cut away from them, choosing the thinner back streets that ran behind warehouses and shuttered shops. He knew how to move around watchful eyes because he spent his life trying not to be seen unless he chose it.

The image of Emma's penthouse kept replaying in his mind. She was slumped against the pillows, her leg stitched and stained, her eyes glassy with exhaustion and pain, and even then, she tried to apologize for drawing him back into her world. He told her to rest, to not open the goddamn door for anyone. He locked the deadbolt and heard the lock engaging as he walked into the hallway, but he knew now that it was nothing more than a fragile seal. Whoever took her waited for the exact moment he left, waited for that exact span of minutes, and known the building well enough to move in and out without leaving anything but destruction.

He turned deeper into one of Houston's industrial districts, where the character of the city changed with a grim honesty. Storefront glass gave way to corrugated metal, and concrete gave way to cracked asphalt and patches of broken gravel. The air took on a different quality with scents of oil, old water, and rust that had soaked into the bones of the area for decades. Tall cranes loomed against the sky like skeletal constructs frozen in mid-gesture, their shapes cut through the orange reflection of refinery fires that burned without pause beyond the low skyline.

The Serpent's Veil existed in this landscape not as a business but as something parasitic and rooted, growing rot and machinery the way fungus grows around buried wood. The green steel door he sought clung to the back wall of a long warehouse, a serpent was spray-painted around the hinges peeled in ragged strips, which made it look as though the snake were shedding its skin in slow, diseased patches.

The light above the entry buzzed and flickered, and each time it dimmed, the door seemed to recede a little farther from the world everyone else used. Brody pulled the car into the gravel near the entrance, killed the engine, and stepped out into the thickness of the night air.

After checking the Ruger, thumbing open and closing the Spyderco blade a few times, and tossing the orb back and forth from palm to palm, he approached the door, feeling as though he were walking back into a wound he had already opened once, the night Adrian Kane first stepped into the lights with that dead-looking woman in his arms. Or was she dead? He didn't know but suddenly remembered something about her eyes that reminded him of the witch that he and sister thought they saw in the moonlight the other night.

Brody remembered the way the crowd went silent, the way the lighting display turned into something more than electricity and gels, and the way Kane's eyes found him in the darkness as if he was the only person in the room. That was the night the weird sisters pressed the orb into his hand and spoke of what he might become, the night his life began to tilt toward something nameless. Emma's abduction was a continuation of that tilt rather than a separate event; he knew that if there were any connection between her, the men who took her, and the thing that wore Adrian Kane's face, this was the place to find an answer.

He pushed the door open and stepped inside.

The Veil didn't welcome him; it swallowed him. Heat struck like a damp cloth slapped across his face with the weight of heavy scents of smoke, spilled alcohol, intoxicating fragrances that were applied without restraint, the underlying sourness of bodies moving in the same crowded air for too many years. Colored lights circled the room in slow, hypnotic sweeps, the beams cut across faces and tables in broken patterns that made it difficult to trust what he saw in any one instant. The sound inside the bar had layers: a low bass line vibrating through the floor and into his feet, a tangle of conversations that never quite resolved into anything discernible. There were the occasional sharp sounds of bottles striking counters, chairs scraping the thick wooden floors, laughter that carried a jagged edge rather than relief.

He paused just inside the threshold and allowed his eyes to adapt to the rotating light. The stage dominated one side of the room with a woman of astonishing physique moving around a pole with a tired precision that spoke of repetition rather than inspiration. She had striking red hair that flowed across her shoulders like freshly cut Christmas ribbons, green eyes that looked like dime-sized emeralds.

He didn't recall any dance pole last time he was here. Her body writhed through positions that matched every beat of the deep pulsing house music. Those around her, men and women, were locked in a trance to her body's every move, but the hollowness in her expression belonged to someone who had slipped out of herself and left muscle memory to carry on. The reflective chrome of the pole threw streaks of color across her ivory skin, each new color suggested a different movement.

The bar was a cavern of crimson gloom, red bulbs swinging from overhead chains, casting jittery shadows that danced across scarred oak tables and booths upholstered in faded leather. The air pressed in, heavy and alive, laced with absinthe rot and myrrh, the house music an endless pulse that thumped the edges of sanity.

Patrons hunched in the corners, junkies with hollow eyes, a tattooed brute nursing a glass of green poison, a woman in rags murmuring to an empty chair. But tonight, the place felt wrong, amplified, as if the walls breathed. A gloaming that pooled unnaturally deep. Brody swore he saw everything shift as if on Ecstasy, forming shapes: contorted faces, clawed hands reaching.

He was on this part of the journey, drug free, to remain in top condition to rip apart whatever and whoever crossed his path toward Emma. Dead or alive. So why was his mind shifting?

"Sees you like her, do ya? Ye gawd, she's a true queen. Not The Queen, but one to git your juices edged I see."

The woman at the front of the bar was dressed in deep blue denim rags, her hair a nest of wire and shredded pieces of worn leather in pastel colors. Her face looked a thousand years old with a nose that had to have been broken once for every year.

Brody stared at her.

"Git you a good private one the Crimson Queen, a good deep fucking for a few shillings more."

He cocked his head. "I'm not here for that."

The hag screeched in abhorrent glee. "Ahhhh, something far grittier I see."

"Listen—"

"It's ye who needs to listen." The hag leaned over the bar, stretching out her wretched body as far as she could. She then turned her head and stretched out a hand with fingers so boney they looked like broken pencils sewn together.

Brody followed her direction as the lighting rig over the stage faltered and then surged. For a brief, unnatural moment, the beams converged into a configuration that he knew too well. The shape of the fiery-head dancer on the stage blurred and stretched, and in its place the illusion of Adrian Kane appeared in the light: the tall frame, the impossible shoulders, the suit that looked cut from darkness rather than cloth, the pale, chiseled face and blocked powder-blue hair, the grave face that had studied Brody with clinical interest during their first meeting.

But this time there was no limp form of the woman who had hung in his arms with her head tilted back at an angle that had suggested she was dead. For a split moment, Brody saw himself carrying that same woman down an overlong chapel hallway across the world. Not far from now. He shuttered and snapped to.

Suddenly the pattern broke. The dancer remained alone on the stage again, the lights resumed their lazy spin, and conversations resumed at their previous volume. Brody understood that the bar had just reminded him of what truly ruled this place. Adrian Kane's image lived in the lighting system and in the memory of every regular who had ever seen him carry that woman. Brody remembered the weird sisters had called the woman who was in his arms the first time he saw her, The First Wife. The thought that men who served such a creature could have something to do with Emma's kidnapping was a thought that caused Mister Boogie to want jump on stage and dance alongside the red-headed starlet with emeralds for eyes.

"Thank you, Bridget. That'll be all for now."

Adrian Kane was standing next to the hag he called Bridget. He put his massive hand on her frail body and turned her away then reached it out to shake Brody's.

***

The first thought Detective Heath Spade had after Brody cut the call short was to drive to Hermann Memorial Hospital down the Katy Freeway to see his partner. He knew she would want to hear this regardless of any pain or any lack of sleep. He also knew time was running out, so he called her cell phone instead, hoping to God in fucking heaven above that she'd answer. When she did, she told him to slow things down.

Hayes: Whoa, whoa, whoa, Heath. Jesus, slow it down. I'm still on a slight morphine drip, yo. Just. Slow. It. Down.

Spade: Right, but listen, Hayes, we don't have a lot of time here.

Hayes: You don't have a lot of time. God knows how long I'm gonna be laid up in this casket on wheels.

Spade: Alright, here it is. Do your best to follow along.

Hayes: Sure.

Spade: Brody called me. Just now. He knew I'd know it was him. Has the fuckin' gall to tell me what happened at Numbers was "fun for everyone," or some shit. We go back and forth before he tells me – or asks me – if I could help him. Work with him.

Hayes: Help him with what? Did you tell that fucker he nearly killed me? Did you, Spade?

Spade: Of course I did. What's the matter with you, yes.

Hayes: Ain't nothing wrong with me other than being almost dead. So...what, he thinks all a sudden he's your new partner because he put me in the hospital?

Spade: You're a bit loopy, Christ, I understand, but listen. He told me his sister is gone. Kidnapped. That I was the only person he thought to call. The best person, that he had nothing to lose. Asked me if "I was in."

Hayes: Where was she kidnapped? Where'd this happen?

Spade: I don't know every detail yet, Carmen. Switchboard told me most likely The Four Seasons. Units are on their way there now, but we didn't get nearly far enough before he hung up after telling me he had another lead to follow. That's why I'm calling you, to brainstorm this for a sec. What do you think?

Hayes: Another lead...hmmm, surprised he didn't call me...

Spade: Why would he call you? Think about it.

Hayes: He's clearly one to gloat and taunt. Jesus. The Four Seasons. Emma must have a place there.

Spade: Or had. Doubt she'll ever see it again. May not ever see her again. Whoever took her from Brody has a wicked game. Patient, too, the worst kind.

Hayes: Must be someone close to Emma Madaline. Someone she would have never guessed.

Spade: Who in her inner circle did you vet the most? Who sticks out the most?

Hayes: I don't know, Heath. She's tight with some sleazy mother... Wait. Could it be that obvious?

Spade: Who? Spit it out.

Hayes: Chain Willis is who I'm thinking.

Spade: Willis? You're the one who presented me with intel that has locked these two in cahoots for years. Why him?

Hayes: Is he really such a stretch? I don't think so. Keep your enemies closer and shit. We don't know how many times she rolled him over...or at least in his mind. Or whatever. Look, you're the one who suggested someone close. He's the closest.

Spade: Copy that and good call. I'll put out an APB on Willis asap. Who else? That fucker's not the only close tie to Madalin.

Hayes: You said Brody had another lead. Who could that be and could it be someone also linked to Emma?

They paused in unison, took deep breaths, thinking things over, knowing each other so well they could hear each other's thoughts from a distance. They spent a few minutes in silence, only the background vitals machines from Hayes's room, her television low, whatever program or movie playing, more a soothing hum. Then it hits them both.

Hayes: You thinking what I'm thinking?

Spade and Hayes: Kane.

Spade: But how? Never mind that, *where* is a better question. He's all over the fucking place and nowhere at the same time.

Hayes: Brody say anything specific that could clue us in?

Spade: Yeah, I think so. He mentioned an underground place as if it was the place to be for anything underground. That if I'm as good as everyone says then I'd figure it out. I haven't for some fu—"

Hayes: It's The Veil. The goddamn Serpent's Veil.

Spade: Jesus fuck. Spot on, partner. I'm on it. Knew there was a reason to call you straight out. Now you've got to rest.

Hayes: Rest? I'm all propped up and shit and ready.

Spade: Keep your phone close. I'm out.

Hayes: Heath…watch your six. You're no good if you end up here.

Spade: Copy, over and out.

***

"Do I understand things correctly, that you're here to see me?"

Adrian Kane walked behind the bar dressed in a bright neon pink suit with a black silk tie. He wore a velvet cowboy hat with a neon pink band that wrapped around it several times, studded with brass rivets. A thick stogey hung low between the corner of his lips like it was permanently attached. His voice was deep and throaty with a heavy English accent.

Mister Boogie locked in. “That’s right.”

“You’ve met some of the others who work for me. Go, sit with them. I’ll be there shortly.” Kane pointed toward the back wall of the floor area then disappeared into the back of the house with Bridget clinging to his arm.

Brody moved forward with measured steps. People noticed him and then pretended they didn’t, the way prey animals sometimes refuse to acknowledge a predator at the waterline because acknowledgment invites attention. A barkeep who replaced Bridget began pouring drinks, seemed to recognize him, and immediately looked down again as if the best thing he could do for himself was to make no sudden movements. Brody felt the weight of eyes sliding across his back as he passed, and he knew that word of his presence already spread to everyone who needed to hear it.

Everything felt empty to Brody, but emptiness in this place did not mean absence. He could feel the same cold attention he had felt during that first conversation, as if Kane watched through any reflective surface he pleased and stored details for later use. There was no intention of offering the man anything other than asking for help.

At the farther end of the room, in the deep corner where the light never settled for long, sat the weird sisters who did not belong to the bar so much as the bar belonged to them. Their booth appeared unchanged, the cracked leather holding their shapes as if no one else had ever occupied that space.

Elspeth sat at the outer edge, her narrow face and sharp eyes turned toward him with a faint, knowing smile. Alisa remained straight-backed beside her, her long bony hands folded, her presence radiating heavy authority of judge and juror. Mairi reclined opposite them with apparent ease, though the stillness in her ragged limbs and the intensity of her pale gaze suggested that not a single motion in the room escaped her notice.

Brody approached them with cool ease.

"Ladies."

Elspeth's smile deepened by a fraction.

The sisters cackled in unison, a piercing sound that bounced off the walls, multiplying until it filled the bar like shattering glass. No patron reacted; everyone's eyes glazed, bodies frozen as if entranced. Elspeth leaned close, her shocking breath washing over Brody like grave wind. "Hee, the pup barks bold, his rage a flame, but flames burn out in our domain. Sister lost, her blood calls loud, but answers come shrouded in cloud."

Alisa's freakish eyes gleamed, her yellowed teeth bared in a jagged smile caked with tartar like extra fangs. She unfolded a thin leather cloth on the bar, revealing a strange pattern that was etched with runes that pulsed faintly in the material. Stranger still, the pulse matched the orb's that was alive in Brody's jacket pocket. "The mogul waits in shadows deep, where software code and blood entreat. But entry demands the mark's confession, a drop to feed the dark obsession."

Mairi's whisper coiled around his throat, deceptive silk laced with barbs. "The orb remembers the garden's fall, the stone that crushed, the divine call. Your vow to Her, to Cain's red hand swear deeper now, or lose your stand."

Brody quickly put out his hand. Mister Boogie wanted to pull the Spyderco but restrained. "No more bullshit. My sister's been taken, and the men who did it moved like people who already live in this kind of shit. They knew when to act and where to disappear. That's why I'm here. Your boss motioned me to come see the three of you. So, here we are. Again." The moment Brody said it, he realized the witches were speaking the best clues he'd get that night. But Mister Boogie wanted Kane.

Alisa studied his face as if she were measuring how much of him had already shifted since the last time she saw him.

"Hmmmm. You walked away from her bed. The world wastes no time when someone like you turns his back, even for a moment. Men who catch such openings never fail to walk through them."

"I know what I did." He kept his tone level and refused to defend himself. "I also understand that this bar sits on the same current that runs under the people who took her. Adrian Kane scarred that into my memory the night he stepped out on that stage with...whoever the fuck she was. If there's a thread between him and the men who took her, I want it. The three of you stand closer to him than anyone else who is still technically human. Well...you and that crackhead Bridget."

Mairi's lips curved in a small, ambiguous expression that might have contained pity, respect, or mild amusement.

"'Technically human.' I like that, errr, we like it. So nice you've met our dear Miss Magnus, but it is your speak-easy of his name without hesitation. The first time you heard it, your tongue treated it like something sharp. That is how men usually hold it, when they live long enough to hold it at all. But...tis also a hint of knowledge of another who could be much closer to him. More powerful."

Brody stared at Mairi, keeping his peripheral focused on the other two. "He's aware of me now, and I know enough of who he is. I am not here to dance around your riddles. Why the fuck he sent me over here seems to be more of it."

Elspeth traced a fingertip in a slow circle on the table's surface in a motion that had the unfocused look of someone drawing something that did not fully exist in the visible world.

"You were getting along so cheerfully with our beloved

Bridget Magnus, so it would seem. Now you're here with us, seems you seek his servants rather than the master—"

"Cut the shit. Thought there were only the three of you when we first met, now that nutcase who makes the three of you—Fuck."

The three stared at him in gaping silence, almost in mockery.

Alisa lifted her hand and placed it briefly on the front of his jacket near his collar, an action that could have been mistaken by an observer for a maternal gesture but felt more like a diagnostic check performed on a dangerous experiment. Normally, Brody would have parried the move hard enough to shatter her bones, but instead slowly leaned back, letting her.

"I see everyone's getting quite comfy. Lovely party." Adrian Kane stood behind the weird sisters. His voice mimicked Sean Connery's from his early Bond days.

Brody stared past the hags right into Kane's eyes where Mister Boogie locked in again.

***

Emma had no idea how long she was out or when the violence had stopped destroying her body. Her entire face was beaten to pulp, eyes both so swollen all she could manage were slivers of vision that were blurred with blood and mucus. Her body told her that many ribs were broken, of course her nose from back in the van, her left elbow, possible knee and ankle, but not sure which one. Probably both. She leaked everywhere of cum and piss but kept a private dignity as she gently wiped around privates and body to do what she could to get the shit off. She sobbed quietly and just as gently as to not feel the broken ribs dig deeper into her lungs.

She prayed but not to her God.

"Please...please...please, Rex...please find me...I won't

hold on much longer..."

***

Spade raced down I-10 toward the Washburn Tunnel as fast he dared. It was the fastest way he knew to The Serpent's Veil. He decided against calling anyone else, just yet, for any backup. Carmen would have said differently, but she was laid up, and his hunger for Brody superseded anything logical. He had no idea if The Veil was in fact where he'd find Brody, or if Brody was going there, how long he would stay. Deeper into the unknown equation was Adrian Kane himself, the fucking criminal mastermind behind more Houston shitshows than Spade could ever count. He also knew once he arrived at The Veil, if he even felt things were off, that dispatch could get him backup in plenty of time...before he killed anyone.

Well, at least it was possible.

He cranked up the stereo in the loner undercover unit. His and Hayes's car had been totaled on the evening before 9/11, and his push for a new one still had not gone through.

Drowning Pool's "Bodies" blasted from the stereo, Dave Williams screaming into the night about bodies piling up on unknown floors, being alone with nothing wrong but consumed by hate.

***

Kane spoke quietly to Brody, yet the words carried through the space between them and the weird sisters with unmistakable authority, as though The Serpent's Veil itself had decided to listen.

"Come, follow me. The three of you mind things up here while I'm away."

He turned before Brody could respond and moved toward the rear of the bar, passing behind the sisters' booth and through a narrow corridor partially concealed by a heavy curtain of black chains. Mister Boogie cooly followed, conscious of the way the ambient sound of the Veil changed with every step, the music dulling into a distant vibration that traveled through the soles of his feet rather than his ears. The air grew warmer and thicker with layered scents that suggested incense burned long past its purpose, sweat soaked into stone, and something faintly metallic beneath it all.

At the end of the corridor, Kane placed his hand against a black panel set into the wall, releasing a steel door with a muffled hydraulic hiss. Beyond it, a steep stairwell descended into pitch blackness. The concrete steps were worn smooth at the center by long use, lined with red bulbs set at uneven intervals that distorted depth and distance as they went down. Moisture clung to the walls, and the smell intensified with every step, until Brody felt as though he were being drawn into the body of a living thing.

The stairwell opened into a vast subterranean chamber. Its low ceiling was supported by heavy concrete pillars that were stained royal purple with symbols etched deep into the surface. Chains hung from overhead beams, some fixed in place, others swaying gently despite the absence of any detectable air current. The room pulsed with sound that was not quite music, a slow, percussive rhythm layered with voices that blended chant and moan until it was impossible to distinguish one from the other.

What struck even Mister Boogie were the bodies that filled the space.

Men and women moved together in unhurried, narcotic rhythms, their skin slick with sweat and oil, their faces masked, painted, or partially obscured by ritual markings. Some danced with eyes closed, lost in sensation. Others knelt or lay prone on the concrete, attended by figures who traced symbols across their backs and midriffs with deliberate care. A few stood motionless at the edges of the room, watching with expressions of reverence rather than curiosity, as though witnessing something sacred rather than depraved.

It was devotion stripped of disguise.

Mister Boogie refocused and Brody felt the weight of it press against him, not as shock, more like recognition, a sense that this space existed because it fulfilled some deeper need. He thought about the letter from Conrad Ellington and what Ellington had said. If Ellington was in fact The Ripper. No one looked at him as he passed. Whatever rules Kane governed this place by, they rendered him temporarily irrelevant; Kane's presence alone dictated all limits.

They reached a circular stone table set near the center of the chamber, positioned within a conspicuously empty perimeter that the surrounding demon's lair did not breach. Two chairs waited. Kane seated himself with effortless composure, his neon-pink suit catching the red light and glowing faintly against the darkness. Mister Boogie sat opposite him, aware that the stone beneath his hands was ice cold despite the heat in the room. Behind them and in the farthest corner to their left sat two women at similar stone tables, in stone chairs.

One wore a sheer crimson chemise. Her skin was as white as peals, her jet-black hair so thick and full it appeared painted with a 4-inch brush. A single green spotlight from the opposite corner beamed across her body. She was playing a strange game with the other woman: the starlet redhead dancer from the first-floor pole who was bathed in a purple glow from the purple spotlight rigged from the other corner.

Brody had never seen the game, though; it was some kind of dice game with a thick board that had slats on each side. The redhead tossed her dice into the middle of the board, and soon after, the jet haired one tipped a few of the slats on her left side of the board.

Behind each woman stood a naked a man, each with their wrists handcuffed behind them, wearing only leather helmets covering their entire head and face, and cracked wooden clogs, Japanese Geta. Brody saw both men's ankles and legs were bleeding. Both men were trembling. Brody knew pain and combat so intimately that he recognized the trembling was fear based rather than from pain itself. In front of each of the women on the floor was a turquoise oval button that looked like a large opal, placed closed to their feet.

"Shut The Box."

Brody refocused. "Excuse me?"

"The game they're playing, Shut The Box. Quite old. Popular in the twelfth and seventeenth centuries. Difference here is the beauties you see play for something quite different than—"

"Never heard of it. And I can see what they're playing for."

Kane's earlier deep English tone changed to one that was high pitched and clearly irritated. "Their names are Jaqueline, the redhead beauty you so loved to see on the pole; the other, Lilith...with the night hair. Would you rather watch them play their game or be in your own?"

"Jackie and Lilly's game looks more fun. Some other time, though... Something tells me they're part of it either way."

Kane's grin was wide and crooked, his voice even more overly effeminate, making the optics of Kane's cigar between his lips feel imbalanced and surreal.

"They've been with me quite some time. This is where everyone comes when they are exhausted by the performance of restraint." Kane kept at his whorish sound, his grin wide and crooked. Everything about him seemed to be escalating in intensity.

Brody kept his gaze., Mister Boogie sized everything up. "I don't know what the fuck that means or what you're on, but the black-haired one looks familiar."

"Your business is not with Lilith."

"Right. Let's cut through it. My business is my sister, Emma Madaline. I'm quite sure you know her, how the fuck couldn't you know her? She doesn't belong anywhere near...this." Brody's head moved in a gesture that meant he was overseeing all of it.

Kane tilted his head slowly. "No?" His voice this time was deep and ragged but without the English accent as he looked back at the women playing the game. "So...she looks familiar to you?"

Brody tried to deflect Kane's obvious distraction, but it was too much. He looked over to the women and their game, and this time tried to lock eyes. He felt his heart race but quickly controlled it. He never saw anyone's eyes that color, other than the strange encounter with the woman in the black bikini so many years ago during childhood that she no longer seemed part of his history.

"She might, but we're not talking about her. I came here to ask about my sister, and you can goddamn well answer me. Fuck all about the demon women and Shut The Fucking Box." The sound system's volume increased, as well as the intensity of the different colors colliding from the lighting.

Kane's grin widened even more, if that were possible, as he chuckled deep and bellowing. He then squinted his enormous eyes to deeply focus. "Let me tell you, ole chap, 'bout an order around here that I think you'll find most entertaining. An organized front, if you will. I call it The Order of the Flies. Called such for...well...everything we all know eventually breaks down to the stench and filth of the maggot's desire, which in turn transforms to the fly. Singular and collective."

Brody's own eyes squinted to match Kane's focus. As far as he could tell, the giant man wasn't on any drug nor had alcohol on his breath. Not that it would matter, for Kane's breath smelled of the rot he was talking about.

"I've never heard of such an...order, you call it? But

whatever the hell it is, doesn't make a fuck's difference to me, if that's who took her. And if it did, that means you did."

Kane held out a massive hand in a gesture to continue. Brody saw that Lilith and Jacqueline stopped playing their game and were looking at his and Kane's conversation, the leather-helmeted men behind them remained frozen in fear.

"Go with me, here. Everyone underestimates flies because they mistake refinement for beauty." Kane's voice was calm, instructive. "The fly is a surgeon of decay. It does not tear or rage or improvise. It catalogs weakness, lands where tissue has already begun to fail, and feeds with exquisite efficiency. It vomits to dissolve what it cannot immediately consume, liquefies rotting flesh into something usable, and then drinks what used to be a body. That is sophistication, not savagery. Brutality with purpose. The fly does not destroy indiscriminately. It reduces things to their most base state. No disguise. No sentiment. Just function. That is why they are perfect. They do not hate us, and they do not judge us. They simply arrive the moment we become edible. This is precisely the purpose of The Order of The Flies and what you...young student, are in."

Mister Boogie tapped his fingers on the heavy wood table and signaled to one of the servers walking around. "A double whiskey. Want one?"

Kane scoffed. "This is my house."

"Doesn't mean I can't buy you a round. 'Specially talking about this kind of fuckery."

Kane signaled to the server just the one drink and put his massive hands on his even more massive neck and face, shifting his hat a few times.

"You came back on a hunch. A correct one. I've given you the depth of it and would not have done so had I not thought you're perfectly designed for it. You are. You and your Super id."

Mister Boogie smiled and tossed back the double the moment it arrived.

Kane leaned closer to Brody, putting his hand on his wrist. Mister Boogie knew that Kane would be a tough one to take down if the time ever came. Regardless of Brody's skillset, what and who he killed and had killed, Kane would be a bitch if he could be had at all.

"Last but not least, she'll be back in your journey soon enough." Kane nodded to the Shut The Box contest. "But. You've come to the right place for what's immediate. Once again, that is." He slapped both his knees hard then adjusted his hat one time.

Brody leaned forward slightly, his voice controlled and measured. "Anyone specific in this Order who you can lead me to?"

Kane's enormous hand gently rubbed his squared chin as if in thought. His tone of voice switched again, making Brody wonder how many personalities were living in the giant's upstairs. "Someone she's slighted. Isn't that always the case? Young Emma isn't some angel who's gone around feeding the homeless and teaching the deaf and dumb. A busybody that one is, as you know full well. So, that's been the taker's feeling. Time to pay the ole pipe and organ, how he's seen it. Makes no difference to my bottom line. I've given you everything you need. Now go. Use what I've given you."

Brody knew he never gave Kane his sister's name, but of course, he knew her. Kane knew everyone and everything, which was what Mister Boogie was sizing up in ways he wasn't sure of yet.

Kane's blazing eyes shifted briefly to the chamber around them before returning to Brody, took off the velvet hat and tussled his pastel blue hair a few times before placing the hat back in place so firmly the brim covered his heavy eyebrows.

"Pain draws attention, and attention accelerates change. The men who took her wanted to see what you would become when something precious was not destroyed quickly but cultivated slowly. The Order of the Flies, that's their game."

Brody's jaw tightened. "I should've seen more. Should have seen it."

Kane nodded in patronizing agreement.

Brody licked the inside of his upper lip. "You've been directing this thing..."

Kane almost choked. "Of course, haven't you been listening? I'm behind Every-Goddamn-Thing. With all you know, all you've seen, you can't let emotion drive this thing. You're in it. Who knows how long it will last, but it's going to take some time. So, more specifically, I instigated it. There is a distinction. I've been at the center of provocation since procreation was first tempted by The Master. He's not here right now. I'm sure you can figure he's the center of the first murder and all that jazz." Kane giggled obscenely as the music leveled up again and all the freaks and ghouls and jagged-edged hooligans dancing about also leveled up. Mister Boogie saw them all as possessed; he didn't mind in the slightest.

Brody's hands curled against the edge of the table then reached inside his jacket pocket for the orb, slowly palming it one hand to another, knowing Kane knew all about it, holding Kane's stare. "This was given to me last time I was here, not that you didn't know. I show it as an act of loyalty. I pledge that loyalty to you now. Completely...Just. Direct. Me. To. Her. I'll handle the rest."

Kane interlocked his hands together, his enormous fingers tapping on his fists. "I'm sure you will. So...an exchange, so to speak."

"A transaction. Isn't that what this fucking order is all about?" Mister Boogie's voice cut through all the mayhem like an icy razor.

The sounds of the chamber's chaos grew in intensity; strobe lights and lasers slashed across the walls and floor shattering together and apart; there were also cries of what sounded like wailing that grew louder; could be pleasure or agony.

Kane's reaction remained detached and stoic. "You're catching on. 'A transaction.' Not because it's her, but you, dear boy. You're the prize. Time to earn what's been given to you, my little son. As well as what will be given. What's been given is that orb, yes, what more will be given is its order. The Order of the Flies. The Single Source of Truth."

Brody stood while Mister Boogie slowly shook his head, clearly reaching their own limit. "I'm no one's little anything, motherfucker, and what... I'll manage to handle your fucking fly order."

Kane looked at him with calm interest. "Brave, to come here...to come down here. Yes...The Order. Remember, flies don't come for death, Mr. Brody, they come for weakness. They arrive at the exact moment a body starts negotiating with itself and begins to rot. That hesitation is an invitation. Flies recognize it instantly, because they are honest about what the world is made of. They have no kings, no loyalty, no mercy. Power among them is density and brutality. The thing that rots fastest draws the most bodies. Thus, the order. Brutality. They do not argue or conspire. They gather, then take."

Kane leaned in just enough for the words to feel invasive. "A quick kill means nothing. It teaches nothing. Prolonged suffering creates gravity. It pulls witnesses. It summons agreement. They keep the wound open long enough for the Order to arrive."

His voice dropped, stripped of ornament. "I rule the flies. I create conditions they cannot ignore. Rooms where hope is stripped. Places where decay blossom. When they come, it is not worship. It is confirmation. Everything fails eventually. The flies just have the decency to show up early."

They held each other's gaze while the chamber continued its ritual movement around them, indifferent to the tension at the table. Mister Boogie looked at the giant man, knowing he was something far more than just human.

"Go. Do whatever it takes."

Brody cocked his head and put both his hands behind his back, leaning forward. "I intend to."

"When finished, you'll understand this night changes everything. Go find The Sisters for their final heed. That is all from me. For Now."

With that, Kane stood, still shocking in size to Brody, walked over to where the strange jet-haired woman and redheaded starlet were focused on their next board move, how terrified the cuffed and muffled men behind them stood. When the jet-haired woman tossed her dice, the redhead flipped over several more slats on the same side of the board where the slats covered that side of the board. Shut it, in fact. When she finished, Kane took a few long strides toward the naked man behind the jet-haired, stepped on a foot device in front of the man's feet that opened a manhole-cover sized opening. The helpless man dropped from existence. At least that was the angle Mister Boogie saw. Both women laughed, looked up at Kane, then Kane and the women looked directly over to Brody.

It wasn't Jacqualine's emerald eyes or Kane's blazing sky-blues that matched his powder-blue hair that was so unnerving. Lilith's lavender was the snag.

Brody squinted to see more clearly. His body tenser than expected.

Both women quickly turned back from Brody prepped for another round of the game as Kane motioned for another possible sacrifice to come forward. How many freaks were part of this game, how many fell through those holes into nowhere, and did they die? Though Mister Boogie was curious, time was running on fumes. Every second spent here was more that Brody was certain was being delivered to Emma, with interest at peak high rates.

Brody turned and walked back through the chamber, the crowd parting without awareness as he passed. At the base of the stairs, he paused only long enough to hear Kane's voice follow him through the heavy air.

"We'll be waiting for you."

Brody ascended the stairs without looking back, the door sealed behind him, leaving the subterranean chamber to continue its slow, terrible devotion beneath the city.

***

Elspeth spoke with the clarity Brody had come to expect. "Where they hide are not new maps found in your mind, but your own history's path, already well-defined. The men you seek haunt rust yards, and lots reclaimed; Where city ruins linger, forgotten and unnamed; Police patrol the edges, pretend the centers too tame; Yet Kane knows such places, perfect to leave a stain. There you'll find the clues, in shadows and grime; Where secrets wait, marked by the passing of time."

She regarded him with a seriousness that held no mockery nor would Brody accept any.

"They're not finished with her, men who abuse women as objects do not rush their displays. They prepare the setting, they gather their audience, and they savor each step. Your arrival will not be an interruption they have planned for, but it will be one they deserve."

Alisa continued. "They're not yet finished with her, these men of cruel pride; Their order on display, their shame pushed aside. They set the stage with care, each wicked act portrayed; A crowd is drawn to witness, every moment delayed."

Brody knew there was little time, which existed only because the men in question enjoyed what they were doing too much for any efficient conclusion. The knowledge twisted in his chest like a cold blade; every minute he spent standing here in the Veil stretched Emma's torment that much longer.

Mairi's eyes did not leave his. It was her attempt to provide a tad of hope. "She still lives...but her spirit's fading. Lights are almost out. There must always remain spirit."

Brody absorbed everything with a slow exhale. "I have enough to find her."

"You walk into the places with your eyes closed and your senses open," Elspeth said. "Every choice you make tonight will inform The Master who you are."

Alisa withdrew her hand and folded it with the other. "We do not bless or condemn, we observe. The Veil will feel what you do out there, and so will the things that move above it."

Brody turned away from their booth and walked back through the bar and stepped outside into the night beyond where it felt cooler than it had since the falling of The Towers. Relief of the air on his skin carried its own quiet menace. The warehouses loomed around the lot, and the faint chiming rattle of metal from somewhere in the distance sounded like laughter overheard from behind a wall.

He crossed to the Chrysler and sat for a moment with his hands resting lightly on the steering wheel as he called up the old mental map of the Ship Channel area. The path formed itself with unpleasant clarity: the frontage road, the turn near the flare stack, the sagging chain-link touched by orange light, and the yard where the ground never fully dried. Somewhere inside that maze, men who believed they were beyond consequence hovered over his sister like butchers.

Mister Boogie had other plans and knew the orb would direct. Brody slammed the car in gear toward the place where rust and blood and black gold would soon share the same ground.

He drove as if the freeway were a living thing that needed to be subdued, ripping through the lanes with feral urgency, engine screaming beneath the hood as Houston unspooled ahead of him in a frenzy of concrete, light, and heat. His hands locked the wheel in a fierce grip, because trembling belonged to men who still believed there was room for doubt. There were only velocity and the certainty that if he arrived too late, the world would fracture in a way that wouldn't recover.

Emma's face lived behind his eyes as presence, wounded but defiant, refusing collapse even as pain gnawed at her. He saw her as she must be now, diminished by hands that mistook cruelty for authority, breathless, body failing inch by inch while men congratulated themselves on their own ugliness. That image sharpened into something unbearable, and Brody felt the shift inside him, the unmistakable sensation of a door opening that had never truly been closed.

***

Detective Heath Spade drove like a madman who had already accepted every consequence of what could be going down at The Veil.

The lights on his unmarked sedan cut through freeways and city streets as he threaded lanes with controlled fury, one hand on the wheel, the other clamped around the radio. Houston blurred past him in layers of concrete and night glare, his focus locked on the coordinates repeating in his mind, the shape of a place that did not belong on any map.

"Dispatch, I need eyes near the industrial complex." His voice tight and measured. "Industrial yards, east side. Possible hostage situation with multiple armed suspects. Possible fucking gang."

Static answered first, then hesitation.

"Units are stretched, Detective. Closest patrol is—"

"Too far, start moving them. I'm not waiting."

He merged hard onto the feeder road, tires barking once before settling, and brought the phone up to his ear without taking his eyes off the road.

"Hayes."

"I'm listening." Carmen Hayes spoke as if in a sprint.

"On my way to The Veil. Bad fuckin' vibe that just turned worse. Brody went dark, and the last signal puts him headed straight into something ugly. I'm rolling in hot, but if you want to help and can muster the strength, I need you prepping homicide and tactical. There'll be nothing fucking clean in this one."

A pause followed, brief but weighted.

"What do you think our guy is walking into?"

"Hard to say, hard to imagine what the fuck I'll find."

He ended the call and pushed harder, the city opening ahead of him like a mouth full of razors ambivalent to the size of its next bite.

***

Emma had lost track of time, in fact the distinction of time had lost its meaning as if it had collapsed into something further away than dreams or unconsciousness, a mental and physical fusion into complete anguish that arrived without warning and never fully receded. Her body was broken and torn in a way that went beyond injury, probably beyond repair, as though it was dismantled and reassembled incorrectly, nerves screaming where there should have been silence, joints busted and split where there should have been stability. Each breath dragged across broken ribs and caught on something sharp inside her chest. The effort of breathing alone felt like a task she was failing at more often than succeeding. This blurred and maddening vision drifted in and out of focus, the warehouse ceiling dissolved into smears of shadow and light. When she blinked, she was never certain what version of the room would return.

Her mind was betraying her, every thought fragmented and unfinished, slipping away before she could hold them long enough to form prayer or plan. Names surfaced and vanished. Memories bled into one another, childhood... Numbers...her penthouse...the witch across the sky...her brother, her dear, dear brother folding together into a single, indistinct horror. She understood dimly that this was what it meant to be destroyed, not in the dramatic sense she had always imagined, but in the quiet way where survival was extinguished. She felt herself receding, her grip on reality loosening. The fear was no longer sharp enough to press forward. Somewhere in the distance, men moved around her, their voices thick with anticipation, but they sounded far away, as if she were already underwater. The last thing she held onto, stubbornly and without logic, was the certainty that Rex would come, even as the part of her that understood the world whispered that certainty did not make things true.

Chain leaned close to Emma's bound form, his scarred face inches from hers, breath thick and rank as spoiled meat. She hung against the warehouse beam, zip ties biting into her wrists, blood trickling down her arms, her ruined leg dangling like a broken branch. The fever burned in her eyes, but she still had enough fire to glare back, muffled whimpers barely escaping her mouth.

His thugs—Rico, Tick, Squirrel, and the rest—circled like hyenas, chuckling low, waiting for more instruction. Chain grinned, yellow teeth gleaming under the work lights, and started his tale, voice loud enough for all to hear, each word a knife twist meant to gut her soul before they gutted her body.

"Listen up, boys. Before we finish off this worthless cunt, let me tell you about the real Emma Madalin, the filthy pig who couldn't even keep her own kid from rotting in her shit. Years ago, up in Lake City, me and a buddy from church got sent to check on her sorry ass. Priest heard complaints about the stink pouring from her place, like death and piss mixed in a blender. We slogged through two feet of January snow, freezing our dicks off just to knock on her door, thinking maybe we could save the little girl from her monster mom.

“Husband opens up, lets us in, and the reek hits like a brick. Piles of dirty clothes everywhere, crusted with God-knows-what. Cum stains, food scraps, probably her period blood smeared on everything. Boxes stacked like she’s hoarding her own trash empire. Emma waddles in with the kid, that poor girl looking half-starved and filthy, plops her down on a mound of laundry that’s molded into a nasty bowl crawling with lice, bedbugs, whatever vermin Emma bred in her slop. Kid curls up like a beaten animal, grabs some ragged doll to escape the hell her bitch mom created.

“We sit on stools buried under more crap, and there’s a half-eaten chicken thigh rotting on the couch, no plate, just greasy flesh grinding into the fabric, maggots wriggling in it already. And get this, winter outside, snow piled high, but a swarm of houseflies circling the room, fat and buzzing. Dozens. Means Emma let those disgusting fuckers breed in her rot for months, laying eggs in the trash she never hauled, the spoiled food, the shit she left fermenting. We ask how they’re doing...school...work... She mumbles everything’s fine, like she’s not queen of her sewer.

“Then Emma drops this. ‘Sorry about the mess. I don’t mind clutter, but I can’t stand filth.

“‘Filth?’ The room’s a biohazard toilet, her kid marinating in it, flies feasting, and this lazy slut claims she hates filth? I wanted to puke or grab her by the throat and shove her face in it. Emma, the hypocritical cunt preaching family at church while her daughter starves in squalor, learning to hate the world because her mom’s too busy whoring for dope to clean or care. How do you live like that, Emma? Active in the community, holding a job, and zero fucking awareness? You’re a plague, ruining that child like you ruin everything, turning her into another broken whore just like you.

“Look at her now, fellas. Tied up, fucked up, broken

up. Same filthy slit. Time to finish this fuckshow, make her squeal 'til she screams to death. What do you say?"

The thugs growled, eyes hardening, knives out, closing in as Emma's muffled screams rose, humiliation breaking her before the blades ever could.

***

REO Speedwagon's "Don't Let Him Go" was pushing the Chrysler's speakers to the limit, Kevin Cronin's powerful tenor, drawn-out voice pleading about the loss of a stud who has it all, the drums and power chords sinking deep into the orb that came alive in Brody's free hand, the song itself recorded in such a way the background rhythms and drums and base sounded like they thudded against the speaker walls.

He held the steering wheel tight enough to increase the size of the veins in his hands by double, racing across the night, his voice howling to Cronin's.

Brody cut the engine at the edge of the yard and let the silence settle over him like a held breath. The warehouse ahead stood in a pool of uneven light, its corrugated skin scarred by years of neglect and misuse, the kind of place the city forgot on purpose because remembering it required acknowledging what people did when no one was watching. He knew it was the place.

The silence pressed in, broken only by the occasional pop of gravel under the tires and the orb's faint pulse against his chest. It was cooler now in the late October night, carrying a bite that seeped through the cracks in the windows, but Brody barely felt it. His mind raced ahead to the warehouse the witches had described in their riddles, rust yards, forgotten lots, a place where men like Chain hid their depravities behind chain-link and decay. Mairi had whispered that Emma was alive, but the lights were almost out.

He stepped out of the Chrysler and closed the door softly, not because he feared being heard, but because the act itself marked a transition. What remained would be handled up close and personal.

Brody moved toward the partially open door and paused only long enough to listen. Inside, voices drifted lazily through the gap, thick with confidence, boredom, and stupidity. The cadence of men who were sunk in that stupidity where no consequence other than vile pleasure fueled by their boredom. A giggle cut through the air, followed by a dull impact that made his jaw tighten. He pushed the door open and slipped inside, allowing it to fall back into place behind him without a sound.

The interior smelled of oil, old wood, and blood that had been given time to cool. Work lights hung from exposed beams and cast harsh yellow cones across the concrete floor, leaving the spaces between in shadow. Pallets and rusted machinery created a maze of narrow lanes and dead ends that would have been useful if anyone inside had expected resistance. Brody would use them with ease in ways The Chain Gang would never understand much less expect.

His heart stoned over when he saw Emma bound to a steel support near the far wall. Her head sagged forward, chin nearly touching her chest, her tortured body hung in the restraints as if it no longer remembered how to hold itself together. She was bloodied and bruised to unrecognition, her breathing came shallow and uneven, each breath a small, final push to survive. Both eyes were swollen shut, her lips split wide and crusted, jaw loose, her arms and legs useless.

Mister Boogie felt the room narrow around that single POV and took over.

No rush. He let his gaze move deliberately, cataloguing the men between him and Emma, counting them with cool precision. There were twelve, spread in loose clusters, their postures relaxed, their weapons present but not yet urgent. Mister Boogie figured the tat-sleeved one was Chain, who stood slightly apart from the rest, his weathered face catching the light, his smile already forming as he noticed the interruption.

Emma's head lifted a fraction, as if drawn by instinct. Her eyes struggled to focus and slid past Brody once before snapping back, recognition breaking through the haze. A tiny relief flickered there but was quickly chased by fear from the ruin the men had done to her.

Brody stepped fully into the light and slowly walked over to his sister as the men allowed it while watching carefully. He knelt beside her, his iron hands gently tracing her broken face, body, legs. His life was one of pure violence, but he'd never seen someone so badly damaged other than with heavy gunfire.

The moment Emma attempted to speak he gently put his finger to her destroyed mouth.

"Shhhh, little sister. Stay with me here for just a while longer. Mister Boogie is here...and so am I."

Emma's head moved slightly as Brody pulled out the Spyderco and cut the ties that bound her, slipped it back into is back pocket, moved her body to the most comfortable position possible, though he knew none existed. He touched her hair softy then Mister Boogie stood and faced the crowd, stepping forward, letting his boot scuff deliberately.

Conversation simmered. One of the men laughed uncertainly, as though waiting for the moment to become funny again. Another raised a pistol halfway, looking to Chain for permission.

Chain's smile widened. "You've gotta be her brother."

Brody stared blankly before Mister Boogie interjected. "Her Savior."

The distance to the nearest man collapsed with startling speed, and the first strike landed with decisive force, snapping the man's balance and sending him crashing backward before his brain could process the impact. Brody followed through without pause, turning the fall into finality, and the sound of the body hitting concrete stripped the laughter from the room. He pivoted and shifted in a single movement while delivering a side kick into the man's neck, breaking it instantly. Though dead, Brody frog leaped onto the man's body in the mount position followed by four jabs to the dead man's face that sounded like rapid-fire gun shots.

Shouts erupted. Someone's gun came up. Brody caught the movement instantly in his peripheral and effortlessly jumped up and shifted in plenty of time for the shot to scream past him and careen into metal. He drove forward through the opening, pivoted, and delivered a spinning back kick that caught another man across the jaw with concussive precision. Brody knew he shattered the thug's teeth as he dropped in a cartoonish thud.

Mister Boogie scanned the entire area with camera eyes as Brody flowed through the space with relentless momentum and spectacular aerial movement as he dove to a hand stand then moved his legs and abs in masterful front flips where the distance to opponents closed instantly. When landing in solid frame positions, he pivoted and L-stepped back and forth to deliver jabs, snapping heads back, cross shots that snapped collar bones and necks, double-axle spin kicks, breaking ribs like pencils; spinning back kicks and fists that struck their mark with lethal accuracy.

During it all, a thick and powerful man was able to rush him clumsily, arms locking around Brody's torso in a desperate attempt to restrain what he did not understand. Brody dropped his weight, twisted through the grip, and sent the man headfirst into a stack of pallets that collapsed under the impact, wood splintering and falling around a body that would not move again. Brody followed the man's crashing body and dove into a somersault that ended with a low kick that caved in the man's teeth and nose.

Gunfire cracked again, closer this time. Brody felt heat tear across his shoulder, pain blooming sharp and bright, a sensation that stripped the last unnecessary thought from him. Pain became information that narrowed him. He saw the shot came from a bald fuck who looked more stupid than dangerous.

Mister Boogie pulled out the Ruger and fired three quick shots dead center into the gunman's forehead as he fell back like large sack of down. He then drew the Spyderco in one fluid motion and stepped into the next wave of men as if the blade itself had summoned him forward. Steel flashed under the work lights. Brody moved his body in a dance-like performance that faked out anyone coming at him, leaving openings for long deep slashes across stomachs, insides of thighs, underneath armpits, and deeper slashes still across chests and shoulder muscles. Slashing where resistance began and ended movement before it could become momentum, the serrated blade also slashing necks, abs, and asses.

Every elbow strike, knee strike, fan and side and roundhouse kick landed in exactly the intended area of every link in Chain's gang. Brody lost track of time but knew the carnage he was creating took exactly the needed time to completely break down Chain's entire crew. For Mister Boogie it didn't take nearly long enough; he wanted everything to simmer and deepen.

***

Spade floored the unmarked sedan through the end of Montrose's long twisted streets, siren off but lights flashing blue and red against the night. The radio crackled with dispatch chatter, units stretched thin, no backup close. His gut twisted. Brody's call had been desperate, the son-of-a-bitch slipping away once again.

He took in deep breaths pushing the sedan to its limit toward The Serpent's Veil.

"I'll chase you all night long, motherfucker."

He skidded to a stop outside the Veil's warehouse

façade, gun drawn as he approached the unmarked door. It groaned open to absinthe fumes and red gloom. Empty booths, a few junkies slumped, no sign of Brody. Three hags stood behind the bar and watched him with black eyes, smirking, giggling. Obscenely so. Spade had never seen such women.

To the left of them, more toward the entrance and lobby was another woman who looked and felt far older than three behind her and standing off to side. She had an enormous nose, weathered and torn, her skin more so.

"Trouble is ye seek? Eh, always trouble on top of trouble." Her voice sounded perpetually burnt and smelled of rot.

Spade looked up and down her face and body, disgusted. He was out of breath but had to start somewhere. "I'm looking for someone."

The one in the middle jolted her boney head forward, grasping the bar with terrible fingers. "Gone, lawman. The marked one seeks his thread." Her foul breath wafted.

Spade was having none of it as he pulled his badge and wagged his gun. "I have no idea what the fuck that means nor do I give rat's fuck how old you are. I'll break your scrawny neck if you come at me again with any bullshit. You or your shitbag grannies." Spade put away his badge and held the Glock in a two-hand grip, waist level.

A giant appeared from where Spade mapped out, he couldn't tell. "Now, now, now, Detective. There's no need for that, please put it away. We'll be more than pleased as the punch to sell any answer to any question. Don't mind them."

He stood seven feet, easily, wore black leather chaps, steel-tipped alligator boots, black leather trench coat with a velvet red cowboy hat. He was the largest man Spade had ever seen, and he'd seen Shaquille O'Neil once play his Rockets when LA was in town.

This motherfucker looked bigger. To each side of him

were two of the most starlet-looking women he had ever seen, one to his left with pitch black hair in a see-through canvas; the one to his right with fiery red hair wearing only a thong and heels. The redhead's eyes looked like emeralds, the dark head wore even darker sunglasses.

Spade had never in his life seen Kane. Only stories. Few photos. But this monster had to be him.

"How 'bout it, Tall Cool One. Gotta feeling you know who I need."

The giant took another step forward. "He's headed east. Shipping area. But that's a drive from here, gunman."

The dark-haired woman took a few steps past the giant, crossed her ivory arms with black taloned nails that looked to sink into her forearms. "You'll never catch him. It's not his time, and you're not the right lawman." Her voice was heavy and raspy.

"How 'bout everyone stop calling me fucking lawman and shit." Spade kept the Glock out. The woman suddenly unnerved him more than the giant.

"As our Master said, look to the ships...but as I said, you're the wrong cop to do the trick."

Before Spade could retort, the giant was in his immediate space, towering over him. "Run along now, little copper. You've got quite the gander chase. Run along."

Tension coiled Spade's breaking point. No way he was going to back down to the giant. He looked up and held eye contact under Kane's brim and stuck the barrel of the Glock right above the belt buckle, backing up a step for room enough to move. Spade's adrenalin was pumping full-force, eliminating any caution of his injuries. "I'll fill your freakish belly with this entire fucking mag, Cowboy."

Kane smiled while looking down at the cop as Lilith took a few steps forward, put her hand gently on Spade's forearm and with her other put her index finger to her blood-red lips in a "shush" gesture.

"He's. Not. Here."

Spade had no idea how many steps ahead Brody was but knew what the strange woman said was the play. He also knew the body count would rise.

***

More screams rose and cut off abruptly as Brody redirected and finished motion upon motion striking into the crew's bodies and body parts without flourish. One man, who Mister Boogie remembered Chain calling him "Tick," managed to rush from the side, desperation driving him faster than logic. Brody turned through the attack, driving a deep side kick into the man's chest that lifted him off his feet and deposited him in a broken heap of pallets near the wall. Brody felt the sternum crack with the perfect strike. Keeping up the dizzying pace, he picked up one of the broken pallets and smashed it to pieces over Tick's body, finally taking one of the pallet boards to beat his head to pulp and bone fragments before tossing the piece of wood away in irritation.

The Ruger came out, again, when space opened more between surviving bodies that were either crawling or writhing inch by inch to escape an onslaught they never fully understood other than they found themselves dying as if they were in a war. Mister Boogie fired with measured certainty and rhythm into each body that he had completely dismantled, slashed to pieces, or broken, each shot placed to end every life but letting the life drain out as slowly as possible. Shots to the neck or stomach or groin, whatever seemed most demeaning.

He also used the Ruger to remove distance when his own hands and feet could not close fast enough, then holstered it again without breaking stride, because proximity was where the room truly belonged to him.

By this time Brody had cut the Chain Gang down to three links including Chain himself. Mister Boogie was saving him for last.

The ones remaining were shouting then abandoning mid-sentence. The two others—he couldn't recall their names—tried to flank Brody but collided with each other in their haste as Brody's body shifted and pivoted in such a way where each of his hands snaked around each of the men's wrists, pulling them together in a single move, causing the violent collision, leaving their positions completely open for a Mister Boogie finish.

He held the men's wrists and hands palms up, breaking the wrists as he moved them around in anguish, helpless on their backs but forced to follow the circular back and forth movements until Brody applied more leverage to shatter the men's elbow joints. The pain was so shocking neither man could scream.

Brody released one of the men's hands and dropped into the mount position on the other, grabbed him by both ears then torqued his head in a move that broke his neck. Mister Boogie finished him off by ripping both ears off, tossed them aside and did the same to the other.

Chain watched in as much awe as horror. When his last man's ears were ripped off his head by the maniac and tossed away as pieces of paper, he looked around the warehouse to take in what had happened to his entire crew. Though Emma's brother was probably severely injured, he had no off switch of any kind.

"Fucking Christ." Chain's own voice startled him as it echoed in the now silent space. He thought he was only whispering.

***

Spade: I just missed that motherfucker, Carmen. Had to have been by fuckin' minutes, but then again, I have no idea.

Hayes: Jesus, Heath, slow down a bit. You're on

hyper drive.

Spade: Yeah, and racing toward the fucking ship channel. Not even sure if that's where our guy is. But with what I just saw it has to be.

Hayes: Nothing at The Veil?

Spade: Oh no, no, no, there was plenty there at that freakshow. Kane himself and three hags that worked with him, although hags isn't quite the word that makes sense. No idea who or what the fuck they were, but the ship channel was what I could get through all the bullshit. But it wasn't Kane or the hags that really tripped me out. Kane had a few women with him. Real starlets. One of them was...Christ, Carmen, I don't know, dark-haired bitch. Really dark but never mind that—

Hayes: Okay, okay, slow down please, God, you're not making any sense, but if it's the ship channel you're heading to, you need some backup, Heath.

Spade: Already on it, partner, just needed to hear you...it...look, you keep me level, Hayes.

Hayes: I know, partner. Keep focused on the fundamentals anything can happen with this bitch.

***

Emma heard much of the violence though it sounded muddled and distant. Hope began to creep back in simply because the violence she heard had stopped coming to her. She used her bloodied hands to gently peel open her eyes to see if she could catch a glimmer of what was taking place. Time had left her. The noise was distorted cracks and breaks and thick enough she could feel it. The glances she did happen to catch were her brother's precise and brutal movements that all looked terrifyingly synchronized. She saw his face only briefly, only a few moments; there was a calm over Rex that was glorified punishment, as terrible and frightful as what was done to her. More so as it terrified and anchored her at the same time. If she would live, this kind of violence would be her new life.

As much brutality as Brody delivered, he was shot not only in the shoulder but took one in the side. A few of the crew were able to land a few kicks and cheap shots here and there from different directions, but nothing debilitating; he had absorbed it, drank it in, adjusted, and continued forward to kill every last one. No draw. No quarter, leaving Chain for last.

When Mister Boogie was finished with Chain's last man, a silence followed, heavy and almost complete. The only sounds came from Emma's ragged breathing from pierced lungs, Chain's quiet hyperventilating as he pushed himself to comprehend what had just happened, Brody's controlled deep breathing, holding each breath in to keep his lungs measured, in control.

Bodies lay scattered across the warehouse floor in twisted, unnatural arrangements. Blood darkened the concrete floors and was sprayed on the beams and walls where Mister Boogie danced. The work lights buzzed faintly, confused by the absence of movement.

Chain's breathing became heavier as he tried to remain composed. He backed away slowly, his smile gone, his eyes wide with a comprehension that had arrived far too late. Brody turned toward him, and something in Chain's posture shifted from bravado to naked survival.

Emma straightened up as much as her battered frame allowed, trying to prop herself up with both hands. She believed all her adrenalin was depleted so the slight resurgence felt like a miracle. She pushed a bit harder to sit up, gutting out the sears of pain that surged through every inch of body.

Brody took notice and took a few steps toward her then stopped in his tracks the moment he saw Chain thinking about making a run for it. He pulled the Ruger and took aim at his forehead. "Don't fucking think of it."

Chain froze in place as Mister Boogie walked over to kneel beside Emma.

"You see...I make all things new again."

Emma turned her head to try and get a better look through her swollen shut eyes. She never heard her brother quote scripture.

With that, he walked over to Chain in a slow strut. "When I'm finished, I'm skull fucking you."

The first blow drove the air from Chain's lungs and folded him forward. The second sent him sprawling across the floor, hands scrabbling uselessly against blood-slick concrete. Chain tried to rise, panic stripping coordination from his movements, but Brody dragged him back by the collar and slammed him into a steel support hard enough to rattle the beam.

Mister Boogie took his time as he beat him with methodical violence, every strike carrying the accumulated weight of Emma's suffering, his nights spent hunting monsters who believed they were clever. Chain's pleas dissolved into incoherent noise. His hands failed him for any protection. His body failed him in stages, each failure punctuated by another blow, another kick, another elbow, until there was nothing left in him that resembled defiance. Brody measured every side kick to various places in Chain's chest, ribs, and sternum. He propped him up at times against the beam to choreograph several spinning back kicks that broke Chain's jaw, shattered teeth, cracked his skull in several places but measured enough to not kill him.

When Brody finally let him fall, Chain collapsed in a broken heap at his feet, breathing raggedly, consciousness flickering in and out like a dying light.

Mister Boogie grabbed him by the sides of the face and jaw. With a violent but precise torque, he broke Chain's neck, paralyzing him instantly. He held Chain up by his hair and pulled out the Spyderco in a single move. Its razor-sharp serrated blade gleamed under the dim light as it cut into the soft neck skin with a jagged tear, ripping through epidermis and dermis in a spray of crimson that soaked the floor. Blood surged from superficial vessels as the serrations ground deeper, shredding the muscles, fibers clinging to the teeth while Chain's head lolled, support collapsing in a gush of warm fluid.

Mister Boogie slowly tore through the common carotid arteries, unleashing rhythmic arcs of bright red blood five feet high, while the jugular veins ruptured in a steady torrent. Finally, the blade mashed the spongy thyroid gland into a slippery pulp of hormones and gore, before finally cracking the vertebra with a sickening snap, the serrations chewing through the remains and severing the spinal cord.

Brody held the head by its roots, looked it over in curiosity, slowly arched his neck back and screamed with a force that he was holding inside since the day their Aunt Anna began everything that led to this moment. When his lungs could no longer push out the scream, he took in another breath as deep as possible and screamed again, feeling his esophagus scrape over, then looked down to the head and ground and controlled his breathing.

Mister Boogie walked back to Emma, head in hand. Standing in front of her he took the head with both hands and moved it close to his groin.

"Don't. Rex...don't."

When Brody heard his sister's whispering and broken plea he realized she was right. He also realized she was dying and it was time to go.

He dropped the head in front of her, landing with a squelchy thud. She could only see it in a blur but still had just enough left to reach out and shove it over a few inches.

He gently picked her up and held her in his arms, keeping her close to his body and with as much tact as possible without reinjuring anything, though he knew any movement could be her last.

"I've got you." His voice steady despite his own pain settling in. "I've got you."

Her head rested against his chest, and for a moment he felt the fragile persistence of her breath. She was alive and nothing else mattered.

He carried her out of the warehouse and into the night, the floodlight humming overhead, insects battering themselves uselessly against the glow. He laid her gently into the large back seat of the Chrysler and moved around to the driver's side, his body aching, his hands bloodied.

Mister Boogie remained, quiet now, watchful, while the city swallowed them and the road opened ahead, carrying brother and sister away from the wreckage and toward whatever came next as the next thing that came to life on the car's stereo was Rush's "The Spirit of Radio," Geddy Lee's high-pitch wail that celebrated radio's power to bring elusive music and create magical moments where there were endless compromises.

***

Detective Spade knew the night had gone too far south before he even shut the cruiser door.

The warehouse sat at the edge of the yard like something abandoned in a hurry, its doors hanging open, light bleeding out in crooked slabs that flattened the gravel and erased depth. No sirens yet, no backup. Yet. No voices on the radio crowding the silence. The city had not caught up to what had happened here, and the delay felt obscene. He stepped out with his weapon already drawn, breath shallow, adrenalin and anxiety masking his injuries. The air carried a smell of pure fear.

Blood. Steel. Burned powder with something sicker beneath it, something inhuman.

The moment he crossed the threshold, sound seemed to die. The warehouse swallowed noise in a way that felt intentional, that was designed to house secrets. Work lights buzzed overhead, their yellow cones revealing only fragments at a time, forcing his eyes to assemble the scene piece by piece. He took two steps inside and stopped.

Bodies lay everywhere that were not piled or staged. They were discarded, flung across the concrete in positions that spoke of motion that was planned execution. One man lay twisted near a pallet stack, spine bent at an angle that made Spade's stomach clench. Another slumped against a steel beam, chest collapsed inward, eyes still open as if surprise had been his final companion, stomach torn open. Blood streaked the floor in wide arcs and jagged lines, tracking paths of movement that had not stopped when the shooting did.

Shell casings glittered under the lights, but they were incidental, punctuation rather than language. The real story was written in bone and tissue.

Spade moved forward slowly, boots sticking faintly as he crossed drying blood. He forced himself to focus, cataloguing injuries the way he had been trained to do even as something inside him resisted. Men's jaws were shattered completely, teeth scattered across the concrete like spilled dice with bloodied roots attached to them. Another lay with broken hands locked around his own throat, fingers pulled apart, as if death had arrived mid-decision. There were boot prints in blood that did not match any pattern of retreat.

Spade wanted to speak but wasn't certain of the words as everything would sound wrong. This was the most deliberate and highly skilled butchering he had ever seen or even read about.

He counted without intending to, his eyes moving automatically. One. Two. Three. He reached twelve and stopped, the number sitting heavy in his chest because it refused to climb higher. Twelve men. All dead. All violently yet professionally destroyed. No signs of panic-driven chaos. Whatever had happened here had moved forward with confidence and control, and the men who died had never found their footing.

Spade reached the far end of the warehouse and felt something inside him give way.

A body lay collapsed near a toppled worktable, slack and empty. The neck ended in a ruined red stump, the cut unmistakable, brutal, and final, no attempt to hide being decapitated. The absence of his head itself dominated the space, louder than any siren could have produced.

Spade stared at the severed neck and felt bile rise in his throat. This was a declaration, almost ceremonial. Whoever had done this had wanted someone to understand what was happening before it ended and had wanted the room to remember it afterward regardless of who would enter.

He lowered his weapon slowly, hands suddenly heavy, forcing himself to breathe. He had seen brutality before, worked scenes shaped by rage, desperation, and stupidity. This was something else. This carried intention with indulgence, violence with controlled chaos. It was personal without being emotional, and that unsettled him more than gore ever could.

He turned and nearly tripped over the severed head. Chain Willis cried tears of blood, his throat a tangle of gore. *Good riddance.* Nearby, cut restraints hung loose from a steel support, ropes cut cleanly rather than torn away. Blood pooled beneath it in dark, uneven patches, with drag marks leading to the center, smeared by something heavy being carried, or dragged.

"He found Emma here. Found his sister and went medieval. Can't say I blame him, but Jesus fucking God..." Spade felt the certainty settle in his chest. The room carried the echo of her suffering, the way some spaces did after violence lingered too long. He pictured her without wanting to, imagined what was done to her; his jaw clenched until it ached. She was alive when this started. Where she was still alive, Spade had no idea other than Brody took her or her body with him.

Spade slowly walked the main warehouse again and looked at the bodies more closely, not as evidence, but as aftermath. Whatever Brody had become tonight, it didn't fit into any category the law recognized. This was vigilantism with bleeding passion that turned to execution shaped by something much colder.

He pulled out his phone and called in every piece of law enforcement, emergency response, fire department, every goddamn one of Houston's finest. Multiple fatalities. Extreme violence. Victims deceased. Scene unsecured. Suspect on the run. He left out the headless part. Some details needed face time before they could be discussed.

He ended the call and dialed again. "Carmen."

Her voice was tired, strained, filtered through hospital quiet. "Heath, I've waited up for you."

"You need to hear this."

A pause. "Give me the Cliff Notes."

"Twelve bodies, their leader, Chain, with his fucking head cut off. This wasn't a hit. It was an erasure."

Silence stretched on the line. He could hear the distant beep of monitors behind her breath. "Now what?"

Spade looked across the warehouse one last time, at the blood, the bodies, the restraints, the missing head.

"Well, partner, all I know is this isn't over. Not for him. Not for us."

She exhaled slowly. "Sorry I'm not there."

"Get more rest, Carmen. You don't realize how much you're gonna need it."

Spade ended the call and stood alone in the warehouse, the weight of the scene pressing in on him. Outside, the yard lights hummed. Insects gathered, drawn by the scent of death, already beginning their quiet work. The city would arrive soon, with tape and forms and explanations that would never fit. He remembered Kane's lecture of The Order of the Flies and knew he just walked across it. Whether it was how Kane intended it, Spade believed he would never know.

He took one last look around, committing the details to memory in a way he knew would follow him home and maybe in a way that would live with him to his own grave. It was a moment he, the law, was chasing something where his laws would never apply much less work.

It was the first time in Spade's career where he began to doubt he'd live through it.

6: TROPHIES

Brody drove without consequence as the city spooled ahead of him in a bloody ribbon that was drying too slowly. Houston at night could masquerade as anything needed: glittering and alive from a distance, then rotten and intimate the moment anything dropped into its veins. Service roads and frontage lanes and anonymous stretches where streetlights didn't so much illuminate as interrogate.

In the rearview mirror, Emma lay across the backseat where he had positioned her, her body angled so she could breathe, her head supported by his bloodied folded leather jacket that reeked with the metallic note of blood that would not wash out of anything tonight. She looked less like a person and more like the aftermath of what just took place.

She had a field of injuries, bruises layered across her skin in dark, and the swell of her face was wrong all over. Her wrists and ankles bore the brutal geometry of restraint, the skin broken and swollen where cord or tape had cut in. There were other marks too, subtler and more telling, the kind that spoke of intention rather than accident.

He released all the terrible images at the hands of those he just systematically destroyed. Imagination was a luxury for people who could afford to fall apart; Mister Boogie would never fall apart. Brody knew all too well the kind of men who brutalized Emma. He knew their mythology; the stupid fraternity of predators who believed violence made them larger than life when in truth it only proved their weakness.

Chain's crew, every one of them, was the same species:

confident in numbers, pitiful alone, laughing when cruelty became communal, and certain that the world would let them continue because the world always did.

He killed them all tonight in a cinematic storm of rage where everything blurred into noise and shadow. He killed them with control, sequence, purpose: each man reduced to a problem, each problem solved. Even the memory of it didn't bring heat to his face or tremor to his hands. It brought only a quiet, sterile satisfaction, the same feeling he'd had at Kelly Manson's estate when he had cleaned, erased, corrected, when he had discovered that his mind, under the pressure of blood and consequence, became clearer, laser focused. That was the difference between a killer and a craftsman. Chain's crew had been thugs, animals with jokes. Mister Boogie was something else entirely. A roar of precision and discipline.

The immediate problem was getting Emma help. Regardless of the damage they both were suffering—though he knew Emma was dying—hospitals were out. There would be a paper trail that would turn blood into all the evidence Detective Spade would ever need.

Still, the other truth was digging into his own ribs: her injuries would kill her if he made any wrong move. The feverish sheen of her skin, the ragged breath, the way her body kept attempting to curl inward despite the pain were signs he couldn't ignore for a second longer. He cleaned endless wounds before, stitched himself up a hundred thousand times. Emma was wholly damaged. And for the first time tonight, Brody felt something that had nothing to do with fear and everything to do with consequence: He could lose her, which sharpened the air inside the Chrysler.

The Houston night moved on around the car as Brody pushed on as the Chrysler's interior became a closed system, every movement threatening Emma's failing body that was fighting blindly now, spending itself with no understanding of whether there would be anything left when arriving at wherever the fuck it was Brody was taking them.

The longer he drove the more he understood that whatever he did next would not simply determine whether Emma lived or died. It would determine what kind of world he was willing to move inside from this point forward, what systems he accepted as legitimate, and which thresholds he was prepared to cross without pretending they were temporary.

Hospitals were meaningless; he left behind their world of paperwork and redemption for good. Was it the world of Conrad Ellington? Of Jack the Ripper come full circle? Mister Boogie smiled at the thought.

He reached for his phone and called The Veil; hearing Kane answer was no surprise.

His voice was fully formed, unhurried, carrying the faint suggestion of amusement that came from never being surprised by human behavior. Brody didn't need to say a word about what happened. He spoke only in terms of outcome and immediate needs, that he needed an emergency place where Emma would have at least a chance to survive. Kane listened in silence, and Brody could feel that listening was something active, evaluative.

Kane offered no comfort or reassurance, but to narrow the path even further, words landed as correction and condescension, as if Brody had been circling an answer long enough, and it was time to step directly into it. No medicine, no recitation of credentials, no guarantee of safety. His voice deep and overly effeminate.

Kane: I have a place to take the young Emma Madalin. Perfectly safe. And yes...I realize time is of the utmost criticality.

Brody: Of course you do, you fucking lunatic. You knew about the whole goddamn setup.

Kane: I also knew you'd come away like the striking

champion that you are. I must say, you did not disappoint.

Brody: Glad I'm such an attraction. Where am I taking her?

Kane: She's called Dr. Jacqueline Penault.

Brody: She's "called" that or is she a fucking doctor?

Kane: Of sorts...yes. But I sense time is lacking to be choosey. Am I reading that right?

Brody: Who is she?

Kane: There's no time for vetting.

Brody: Who...is she?

Kane: You saw her your last visit, Mr. Brody. Or...is it Mr. something else? Don't answer. She was playing the board game you were so fond of with our beloved Lilith.

Brody: The dancer?

Kane: Not sure if it's really dancing that she performs now is it. It's you who does the dancing.

Brody: Jesus... Fuck...

Kane: Stop. To be clear, Miss Madalin will be in fine hands with Dr. Penault. I believe you're familiar with the River Oaks part of town, am I correct? Little run-in with another doctor out that way just before our towers were destroyed, yes?

Brody: Address.

Kane gave Brody the address and the gate code to Dr.

Penault's place. When the call ended, the absence of his voice felt like a seal snapping shut, and Brody drove with a new understanding of inevitability, his route altering automatically as if the address Kane gave brought back the instant memory of being strapped in Dr. Manson's chair just a tad before Mister Boogie found his way.

Jacqueline Penault's home wasn't far from Dr. Kelly Manson's, and when Brody saw it, he didn't believe for a moment it wasn't one more of Kane's pleasure domes.

The gate did not announce itself theatrically as many estates in the area did. It appeared with understated authority of something that assumed recognition, iron rising from stone with cameras that tracked the Chrysler's approach in patient, calibrated arcs. Brody slowed and stopped, lowering the window only enough to speak when prompted. He offered only the code as Kane said, the desperate breathing of Emma the constant background noise.

The gate opened to a driveway curved through landscaping that felt almost aggressively composed, trees trimmed to suggest naturalness while betraying the meticulous control beneath it. The house emerged gradually, its scale revealed by increments rather than spectacle, symmetrical and assured, lit with golds and reds from the outside, as well as within. Brody parked and shut off the engine, and the silence pressed against him with a weight that made the city beyond the walls feel irrelevant.

He checked on Emma before getting out of the car, gently shutting the driver's door and walking a few steps toward the estate's entryway, walking more gingerly than anticipated as his own wounds and pain continued to set in.

The front door opened.

Dr. Penault stepped into view with the same unhurried precision he remembered yet stripped now of performance context but unchanged in essence. Without the thundering house music of The Veil her presence was even more pronounced, walking with authority. "So nice to see you again. We didn't have the chance to speak when I last saw you." Her voice was deep and throaty, but not a smoker's voice. Brody knew the difference.

"I was told to come here, that you'd be able—"

Penault slowly raised a finger. "Of course. I've been expecting you. Bring her inside." It wasn't a request or a command but more an instruction that assumed compliance. Brody followed without resistance, lifting his sister with the same careful discipline that had governed every movement of the violent and terrible night.

The interior of the estate revealed itself as something closer to a private institution than a home, its elegance of comfort was something Brody never saw, something Mister Boogie wanted to bathe in.

She guided him with minimal words, directing him toward a prepared space that felt neither improvised nor hospitable, and when he laid Emma down, Penault's hands were already moving, efficient and unafraid, touching injury without apology or hesitation.

Brody stood back, not because he was told to, but because he understood instinctively that whatever work was being done, he was a spectator. His eyes then locked on two paintings that dominated Penault's living room the way an altar dominates a chapel. They were enormous, rising from the floor to near the ceiling, their frames heavy and dark.

The first one was called *The Whore of the Earth*. The grand room was arranged around both paintings with quiet submission, the furniture pulled back as if in deference, the lamps angled not to illuminate but to avoid competing with its luster.

At its center sat Lilith, enthroned and eternal, her body rendered with a reverence that bordered on blasphemy. She was voluptuous without softness, beautiful without warmth, her presence so complete it erased any need for motion. Her lavender eyes, luminous and depthless; they did not look outward so much as inward, studying the viewer with the calm intimacy of a being who already knew the outcome. Her skin glowed pale and flawless, untouched by the ruin she presided over, and her mouth curved into a knowing that required no smile.

Scarlet draped her body in heavy folds, the fabric pooling around her like congealed sin, and in one hand she held a chalice brimming with a dark, viscous substance that caught the light like oil. Around her neck hung a chain of symbols rendered with meticulous cruelty: crowns stripped of authority, crosses fractured and inverted, halos cracked and dulled. They were ornaments where each one a conquered belief rather than a conquered life.

Beneath her throne the world collapsed. World-renowned cities burned along the lower edge of the canvas, towers buckling inward, streets choked with figures rendered just clearly enough to display panic and hopelessness. Kings knelt. Beasts devoured one another. Angels fell without flame or drama, their wings folding in acceptance of the horror. Serpents coiled at her feet, their scales catching the same lavender light as her eyes, and from the ruptured ground rose hands by the thousands, reaching not for salvation but for permission.

It was the stillness that made the painting unbearable, not its violence. Lilith did not rage or judge. She reigned. There was no moral compass at work, only the certainty of dominion, the calm of a being who controlled corruption as the world's most honest form. It was not a warning but an instruction.

The other painting, facing it across the length of the room, was *The Pig of the Earth.*

This canvas produced silence through revulsion. Where *The Whore of the Earth* ruled in composed inevitability, the Pig convulsed, its presence warping the space around it as if the walls themselves were resisting what they had been forced to contain. Its frame was thicker and more brutal, the wood scarred and darkened like something salvaged from a slaughterhouse rather than a gallery. Brody noticed the air nearest the painting felt warmer, faintly rancid, carrying a stench his mind rejected even as he recognized it.

The pig at the center of the canvas was vast, grotesquely swollen, its flesh rendered with a devotion to texture that bordered on obscenity. Its body was distended beyond any natural proportion, skin stretched taut and veined, slick with a sweat, blood, and bile fused into a single substance. The eyes were the worst of it, human in their awareness, fevered with possession, rolling white and red as if too many voices were pressing outward from behind them, each desperate for acknowledgement. The snout gaped open in a soundless scream, teeth crooked and bared, saliva and filth cascading downward in thick ropes that pooled beneath its hooves.

The scripture was unmistakable. Behind the pig rose the cliff, jagged and unforgiving, its edge crowded with the bodies of other swine frozen in the instant of obedience. They fell headlong into annihilation, legs splayed, mouths open, the herd captured as a mass exodus of flesh driven by command rather than will. Above them the sky churned with bruised clouds, heaven folding inward on itself as if recoiling from the consequence of its own authority.

What elevated this pig from sacrifice to abomination was the way the demons roamed about it. They were not depicted as entering or leaving but as emerging, pressing outward through flesh as though the animal were a womb rather than a vessel. Faces distorted the surface from within, muscle and fat reshaped into masks of agony and ecstasy. Hands clawed beneath translucent skin, fingers splayed and grasping for permanence. Ancient, fractured words were etched into the hide like brands, the language of Legion made visible and eternal, a gospel written in meat.

While the herd obeyed and hurled itself into oblivion, this one creature remained, rooted at the precipice, its hooves sunk deep into stone as if the cliff itself had yielded to its weight. Its gaze was not fixed on Christ, who appeared only faintly in the far distance, diminished and almost incidental. It was turned instead toward the opposite wall, toward the *Whore of the Earth.*

This was the demon that survived obedience as a remnant that learned from command rather than submitting to it. Where Lilith ruled through sovereignty and stillness, the Pig endured through contamination and weight. One ruled over the hell while the other ravaged it. One was crowned. The other was burdened. Together they formed a complete theology of horror, not as chaos, but as a system.

Standing between the two paintings, Brody understood that Penault's house was some kind of cathedral of the damned. These were not warnings hung for contemplation. They were coordinates asking how far he was willing to go. Mister Boogie slowly grinned as he felt deeply intertwined in all of it.

She dismissed Rex Brody from the room without explanation as he stepped into an enormous corridor feeling everything begin to shift. Control had not been surrendered so much as transferred, the knowledge unsettling, even for Mister Boogie. But he smiled anyway despite his own pain.

He stood there alone, the night sealed outside the walls, his sister beyond a closed door, and felt the final recognition take hold: that whatever he now was would be a reckoning even more exacting than violence alone.

The air in the corridor was still and, in that stillness, Mister Boogie began to listen for what came next.

***

Detective Spade sat in the washed-out light of his office, as if the bulb above him were an interrogation lamp, and he was the one being questioned by the case, by the city, by the slow, inexorable maniac killer that Rex Brody had become. The air smelled like stale coffee and disinfectant, the institutional perfume of men who lived too long in rooms where other people's disasters were hurriedly splashed all over typing paper.

On his desk, the scene photos from Chain's operation were spread like obscene tarot cards: bodies arranged by brutal moves with precise intention, violence rendered with a chaotic method that unnerved him most because method meant mind, and mind meant trajectory, and trajectory meant the kind of predator who was never caught while chasing, because chasing only poured gas on the fire. Spade stared at the grainy printouts until the details began to warp, until the blood became less a fluid and more a signature.

He pushed the photographs away and tried to think like a man who still believed in law. Rex Fucking Brody certainly didn't, and Spade wondered how deeply the sister felt the same way.

It was his fault Carmen was in the hospital, and that fact sat in him like a second injury, a private wound he could not cauterize with anger. He had departments wanting answers, supervisors wanting timelines, a city that liked its monsters simple so it could pretend it knew what to do with them.

Brody was now a contract killer signing off on contracts written by his own hand. Spade had no clue of Brody's past, not really. Fucked up childhood like everyone else, but the Brody Spade felt now moved through Houston like a human fucking wrecking ball with a heartbeat. He understood that if Brody had taken his sister back, he had not taken her back to return her to her world. He would take her to his.

Spade leaned back, rubbing his face, then forced himself to sit up as if posture could summon clarity. He pulled up the map on his computer, the web of Houston streets and neighborhoods flattening into a grid that tried to be rational. He started listing what he knew rather than what he feared. Brody took down Chain's crew in a way that Spade couldn't imagine. It meant Brody did what he always did when the world cornered him: he made it smaller by removing everything in his way. It also meant the police were now dealing with someone who they had no idea how to handle. They would have to learn as they went along. Spade shook his head at the thought of how many were going to die, and not just police.

Of course, Brody wouldn't take his sister to a hospital nor to anyone who could be subpoenaed.

Spade stared at the map and thought of River Oaks not because he had any evidence, but because River Oaks was where people hid in plain sight, behind gates and hedges and the assumption that nothing truly terrible ever happened where money lived. Plus, there was Brody's history there with the Dr. Kelly Manson brutality. Trauma had gravity, and gravity pulled people back to similar places. Spade circled the neighborhood with his cursor and felt the familiar frustration of being a man who needed warrants in a world where paperwork was meaningless to monsters.

He picked up his phone and dialed a number he hated to dial, because it belonged to the kind of unit that treated everything like a hunt and everyone like prey. Fare more so than Homicide. The voice on the other end was clipped and impatient.

"I need eyes," Spade said. "Quiet ones. I don't want uniforms spooking him."

"You got a location?"

Spade looked at the map again, at his own circle, at the emptiness of intuition pretending to be a lead. He swallowed.

"I have a hunch on our man who doesn't like any loose ends."

The voice laughed dryly. "That's not actionable."

"It's what I have. Watch River Oaks. Watch the private clinics. Watch the gated estates. Anything that looks like money and secrecy. Our guy is trying to keep someone alive, so he's going to someone private."

A pause, then: "And if we find him?"

Spade stared at the photos again, at the method, at the quiet cruelty of precision. He thought of Carmen's face under hospital lights. He thought of Emma, whoever she was now, whatever had been done to her.

"If you find him," Spade said, voice low, "you call me first. You do not engage him like he's a standard fugitive. You do not corner him in public. You do not turn this into a spectacle."

"Because?"

"Because he will burn the entire city down just to make a point," Spade said, and the words felt true in a way that chilled him. "And right now I don't even know what point he thinks he's making."

He ended the call and sat very still, listening to the quiet of his office, realizing with a sudden heaviness that the case had already moved beyond him. The law was a net designed to catch ordinary men. Brody was no longer ordinary. Spade could feel the city shifting in response, like an animal sensing a predator in its bloodstream. He put his hands flat on the desk as if anchoring himself to something solid, and he told himself that he would find Brody because that was what he did, that was who he was, that was the only way to keep the world from becoming whatever Brody wanted to remake it into.

But even as he made the promise, he felt it: a quiet dread that Brody was no longer hiding.

Brody was building.

***

In the corridor outside Emma's room, the silence had a composure that felt practiced, as though the house itself had learned to hold its breath. Brody stood with his hands loosely at his sides, his posture deceptively relaxed, yet every muscle in him remained calibrated for instant violence. The walls around him were elegant in a way that suggested money had been used, not for comfort but for control, the surfaces too clean, the lighting beautifully intentional, the air carrying a faint medicinal note beneath a floral sweetness that never quite resolved into any flower he could name. It was the smell of order applied to the body, the scent of someone who believed in cleanliness, not as hygiene but as doctrine. He listened for Emma's breathing through the door and heard nothing distinct, only the soft insinuation of activity inside: the creak of a bed frame, the whisper of fabric, the quiet click of something metal set down carefully. The sounds were unsettling.

His pains began to rise in the absence of adrenaline, not as a dramatic flair but as a slow, deep insistence that certain bruises were now ready to speak, and certain cuts had decided they mattered. His knuckles were swollen, the skin split in places from impact with flesh and bone, and beneath the clean composure of his face there was a thin, bright line of strain that came and went as he breathed. Mister Boogie enjoyed the pain as it was proof that the night was real. Still, he could feel a faint, grim satisfaction in the way his body complained.

The door opened without warning, and Dr. Penault appeared in the gap as if she had been there the entire time, and the corridor had simply been waiting for her to reveal herself. She wore a robe that looked like something medical without being medical, a garment that suggested function, and her hair was pinned back too tight. Her face held no softness and no cruelty, only a kind of calm that belonged to people who were comfortable with the body's worst truths. She looked at Brody, and her gaze did not linger on his expression. She took in his hands, the faint discoloration along his jaw, the way his shoulders sat slightly off center, and then she moved on as if cataloging a damaged object whose function still mattered.

"She's stable."

Brody felt the sentence land in him with a relief so

sharp it almost resembled pain.

"How stable?"

Penault's eyes held him with mild interest, as though she were measuring his ability to tolerate the truth. "Stable enough to stop slipping. Not stable enough for you to pretend she's out of danger."

He nodded once.

She stepped into the corridor fully and closed the door behind her with the quiet finality of a seal. "Wash. Not because blood offends me. Because it invites attention, and attention is the cheapest form of misfortune."

"I don't even know what that means, and I'm not leaving her."

Her expression barely shifted, yet the air around her tightened as if the house itself had taken her side. "You're not leaving the property. If you want to guard her, I want you clean."

There was a firmness in her that did not come from volume but from certainty. Brody understood it as it was the same certainty he felt when he decided every last fucking link in Chain's crew would break, a certainty of a someone who would never negotiate with necessity.

He followed her down the corridor; as they walked, the house revealed itself in glimpses of rooms that looked too composed to be lived in, furniture arranged with an eye for symmetry rather than comfort, art on the walls that matched the horror of the massive Lilith and Pig paintings. Everything about the estate was emersed in refined dread. Brody could feel it pressing against him, evaluating him, asking silently whether he belonged in spaces where everything was curated and nothing was accidental.

Penault guided him into a bathroom that was larger than most living rooms, marble and chrome and an almost surgical brightness. She set a folded towel on the counter, then placed a small kit beside it with gauze, antiseptic, bandage wrap. The supplies looked expensive in the way everything here looked, not because cost mattered, but because the owner of the estate believed quality was a form of authority. Brody still couldn't decide if Penault was the owner or Kane.

"Wash and wrap your hands and return to the sitting room across from her door. If I need you, I'll call. If you interrupt me, I'll remove you from the corridor."

Brody met her gaze. "Try."

Penault held his eyes without flinching. "You're still thinking you're in charge."

Mister Boogie kept the stare. "You're still thinking I'm not."

She scoffed and left him there, the door closed behind her with the same quiet finality, leaving Brody alone with running water and a mirror that reflected a man who looked less like an injured savior and more like a predator who had wandered into a cathedral. Strangely, he thought of the image he had about such a cathedral somewhere far from here with no idea what it meant.

He washed slowly, letting the water run over his hands until the blood loosened and slid away in pink threads that disappeared down a drain too clean to deserve them. He scrubbed beneath his nails, cleansed the cuts, wrapped his knuckles with practiced efficiency, the same motions he had used in gyms and back rooms and nights that always ended with someone else busted to pieces. When he finished, he stared at his reflection and saw a face that no longer belonged to the young man who once thought violence was a reaction rather than a craft. He saw a face that had accepted the idea of inheritance, not as romance, but as biology, as lineage, as fate written in muscle memory. Conrad Ellington. Jack the Ripper. Names that tasted like myth and blood, names that suggested the past did not die so much as change bodies.

He left the bathroom and returned to the corridor as instructed, because instructions mattered here, and he was not foolish enough to challenge a system while his sister lay inside it.

The sitting room across from Emma's door was dim, lit by lamps that produced a warm amber glow, the kind that made skin look softer than it was. Mister Boogie sat in an armchair that felt too expensive to be comfortable and waited. The waiting was the hardest thing he had done all night. He listened to the house, to the faint creaks of its structure settling to the distant hush of Penault moving inside the room with Emma, to the small clinks and murmurs of medicine being practiced like ritual. In that listening, he began to feel something else beneath the relief: a subtle dread that survival was not the end of the story. Survival was only the opening.

The door to Emma's room opened again, and Penault appeared, her hands clean, her sleeves rolled back slightly. She carried herself as if she had just completed a procedure and found it satisfactory.

"She's sleeping. Repairing."

Brody rose. "I want to see her."

She considered him, then nodded once. "Sure. But briefly."

He entered the room and the sight of Emma, even in softened lamplight, struck him with a quiet violence all its own. She lay on the bed, her face turned slightly to one side, bruising visible beneath the thin veil of a clean sheet drawn up to her chest. She had cleaned her as much as she could be cleaned without erasing the truth. Bandages wrapped her wrists and ankles, neat and clinical. An IV line ran into her arm with understated precision, and the slow drip of fluid felt like a fragile promise. Her breathing had steadied, still shallow but less desperate, as though her body had accepted that, for the moment, it was safe enough to stop fighting the air.

He stood beside the bed and looked down at her, and for a moment he felt something close to tenderness attempt to surface. He crushed the feeling immediately as it was dangerous and made people careless. He would never be careless again.

Penault watched him from the doorway, her presence felt without intrusion. “Don’t touch her yet. She needs her own skin to feel like it belongs to her.”

Brody withdrew his hand before he realized he had lifted it. He stepped back into the corridor, and Penault closed the door again.

“She’ll be hungry and not just for food but meaning.”

“What are you talking about?”

Penault’s gaze sharpened slightly, as if she were amused by how literal he could be when he wanted to avoid emotional language. “Most people don’t survive what she survived and return to innocence. Not that anything about her was innocent.”

“You’re really going there right now? Really? You don’t know a fucking—”

“Hush now. No need for anything tighter than it already is. I know that your sister is not the type to choose ruin. Nor you.”

Penault’s lips curved into something that was not quite a smile. “I know bodies. Perhaps just as well as you do. And I know what certain bodies do when they are wounded beyond dignity. They become weapons, Rex. You’re the last person I should be saying that to.”

The use of his name didn’t feel intimate or friendly, but as if she were testing how he reacted to being named by someone who didn’t fear him. He said nothing. He’s the one who called Kane, not the other way around. Or was it that way all along? Regardless, the infrastructure was already moving.

Penault gestured toward the sitting room. “Wait here again, if she wakes in panic, I’ll handle it. If she wakes in clarity, you may speak with her but understand this...what you say to her in the first hours will become a kind of scripture.”

Brody waited again. His mind began to lay out the future the way it laid out a crime scene, ordering it into steps and sequences. Emma would heal quickly enough, that much he knew, especially under the witchcraft of Penault, a craft he was beginning to fully accept, to embrace. That was the purpose of this place, and Brody understood it. He had lived his own pain in a way that had always felt endless; he knew his sister had lived the same. They both had to embrace the witchcraft of not only Penault but everything that took place at The Serpent's Veil. They were part of it, and Mister Boogie felt even more alive than when he had Chain's head in his hands.

When the door finally opened, it was Emma who appeared, taking Brody off guard. She moved slowly, but under her own command, wrapped in a robe that was too elegant for the reality of her injuries. Her hair was damp, freshly washed, and the clean scent of it struck Brody in the same way the bandages had: as proof that someone had tried to return her to humanity without pretending it was intact. She didn't look at the floor or flinch at the corridor's shadows. She walked as though she had already decided she would not be ashamed of anything.

Her eyes found him immediately, and what lived in those eyes was not confusion or fragility. It was a bright, controlled hatred that looked frighteningly lucid, as if the violence done to her had burned away everything in her soul that might have hesitated to become what she now needed to become.

Penault remained behind her like a quiet sentinel, watching in silence.

Emma sat in the chair opposite Brody and simply stared at him, and in that stare Brody felt her making an inventory of him, confirming that he was real, confirming that she had not hallucinated his return or her being saved from the hell in the warehouse, scoping every inch of him to make sure the world had not stolen him.

Brody reached over and carefully put his hand on her knee. "What do you want to do?"

Emma took in a deep enough breath, and Brody saw how much pain it was causing her, as if the breath would shatter another rib. When she let it out, Brody sat back and folded his arms and waited.

He knew when she spoke that her pain had harnessed into something he'd never expected. "Burn it. Starting with our dear Aunt Anna."

Brody's throat tightened slightly. Mister Boogie smiled more slightly.

Emma leaned forward, her motion slow, careful, disciplined, as if pain were now something she handled rather than it handling her. "I want everyone to suffer the way I did." It was a stark honesty that made the sentence feel like a law. Her mouth twitched into contempt for the idea of limits.

Brody's mind moved immediately, cataloging the first target. "You know where she is?"

Emma nodded. "And Rachel."

Brody hadn't thought of the caseworker since the day the family was torn apart. Mister Boogie wondered why she had been forgotten. A mistake that wouldn't be missed. The sound of her name created a tidal wave of rage.

Penault shifted slightly in the doorway, her presence still silent, still watching, and Brody understood that she was part of everything unfolding. This was the place that created vengeance.

Emma sat back, exhaling slowly.

"They thought they owned us, that they could take us and break us and build us back into whatever they wanted, and we would thank them for it. I want them both to understand they were never holding any leash."

Brody listened because interruption would only fracture the clarity he could feel crystallizing in her. She wasn't rambling but assembling her anger into shape, and shape was power.

"You've kept track of Rachel?"

Emma's gaze sharpened. "Isn't it perfect?"

Brody sat back. Clean. Perfect. The same language he used when he erased himself from scenes, when he made violence look inevitable rather than messy. He saw, in that moment, what had changed most profoundly: Emma was no longer a person he needed to protect from his darkness. She now spoke darkness fluently. He kept staring at her, noticing something else had changed.

"Your eyes are different."

She stared back. "How so?"

"The color. The color has changed."

"Changed to what?"

Brody cleared his throat. "Well...a shade like the woman you talked about back at Houston's. Like the woman I saw sitting with her at The Veil." Brody turned his head to Penault as she stepped forward, entering the room's triangle of tension with calm authority.

"Changes always take place during healing, but there's still some time needed."

Brody's eyes narrowed. "How much time?"

"Never mind that," Emma said. "Enough time for the perfect plan." Her voice lowered again, nearly a whisper, as if she were speaking into the future itself. "I want them to see everything."

Outside the estate walls, Houston continued to live and glitter and pretend, unaware that a new configuration of violence was being refined in a quiet room behind a closed gate. Behind another closed door, Emma's body kept healing under Penault's hands while Mister Boogie prepared a ritual.

***

Anna St. Claire arrived believing, as she always had, that the world still bent toward her when she applied the correct pressure. She parked beneath the unfinished structure of a newly designed downtown monolith because Emma had chosen that building with care, and because she knew Anna would soon office here. She had Chain Willis, of all people, follow her aunt before her brother dismembered him and his crew. Emma had learned of their aunt's every move.

Anna trusted concrete and elevation and isolation. They suggested authority without witnesses and privacy without vulnerability. The city at night had always given her what she needed, distance disguised as safety and the reassuring sense that no one important was close enough to interfere.

She stepped out of her Lexus, dressed to kill, coat tailored, posture composed, her face already assembled into the expression she used when she intended to correct someone and walk away unscathed. Not a care in the world of how many people she had fucked over in her family, her friends, her colleagues just so long as it served her soulless agenda.

She noticed the smell of the vagrant before she noticed the filth and silt of his presence. It was enough to make her gag, cutting through the thickness of downtown Houston's perpetual grimy air.

He was dressed as any other homeless leach: layer upon layer of cheap shirts under a piss and shit stained linen shirt-jacket, jeans stiff with layers of dirt and blood, thick-soled black shoes that were coming apart. But why was he here? In her building where the fresh parking lot concrete still looked wet.

Anna immediately went for her mace in her Louis Vuitton mini purse.

"Hey...whoa now, I don't want any trouble. Not lookin' for any wrongdoing." The man's voice was ragged and weak. Anna swore she could smell his breath over his own hellish stink.

"How did you get in here? What are doing here?"

The man put up both hands, his fingers wiggling about

in fingerless cloth gloves that hadn't been washed since they came off the manufacturing line. "Don't spray that at me. I was told to be here. It was specific that I'd be paid to be here, to be part of something, I don't know, lady, and I don't think I want to know."

Anna held her mace out like it was a handgun as she took a few steps forward. She was Anna St. Claire, VP of Finance at one of Houston's premier risk management firms, Ganger and Brahms. She cared less about fucking her way to the top. In fact, it had always given her pure joy and confidence every time some idiot corporate warmonger wanted to get her panties off, and she ended up making him think it was because she wanted him sexually. Anna's entire life was fueled by what would give her the most power. She had fucked over family, friends, colleagues, whoever was in the way. Handling some maggot on Houston's streets who slugged his way into her new building was the least of her worries.

"What's your name?" She stopped with a sudden jolt of anger, tsking. "Never mind that. I'm sure you'll be delighted to be back in county jail just as soon as I can get the police here. You stay right there." Anna fumbled in her LV bag for her cell phone when suddenly some of the long-light ceiling fixtures were shot out, shards of glass and plastic ricocheting and echoing through the vast empty lot.

Then the parking garage lights went completely out.

***

Downtown Houston at night had a way of looking like a city that had already been evacuated, its towers lit like reliquaries while the streets below emptied into long corridors of glass and concrete where footsteps sounded too loud and too singular. Houston wasn't peaceful. It was watchful. It was an instrument waiting to be played by whoever arrived with intention.

Rex and Emma drove without headlights for the last block, coasting through a seam of darkness between two buildings where the lamps had been broken or removed or simply never repaired, when she signaled him to turn into one of Houston's newest skyscrapers. Brody's rental felt like a violation of the stillness, even with the engine throttled low, and he took a narrow service entrance into the building's parking garage that belonged to banks on paper, to redevelopment proposals, to city plans and insurance policies, to the physical world where it would one day belong to pigeons and wind and the slow accumulation of grime. But tonight, it belonged only to those who had permission or those who were giving permissions.

Or, in Roger Denison's case, where permission was directed by Rex Brody.

Emma's direction was to park on the third level where gorgeous new concrete guardrails carried the instant odor of wealth and power. Beyond the open sides of the garage, downtown's lights glittered as if nothing could ever rot there, as if money itself could ward off entropy.

Brody stepped out and stood for a moment with the door open, knowing that Denison would be exactly where he was told. Nothing else moved except the distant hum of the freeway and the occasional hollow metallic clatter of a loose sign shifting in the wind. He closed the door softly, turned to Emma who was now dressed in similar fashion to Penault, the hood shadowing the upper half of her face while the rest remained visible enough to announce that she was alive and well. Her body still carried the residue of what had been done to her as a quiet distortion of movement. Mister Boogie was pleased with her healing.

She stepped out of the car and stood beside him with a stillness that was almost frightening, her changed eyes tracking the emptiness of the garage as if she were studying a room before selecting where she wanted to place a match.

Brody carried a duffel bag that looked ordinary enough

to be dismissed by anyone. It held a change of clothes, a top hat and white glove, plenty of .22 long round ammunition, a high-powered light beam, and a tape deck he purchased at a local pawn shop just before he and Emma left Penault's estate.

He walked ahead, his footsteps measured, the bag swinging at his side with controlled weight; he felt Emma follow him without hesitation. They moved along the garage's interior wall toward a stairwell that led down to a lower level where the newly installed lights were low and sensual in Houston's newest steel tuxedo.

The board was already there.

It leaned against the concrete wall of the garage like something temporary and obscene, a slab of cheap particle board braced from behind with crude lumber that had been cut without care for symmetry or finish. Its surface was raw and fibrous, already scarred from transport, the edges chipped, the corners blunted where it had been dragged across cement.

Rex stepped toward it and pressed his palm flat against the surface as if greeting an accomplice. Emma had the fluorescent lights overhead turned back on and washing everything in a sterile white glare that erased warmth from the air and flattened shadows into sharp planes. The garage hummed with mechanical indifference. Down here, the world narrowed to concrete, breath, and intention.

Emma held back several paces, her posture still and composed. Roger Denison hovered near a column, his shoulders rounded inside layered coats, eyes fixed on Brody as though he were watching a sermon rather than a crime. He still had no idea what he was doing there and things were becoming far more complicated than he ever wanted.

Brody tested its balance with deliberate pressure, adjusting the brace until it stood square and unyielding. His movements were measured, almost reverent. Anna was becoming just as confused as Denison, as the man dressed in a top hat and white glove had the strangest presence she ever remembered in a man. She was instantly unnerved, which was something she never expected.

When Brody turned toward Anna, the geometry of what was about to happen had already settled into place for Mister Boogie. The moment she attempted to point the mace toward the man, he moved with a speed and agility that terrified her, knocking the mace from her hand hard enough to where she thought her wrist broke.

Mister Boogie forced her back against the board. When Anna attempted to resist and move away, he hit her perfectly in the ribs and sternum, watching her fall to the ground in such fierce pain she felt crippled. Brody stood over her watching her body do whatever it could to regain some kind of composure. When Anna was able to look up to the man he smiled at her.

"Hello, Aunt Anna."

Her face wrinkled in confusion and awareness at the same time. Regardless of the pain, the reality of her nephew standing over her was shocking enough that her body overlooked the pain.

"Rex?" For the first time ever, she was surprised by her own voice.

Brody kneeled to meet her face.

"That's right. But not just me." He extended his arm toward Emma. "Your niece is here, too. We thought it was time for a family reunion."

Emma stayed her ground and simply nodded for Rex to continue. Anna looked to her and saw a woman who was more striking than herself. More striking than she'd ever been. She shook her head a few times, trying to regain composure and dignity, wondering how in the hell this was happening.

"I don't understand, Rex, what this is, what you're—"

"Oh, but you will."

Brody lifted his aunt off the ground with such ease and

power that Anna believed his strength would kill her before she had a chance to use any of her negotiating skills.

Denison kept watching in astonishment of what was unfolding, still clueless why he was there.

Brody extended her arms outward until her shoulders felt they'd tear. He secured her wrists and ankles with the zip ties through pre-cut holes in the board, molding her into the shape he wanted. She continued to struggle at first, twisting against the pressure, her breath rising in broken gasps that dissolved into the hollow acoustics of the garage.

Mister Boogie stepped back to study her. The pose was important regardless that she was now secured. He adjusted her left arm slightly higher, correcting the angle until the line from wrist to shoulder satisfied him.

"Keep it here."

"I don't know what this is, Rex, but I'm not just—"

Brody slapped her face with the gloved hand as to not break the skin. He touched his forehead to hers.

"Not another word or I'll gut you here and now." Brody had the Spyderco knife opened, the blade on the side of her neck, the serrated edge causing instant blood drops.

"You know good goddamn well what this is all about." Emma's voice was just enough to keep Anna from any further struggle or injury from God knows what Rex was going to do.

Brody took a step back, tilted the top hat, keeping the blade out in front of his body. He reached over and tilted her chin upward, exposing her throat to the fluorescent glare. The light drained color from her skin and cast hard shadows beneath her ribs. She looked less like a woman and more like an object pinned in place for examination.

"Emma...you're such a beauty. Your eyes." It was the best Anna could muster under such severe stress and fear. Rex terrified her, but maybe if she could reach Emma there could be a chance to survive.

Brody listened without reaction as Emma put her index

finger to her lips. Anna was right: Emma was a beauty. He'd never noticed it until now. He also focused on his sister's eyes, realizing her change was escalating.

"You lied to us. It was you who tore us apart. We have no idea where our brother, Don, is, but this is what we have right now. The three of us."

Emma walked into the immediate space of Anna's crucified body right next to Rex. "Soon, it will just be the two of us." Emma put her hand on Rex's shoulder and leaned in to kiss his face. "Whoever that was in the warehouse, let him take over." Emma walked back to where she stood when watching the events unfold without another word to her Aunt Emma.

Mister Boogie tilted the top hat a bit more, took a few steps back and gave the signal to Roger Denison to play the tape in the cheap tape recorder. Though Denison still had no idea what his part in all this was he followed orders, clicked the play button on the tape deck Brody had given him from the duffle bag. KC and the Sunshine Band's "I'm Your Boogie Man" filled the garage with a cheap echo that filled the area.

Mister Boogie marked her with controlled precision, opening narrow lines that would not kill instantly but would not close either. The blood surfaced slowly, dark and deliberate, and began its downward course. It traced along her arms and collarbone, collected at the base of her throat, and fell in measured drops against the wood behind her. The board absorbed it greedily, the cheap fibers darkening and swelling as if eager to participate.

Anna's resistance weakened as shock settled into her muscles. Her breathing fractured into shallow pulls. Her eyes widened, not with hysteria but with dawning comprehension that she had been reduced to a symbol.

The bass line of "I'm Your Boogie Man" rolled into the garage, tinny yet insistent, the rhythm bouncing off concrete pillars and returning distorted. The brightness of the melody felt obscene against the metallic scent in the air. The lyrics slid through the space with predatory promise.

Mister Boogie began to dance, his hips swayed in time with the beat. His shoulders rolled with controlled sensuality. He circled her body slowly, his boots gliding across the concrete in rhythm. There was no frantic energy, only enjoyment, but it was disciplined and elegant. He mouthed the lyrics toward her as if they were vows spoken intimately.

He leaned in close during the chorus, his breath brushing her ear, then withdrew and spun away again, hands lifting and cutting through the air as though conducting the scene. His shadow passed over her repeatedly, merging with her outline against the wall.

Emma stared in amazement.

Her gaze tracked every movement. She watched her brother not with fear but with awe. Something inside her had already aligned with this moment long before the board had been purchased. She understood that this was some kind of declaration that the whole world would hear.

Denison shifted unsteadily, sweat beading at his temple despite the cool air. He looked toward the elevator doors, toward the ramp, toward any sign that the outside world might intrude. Nothing did. The garage remained sealed in fluorescent stillness.

Anna's strength diminished steadily. Her head sagged, then lifted weakly, then sagged again. Blood continued its slow descent, darkening the board, pooling at her feet. Her fingers twitched once against the restraints before falling limp.

The song continued, relentless.

Mister Boogie moved closer one final time and placed his hand lightly against her chest. He felt the rhythm beneath his palm, counted it, measured it, then removed his hand as the beat of the music overtook the fading pulse beneath his fingers.

He stood before Anna's crucified body and regarded it one final time, not with triumph but with the calm appraisal of a man confirming a design that was perfectly executed. The body hung like scripture for a world that would not understand its true language. In the morning, his hope was that the city would awaken to a new panic. The news would speak of ritual. The department would hunt the wrong man. Detectives Spade and Hayes would feel the shift and try to name it, and naming it would save no one, but it would keep him alive.

Brody turned away and walked toward Emma, her eyes remained fixed on the body as he approached. Only when he was close did she look at him. In her gaze there was no gratitude. There was no collapse into softness. There was only a fierce, disciplined alignment that felt like a vow. Brody did not ask her how she felt. He took her gently by the elbow and guided her toward the stairwell, leading her out the way they had come, their footsteps swallowed by the garage's cavernous quiet.

"Wait here a minute." Brody walked over to Denison.

"Stay here. Don't think of fucking moving. This is all part of the show." He pulled out a thousand dollars cash and placed in Denison's filthy hand.

"That was a show of some kind?"

Brody nodded, put his hand on Denison's shoulder with a grip hard enough to let the vagrant know he could shatter the bone at will. "That's exactly what it was. Be well, old timer. Keep your burner with you."

Denison nodded not saying a word as he felt for the burner phone in his ragged, over-sized jeans.

Brody and Emma moved upward through the stale air, toward the level where the Chrysler waited, toward the city's glow, toward the world that would wake in a few hours and knowing its danger level had just been turned up a level. When they reached the car, Brody paused and looked out at downtown's lit towers, those monuments to commerce and denial. The city looked untouchable from a distance. It always did. But he knew now, in his bones, that cities were fragile things held together by agreements no one remembered making. Break enough of those and the entire structure began to tremble.

Emma slid into the passenger seat without a word. Brody started the engine and drove out of the garage, the gate of the city opening for him with indifferent ease. Behind them, in that dead structure, a woman hung crucified against concrete, her blood cooling as the false story would take root around her. Houston's skyline receded behind them, Brody felt the next scenes already forming in the same calm, inexorable way hunger forms, because doctrine, once begun, did not stop at one offering.

***

BREAKING NEWS
Front Page Exclusive – The Houston Post
December 22nd 2008
NEW DETAILS EMERGE IN HOUSTON SERIAL KILLER CASE
By Houston Post Editorial Staff

Houston homicide detectives are quietly reopening and recontextualizing a series of killings dating back to late October 2001, raising the possibility that multiple murders long treated as isolated, resolved, or unrelated may represent the early phase of a serial pattern spanning more than seven years.

The renewed inquiry centers on the deaths of Tina Parker, 41; Leslie Ames, 38; Rachel Martin, 44; and Anna St. Claire, 46, whose murders occurred within a compressed time frame during the fall of 2001, a period when law enforcement agencies nationwide were operating under extraordinary strain in the weeks following the September 11 terrorist attacks.

Authorities now say that fragmentation, combined with premature conclusions in at least two cases, may have obscured a broader structure.

"These were not spontaneous crimes," said Detective Heath Spade, who has been leading the investigation alongside Detective Carmen Hayes since 9/11. "What we are seeing now is discipline. Control over environment, control over timing, and consistency in how scenes were managed. That kind of repetition does not occur by chance."

FOUR WOMEN, ONE PATTERN

Parker's body was discovered shortly before dawn inside an unfinished parking structure east of downtown Houston in late October 2001. Less than two hours later, Ames was found inside a vacant industrial property several miles south. Though investigators have declined to release specific details regarding body positioning or injuries, police confirmed that both scenes exhibited what they now describe as ritualized consistency.

Preliminary findings from the Harris County Medical Examiner's Office indicate the victims sustained comparable injuries, though full autopsy reports remain sealed as part of the active review.

At the time, both cases were investigated aggressively but separately. Detectives say the operational reality of late 2001, when local departments were balancing routine homicide work with expanded federal coordination and terrorism preparedness, contributed to a siloed approach.

"When you do not yet know you are looking at a series, you do not look laterally," Hayes said. "You close what you can close."

That approach extended to the death of Anna St. Claire, whose murder occurred months later and was publicly attributed to Roger Denison, a transient individual arrested after personal belongings and handwritten materials were recovered near the scene. Denison was charged, and the case was widely regarded as resolved.

Investigators are now questioning that resolution.

THE DENISON QUESTION

According to sources close to the investigation, elements of the St. Claire scene share structural similarities with the Parker and Ames murders that go beyond coincidence. Detectives would not specify those elements but confirmed that the consistency has prompted a formal reassessment of Denison's role.

"The issue is not whether Denison was present in the area," Hayes said. "The issue is whether the scene itself reflects his behavior or someone else's."

Police emphasized that Denison remains a person of interest, but officials stopped short of reaffirming his responsibility for St. Claire's death, signaling a notable shift in the department's position.

Rachel Martin's case adds further complexity.

THE CASEWORKER

Martin was a senior family services caseworker whose professional responsibilities placed her at the center of some of Harris County's most contentious custody disputes and emergency removals. Her work required frequent interaction with families under investigation and individuals facing court-ordered separation.

Colleagues described Martin as procedural, unyielding, and deeply committed to institutional process.

"She believed the system worked if you followed it exactly," said a former coworker who requested anonymity. "Rachel enforced policy even when it made people angry."

Martin was found dead several months after the Parker and Ames murders. Like St. Claire's case, her death was initially treated as isolated and resolved without public linkage to other homicides.

Detectives now say that assumption may have been premature.

Investigators are reviewing whether Martin's professional activities brought her into contact with individuals later connected to other scenes, or with someone who would go on to demonstrate repeated access, control, and familiarity across multiple environments.

"This is not about fault," said Spade. "It is about understanding victimology. Who someone was and what they did matters when you are trying to identify motive and opportunity."

A BROADER RECKONING

The renewed focus on the four women's deaths comes amid various investigation into the ritual murders that have taken place from Houston to Lake City. Ritual murders of young women being secured on particle board backdrops, bodies in an X position, wrists and sides of their necks cut to bleed out. The problem has been each of these killings have all been allegedly done by street vagrants found in the immediate scenes.

Also back in 2001 are the killings of Chain Willis and eleven members of his criminal organization. While police initially characterized those deaths as underworld retaliation, detectives now say aspects of the scenes do not align with typical gang violence.

"In retaliatory violence, you expect speed and disorder," said one law enforcement source. "Some of what we observed suggested time, familiarity, and restraint."

Spade and Hayes declined to confirm whether the Willis killings are directly linked to the earlier murders or current ones but acknowledged that investigators are examining whether the same offender may have intersected with Willis's network, either to eliminate witnesses or to exploit existing criminal infrastructure.

Detectives are mapping locations, transportation routes, and known associates tied to Willis's operation and comparing them with the sites connected to Parker, Ames, Martin, and St. Claire. Surveillance footage gathered during the Willis investigation is also being reanalyzed for recurring vehicles, individuals, or behavioral markers.

"We are not drawing conclusions," Spade said. "But ignoring overlap would be irresponsible."

A SEVEN-YEAR ITCH

While officials have not formally classified these cases as a serial homicide investigation, sources indicate detectives are quietly cataloging additional unsolved killings dating back to 2001 that share similar structural characteristics.

Investigators say the pattern is not defined by victim demographics alone, but by scene discipline, symbolic repetition, and deliberate control. Police emphasized that no new suspects have been publicly identified, and that all persons previously named in connection with these cases remain under review.

Authorities are urging anyone with information related to the movements of Tina Parker, Leslie Ames, Rachel Martin, or Anna St. Claire, or with knowledge of Chain Willis and his associates, to contact the Houston Police Department's homicide division.

"This is not about reopening old wounds," said Hayes. "It is about making sure we are not protecting the wrong narrative."

The investigation remains active.

Spade: Have you read the fucking latest from The Post?

Hayes: Just finished it.

Spade: No fucking word about Doctor Kelly Manson or Chelsey Bingham. Not a fucking word about it.

Hayes: Or the woman killed at the library.

Spade: Can't remember her name.

Hayes: Jennifer Armstrong.

Spade: Right. He killed her the same day as Manson and Bingham.

Hayes: Technically the next day.

Spade: Whatever. Point is, Hayes, this article leaves out way too fucking much and nothing that leads to anything we've been tracking all these years.

Hayes: Paper's always been that way. Why are you so wound up about this piece?

Spade: Why now is why?

Hayes: Listen, Heath, I'm tired. It's Christmas time and this just isn't at the top of my list right now. What's the real reason you're calling? You've got something you're onto, then let's hear it.

Spade: He's gone, Hayes. They're both gone. Out of the country. No way they're still here. Not for now at least. I feel it.

Hayes: Okay...so...where? What part of the world are you going to race off to?

Silence.

Hayes: Heath, are you there? Want to fill me in so I can get back to my holiday cheer?

Spade: Sorry, just thinking it through. That's why I called because you always help me think it through.

Hayes: Fine. Why don't we look at the obvious places. Brody and Madalin would go...someplace that's glamour and glitz, am I right?

Spade: Can't imagine them hiding out in The Middle East.

Hayes: Well, not so fast. We know Brody spent a lot of time in Cambodia.

Spade: That's the not the fucking Middle East.

Hayes: Course not, but it's also not Europe or Canada or Australia. Don't seem such places would be to Emma Madalin's liking.

Spade: Right. So...Canada? Vancouver? Prague? Spain, Carmen?

Silence.

Spade: Hayes?

Hayes: You called me to brainstorm.

Spade: Well?

Hayes: France. You said you have a feeling they're gone, gotta be France and there's only one place in France that even matters.

Spade: Understood, partner. Get back to your holiday festivities.

***

The rain had stopped an hour before Emma arrived, but

the streets of Saint-Germain still held its glorious shine, reflecting café lights in trembling ribbons across the pavement. The air in Paris carried a cool softness that Houston never possessed, a restraint that felt almost polite.

Emma paused across the street from Café de Flore and peered through the window before crossing. She saw Detective Heath Spade sitting alone at a small marble table near the glass, a demitasse untouched in front of him. He looked the same as he had in Houston ten years earlier, except harder, deeply weathered. His posture remained upright, controlled. He was not a man who slouched into comfort.

When she stepped inside, he saw her immediately; no flicker of surprise in his face, just pure recognition. "Miss Madalin."

"Don't be formal with me, detective." She slid into the chair across from him without waiting for an invitation.

"Fine. Emma."

A young model-type waiter hovered around them instantly. Emma ordered espresso in careful French. Spade waited until the man moved away before speaking again. "How'd you know I'd come here? That you knew I was here?"

"I get information same as you, detective, and I'm just as resourceful. How do you know you're not the one who's being hunted all this time? Ever think of it that way?"

Spade's mouth curved faintly, not quite a smile. "You know I've got enough on your brother to extradite him. I don't on you, but I've got enough for him. You already know this or you wouldn't be here talking to me, if that was some pipedream. He'll be extradited back to Houston. French police are arrogant but not stupid. Being part of such an international arrest, how can they help themselves? That's why you're here."

Emma leaned back, studying him as though evaluating the lines of a building she had not visited in years. "I'm here because you never understood him. And...because I know where he is."

"You're not turning him in. You're protecting him, and I understand him well enough to catch him."

"You'll only catch him if he wants to be caught."

Spade didn't respond immediately. He stirred his coffee slowly. Outside, a couple hurried past beneath a shared umbrella. Inside, the low murmur of conversation filled the room without intruding.

Emma's espresso arrived. She wrapped her fingers around the small porcelain cup without drinking. "You've been chasing him for seven years. You needed a victory after so much loss."

His eyes stayed on her. "I don't believe in winning. I believe in finishing."

She scoffed. "Is that what you call this? Finished?"

Spade leaned forward slightly. "Your brother murdered multiple people across state lines. He staged scenes, framed the homeless. This ends with him in prison, or it ends with him dead. Those were always the only two outcomes."

Emma slowly shook her head. "That's all theoretical, and you goddamn well know it, detective. You think this is about outcomes. Always have. You see a body, you see a statute, you see a file number, case number. You never see the architecture."

"Architecture." Spade repeated it evenly.

"Yes. Structure. Intention. He was building something. And he will continue to build something. You'll never keep him in a cell. You've got nothing to keep him."

"He's a cold-blooded killer."

Emma cleared her throat. "He is a corrector. Correcting shit that needed it a long time ago."

Spade's expression hardened slightly. "Right. Goes back to your aunt. Your family being torn apart. Spare me, Emma, we've all had bad shit happen. He just made things a lot fucking worse."

She took a long sip of her espresso while looking over his weathered face. She almost felt sorry for him.

"Let me continue. There is also a shit load of random killings that I happen to believe are all part of Rex Brody's full *vision*, if you will. Woman murdered in Arizona for no apparent reason...at an Indian burial site. I happen to believe it was because she was irritating your brother. Was on her cell phone when she shouldn't have been. A couple in a movie theater who had their throats slit for what I think was nothing more than the crime of talking during the movie. Got a few eyewitnesses who describe someone like Brody there."

Emma laughed slowly in mockery. "Really, detective? All these dots you're trying to connect with no aim, no angle, no reason but to, what? Toss red herrings into the mix?"

"Doesn't mean I'm wrong, and you know it, and I'm not finished. Had a blood bath at a local grocery store in Lake City less than a year ago. Something close enough to remind me of Chain Willis and crew. Even the savior part. Group of punk ass bitches giving a single woman and her daughter a really hard time. Gettin' nice and ugly with both of them. Just so happens some mystery man was shopping next to the scene, saw what was going' down, and before the thugs knew what end of their asses were up, were taken out as fast as their mouths and hands were poppin' off at the woman and child. But that's not the bitch of it, Emma. Guy takes out the mother, too, because, apparently, she was a bad fucking mother to get them in the situation in the first place. Girl lived through the whole thing. Name's Tori Paisley. I kept tabs on her. But I've got a hunch that tells me you just don't want to know all of it."

She held his gaze. "Doesn't matter what I believe. I'm asking you to admit that you see his discipline. That part of you respects it."

Spade's silence lasted long enough that the waiter glanced over, uncertain whether the table required attention. The detective finally broke in. "I respect his intelligence. Not the same thing."

Emma nodded slowly. "That's all he ever wanted from you."

"What a curious statement."

"You studied him the way he studied you. You read the patterns. So did your partner. You both anticipated him. You stayed with the case long after everyone else would have long ago given up. You made him real."

Spade exhaled quietly. "Why are you really here, Emma?"

She leaned back, letting the question settle. "You already said it's to protect him. Because he's going to prison, and you're gonna parade him through Houston as the monster you finally captured. Because you'll build your press conference carefully, and you'll speak about justice and persistence."

"He doesn't need my help to look monstrous."

"He needs context."

"That doesn't excuse what he did."

"But you can't prove all that you say."

"I've got enough to start." Spade's voice tightened for the first time.

Emma's gaze softened, but not her tone. "I'm asking you to tell the truth about him."

Spade's brow furrowed. "He's a serial killer."

"Ha. You can't go there, and you fucking know it. He was forged a long time ago. You only saw pieces of it. At Numbers, how controlled he was. Every scene had meaning. He was and has been disciplined chaos, responding to something that shaped him long before you knew his name."

Spade watched her carefully. "Childhood trauma?"

"I am not blaming, only explaining."

Spade leaned back. The café light reflected faintly in the window behind him, doubling his outline against the night. "You want me to humanize him."

"He protected me, detective. He. Saved. My. Life.

From fucking animals."

Spade's expression shifted. "I know that, Emma. I'm sure what happened was—"

"You've no clue."

Spade studied her face. "No. I don't. But I saw what was left behind. Are you not afraid of any of it?"

Emma stared blankly. "None of it."

Spade's tone cooled. "So...you're admitting knowledge of that crime."

She shook her head slowly and took another drink.

"Let me tell you something, Miss Madalin. He'll spend the rest of his life rotting in a cell if it's the last goddamn thing I do on this earth."

She continued shaking her head with the same blank stare.

Spade leaned forward again, lowering his voice. "Your brother orchestrated spectacle. He wanted attention. He left signatures. He cultivated myth. And I'm gonna prove it."

The café door opened, letting in a draft of icy air and the faint scent of rain-washed stone. Emma watched a waiter light a cigarette outside for a pair of tourists. The world moved on, unaware of the conversation unfolding in its midst.

"You love him." Spade's voice had softened.

"Of course."

"And you believe that love somehow redeems him."

"I believe love explains him."

Spade's jaw tightened. "Go on, then."

Emma leaned forward, mirroring his posture. "We're not born violent, detective. He was taught containment and silence. He was taught that weakness invites annihilation. Every act you cataloged as escalation was correction in his mind. Every so-called ritual you fantasized about in your psychopathy. Maybe it was structure. You chased a monster. I lived with a brother."

"Rex Brody enjoyed it."

"And that terrifies you, because enjoyment implies choice...agency"

Spade held her gaze. "It better terrify you, lady."

Emma leaned back and lit a long cigarette.

Spade did the same with a Marlboro Red, sat back slowly, absorbing the weight of her loyalty. "You understand that if evidence surfaces tying you to anything, I'll not hesitate to go after you just as hard."

"I'd expect nothing less. But you still can't seem to wrap your head around what we've been talking about."

The waiter returned to refill water glasses. Neither of them thanked him.

Spade studied her one final time. "This is going to end."

She leaned into his space. "This is never going to end."

The hardened detective chuckled and took a last drag on his Marlboro. "You both chose Paris because you knew I'd follow."

"He wanted you to see him somewhere beautiful. I'm also sure your partner suggested you to come here."

Spade regarded her carefully ignoring the jab. "Beauty matters to him?"

"It always has."

They stood facing one another, two survivors of the same long pursuit from opposite sides of its moral divide.

"You're not like him."

Emma's expression remained unreadable. "Don't be so sure, detective. You didn't win."

Spade turned toward the door, then stopped. "Is that why you wanted to meet tonight, to tell me that?"

Emma held his gaze. "Sainte-Chapelle. Midnight. He'll turn himself in peacefully."

Spade stepped out into the Paris night, the door closing softly behind him. It was almost over. He dug out his phone and called it in.

Emma remained inside for a long moment as the city hummed beyond the glass, indifferent and luminous. She lifted her espresso cup and drained the last of it, the bitterness settling deep in her throat.

They could cage his body and try to catalog his crimes. But they would never unmake what he built...or what he had built in her.

***

By the time Brody entered the Sainte-Chapelle, Paris had already decided it was done with him.

The city outside was awake but indifferent, the usual low churn of footsteps and traffic and conversation spilling across stone and water, the sound of a place that had survived too much history to care about one more man arriving at its threshold. He passed through the guards without resistance, a solitary figure moving into a cathedral built, not to comfort but to intimidate, a structure meant to remind anyone standing inside it how small they were in the presence of something eternal.

The doors closed behind him with a long, thudding echo that went on and on as if Christmas Eve would never end, and no Christ would come to the world to save it.

Inside, the Sainte-Chapelle stood empty. Just space and color and height, the long vertical ascent of stained-glass windows climbing toward a ceiling that seemed to recede endlessly in purples and deep reds. Biblical scenes burned in blue and red and gold, saints frozen in glass, martyrs rendered beautiful in their suffering, violence sanctified through art and distance.

Brody walked down the center aisle, wondering what to expect. When Kane had helped him leave the states with Emma, it was under the agreement that on this night, Christmas Eve in Paris at the Sainte-Chapelle, he would find his new contract, his new path.

His footsteps echoed softly, controlled, his pace unhurried. He wore no disguise, no costume, no hat. He needed no one. Not even Emma. That chapter of his life had closed. Mister Boogie was ascending to a new level.

He stopped halfway down the aisle and looked up in marvel. Christmas Eve in Paris carried a different kind of light. The sun had dropped low, hovering at the edge of departure, and what remained filtered sideways through the towering stained-glass walls. The panels rose like vertical seas of deep reds, violent blues, gold leaf burning through scenes of prophecy and slaughter. Winter light sharpened everything to a slow cutting glow.

The height was disorienting. The chapel didn't feel constructed so much as suspended. Slender columns lifted into vaulting ribs painted a midnight-blue so dark it resembled the sky outside, punctured with gold fleur-de-lis that caught the fading light and held it. The ceiling seemed less like a roof and more like an inverted firmament pressing down in silence.

He stepped forward, boot striking the stone with a sound that cracked through the nave and climbed, clean and unsoftened, all the way to the vault before returning to him sharpened. It was an echo that studied him before giving itself back.

He walked down the center aisle alone. Or so he thought.

No pews crowded the space to absorb the rhythm. The aisle ran long and deliberate toward the altar, a narrow path bordered by walls that were no longer walls, but scripture rendered in fire and glass. Creation, betrayal, crucifixion, judgment of every horror preserved in jewel tones that refused to fade. The winter light moved through them slowly as the sun slipped lower, and the scenes seemed to breathe.

Red spilled across the stone floor and climbed his coat in fractured geometry. Blue pooled at his boots. Gold traced the bones of his hands. He slowed his pace, allowed it to measure him.

Outside, somewhere beyond the thick medieval walls,

a choir began singing "Silent Night." The melody drifted faintly through stone, barely audible, distorted by distance. The irony amused Mister Boogie. The chapel held its own silence, and it was not the kind that comforted.

When he struck the stone harder with his heel, the report rang out like a pistol shot. The sound ricocheted through glass and iron tracery, then returned thin and precise. For a moment, the colored saints seemed to lean inward. Martyrs with serene faces bathed in crimson. Apostles lifting palms in frozen testimony. The rose window at the western end blazed in circular symmetry with Christ enthroned, the dead rising in concentric arcs, the damned spiraling downward in stylized flame.

Brody walked until he stood beneath that rose, the entire chapel aligned around him.

It was a merciless geometry, vertical lines drew the eye upward, converging ribs meeting like blades. The glass walls offered no shadows deep enough to claim a man. Even alone, he was displayed and rendered small against a structure designed to preserve relics and proclaim eternity.

It was the night devoted to birth of innocence that would grow to the ultimate power, all of it the idea that salvation enters the world quietly, wrapped and fragile, but it went out with blood and thunder

He felt all of it.

The air pressed against his lungs as though the chapel were aware of him. His breath appeared faintly in the cold, lingered for a second, then dissolved. The silence thickened between his footsteps. He turned slowly and looked back down the length of the nave, seeing the aisle stretch behind him like a blade laid flat. The colored light was thinning now. The reds darkened to something arterial. The blues deepened toward indigo. Gold thinned into narrow lines along the ribs of the vault.

Outside, bells began again; midnight approaching.

He imagined the city kneeling in fragments, families

gathered around tables, lovers exchanging quiet promises, priests lifting chalices beneath warm electric light. The world rehearsing its belief in renewal. Mister Boogie knew better.

Sainte-Chapelle was built to house relics: the Crown of Thorns, splinters of sanctified wood, fragments of bone believed holy because they endured. The entire structure existed to elevate what was broken and declare it sacred.

Rex understood that instinct intimately; Mister Boogie understood it as a war cry.

They had both curated their own collection across the country. Not always objects, but sometimes moments and expressions. The precise second comprehension of dreadful fate bloomed in another human being's eyes. Silence after impact. The weightless clarity that followed. Those were also relics for the ages, and ones the cops would track for years to come.

Brody stepped forward again and mounted the shallow steps before the altar. The final light of the evening cut through the glass and struck him full across the chest. For a brief, suspended second, he stood divided by color: half drenched in crimson, half submerged in blue. The chapel held him there in luminous judgment.

The interior dimmed in stages. The stained glass smoldered. Outside illumination faded into city glow and winter sky. The chapel's vast height receded into shadow, though the gold stars above retained a faint, stubborn glint.

Midnight bells rang across Paris.

The glass told stories he knew well. Sacrifice. Betrayal. Judgment. Blood transmuted into meaning. Men broken and exalted in the same breath. He had spent years dismantling myths like these, repurposing them, dragging them out of sanctuaries and into parking structures and alleys and unfinished buildings. Yet standing here, beneath this cathedral of narrative, he felt recognition.

"You made it." The voice cut through the chapel's

chambers in a velvet rip with an echo that overcame the Christmas bells.

She stood near the pulpit, where the floor rose slightly and the light gathered more densely, the colors from the windows folding over her body as if the glass itself had decided to claim her. She wore a crimson fitted dress and a crown of thorns. Her presence bent the space around her without effort.

Brody knew it was Lilith from The Serpent's Veil and could have been the woman from the bayou those many years ago. The woman from Kane's arms who had offered him murder like mercy when he was still a child.

Her eyes were the same impossible violet.

"We all come to places like this at the end. Men do. Churches. Courts. Ruins. Somewhere tall enough to make them feel absolved. But men like you...they come to places like this for a new beginning."

Mister Boogie faced her with full curiosity; Brody did with full adornment. Maybe it was atonement for both.

For a long moment, neither of them spoke. The silence between them felt like a long-lost reward.

She stepped down from the pulpit and moved toward him, her footsteps soundless against the stone. The colors shifted across her face as she walked, saints bleeding into demons, halos dissolving into shadow, the glass unable to decide what story it wanted to talk about her.

Brody watched her approach without tension but with a hunger and a fear.

"I thought I saw you once before when I was a child. I was with my brother."

"Maybe you did." Her voice was more striking than her appearance, which Mister Boogie found intoxicating.

"You were the one in Kane's arms at The Veil."

Lilith smiled and pulled down the crown of thorns enough to cause blood to trickle down her ivory face. "Yes."

"He carried you like you were the most precious being

on earth."

She stepped forward two steps in pure grace. "I am."

She walked to stand in front of him, close enough now that he could feel her warmth, smell her endless fragrance, yet sense that strange absence she had always carried, as if the air refused to cling to her. "You have learned what you needed."

Mister Boogie cocked his head. "Now what?"

Lilith's smile deepened, approving.

Behind them, unseen but present, the city shifted. Silently, Paris police cars converged on the Sainte-Chapelle. Somewhere beyond the cathedral walls, Detective Spade stood waiting with the patience of a man who understood that timing mattered more than speed. He had followed Brody across years, across the country, across an ocean, and now he waited without triumph, knowing this was not an arrest that could be rushed.

Inside the Sainte-Chapelle, time held.

Lilith tilted her head slightly, studying Brody with the same appraising gaze she had used on him decades earlier when he was smaller and shaking and furious and unformed. "You are going to do exactly what you were made to do. Exactly as your own blood once did. You read the letter. I'm here to authenticate it."

"My sister once said we had to burn it, all of it."

"She was right." Lilith put a cold iron hand on his shoulder. Brody was taken aback but not Mister Boogie. "It's time to continue."

Her gaze softened then, not with pity, but with something closer to intimacy. She stepped closer still, took off the crown of thorns and placed it on the floor, wiped the blood from her forehead as if erasing it, their bodies nearly touched. "This is better left here. Carry me. Just as Kane did. Carry me down the aisle toward the end of the world."

Brody hesitated only long enough to understand it was all about symmetry. About continuing a circuit that had been open since the first time he had seen her stretched beneath the sun, offering violence like a gift.

He bent and slid one arm beneath her knees, the other around her back.

She weighed nothing.

As he lifted her, the cathedral seemed to exhale. The stained glass flared, colors spilling across the floor in fractured patterns that looked like blood when they crossed his shoes. She stretched her head back low toward the ground, her arms dangling as if dead, her eyes half-lidded, content.

For a moment, he thought of Kane and the night he first understood the hierarchy he was entering.

He turned and began to walk with her in his arms. Each step down the aisle felt deliberate, ceremonial, as if the cathedral itself were counting them. Saints watched from glass as a man carried something older than any doctrine past their frozen martyrdoms. Judgment remained suspended, undecided.

Mister Boogie stopped at the doors. “This is where I leave you.”

Her lavender eyes locked onto his.

She smiled, that same quiet, knowing curve of lips as he lowered her gently, setting her on her feet. For a heartbeat, she remained close, one hand resting against his chest.

“You’ll see me again. Working for me.”

Brody took a step back and did a slow courtesy bow.

She stepped back, already dissolving into the cathedral’s light, becoming indistinguishable from the color and shadow that had birthed her.

Brody pushed the doors open and stepped into the Paris night air. Blue on white police cars jammed the street, parked every-which-way, lights flashing. Cops took defensive positions; no guns were visible. Detective Heath Spade stood across the street, talking on his mobile phone.

They looked at each other without animosity; two men

who understood that the story they had been orbiting was now complete.

Spade nodded to Brody and returned to his phone call. “Marion, you were saying something about your brother, Steven Paul, right?”

“He’s been arrested again.”

“Then I think you should know I’ve got this high-profile intake coming in. Harris County.”

“Rex Brody?”

“Yep, that’s the one. Maybe do what you need to, to keep this one away from him. Gotta go.” He ended the call, walked across the Christmas dark, and stopped a few feet in front of Brody. Interpol had given him the honor of making the arrest. “Rex Brody. You’re being extradited to the United States.”

Mister Boogie nodded once.

The police took him into custody, normal procedure, handcuffs, pat down. No resistance. They spoke in French. As the cops put him in the back seat, Brody hesitated long enough to cast a sly smile toward Spade.

Doors closed.

The car sped away from the Sainte-Chapelle.

Spade watched as Paris swallowed them whole.

Behind him, the Sainte-Chapelle stood unchanged, its glass still glowing, its stories still frozen, its judgment still deferred.

And somewhere inside that cathedral, for just a moment longer, the echo of footsteps faded, as if something ancient had finally been carried out of the light and into the darkness forever.

About the Author

Dean Patrick was born and raised in Houston, Texas. Educated at The University of Houston with Masters Degrees in Professional Writing and Literature, he works as a writer for a Houston-based orthopedic center and for software technology companies in the Salt Lake City area. He lives in Morgan, Utah, on a small ranch with his wife, Lisa. To this day, he considers his sobriety his greatest victory.

Be sure to read books #1 and #2 in Dean Patrick's Terra Drake Horror Series

#1: The Lady Mephistopheles

Stephen Paul is a raging alcoholic whose addiction suddenly manifests itself, one cold Utah night, in the form of a beautiful woman. Terra Drake, at first, seems warm and inviting, but she soon shows him the horrors she'd beset upon his small town, the murder of his next-door neighbor, the bewitching of his hairstylists, the freakshow the county fair had become, and the damnation of his priest in the new Church of Flies. She's in cahoots with another demon, the Hooded Darkness, who stalks him at every turn, and the more he drinks, the more horror he sees and the more he blames them for the misery that has befallen small-town America. As his warnings to citizens and friends go unheeded, he strikes out on his own to defeat this ultimate evil, to save the world before hell itself comes calling.

#2: Terra's Sabbath

Homicide Detective Marion Paul, on a quest to discover why his brother drank himself to death, steps into an obscene world of witchery and Satanism that plagues Small Town America, where the demon woman, Terra Drake, orchestrates the murders of its citizens and the enslavement of their children. The trail of blood and death traces back to Biblical times, and her hand has touched the most notorious of serial murderers throughout history. Marion, having seen the worst of human nature, rushes headlong into her cult of witches and werewolves against which he has no defense, not by gun, knife, or fists, a nightmarish battle that tests his sanity and entraps his family. Should he lose this cat-and-mouse trial of wits and courage, everyone he loves will surely die.

#3: The Harlot and the Beast

Detective Marion Paul, desperate to save his kidnapped daughter and girlfriend, must run a gauntlet of apocalyptic horrors and psychopathic killers to untangle a twisted web of clues, all mired in a warped arena of psychological torment, deception, and numbing mind control meant to keep him a bay and drive him insane. Jack the Ripper incarnate Rex Brody and the wolf-beast Adrian Kane are determined to sacrifice the ones Marion loves in a bloodletting ceremony to the harlot Terra Drake. She's the personification of beauty in the flesh and ugliness of spirit, and she wants humanity to bow down to Her in worship. Now, as his hometown of Duncan, Utah, is invaded by witches and ghoul-elves, and the cauldron fires leap and roar, he takes a stand against evil...for his loved ones, his home, and the rest of us in small-town America.

www.ingramcontent.com/pod-product-compliance
Lightning Source LLC
LaVergne TN
LVHW020655110826
845149LV00012B/2009